DAVID MARCUS

David Marcus was born in Cork, read Law at University College, Cork, and King's Inns, Dublin, and was called to the Irish Bar in 1945. The following year he founded *Irish Writing*. In 1954, shortly after the publication of his first novel, *To Next Year in Jerusalem*, he went to live in London, where he spent the next thirteen years. He then returned to Ireland and joined *The Irish Press*, where he was Literary Editor from 1968 to 1986 and in which he founded *New Irish Writing*, a weekly page of short stories and poetry which became a national institution.

David Marcus has had many stories and poems published in Ireland, Britain and the U.S.A., and has translated the 1,000 line, eighteenth-century Gaelic poem *The Midnight Court*, edited several anthologies of Irish stories, and in recent years has published two further novels and a collection of his own short stories.

sceptre

STATE OF THE ART

SHORT STORIES BY THE NEW IRISH WRITERS

Edited and Introduced by
David Marcus

Selection and introduction copyright
© David Marcus 1992
For individual copyright in the stories see page 375

First published in Great Britain in 1992 by Sceptre Books

A Sceptre original

Sceptre is an imprint of Hodder and Stoughton Paperbacks, a division of Hodder and Stoughton Ltd

British Library C.I.P

State of the Art: Short Stories by New Irish Writers
  I. Marcus, David
  823.0108 [FS]

ISBN 0-340-57400-3

Printed and bound in Great Britain for Hodder and Stoughton Paperbacks, a division of Hodder and Stoughton Ltd, Mill Road, Dunton Green, Sevenoaks, Kent TN13 2YA. (Editorial Office: 47 Bedford Square, London WC1B 3DP) by Clays Ltd, St Ives plc. Photoset by Rowland Phototypesetting Ltd, Bury St Edmunds, Suffolk.

CONTENTS

STATE OF THE ART

INTRODUCTION

The modern short story is a *genre* in which, quite early in this century, the work of Irish writers attracted world-wide acclaim. World-wide, that is, apart from Ireland itself. As Frank O'Connor, one of the short story's greatest practitioners, declared in a talk delivered to the Dublin PEN in 1964, '. . . the real attitude to literature in this country is . . . [that] writing is a sin, and the writer is a sinner . . .' O'Connor died before the end of that year, but had he lived to the end of the decade he would have been able to observe not only the birth of a new Ireland in which not a few of its emerging writers were destined to achieve a status akin to literary beatification, but an Ireland soon to be rehabilitated as a state in which the art of the short story would once again flourish. To display the state of that art in Ireland now is the object of this anthology devoted to the work of writers whose stories did not begin to appear until late in the '60s. Such writers are many in number, too many, indeed, to fit into a single volume – hence the exclusion of all those who, up to the early months of 1991, had not published at least one collection.

The question begged by this anthology is, of course, in what way did the Irish short story of the '70s and '80s differ from that of earlier decades. The '60s saw the beginning of mould-breaking changes in the pattern of Irish life: economic emphasis shifted from agriculture to industry, population moved from country to city, the rise of women's lib injected a new ferment and concern into social affairs, the spread of television loosened inhibitions far more than drink ever had, and in other vital areas – most particularly in education – fresh, forward-looking ideas brought about what many commentators recognised as a peaceful social revolution.

A social revolution provides an ideal stimulus for new directions in art and culture. For the Irish short story, however, there was a problem: no indigenous market existed. Without a market, how were new short story writers to be encouraged? The half-dozen or so Irish literary periodicals of the '40s and '50s had disappeared, and access to the pages of British and North American magazines was virtually impossible for beginners, few of whom in any event were able to find and study such publications. And then two things happened, the first giving rise to the second. In 1968 the national daily newspaper, *The Irish Press*, launched 'New Irish Writing', a weekly page of short stories and poems, inviting not only unknowns, but seeking to establish standards for them to aim at by also regularly publishing work by Ireland's leading writers. Within a few years came the second boost for the Irish short story when the publishers, Poolbeg Press, assisted by the republic's Arts Council, embarked on a policy of bringing out collections of short stories by many whose first work had appeared in 'New Irish Writing'. Additionally, the prestigious House of Hennessy, purveyors of the famous brandy, sponsored annual Literary Awards for the best-adjudged stories by new writers published in the 'New Irish Writing' page.

That the provision of such a platform would result in the emergence of many previously unpublished, highly talented short story writers was no great surprise, but that half of them would be female was unforeseen. For the first time in the Irish short story the voice of women, unrestrained and in chorus, was heard loud and clear. Issues of social and sexual exploitation, previously unmentioned and unmentionable, constituted their main material, and while such issues were also being discussed in the feature pages of the national newspapers now that women's lib had swept away traditional taboos, the transmutation into literature of authentic experience from a hitherto hidden realm gave the Irish short story a new immediacy.

In what other ways did the Irish short story of the '70s and '80s differ from that of earlier decades? As might be expected, traditional treatments had to make some room for ways of projecting voices and views which reflected the adoption of contemporary *mores* from the outside world. Not that tradition was completely abandoned – sometimes the new freedom allowed writers of the old school to wrap conventional forms around unconventional themes with provocatively piquant results. By and large, however, the three tyrannous S's of Irish life – sin, soil and sex – on which so many writers had relied, underwent a metamorphosis and important earlier standbys either lost their validity or became just clapped out. The priest as an authoritarian monitor of mind, movement and muscle, virtually disappeared, religious belief itself being now questionable and the sacerdotal role and writ a matter for examination; reminiscences of brutal school beatings by Christian Brothers faded away with the decline or demise of its sufferers; maudlin anecdotes about village simpletons had had their day; the Troubles in Northern Ireland were more demanding than the remote 1920s struggle for independence; poverty-driven lifelong exile to the USA was replaced by periods of wandering and/or working in Britain and Europe punctuated by flying visits home; the diurnal drudgery of rural farm and village life, though retaining the loyalty of some of the older, longer-memoried chroniclers, seemed now much less relevant or interesting than the reports of the growing urban school through whose narratives four-letter words flickered like electric shocks.

Some commentators may say that the Irish short story has lost its individuality. If it has, then it has only insofar as Irish life has lost its individuality. Be that as it may, I believe this anthology will illustrate that the state of the art in Ireland is as healthy today as it ever was. And considering that another anthology, just as fresh, exciting, and lengthy, could be assembled from the work of writers I have had to omit, the resurgence of the Irish short story seems assured for the foreseeable future.

David Marcus
1992

NIGHTWIND

JOHN BANVILLE

Born 1945, in Wexford, John Banville's first book, *Long Lankin* (1970), was a collection of linked stories. He has since written seven novels and is regarded as one of the leading novelists of his generation. He won the James Tait Black Memorial Prize in 1976, the Guardian Fiction Prize in 1981, and the GPA Irish Fiction Award in 1989 for *The Book of Evidence* which had been short-listed for the Booker Prize. He is Literary Editor of *The Irish Times*.

He shuffled down the corridor, trying the handles of the blind white doors. From one room there came sounds, a cry, a soft phrase of laughter, and in the silence they seemed a glimpse of the closed, secret worlds he would never enter. He leaned against the wall and held his face in his hands. There were revels below, savage music and the clatter of glasses, and outside in the night a wild wind was blowing.

Two figures came up from the stairs and started toward him. One went unsteadily on long, elegantly tailored legs, giggling helplessly. The other leaned on his supporting elbow a pale tapering arm, one hand pressed to her bare collarbone.

– Why Morris, what is it?

They stood and gazed at him foolishly, ripples of laughter still twitching their mouths. He pushed himself away from the wall, and hitched up his trousers. He said:

– 'S nothing. Too much drink. That you David?

The woman took a tiny step away from them and began to pick at her disintegrating hairdo. David licked the point of his upper lip and said:

– Listen Mor, are you all right? Mor.

– Looking for my wife, said Mor.

Suddenly the woman gave a squeal of laughter, and the two men turned to look at her.

– I thought of something funny, she said simply, and covered her mouth. Mor stared at her, his eyebrows moving. He grinned and said:

– I thought you were Liza.

The woman snickered, and David whispered in his ear:

– That's not Liza. That's . . . what is your name anyway?

– Jean, she said, and glared at him. He giggled and took her by the arm.

– Jean, I want you to meet Mor. You should know your host, after all.

The woman said:

– I wouldn't be a Liza if you paid me.

– Mother of God, said Mor, a bubble bursting on his lips.

David frowned at her for shame and said:

– You must be nice to Mor. He's famous.

– Never heard of him.

– You see, Mor? She never heard of you. Your own guest and she never heard of you. What do you think of that?

– Balls, said Mor.

– O now. Why are you angry? Is it because of what they are all saying? Nobody listens to that kind of talk. You know that. We're all friends here, aren't we, Liza –

– Jean.

– And this is a grand party you're throwing here, Mor, but no one listens to talk. We know your success is nothing to do with . . . matrimonial graft.

On the last words the corner of David's mouth moved as a tight nerve uncoiled. Mor looked at him with weary eyes, then walked away from them and turned down the stairs. David called after him:

– Where are you going, man?

But Mor was gone.

– Well, said the woman. Poor Mor is turning into quite a wreck. These days he even has to pretend he's drunk.

David said nothing, but stared at the spot where Mor had disappeared. The woman laughed, and taking his arm she pressed it against her side and said:

– Let's go somewhere quiet.

– Shut your mouth, David told her.

Downstairs Mor wandered through the rooms. The party was ending, and most of the guests had left. In the hall a tiny fat man leaned against the wall, his mouth open and his eyes closed. A tall girl with large teeth, his daughter, was punching his shoulder and yelling something in his ear. She turned to Mor for help, and he patted her arm absently and went on into the drawing room. There in the soft light a couple were dancing slowly, while others sat about in silence, looking at their hands. In the corner a woman in a white dress stood alone, a little uncertain, clutching an empty glass. She watched his unsteady progress toward her.

– There you are, he said, and grinning he touched the frail white stuff of her gown. She said nothing, and he sighed.

– All right, Liza, so I'm drunk. So what?

– So nothing. I said nothing. Your tie is crooked.

His hands went to the limp black bow at his neck, and went away again.

– It's coming apart, he said. The knot is coming apart.

– Yes.

He held her eyes for a moment, and looked away. He said:

– You have a sobering effect, Liza. How do you live with yourself?

– You always pretend to be drunker than you are and then you blame me. That's all.

– You know, I met a woman upstairs and thought it was you. She was laughing and I thought it was you. Imagine.

He put his hands into the pockets of his jacket and looked at the room. The couple had stopped dancing, and were standing motionless now in the middle of the floor, their arms around each other as though they had forgotten to disentangle them. Mor said:

– What are they waiting for? Why don't they go home?

– You hate them, Liza said. Don't you?

– Who?

– All of them. All these people – our friends.

He looked at her, his eyebrows lifted.

– No. I'm sorry for them – for us. Look at it. The new Ireland. Sitting around at the end of a party wondering why we're not happy. Trying to find what it is we've lost.

– O Mor, don't start all that.

He smiled at her, and murmured:

– No.

David put his head around the door, and when he saw them he smiled and shot at them with a finger and thumb. He crossed the room with exaggerated stealth, looking over his shoulder at imaginary pursuers. He stopped near them and asked from the corner of his mouth:

– They get him yet?

– Who? said Liza, smiling at his performance.

Mor frowned at him, and shook his head, but David pretended not to notice.

– Why, your murderer, of course.

Liza's mouth fell open, the glass shook in her hand, and then was still. David went on:

– You mean you didn't know about it? O come on now, Liza, I thought you and Mor had arranged it. You know – we've got everything at our party including a murderer loose in the grounds with the cops chasing him. You didn't know, Liza?

– Shut up, David.

– O excuse me, said David, grinning, and coughed behind his hand. Liza turned to him.

– David, what is this joke all about? Seriously now.

– Well Liza, it's no joke. Some tinker stabbed his girlfriend six times in the heart tonight. The guards had him cornered here when the rain came on. The way I heard it they left some green recruit to watch for him while they all trooped back to Celbridge for their raincoats. Anyway, they say he's somewhere in the grounds, but knowing the boys he's probably in England by now. Come over to the window and you can see the lights. It's all very exciting.

Liza took a drink and laid down her glass. She said quietly, without raising her head:

– Why didn't you tell me, Mor?

– I forgot.

– You forgot.

– Yes. I forgot.

David looked from one of them to the other, grinning sardonically. He said:

– Perhaps, Liza, he didn't want to frighten you?

Mor turned and looked at David, his lips a thin pale line.

– You have a loud mouth, David.

He moved away from them, then paused and said:

– And uncurl your lip when you talk to me. Or I might be tempted to wipe that sneer off your face.

The smile faded, and David said coldly:

– No offence meant, Mor.

– And none taken.

– Then why are you so angry?

Mor laughed, a short, cold sound.

– I haven't been angry in years.

He stalked away, and in silence they watched him go. Then Liza laughed nervously and said:

– Take no notice of him, David. He's a bit drunk. You know.

David shrugged his shoulders and smiled at her.

– I must go home.

In the hall Liza helped him into his coat. He said lightly:

– Why don't you come over to the house and visit me some day? The old bachelor life gets very dreary.

She glanced at him with a small sly smile.

– For what? she asked.

He pursed his lips and turned to the door. With his hand on the lock he said stiffly:

– I'm . . . I'm very fond of you, Liza.

She laughed, and looked down at her dress in confusion.

– Of me? O you're not.

– I am, Liza.

– You shouldn't say things like that. Good night, David.

But neither moved. They stood and gazed at each other, and Liza's breath quickened. She moved swiftly to the door and pulled it open, and a blast of wind came in to disturb the hall. She stepped out on the porch with him. The oaks were lashing their branches together, and they had voices that cried and groaned. Black rain was falling, and in the light from the door the lawn was a dark, ugly sea. She opened her mouth to speak, closed it, then turned away from him and said:

– Call me.

She stood very still and looked out at the darkness, and the damp wind lifted her hair. David moved to touch her, and dropped his hand. He said:

– I'll call you tomorrow.

– No. Not tomorrow.

– When?

– I must go, David.

With her head bent she turned and hurried back along the hall.

All the guests had left the drawing room, and Mor sat alone in a high, winged chair, a glass in his hand and a bottle beside him on a low table. His tie had at last come undone, and his eyes were faintly glazed. Liza went to the couch and straightened a cushion. From the floor she gathered up a cigarette end and an overturned glass. He watched her, his chin on his breast. He said thickly:

– What's wrong with you?

– Nothing. Have they all gone?

– I suppose so.

She went to the tall window beside his chair and drew back the curtains. The wind pounded the side of the house, and between gusts the rain whispered softly on the glass. Down past the black, invisible fields, little lights were moving. She said:

– I wonder why he killed her.

– They say he wanted to marry her and she wouldn't have him. I think she was maybe a man-eater. A tart. He killed her. Happens every day, these days.

There was silence but for the wind and rain beating, and the faint sighing of the trees. Mor said:

– I suppose David made his usual pass?

She moved her shoulders, and he grinned up at her, showing his teeth. She said:

– He asked if . . . he asked me to go with him. Tonight. He asked would I go with him.

– Did he, now? And why didn't you?

She did not answer. He poured himself another drink.

– I know how David's mind works, he said. He thinks I don't deserve you. He's wrong, though – God help me.

– You have a nasty mind.

– Yes. Though he must have been encouraged when I took the job. That sent me down a little farther.

He looked at her where she stood in the shadows watching the night. He frowned and asked:

– Do you despise me too?

– For taking the job? Why should I? Are you ashamed?

– No, no. Your father is very good to do so much for me. Yes, I'm ashamed.

– Why?

– Don't act, Liza.

– It was your decision. If you had kept on writing I would have stood by you. We would have managed. Daddy could have –

She bit her lip, and Mor laughed.

– Go on, he said. Daddy could have kept us. You're right. Kind, generous daddy would have come along with his money-bags to sour our lives. Where's the use in talking. Me a writer? I'd be laughed out of the county. The bar in the Grosvenor Arms would collapse after a week of the laughing. Did you hear how mad Mor knocked up old man Fitz's daughter and moved into the big house and now says he's writing a book? Did you ever hear the likes? No, Liza. This place produced me and will destroy me if I try to break free. All this crowd understands is the price of a heifer and the size of the new car and the holiday in Spain and those godblasted dogs howling for blood. No.

She said quietly:

– If you hated these people so much, why did you marry into them?

– Because, Liza my dear, I didn't know I was marrying into them.

There was a long silence, then Liza spoke:

– It wasn't my fault he died, she said, sadly defiant.

Mor turned away from her in the chair and threw up his hands.

– Always, he said. Always it comes to your mind. Blaming me.

She did not speak, and he leaned towards her, whispering:

– Blaming me.

She joined her hands before her and sighed, holding her eyes fixed on the dark gleam of the glass before her. He said:

– Well why don't you just trot along now after old David there. Sure maybe he can give you a better one. One that will live longer and make you happy.

She swung about to face him. Her eyes blazed, and she said:

– All right then, Mor, if you want a fight you'll get one.

For a moment they stared at each other, and her anger went away. She turned back to the window.

– Well? Mor asked, and the word rang in the silence. She lifted her shoulders slowly, allowed them to fall. Mor nodded.

– Yes, he said. We've had it all before.

He stood up unsteadily, pressing his fingers on the arm of the chair for support. He went and stood beside her at the window. She said:

– They're still searching. Look at the lights.

Side by side they stood and watched the tiny flashes move here and there in the dark. Suddenly she said:

– If he got to the stables he could come in through the side door. If he did I'd hide him.

He stared at her, and feeling his eyes on her she set her mouth firmly and said:

– I would, I'd hide him. And then in the morning I'd get him out and bring him to Dublin and put him on the boat for England, for Liverpool or some place.

She reached out blindly and took his hand. There were tears on her face, they fell, each gathering to itself a little light and flashing in the darkness of the window.

– We could do that if he came, couldn't we, Mor? It wouldn't be a bad thing to do. It wouldn't be a crime, I mean, would it? Out there in the dark with the rain and everything and thinking about all the things – thinking and thinking. It wouldn't be wrong to help him, Mor?

He took her in his arms and held her head on his shoulder. She was trembling.

– No, he said softly. It wouldn't be a bad thing.

She began to sob quietly, and he lifted her head and smiled at her.
– Don't cry, Liza. There now.

The door-bell rang, and her eyes filled with apprehension. Without a word she moved past him and left the room.

Mor stood and looked about him. Long ago when he first saw this room he had thought it beautiful, and now it was one of the few things left which had not faded. The shaded lamps took from the warm walls of lilac a soft, full light, it touched everything, the chairs, the worn carpet, with gentle fingers. On the table beside him a half-eaten sandwich lay beside his bottle. There was an olive transfixed on a wooden pin. Muted voices came in from the hall, and outside in the fields a shout flared like a flame in the dark and then was blown away. Mor lifted his glass, and when the amber liquid moved, all the soft light of the room seemed to shift with it. He felt something touch him. It was as though all the things he had ever lost had now come back to press upon his heart with a vast sadness. He stared at the table, at the little objects, the bread and the bottle, the olive dead on its pin.

Liza came back, her hands joined before her, and the knuckles white. She stopped in the middle of the room and looked blankly about her, as if she were dazed.

– What is it? he asked. Who was at the door?
– A guard.
– What did he want?
– What?
– What did he want? The guard.
– O, the guard. He wanted to use the 'phone.

She looked at him, and blinked rapidly twice.
– They found him, she said. He hanged himself in the long meadow.

She examined the room once again with vague eyes, then she sighed, and went away. He sat down to finish his drink, and after a time went out and climbed the stairs.

Liza was lying in bed, the lamp beside her throwing a cruel light over her drawn face. He sat beside her and watched her. Her eyes were open, staring up into the dimness. In the silence there was the sound of the rain against the window. She said, so softly he barely heard her:
– We missed so much.

He leaned down and kissed her forehead. She did not move. He put his hand over her breast, feeling the nipple cold and small through the silk of her nightgown.
– Liza.

She turned away from him, and when she spoke her voice was muffled by the sheets.

– Bring me a glass of water, Morris. My mouth is dry.

He moved away from her, and switched off the light. He went down the stairs in the darkness, the air cold and stale against his face. On quiet feet he returned to the drawing room and poured another, last drink. Then he went and stood at the dark window, and listened to the wind blowing in the trees.

SHEPHERD'S BUSH

People looked very weary, May thought, and shabbier than she had remembered Londoners to be. They reminded her a little of those news-reel pictures of crowds during the war or just after it, old rain-coats, brave smiles, endless patience. But then this wasn't Regent Street where she had wandered up and down looking at shops on other visits to London, it wasn't the West End with lights all glittering and people getting out of taxis full of excitement and wafts of perfume. This was Shepherd's Bush where people lived. They had probably set out from here early this morning and fought similar crowds on the way to work. The women must have done their shopping in their lunch-hour because most of them were carrying plastic bags of food. It was a London different to the one you see as a tourist.

And she was here for a different reason, although she had once read a cynical article in a magazine which said that girls coming to London for abortions provided a significant part of the city's tourist revenue. It wasn't something you could classify under any terms as a holiday. When she filled in the card at the airport she had written 'Business' in the section where it said 'Purpose of journey'.

The pub where she was to meet Celia was near the tube station. She found it easily and settled herself in. A lot of the accents were Irish, workmen having a pint before they went home to their English wives and their television programmes. Not drunk tonight, it was only Monday, but obviously regulars. Maybe not so welcome as regulars on Friday or Saturday nights, when they would remember they were Irish and sing anti-British songs.

Celia wouldn't agree with her about that. Celia had rose-tinted views about the Irish in London, she thought they were all here from choice, not because there was no work for them at home. She hated stories about the restless Irish, or Irishmen on the lump in the building trade. She said people shouldn't make such a big thing about it all. People who came from much farther away settled in London, it was big enough to absorb everyone. Oh well, she wouldn't bring up the subject, there were enough things to disagree with Celia about . . . without searching for more.

Oh why of all people, of all the bloody people in the world, did she have to come to Celia? Why was there nobody else whom she could ask for advice? Celia would give it, she would give a lecture with every piece of information she imparted. She would deliver a speech with every cup of tea, she would be cool, practical and exactly the right person, if she weren't so much the wrong person. It was handing Celia a whole box of ammunition about Andy. From now on Celia could say that Andy was a rat, and May could no longer say she had no facts to go on.

Celia arrived. She was thinner, and looked a little tired. She smiled. Obviously the lectures weren't going to come in the pub. Celia always knew the right place for things. Pubs were for meaningless chats and bright, non-intense conversation. Home was for lectures.

'You're looking marvellous,' Celia said.

It couldn't be true. May looked at her reflection in a glass panel. You couldn't see the dark lines under her eyes there, but you could see the droop of her shoulders, she wasn't a person that could be described as looking marvellous. No, not even in a pub.

'I'm okay,' she said. 'But you've got very slim, how did you do it?'

'No bread, no cakes, no potatoes, no sweets,' said Celia in a business-like way. 'It's the old rule but it's the only rule. You deny yourself everything you want and you lose weight.'

'I know,' said May, absently rubbing her waistline.

'Oh I didn't mean *that*,' cried Celia horrified. 'I didn't mean that at all.'

May felt weary, she hadn't meant that either, she was patting her stomach because she had been putting on weight. The child that she was going to get rid of was still only a speck, it would cause no bulge. She had put on weight because she cooked for Andy three or four times a week in his flat. He was long and lean. He could eat for ever and he wouldn't put on weight. He didn't like eating alone so she ate with him. She reassured Celia that there was no offence and when Celia had gone, twittering with rage at herself, to the counter, May wondered whether she had explored every avenue before coming to Celia and Shepherd's Bush for help.

She had. There were no legal abortions in Dublin, and she did not know of anyone who had ever had an illegal one there. England and the ease of the system were less than an hour away by plane. She didn't want to try and get it on the National Health, she had the money, all she wanted was someone who would introduce her to a doctor, so that she could get it all over with quickly. She needed somebody who knew her, somebody who wouldn't abandon her if things went wrong, somebody who would lie for her, because a few lies would have to be told. May didn't have any other friends in London. There was a girl she had once met on a skiing holiday, but you couldn't impose on a holiday friendship in that way. She knew a man, a very nice, kind man who had stayed in the hotel where she worked and had often begged her to come and stay with him and his wife. But she couldn't go to stay with them for the first time in this predicament, it would be ridiculous. It had to be Celia.

It might be easier if Celia had loved somebody so much that everything else was unimportant. But stop, that wasn't fair. Celia loved that dreary, boring, selfish Martin. She loved him so much that she believed one day he was going to get things organised and make a home for them. Everyone else knew that Martin was the worst possible bet for any punter, a Mammy's boy, who had everything he wanted now, including a visit every two months from Celia, home from London, smartly-dressed, undemanding, saving away for a day that would never come. So Celia did understand something about the nature of love. She never talked about it. People as brisk as Celia don't talk about things like unbrisk attitudes in men, or hurt feelings or broken hearts. Not when it refers to themselves, but they are very good at pointing out the foolish attitudes of others.

Celia was back with the drinks.

'We'll finish them up quickly,' she said.

Why could she never, never take her ease over anything? Things always had to be finished up quickly. It was warm and anonymous in the pub. They could go back to Celia's flat, which May felt sure wouldn't have even a comfortable chair in it, and talk in a business-like way about the rights and wrongs of abortion, the procedure, the money, and how it shouldn't be spent on something so hopeless and destructive. And about Andy. Why wouldn't May tell him? He had a right to know. The child was half his, and even if he didn't want it he should pay for the abortion. He had plenty of money, he was a hotel manager. May had hardly any, she was a hotel receptionist. May could see it all coming, she dreaded it. She wanted to stay in this warm place until closing-time, and to fall asleep, and wake up there two days later.

Celia made walking-along-the-road conversation on the way to her flat. This road used to be very quiet and full of retired people, now it was all flats and bed-sitters. That road was nice, but noisy, too much through-traffic. The houses in the road over there were going for thirty-five thousand, which was ridiculous, but then you had to remember it was fairly central and they did have little gardens. Finally they were there. A big Victorian house, a clean, polished hall, and three flights of stairs. The flat was much bigger than May expected, and it had a sort of divan on which she sat down immediately and put up her legs, while Celia fussed about a bit, opening a bottle of wine and putting a dish of four small lamb chops into the oven. May braced herself for the lecture.

It wasn't a lecture, it was an information-sheet. She was so relieved that she could feel herself relaxing, and filled up her wineglass again.

'I've arranged with Doctor Harris that you can call to see him tomorrow morning at 11. I told him no lies, just a little less than the truth. I said you were staying with me. If he thinks that means you are staying permanently, that's his mistake not mine. I mentioned that your problem was . . . what it is. I asked him when he thought it would be . . . em . . . done. He said Wednesday or Thursday, but it would all depend. He didn't seem shocked or anything; it's like tonsillitis to him, I suppose. Anyway he was very calm about it. I think you'll find he's a kind person and it won't be upsetting . . . that part of it.'

May was dumbfounded. Where were the accusations, the I-told-you-so sighs, the hope that now, finally, she would finish with Andy? Where was the slight moralistic bit, the heavy wondering whether or not it might be murder? For the first time in the eleven days since she had confirmed she was pregnant, May began to hope that there would be some normality in the world again.

'Will it embarrass you, all this?' she asked. 'I mean, do you feel it will change your relationship with him?'

'In London a doctor isn't an old family friend like at home, May. He's someone you go to, or I've gone to anyway, when I've had to have my ears syringed, needed antibiotics for flu last year, and a medical certificate for the time I sprained my ankle and couldn't go to work. He hardly knows me except as a name on his register. He's nice though, and he doesn't rush you in and out. He's Jewish and small and worried-looking.'

Celia moved around the flat, changing into comfortable sitting-about clothes, looking up what was on television, explaining to May that she must sleep in her room and that she, Celia, would use the divan.

No, honestly, it would be easier that way, she wasn't being nice, it would be much easier. A girl friend rang and they arranged to play squash together at the weekend. A wrong number rang. A West Indian from the flat downstairs knocked on the door to say he would be having a party on Saturday night and to apologise in advance for any noise. If they liked to bring a bottle of something, they could call in themselves. Celia served dinner. They looked at television for an hour, then went to bed.

May thought what a strange empty life Celia led here far from home, miles from Martin, no real friends, no life at all. Then she thought that Celia might possibly regard her life too as sad, working in a second-rate hotel for five years, having an affair with its manager for three years. A hopeless affair because the manager's wife and four children were a bigger stumbling-block than Martin's mother could ever be. She felt tired and comfortable, and in Celia's funny, characterless bedroom she drifted off and dreamed that Andy had discovered where she was and what she was about to do, and had flown over during the night to tell her that they would get married next morning, and live in England and forget the hotel, the family and what anyone would say.

Tuesday morning. Celia was gone. Dr Harris's address was neatly written on the pad by the phone with instructions how to get there. Also Celia's phone number at work, and a message that May never believed she would hear from Celia. 'Good luck.'

He was small, and Jewish, and worried and kind. His examination was painless and unembarrassing. He confirmed what she knew already. He wrote down dates, and asked general questions about her health. May wondered whether he had a family, there were no pictures of wife or children in the surgery. But then there were none in Andy's office, either. Perhaps his wife was called Rebecca and she too worried because her husband worked so hard, they might have two children, a boy who was a gifted musician, and a girl who wanted to get married to a Christian. Maybe they all walked along these leafy roads on Saturdays to synagogue and Rebecca cooked all those things like gefilte fish and bagels.

With a start, May told herself to stop dreaming about him. It was a habit she had got into recently, fancying lives for everyone she met, however briefly. She usually gave them happy lives with a bit of problem-to-be-solved thrown in. She wondered what a psychiatrist would make of that. As she was coming back to real life, Dr Harris was saying that if he was going to refer her for a termination he must know why she could not have the baby. He pointed out that she was healthy, and strong, and young. She should have no difficulty with pregnancy or birth. Were there emotional reasons? Yes, it would kill her parents, she wouldn't be able to look after the baby, she didn't want to look after one on her own either, it wouldn't be fair on her or the baby.

'And the father?' Dr Harris asked.

'Is my boss, is heavily married, already has four babies of his own. It would break up his marriage which he doesn't want to do . . . yet. No, the father wouldn't want me to have it either.'

'Has he said that?' asked Dr Harris as if he already knew the answer.

'I haven't told him, I can't tell him, I won't tell him,' said May.

Dr Harris sighed. He asked a few more questions; he made a telephone call; he wrote out an address. It was a posh address near Harley Street.

'This is Mr White. A well-known surgeon. These are his consulting-rooms, I have made an appointment for you at 2.30 this afternoon. I understand from your friend Miss . . .' He searched his mind and his desk for Celia's name and then gave up. 'I understand anyway that you are not living here, and don't want to try and pretend that you are, so that you want the termination done privately. That's just as well, because it would be difficult to get it done on the National Health. There are many cases that would have to come before you.'

'Oh I have the money,' said May, patting her handbag. She felt nervous but relieved at the same time. Almost exhilarated. It was working, the whole thing was actually moving. God bless Celia.

'It will be around £180 to £200, and in cash, you know that?'

'Yes, it's all here, but why should a well-known surgeon have to be paid in cash, Dr Harris? You know it makes it look a bit illegal and sort of underhand, doesn't it?'

Dr Harris smiled a tired smile. 'You asked me why he has to be paid in cash. Because he says so. Why he says so, I don't know. Maybe it's because some of his clients don't feel too like paying him after the event. It's not like plastic surgery or a broken leg, where they can see the results. In a termination you see no results. Maybe people don't pay so easily then. Maybe also Mr White doesn't have a warm relationship with his Income Tax people. I don't know.'

'Do I owe you anything?' May asked, putting on her coat.

'No, my dear, nothing.' He smiled and showed her to the door.

'It feels wrong. I'm used to paying a doctor at home or they send bills,' she said.

'Send me a picture postcard of your nice country sometime,' he said. 'When my wife was alive she and I spent several happy holidays there before all this business started.' He waved a hand to take in the course of Anglo-Irish politics and difficulties over the last ten years.

May blinked a bit hard and thanked him. She took a taxi which was passing his door and went to Oxford Street. She wanted to see what was in the shops because she was going to pretend that she had spent £200 on clothes and then they had all been lost or stolen. She hadn't yet worked out the details of this deception, which seemed unimportant compared to all the rest that had to be gone through. But she would need to know what was in the shops so that she could say what she was meant to have bought.

Imagining that she had this kind of money to spend, she examined jackets, skirts, sweaters, and the loveliest boots she had ever seen. If only she didn't have to throw this money away, she could have these things. It was her savings over ten months, she put by £30 a month with difficulty. Would Andy have liked her in the boots? She didn't know. He never said much about the way she looked. He saw her mostly in uniform when she could steal time to go to the flat he had for himself in the hotel. On the evenings when he was meant to be working late, and she was in fact cooking for him, she usually wore a dressing-gown, a long velvet one. Perhaps she might have bought a dressing-gown. She examined some, beautiful Indian silks, and a Japanese satin one in pink covered with little black butterflies. Yes, she would tell him she had bought that, he would like the sound of it, and be sorry it had been stolen.

She had a cup of coffee in one of the big shops and watched the other shoppers resting between bouts of buying. She wondered, did any of them look at her, and if so, would they know in a million years that her shopping money would remain in her purse until it was handed over to a Mr White so that he could abort Andy's baby? Why did she use words like that, why did she say things to hurt herself, she must have a very deep-seated sense of guilt. Perhaps, she thought to herself with a bit of humour, she should save another couple of hundred pounds and come over for a few sessions with a Harley Street shrink. That should set her right.

It wasn't a long walk to Mr White's rooms, it wasn't a pleasant welcome. A kind of girl that May had before only seen in the pages of fashion magazines, bored, disdainful, elegant, reluctantly admitted her.

'Oh yes, Dr Harris's patient,' she said, as if May should have come
in some tradesman's entrance. She felt furious, and inferior, and sat
with her hands in small tight balls, and her eyes unseeing in the
waiting-room.

Mr White looked like a caricature of a diplomat. He had elegant
grey hair, elegant manicured hands. He moved very gracefully, he
talked in practised, concerned clichés, he knew how to put people at
their ease, and despite herself, and while still disliking him, May felt
safe.

Another examination, another confirmation, more checking of
dates. Good, good, she had come in plenty of time, sensible girl. No
reasons she would like to discuss about whether this was the right
course of action? No? Oh well, grown-up lady, must make up her own
mind. Absolutely certain then? Fine, fine. A look at a big leather-bound
book on his desk, a look at a small notebook. Leather-bound for
the tax people, small notebook for himself, thought May viciously.
Splendid, splendid. Tomorrow morning then, not a problem in the
world, once she was sure, then he knew this was the best, and wisest
thing. Very sad the people who dithered.

May could never imagine this man having dithered in his life. She
was asked to see Vanessa on the way out. She knew that the girl
would be called something like Vanessa.

Vanessa yawned and took £194 from her. She seemed to have
difficulty in finding the six pounds in change. May wondered wildly
whether this was meant to be a tip. If so, she would wait for a year
until Vanessa found the change. With the notes came a discreet printed
card advertising a nursing home on the other side of London.

'Before nine, fasting, just the usual overnight things,' said Vanessa
helpfully.

'Tomorrow morning?' checked May.

'Well yes, naturally. You'll be out at eight the following morning.
They'll arrange everything like taxis. They have super food,' she
added as an afterthought.

'They'd need to have for this money,' said May spiritedly.

'You're not just paying for the food,' said Vanessa wisely.

It was still raining. She rang Celia from a public phonebox. Everything was organised, she told her. Would Celia like to come and have
a meal somewhere, and maybe they could go on to a theatre?

Celia was sorry, she had to work late, and she had already bought
liver and bacon for supper. Could she meet May at home around nine?
There was a great quiz show on telly, it would be a shame to miss it.

May went to a hairdresser and spent four times what she would
have spent at home on a hair-do.

She went to a cinema and saw a film which looked as if it were
going to be about a lot of sophisticated witty French people on a yacht
and turned out to be about a sophisticated witty French girl who fell
in love with the deck-hand on the yacht and when she purposely got
pregnant, in order that he would marry her, he laughed at her and the
witty sophisticated girl threw herself overboard. Great choice that,
May said glumly, as she dived into the underground to go back to the
smell of liver frying.

Celia asked little about the arrangements for the morning, only
practical things like the address so that she could work out how long
it would take to get there.

'Would you like me to come and see you?' she asked. 'I expect
when it's all over, all finished you know, they'd let you have visitors.
I could come after work.'

She emphasised the word 'could' very slightly. May immediately
felt mutinous. She would love Celia to come, but not if it was going
to be a duty, something she felt she had to do, against her principles,
her inclinations.

'No, don't do that,' she said in a falsely bright voice. 'They have
telly in the rooms apparently, and anyway, it's not as if I were going
to be there for more than twenty-four hours.'

Celia looked relieved. She worked out taxi times and locations and
turned on the quiz show.

In the half light May looked at her. She was unbending, Celia was.
She would survive everything, even the fact that Martin would never
marry her. Christ, the whole thing was a mess. Why did people start
life with such hopes, and as early as their mid-twenties become beaten
and accepting of things. Was the rest of life going to be like this?

She didn't sleep so well, and it was a relief when Celia shouted that
it was seven o'clock.

Wednesday. An ordinary Wednesday for the taxi-driver, who
shouted some kind of amiable conversation at her. She missed most
of it, because of the noise of the engine, and didn't bother to answer
him half the time except with a grunt.

The place had creeper on the walls. It was a big house, with a small
garden, and an attractive brass handle on the door. The nurse who
opened it was Irish. She checked May's name on a list. Thank God it
was O'Connor, there were a million O'Connors. Suppose she had had
an unusual name, she'd have been found out immediately.

The bedroom was big and bright. Two beds, flowery covers, nice furniture. A magazine rack, a bookshelf. A television, a bathroom.

The Irish nurse offered her a hanger from the wardrobe for her coat as if this was a pleasant family hotel of great class and comfort. May felt frightened for the first time. She longed to sit down on one of the beds and cry, and for the nurse to put her arm around her and give her a cigarette and say that it would be all right. She hated being so alone.

The nurse was distant.

'The other lady will be in shortly. Her name is Miss Adams. She just went downstairs to say goodbye to her friend. If there's anything you'd like, please ring.'

She was gone, and May paced the room like a captured animal. Was she to undress? It was ridiculous to go to bed. You only went to bed in the day-time if you were ill. She was well, perfectly well.

Miss Adams burst in the door. She was a chubby, pretty girl about twenty-three. She was Australian, and her name was Hell, short for Helen.

'Come on, bedtime,' she said, and they both put on their night-dresses and got into beds facing each other. May had never felt so silly in her whole life.

'Are you sure we're meant to do this?' she asked.

'Positive,' Helen announced. 'I was here last year. They'll be in with the screens for modesty, the examination, and the pre-med. They go mad if you're not in bed. Of course that stupid Paddy of a nurse didn't tell you, they expect you to be inspired.'

Hell was right. In five minutes, the nurse and Mr White came in. A younger nurse carried a screen. Hell was examined first, then May, for blood pressure and temperature, and that kind of thing. Mr White was charming. He called her Miss O'Connor, as if he had known her all his life.

He patted her shoulder and told her she didn't have anything to worry about. The Irish nurse gave her an unsmiling injection which was going to make her drowsy. It didn't immediately.

Hell was doing her nails.

'You were really here last year?' asked May in disbelief.

'Yeah, there's nothing to it. I'll be back at work tomorrow.'

'Why didn't you take the Pill?' May asked.

'Why didn't you?' countered Hell.

'Well, I did for a bit, but I thought it was making me fat, and then anyway, you know, I thought I'd escaped for so long before I started the Pill that it would be all right. I was wrong.'

'I know.' Hell was sympathetic. 'I can't take it. I've got varicose veins already and I don't really understand all those things they give you in the Family Planning clinics, jellies, and rubber things, and diaphragms. It's worse than working out income tax. Anyway, you never have time to set up a scene like that before going to bed with someone, do you? It's like preparing for a battle.'

May laughed.

'It's going to be fine, love,' said Hell. 'Look, I know, I've been here before. Some of my friends have had it done four or five times. I promise you, it's only the people who don't know who worry. This afternoon you'll wonder what you were thinking about to look so white. Now if it had been terrible, would I be here again?'

'But your varicose veins?' said May, feeling a little sleepy.

'Go to sleep, kid,' said Hell. 'We'll have a chat when it's all over.'

Then she was getting onto a trolley, half-asleep, and going down corridors with lovely prints on the walls to a room with a lot of light, and transferring onto another table. She felt as if she could sleep for ever and she hadn't even had the anaesthetic yet. Mr White stood there in a coat brighter than his name. Someone was dressing him up the way they do in films.

She thought about Andy. 'I love you,' she said suddenly.

'Of course you do,' said Mr White, coming over and patting her kindly without a trace of embarrassment.

Then she was being moved again, she thought they hadn't got her right on the operating table, but it wasn't that, it was back into her own bed and more sleep.

There was a tinkle of china. Hell called over from the window.

'Come on, they've brought us some nice soup. Broth they call it.'

May blinked.

'Come on, May. I was done after you and I'm wide awake. Now didn't I tell you there was nothing to it?'

May sat up. No pain, no tearing feeling in her insides. No sickness.

'Are you sure they did me?' she asked.

They both laughed.

They had what the nursing-home called a light lunch. Then they got a menu so that they could choose dinner.

'There are some things that England does really well, and this is one of them,' Hell said approvingly, trying to decide between the delights that were offered. 'They even give us a small carafe of wine.

If you want more you have to pay for it. But they kind of disapprove of us getting pissed.'

Hell's friend Charlie was coming in at six when he finished work. Would May be having a friend too, she wondered? No. Celia wouldn't come.

'I don't mean Celia,' said Hell. 'I mean the bloke.'

'He doesn't know, he's in Dublin, and he's married,' said May.

'Well, Charlie's married, but he bloody knows, and he'd know if he were on the moon.'

'It's different.'

'No, it's not different. It's the same for everyone, there are rules, you're a fool to break them. Didn't he pay for it either, this guy?'

'No. I told you he doesn't know.'

'Aren't you noble,' said Hell scornfully. 'Aren't you a real Lady Galahad. Just visiting London for a day or two, darling, just going to see a few friends, see you soon. Love you darling. Is that it?'

'We don't go in for so many darlings as that in Dublin,' said May.

'You don't go in for much common sense either. What will you gain, what will he gain, what will anyone gain? You come home penniless, a bit lonely. He doesn't know what the hell you've been doing, he isn't extra-sensitive and loving and grateful because he doesn't have anything to be grateful about as far as he's concerned.'

'I couldn't tell him. I couldn't. I couldn't ask him for £200 and say what it was for. That wasn't in the bargain, that was never part of the deal.'

May was almost tearful, mainly from jealousy she thought. She couldn't bear Hell's Charlie to come in, while her Andy was going home to his wife because there would be nobody to cook him something exciting and go to bed with him in his little manager's flat.

'When you go back, tell him. That's my advice,' said Hell. 'Tell him you didn't want to worry him, you did it all on your own because the responsibility was yours since you didn't take the Pill. That's unless you think he'd have wanted it?'

'No, he wouldn't have wanted it.'

'Well then, that's what you do. Don't ask him for the money straight out, just let him know you're broke. He'll react some way then. It's silly not to tell them at all. My sister did that with her bloke back in Melbourne. She never told him at all, and she got upset because he didn't know the sacrifice she had made, and every time she bought a drink or paid for a cinema ticket she got resentful of him. All for no reason, because he didn't bloody know.'

'I might,' said May, but she knew she wouldn't.

Charlie came in. He was great fun, very fond of Hell, wanting to be sure she was okay, and no problems. He brought a bottle of wine which they shared, and he told them funny stories about what had happened at the office. He was in advertising. He arranged to meet Hell for lunch next day and joked his way out of the room.

'He's a lovely man,' said May.

'Old Charlie's smashing,' agreed Hell. He had gone back home to entertain his wife and six dinner guests. His wife was a marvellous hostess apparently. They were always having dinner parties.

'Do you think he'll ever leave her?' asked May.

'He'd be out of his brains if he did,' said Hell cheerfully.

May was thoughtful. Maybe everyone would be out of their brains if they left good, comfortable, happy home set-ups for whatever the other woman imagined she could offer. She wished she could be as happy as Hell.

'Tell me about your fellow,' Hell said kindly.

May did, the whole long tale. It was great to have somebody to listen, somebody who didn't say she was on a collision course, somebody who didn't purse up lips like Celia, someone who said, 'Go on, what did you do then?'

'He sounds like a great guy,' said Hell, and May smiled happily.

They exchanged addresses, and Hell promised that if ever she came to Ireland she wouldn't ring up the hotel and say, 'Can I talk to May, the girl I had the abortion with last winter?' and they finished Charlie's wine, and went to sleep.

The beds were stripped early next morning when the final examination had been done, and both were pronounced perfect and ready to leave. May wondered fancifully how many strange life stories the room must have seen.

'Do people come here for other reasons apart from . . . er, terminations?' she asked the disapproving Irish nurse.

'Oh certainly they do, you couldn't work here otherwise,' said the nurse. 'It would be like a death factory, wouldn't it?'

That puts me in my place, thought May, wondering why she hadn't the courage to say that she was only visiting the home, she didn't earn her living from it.

She let herself into Celia's gloomy flat. It had become gloomy again like the way she had imagined it before she saw it. The warmth of her first night there was gone. She looked around and wondered why Celia had no pictures, no books, no souvenirs.

There was a note on the telephone pad.

'I didn't ring or anything, because I forgot to ask if you had given your real name, and I wouldn't know who to ask for. Hope you feel well again. I'll be getting some chicken pieces so we can have supper together around 8. Ring me if you need me. C.'

May thought for a bit. She went out and bought Celia a casserole dish, a nice one made of cast-iron. It would be useful for all those little high-protein, low-calorie dinners Celia cooked. She also bought a bunch of flowers, but could find no vase when she came back and had to use a big glass instead. She left a note thanking her for the hospitality, warm enough to sound properly grateful, and a genuinely warm remark about how glad she was that she had been able to do it all through nice Dr Harris. She said nothing about the time in the nursing-home. Celia would prefer not to know. May just said that she was fine, and thought she would go back to Dublin tonight. She rang the airline and booked a plane.

Should she ring Celia and tell her to get only one chicken piece? No, damn Celia, she wasn't going to ring her. She had a fridge, hadn't she?

The plane didn't leave until the early afternoon. For a wild moment she thought of joining Hell and Charlie in the pub where they were meeting, but dismissed the idea. She must now make a list of what clothes she was meant to have bought and work out a story about how they had disappeared. Nothing that would make Andy get in touch with police or airlines to find them for her. It was going to be quite hard, but she'd have to give Andy some explanation of what she'd been doing, wouldn't she? And he would want to know why she had spent all that money. Or would he? Did he even know she had all that money? She couldn't remember telling him. He wasn't very interested in her little savings, they talked more about his investments. And she must remember that if he was busy or cross tonight or tomorrow she wasn't to take it out on him. Like Hell had said, there wasn't any point in her expecting a bit of cosseting when he didn't even know she needed it.

How sad and lonely it would be to live like Celia, to be so suspicious of men, to think so ill of Andy. Celia always said he was selfish and just took what he could get. That was typical of Celia, she understood nothing. Hell had understood more, in a couple of hours, than Celia had in three years. Hell knew what it was like to love someone.

But May didn't think Hell had got it right about telling Andy all about the abortion. Andy might be against that kind of thing. He was very moral in his own way, was Andy.

TECHNICAL DIFFICULTIES
AND THE PLAGUE

CLARE BOYLAN
Born in Dublin, 1948, Clare Boylan was for many years one of Ireland's
leading journalists before turning to full-time creative writing. Her first
novel came out in 1983 and she has since published three further
novels and two collections of short stories, *A Nail In The Head* and
Concerning Virgins.

The things women do to their children. I know a woman who called her children Elgar and Mozart. Elge and Moze, they are now. But children can be cruel too.

I called my children Robin and Rosemary, nice names for nice children. It suits their pink cheeks and the light curl of their gold-brown hair. I can say without exaggeration that I gave up everything for them. I gave up the chance of a good career and stayed with my husband, who was never the life and soul of the party. After all that, what do you think they did? They never came.

I don't often brood but I am sitting alone at a cafe in a foreign country and a strange man has just sat down beside me, so you can excuse my mind for running riot. Robin and Rosemary. Their little ghosts do not haunt me but I feel the weight of their ingratitude. I waited so long for them. Everything was ready. I had my insides checked out. They were like a new pin. My husband had his sperm inspected for short measure, but he had been packed to capacity. The little bastards simply couldn't be bothered to turn up.

There is something familiar about the man but I expect that's just my imagination.

You know how it is when you're on your own in a strange place; first there is the giddy freedom. Then you start peering into your handbag. After that you begin imagining things about the people around you.

What annoyed me about Robin and Rosemary is the fact that they were so much Desmond's children – not really mine at all. That business of keeping me waiting, they got that straight from their father. All through our marriage he has been vanishing on mysterious errands, leaving me sitting at home or in the car, or God knows where. He says he has to go and buy a paper or get some money or relieve himself, but he takes so long one feels he must have negotiated the purchase of Times Newspapers or held up the bank. Who knows what

he does to relieve himself. Once I accused him of spending time with
other women. His response irritated me so much that I seriously
thought of leaving him. 'Who'd have me?' he said, and he laughed at
both of us.

You won't guess where I am now. I am on the Piazza del Campo
in Siena, at that restaurant with the blue and white awning and tables
on the shady side of the square. It is a sunny spring morning and we
came here to have a look at the Etruscan Museum and then a lunch
of asparagus at Guido's. Suddenly Itchy Britches got up and said he
had something to see to. 'Don't be long,' I begged him, but you might
as well ask Dustin Hoffman not to be short.

This man who has sat down beside me is not unlike Dustin Hoffman.
He is dark with a kind of nervous mouth that twitches into a smile
when he catches me looking at him. He smokes a lot. In spite of his
nervousness he does not look away.

He has a way of holding one's gaze, of drawing you deep into those
Amaretto-coloured eyes. People change but their eyes never change.
At first I didn't recognise him because of his clothes. He is much
richer than he used to be, bits of Gaultier and Cartier stuck all over
him. It was only when I found myself wandering into those pools of
peat-coloured velvet and I suddenly tripped over my own entrails that
I realised who had sat down beside me. 'Jesus Christ,' I muttered.
The man laughed. Giorgio – that's his name – laughed. It gave me a
chance to compose myself. I leaned back, took one of his cigarettes
and held my hand steady to light it. 'Hi!' I said. He beamed at me
(that slightly rueful, vaguely wolfish grin) – 'Don't I know you from
somewhere?' Two can play at that game. I studied him, as if my life
was an endless queue of Dustin Hoffman lookalikes awaiting identification. 'Somewhere,' I said remotely. 'Well, you're looking good,' he
laughed.

Now that is the truth. In spite of everything I look all right. I'll tell
you something. Any woman can look terrific. All you need is a lot of
money. I got that from my parents.

I deserved it after what they did – or rather, tried to do – regarding
my upbringing. Well, they died young, which shows that there is a
God in heaven. Anyway, you have to get your hair done once a month
at the most expensive place in town, and tip too much which ensures
you are always dealt with by the head honcho. You need four trips to
the sun a year. My legs are brown all year long. They never peel.
You have to have fantastic clothes. Men say they don't notice clothes
and it's true. It's not the clothes they notice but a total effect. Getting

the right clothes is my neatest trick. I go into one of those expensive boutiques where the girls are always dressed in tight pants and angora sweaters with silver inserts, and I say: 'Look, I'm having an affair with this amazing guy and I need something really special to wear.' Young girls are very creative in the arena of sex. They take on the part and pick out something for you as if they were the ones having the affair. They're used to the clothes. They know how they sit. Depend upon it, you'll walk out with something good. There is a drawback to this sort of transaction. Quite often the girls are very forward and will ask you questions of an intimate nature. I find it's best to just invent a whole scenario, because otherwise they lose heart and will dump you with something in apricot pleated chiffon which makes your bottom look like a pyjama case.

Today I am wearing black linen with big bone buttons, open almost to the thigh. There is a chunk of gold jewellery on one shoulder and my hair partially hides this from view.

My hair comes down in very pretty strings of mouse and yellow colour with intriguing threads of silver and gold. On top it looks as if it was caught in the wind, but only in the right direction. My face is doing well for its age. I have a slight squint, but men seem to find this attractive, and small neat white teeth and a plump sort of mouth.

I wish my husband could see me now. The way this handsome foreigner – my ex-lover in case you hadn't guessed – is looking at me, would drive even the most yellow-blooded husband to a frenzy of fury. He has ordered coffee and brandy for us and is talking about Siena, but his eyes are saying that somewhere under that thatch of rumpled-looking brown hair there is a hand reaching out to undo the next button on my skirt and slide in to feel the skin of palest primrose silk which is all there is between me and decency.

Do lovers know when seduction begins? He is telling me about the Palio, but every word he uses is passion, frenzy, sweat, climax. His brown hand beats the table as he talks of rolling drums and clanging bells, of plot and prayer and pantagruelian feasts.

Swirling through the ancient streets come mace bearers, flag bearers, trumpeters, palace musicians; captains, centurions, district representatives, drummers, flag bearers, pages. There are the knights of the Lion, Bear, Strong Sword, Viper and, of course, the Cock. By the time the riders enter, the surging crowd is delirious with excitement. 'But it only lasts a minute,' I say, 'the Palio. What do all those people do afterwards?'

'They get drunk,' he says. 'They go home and make love.'

'All those poor tourists,' I shake my head; 'having to go home to
Stockholm and Texas and Hong Kong and Canberra to make love.'

He laughs. 'They should come to live in Siena like me.'

'Oh, you live here now?' I am all coyness and politeness. Who
writes the lousy scripts?

He is lucky enough, he tells me, to live right inside the walls on the
Via della Galluzza, a preserved medieval street spanned by eight
arches draped with authentic washing. His little house is dark, so he
has chosen three small pieces of art – a terracotta urn from the
Roman period, a fifteenth-century manuscript and a small religious
painting attributed to Sodoma – and illuminated only these.

'The effect,' he says, 'is . . . intimate. I think you would like it.'

'Are you saying you'd like to show me your etchings?'

'No,' (How can so bad a man manage to look so ingenuous?), 'I'd
like to make love to you.'

Strolling beside him across the square which is not a square but the
shell of a scallop, I remember what it was about him that delighted
and enraged me. Giorgio was never in a hurry. Having made me ready
for love he seems to have forgotten he ever mentioned it. He has
separated himself from me. He is showing off. He asks me how well
I know Siena. Siena is a convent, he says, Florence a salon, Venice
a whorehouse. Do I know Lorenzetti's 'Madonna of Milk' in the Arch-
bishop's Palace? Have I ever used that slot machine in the cathedral
that gives you an English commentary when you put in a coin? He has
treats in store for me. Treats. His teeth flash on the word. I could
kill him.

Time is not as important now as it used to be. I seem to have put
in half a lifetime of waiting. When I was young it was everything.
Opportunities came like comets, burning themselves out in a blazing
trail. Even memory turns to ash. I can scarcely remember my time
with Giorgio, except as a little ache of regret and some even tinier
twinge of irritation.

What went wrong? We could have been married. Think what our
children would look like.

All the same, I can see why he would earn his place in the Good
Lovers' Guide. He is clever. He is a tease. When I ask a question he
pretends he cannot hear and leans so close my mouth is on the hair
that curls softly around his ear. When he guides me across the street,
his hand is on the base of my spine, almost on my backside. He may
have forgotten that he invited me to be seduced, but he makes it
impossible for me to forget.

By now you must be wondering what happens when my husband gets back. Believe me, I would be grateful for a small fit of jealous rage. He'll have a drink, look at his watch, order something to eat. If I haven't returned by the time he's eaten, he'll have another drink, start falling asleep and then go back to the hotel for a siesta. When I get back he'll ask me if I had a nice day.

To hell with husbands. We step out of the sunshine and into the chill of the Duomo. It takes a moment of getting used to, like when you first slide into bed and the cool sheets electrify your skin. The sweat beneath my arms goes cold, my slippery feet begin to reassert their grip on sandals.

Then comes a rush of heat as Giorgio turns to kiss me. Right there in the blazing gloom of the cathedral, with crepe-soled tourists and evil-eyed old black-clad women, his lips are on mine and it is like the first taste of a fresh fig. I am crippled by want. I cannot move. He strides off between the black and white striped marble pillars, which make a perfect designer backdrop for his soft wool clothes. I run to catch him. The feeble clap of my sandals proclaims the weakness of my sex. He is making a phone call, no, putting money in something. I touch his arm. Instead of the embrace I need, he is clamping earphones on my head.

The device is ordinary enough. A selection of slides appears on a screen and a commentary gives you all the most boring details – which century, what pope, how valuable. But the voice! This is the English commentary and the voice is that of the young queen at her coronation – a butterfly packed in ice. I am mesmerised, I am outraged. Is this his idea of a joke, to invade me with virgin purity so that I will feel like the sordid sweaty tourist I am? I glare at him. He is smiling, the bastard. The young queen is telling me about the construction of the New Duomo. It was a fantastic project, intended to cover the whole area of the Campo. Heaven was to be pierced by the spire, tall and blinding with its stripes of black marble and layers of squinting windows.

Great slabs of black marble flew on their high scaffolding like fragile compact discs. Wafers of glass quivered and snapped in the breath of a capricious God.

Why do people always want the impossible? You might as well ask why love never lasts. But that is not the problem. When a love affair ends, there is no more to be said. The real question is, why do love affairs fail to end? Look back on any you've been lucky enough to suffer, and you'll never be able to remember what went wrong. You

can waste a whole lifetime in retrospective rehearsals, trying to locate
some tiny draught that snuffed out the inferno, convinced that but for
that dress or this word, you could have had happiness as long as you
lived.

I look at Giorgio with his amused grin and his brown self full of
essential maleness as a truffle is full of its fragrance. My perfect twin.
He even knows how to take the starch out of me, how to make me
female and vulnerable. I am wistful and quivering, in need of making
love as much as sex. How did it end?

'Unfortunately it never reached completion,' the young queen is
telling me, although of course she is talking about the Duomo. 'This
was due to technical difficulties . . . and the plague.'

I have an unfortunate laugh. I holler. Giorgio still has his wry smile
but I holler.

One hundred and seventy-two popes and thirty-six emperors gaze
down at me furiously from the walls.

Afterwards we plod up the steep streets through the Jewish quarter, past the church of San Girolamo, and the Via dei Servi to the
church of St Mary of the Servants and the Piazza Allesandro Manzoni.
From here, the whole city is laid out like a delicate antipasto, the little
pink roof tiles as dainty as overlapped slices of carpaccio. The spire
of the Duomo is a pencil sketch by Ruskin beneath a stockinged lens
of a sky.

As you get older you need a lover to aid long-distance vision, the
same way you need glasses. Your sight gets clouded by specks of
disaster. You see a child walking on a wall, trying to kill itself. You
notice some woman, who has been wrenched and wrung by sorrow
until even her feet won't set themselves down straight, and you think
'My God, she's younger than me.' The protection of an admirer makes
all these things irrelevant and therefore invisible. I suppose there is
violence and discontent and poverty and jealousy in the narrow streets
that lead down to the Campo, but all I can see is a vision of heaven.
There is a faint nagging irritation behind the bridge of my nose, but
you get that from wearing spectacles too.

The celestial effects department have also been at work in Giorgio's
little house. The lighting is lovely. Imagine a cathedral that was warm
instead of cool, that had soft furniture to sink into, that led on to a
flowery courtyard behind. It's like a painting – a Turner – where
nothing quite exists but is defined by light. I suppose it might seem
gloomy in different circumstances.

He tells me to take off my dress and leaves me on a black sofa while he goes to open some wine. Brown skin and primrose silk panties look lovely in this light.

He brings wine that glows like candlelight. We kiss until I reach a slow rolling boil and then he takes off his clothes and what remain of mine. Unencumbered by worldly goods and hand in hand and toe to toe, we are about to fly into heaven.

'You know,' Giorgio smiles, 'this doesn't feel quite right.'

'It feels right to me,' I say as nicely as possible. 'What's the matter?'

He removes the top half of his torso from mine and bends to the floor for his glass of wine. 'I don't know your name.'

The nagging in my nose spreads upwards and becomes a pulsing band across my forehead. 'Call me Mrs Henebry, Giorgio,' I say. 'That's my married name, if that's what you wanted to know.'

'All right, Mrs Henebry,' he says slowly: 'but my name's not Giorgio. It's Leonardo.'

Giorgio has commenced a feathery, circular massage but the magic has gone. I can't concentrate. I can't stand a mean-spirited man.

'Listen!' I sit up so rapidly that his chin hits my forehead. 'You don't have to protect yourself from me. You don't have to change your identity in case I have you traced or something. I'm not after you – not this time.'

'It's all right, dear Mrs Henebry,' Giorgio strokes my hair. He kisses my eyes. 'I only want to make you happy.'

He's a complex sort of person. I suppose I should enjoy myself, since I don't often get the chance. I'm not young and vulnerable any more. Why the hell should I care about his games so long as I have the company of his pleasure? All the same, I feel I owe it to my younger and more fragile self not to let him get away with it. He hasn't even bothered to change his lines. 'I only want to make you happy.' That's exactly what he said to me the first time.

'Why didn't you marry me, Giorgio?' I say. 'When we were young?'

He gives me an odd, assessing sort of look. 'It is a pity, but alas I did not know you then.'

'How much does it take to know me? You took away my innocence. I gave you my trust.'

He sits up. He shrugs. Naked, he lopes off to look for cigarettes. 'I don't know what you are playing at, but I have never met you in my life before.' When he returns he perches on an edge of the furniture and lights a cigarette. He is back in his leisurely mood. He seems to have forgotten there is a naked woman waiting for him on the sofa. 'You know, Mrs Henebry,' he says; 'you worry me a little. Perhaps you are the kind of woman who makes love to a man and afterwards says she was raped. I think maybe you take your fantasies a little too seriously.'

'What do you mean fantasies, Giorgio?' By now I am furious. 'You think it's some sort of fantasy that we met in Florence as students and you made me your lover and promised to marry me?'

'My name is Leonardo.' He leaves his cigarette poised in his mouth while he bends to retrieve his trousers from the floor and puts them on with a carefulness that indicates an appreciation of his own body. The fall of brown hair over his forehead still tugs at my heart. 'I am thinking,' he says, 'perhaps you are a little confused.'

'Confused?' I reach out and smack him smartly across the face. It isn't the word. It's the awful sliding sense of déjà vu.

All day he has been undermining me but now he has taken me right back. Suddenly I remember everything. Naturally I was confused. I was nineteen and an orphan and had given him all my confidence. I kept nothing from him. 'It was Aunt Lilian, wasn't it? That's why you left me. It was after I told you about our family skeleton – poor loony Aunt Lil. You thought our children might turn out to be nut cases. You thought I might have caught the weird streak.'

He gets up quickly and walks across the room, shrugging into his shirt, buttoning up, protecting himself. 'You're crazy,' he mutters.

There comes a point in life (I believe this happens to most women) where you simply are not prepared to put up with one more single piece of insulting behaviour from any man whatsoever. Feeling perfectly calm, I climb off the sofa and silently cross the floor, pluck the terracotta urn from the Roman period out of its illuminated niche and break it over the back of his head. It is heavy. I didn't think it would break. 'Sorry,' I say to the figure on the floor, 'about the urn.'

Later on, back at the cafe on the Campo, I wonder if he was alive or dead. There was an oddly permanent look to his expression of surprise. Thinking about that *maschera*, I begin to wonder if it really was Giorgio. The eyes were definitely the same, but now I seem to recall that Giorgio had a deep cleft in his chin.

However, there are other things to preoccupy me. I see Desmond lumbering across the square in the afternoon heat. I am almost glad to see him. I will overlook his awful jacket like an ice-cream sales-man's, his squeaky shoes and the thinning patch on top of his head. To look at me nobody would believe that I was waiting for such a second-rate specimen of the male sex but we have been through a lot together. We are veterans of the fertility clinic.

'Where the hell have you been?' I say quite amiably when he slumps opposite me at the table.

Do you know what he does? He doesn't even answer me. He gets up and moves to the next table.

I stand over him like a spider and thump the table until the little wrapped sugars jump in their bowl. 'Desmond?' I say, 'speak to me.'

He looks embarrassed and unhappy, the miserable coward. 'Look,' he whispers, 'you're making a mistake. My name isn't Desmond.'

'Go on,' I yell, commanding an audience as I intend to. 'Tell me now you're not my husband.'

I'm reminded of a figure in a painting by Munch as he flees across the square, his cream jacket flapping, his hands raised in dismay. I feel no remorse. Why would he not have the guts to just say straight out he is not my husband when that is the truth? Actually, for a minute I thought it was Desmond. The light has gone round and the sun is in my eyes.

When I was very young I used to think you could make things happen. I know better now. I was sixteen and entombed in wealthy suburbia by two parents so dull that it is distasteful to think of their part in my existence. I wanted to try my wings, to experiment with life. My parents thought I was crazy. They observed me like a specimen under glass. They wanted me to *see* someone, they said.

What they really wanted was to have me put away. Sadly, they perished in a fire which also took all traces of the ugly house.

After that I thought it was just a matter of getting on with life but I never met anyone to match my pace. I was just passed from one set of fatally indecisive hands to the next, like a bucket in a fire line, destined never to reach the blaze. I waited for my life, for my lover, for my children.

Most of all I waited for my husband whose absences are of such duration and assortment that sometimes, sitting in this hotel lobby or that square, watching the cast change or the weather run through its repertoire, I find myself wondering if he really exists at all.

TRIO

HELEN LUCY BURKE

Born in Dublin, Helen Lucy Burke has had many stories in periodicals and anthologies in Ireland, Britain and Germany since her first publication in *The Irish Press* 'New Irish Writing' in 1969. She has also published a novel and a collection of short stories, *A Season for Mothers*, and in recent years has acquired a formidable reputation as a drama critic and a commentator on restaurants for *The Sunday Tribune*.

Two people, a man and a little boy, were walking quickly along the road. The man had a white stick in one hand. His other hand rested on the boy's shoulder. The boy, too, had a stick, or rather a staff. He was dressed in Scout's uniform. By the look on his face he seemed to be proud of the physical contact with the man, though from time to time to maintain it he had to take a few steps at a jog-trot. He kept up a steady stream of talk to which the man replied at random.

About a hundred yards before the crossroads the repair gang had been at work. Even before they came to the rough place, the man slowed down and began to pat left and right with his stick.

'How did you know the repairs were there?' asked the boy.

'By the sound, by the sound,' said the man, smiling.

'But they don't make any sound.'

'We make it for them,' said the man.

The little boy could make no sense of the reply, and felt the man was making fun of him.

'Close your eyes and listen the next time,' explained the man who sensed the boy's hurt. 'You'll hear your steps getting dull and thumpy.'

It was a mid-afternoon in the end of April. The wind seemed soft but had a concealed edge. When they came to the turning the man let go the boy's shoulder and turned up the collar of his coat. He stood still for a minute or so, with his shuttered face tilted towards the sky.

'It's a blue sky with bits of white,' said the boy importantly. 'Do you know what blue is?'

'Of course,' said the man. 'It's like this.' He whistled a snatch of melody, rather quick and dashing. 'And this is white.' This time the tune seemed to the boy to be very slow and winding.

'How could a tune be a colour?' asked the boy.

'How could it not?' replied the man. 'In that gate, now, and up the drive, and mind you don't trip yourself up on the stone sill.'

As they went through the gate the boy stumbled on the ledge and felt resentfully that the blind man must be laughing at him. Dead leaves from several winters clogged the edges of the drive. He shuffled his feet through them, making a crackling noise like cornflakes. It was a long walk for a shilling, and there would be the calling back for Mr Garvey and leading him to his own house. All the same, he knew it would look good on the report sheet for the Scoutmaster. None of the other fellows would have done anything as charitable or romantic. It was his mother who had suggested it.

'Does your sister walk you here every Saturday just to listen to Miss Moone's gramophone?'

'My sister is a very kind woman to her brother.'

The boy worked this statement out in silence for a minute.

'You must be terrible fond of music,' he said politely. 'They play us music at school sometimes, but it often hasn't any tune at all. I don't call that music. It's just made-up.'

'Ah, that's the best kind,' said Garvey. 'You can fit your own tune to it.'

'Why wouldn't you just turn on the radio?'

'You don't hear chamber-music on the radio,' the man replied absently, 'and anyway she has stereo, which makes all the difference.'

They came round a bend among the trees and the house loomed over them. The man knocked on the door in a knowing-he-was-expected sort of way. Fumbling in his pocket he produced a coin.

'Oh, no,' protested the little boy, shocked. 'It's a shilling, you know, only, a Bob a Job, and I can't take it until I've fully finished and brought you home again. That's the rule.'

The door swung back. In the opening Miss Moone loomed like a tree. Her waving arms of welcome were tossing branches. Her body the trunk of a fir.

The boy got well back behind his companion. He knew Miss Moone, not only because she often halted her cavalry-dash progress into the shops to talk to his mother, but also because several times he had formed part of the yapping band who followed her about shouting 'Big Miss Moone, Ticky tacky toon, Is it cold up in the sky? Reach me down a star.' Now and then she lashed out with her walking-stick at her tormentors. Mostly though she either went on as if she heard nothing, or else just turned and gave them the sort of look that would be pitiful and pleading in a woman half her bulk, but made Miss Moone look like a bullock in the slaughteryard.

'This is Edward,' said the blind man. 'I'm his good deed. Hetty wasn't able to bring me and the road is up along by the cross, so . . .'

He tapped with his stick and laughed. 'Edward will call for me about six o'clock.'

He turned around to Eddie (And how did he know where I was standing? wondered the boy) and gave him a slight slap on the shoulder. It might have been a thank-you or it could have been in joke. The door closed. Through the panes in the upper half he saw the two going up the wide staircase towards Miss Moone's drawing-room, the angles of her figure as clearly defined as a handful of forks through the waves of dimpled glass.

A few drops of rain began to fall as a mat of white fleece swept across the pale yellow face of the sun. Suddenly tired of being a Scout the boy decided to try being an Indian. On soundless moccasined feet he flitted through the deep groves. The hawk-eyes were keen and watchful. No leaf bent. No twig cracked. But the game was quickly discarded as useless. The deserted garden with its unmown grass washing up about the pedestals of the cracked statues could not present even an imaginary hazard without which the game could not be sustained.

From an upstairs room of the square stone house, through an open window a branch of music blossomed.

'Blue and white,' muttered the little boy, shaking his head from side to side in bewilderment. He trotted cautiously to the foot of a chestnut tree which leaned in towards the open window. A stiff mat of thorn and grass provided a hiding-place for his staff. Spitting on his hands he began a struggling climb up the smooth-muscled trunk into the tangle of branches.

'Oh, how I love this early Spring sun,' cried Miss Moone. She led Garvey to a seat on the couch and pressed him into its chintzy depths.

Huge overblown roses on a yellowish background that had once been white. Her dear mother's choice. For a second she admired the splay of her hand against his shoulder, the fingers long and sensitive, the nails well-turned, oh the Moones had always good hands for the old blood showed! Then to provide an excuse for the lingering touch she nudged him gently sideways to where the pool of sunshine poured itself in a shaft of shivering gold on the arm of the couch.

'Feel the heat. Can you feel it, can you feel it?' Her voice had become a serious clarinet as she thought about her own thoughtfulness. For of course blind people are more sensitive to all influences on the remaining senses.

And there to prove it, Garvey was basking in the sunlight like a cat, with such twists and wriggles as if he were stroking himself

against it. From far back in infancy he could remember a genial presence that beat against his eyelids, turning even *his* darkness to a warm
red, before that vestige, too, had faded. But even yet, by tilting his
face to a shadowed sky, he could say to his sighted companions,
'There it is: the sun,' and be more sure than they were.

'A nice, nice, sunshiny room,' he drawled, stretching out his legs
and giving the feet a little pirouette like the beginning of a ballet figure.
'And now, some suitable music?' In a reflective manner he added, 'We
had the Bartok last week.'

Miss Moone recalled, as she invariably did, some details from a
book in her father's library, telling how blind girls in China were urged
into prostitution, the loss of power in one of the senses increasing the
voltage in the others. And men?

This alien fifty per cent of her own race seemed to Miss Moone to
be composed of beings unmoved by the fates which affected women.
Even her father had appeared to her to be of a different species, as
if he had dropped from some other planet and acquired the rudiments
of speech without penetrating to its heart. And yet, with all that,
somehow in the presence of men she felt that it was *she* who was the
intruder, the aborigine who lingered on into the culture of the
invaders. Only Garvey, whom she saw every Saturday, who never
saw her, seemed innocent of threat, perhaps only because his severe
gaze turned always inwards had never seared her huge frame with
the invariable mortifying quiver of, first, surprise, then laughter, which
was dealt out to her by stranger males. Before, that is, they learned
she was the rich Miss Moone.

Oh undoubtedly, she thought, Garvey was different; and you could
never guess by the quietness of him that he was a man at all. She
searched her mind for some delicacy of action that would show him
he was with a finer soul than the common run, for she felt that he had
a sensitive face with traces of hurt on it. Boorish people would have
offended him, even with well-meant sympathy. The thing for her to
do was to offer him what he could enjoy without any allusion to what
he lacked. The Beethoven A Minor Quartet? No, no, that was music
to hear in ecstatic stillness. What she wanted was something knee-
squeezing, a graceful joyous melody at the culmination of which she
could drop a comradely hand on his thigh, confident that the gesture
would not be misunderstood.

The Mozart Quintet – yes, that was it.

A flurry of clarinet notes replied conversationally to the strings as
she threw herself down on the carpet in the pool of sunshine.

'It's just the right kind of music for this room and this time of year,' she murmured, softly as she thought. (Though in fact her murmur, coming from her huge frame, was like the drone of a bassoon.)

His face nodded up and down in reply. It had the wistful knowingness of a Gothic saint in weathered limestone. The eyes were bright blue, and except for a fixity of focus, seemed as capable of vision as her own. Not for him the dark glasses of a conventional blind man; they were only for those sightless horrors whose eyes had wheeled and turned in their heads until they looked like filmy poached eggs; she had seen many of them begging with boxes. And she herself had her own use for dark glasses; great octagonal ones she had for walking in town which rendered her completely invisible, she felt, all six feet three of muscle and bone that separated brindle head from heel; and the dark glasses also helped her hearing into deafness so that she could not hear the catcalls or the muttered jokes.

'The stereo is wonderful,' said Garvey in the pause between the movements. 'We might have them sitting here with us. De Bavier,' he added vaguely, gesturing towards the end of the couch as if the soloist were sitting there.

Miss Moone gave her attention to the music which was rippling through the room in competition with the song of a blackbird who was proclaiming that the chestnut tree and the nest midway up belonged to him, to him, and not the boy huddled in the fork of the tree.

'Do you think he quite had it there? There's another version that I had . . .' Garvey shushed her to silence. He seemed to be inhaling the music through the pores of his skin, leaning slightly forward so that the sunlight fell on half of his head. It brightened the hair it touched to russet while the rest of his head was shadowed black.

Apologetic to his hostess, he said when the movement ended, 'I wanted to get that bit.' He whistled a few notes and patted his chest as if he had stored the melody there.

Oh the pity, oh the pity. Sighing to herself Miss Moone moved over beside the fire and began to remove her clothes. Her melancholy was more pronounced than usual, partly because it was Spring and partly because she had been shopping the previous day for a dressing-gown. As usual she had sought something pink and perhaps frilled, and as usual she had finished up in a man's shop buying a grey hairy thing 'for my brother. About the same size as me.'

The blouse, folded tidily, she hung beside the cherry-coloured cardigan over the back of the chair. She had moved out of the sunlight into the red of the fire. It burnt her shoulder as she stooped forward to unfasten the brassiere which she wore over a woollen vest. Without it, her breasts dropped suddenly and flattened themselves. Until she removed her vest her figure might have been a man's. In bare feet and wearing only a skirt she moved back across the room out of the warm redness into the lemony pallor, the thin April sunlight that had a sour edge of frost to it.

'This is beautiful,' said Garvey dreamily. A Bach cello suite was filling the room with dark sound.

To the boy in the tree it was bewilderment. Hooting sounds going from high to low, that were supposed to be music, and that queer big woman doing rude things. Of course Mr Garvey couldn't actually see the rude things so perhaps they didn't count, really . . . She was bending herself forward and then suddenly drawing herself upright with a snap so that the two long triangular flaps of flesh which hung from each side of her chest tossed in the air. She was so close to Mr Garvey that if he had reached his hand out into the air the flaps would hit him. But Mr Garvey was lying back in the depths of the couch, wearing an expression of great peace on his face though his eyes were wide open and glinting in blue flashes where the light struck them. And now Miss Moone had her back to the window so that Eddie could not make out well what she was at, except that it made him feel all embarrassed like reading those bits out of Bible in class, and wanting to look away, or feeling he ought to, and not being able. Her back was a funny colour, he noticed, and the skin was all slack like the way balloons got when they were left over after Christmas, with little puckered marks and a way the eye had of knowing that they would be unpleasant to the touch. When you poked at them the dent stayed in the surface; his grandmother had been able to do that with her feet before she died. And Miss Moone's back had red marks over it as well. And now, Janey, she was running around the room, in and out between the furniture.

In her own mind she was clothed only in light, on Mount Ida. A Bacchante, a Maenad, a tree-nymph, released every Saturday from the spell of enchantment that held her prisoner to respectability and a jumper and skirt.

She circled the room at a dizzying pace. Oh if Mr Garvey only had eyes and thank God he had not! These Saturdays were all she had to remind her that she was a woman.

'Do you think we could have Haydn? The one we had last week?' asked Garvey. The Bach had frisked to a close.

Miss Moone sped on soundless feet to the chair near the window and paused for breath before answering.

'Oh that Bach. It's like tearing yourself away from Heaven. Yes, of course, I'll get the Haydn.'

The trembling of fatigue in her voice could easily be put down to musical emotion. A very creditable weakness.

Edward craned forward from his perch in the tree. He thought of certain cryptic statements made by his teacher during religious instruction. They began to make sense. Surely indeed something so ugly must be a sin, for surely God had never intended a woman to take up postures like this, whether anyone could see her or not. This lace shawl now – it was even worse than the skin!

Wrapping the folds around her Miss Moone thought of wedding days. It was in fact her mother's combing-jacket. Through its flower pattern her flesh shone pink-beige, and in her ears rang, not Haydn but nuptial music; and as she minced along the carpet a spectral groom, six feet six inches tall, supported her with his arm.

A celadon bowl, filled with narcissi, stood on the corner table. She glided to it, buried her face in the flowers for refreshment, took them from the water and held them to her breast. This was the way she would have stood; these the flowers to sustain her through the ceremony with their dreamy breath; there on the couch was the groom she should have had.

'Ah Miss Moone, I can't think why, but this music makes me think of weddings and flowers and happy spring things. Lambs, birds' nests, tender young girls . . .' His voice trailed away in a dreamy diminuendo.

He had turned his thin face to where Miss Moone was stealthily replacing the flowers in their vase. Once more Garvey had surprised her, for she could have sworn that she made no sound in leaving her place. With awe she remembered the uncanny sense of hearing possessed by the blind, for they can sense you in the far corner of a room by your heartbeats, a peculiar faculty like that of a mosquito for detecting the presence of a blood-bearer. In haste she began to clothe her torso again, as the Angelus rang out from the nearby Roman Catholic church.

Ten minutes later she was conducting Garvey decorously downstairs to where the little Boy Scout waited in the porch.

The two went down the path together. Neither spoke until they were out the gate. Then the boy asked, 'Is Miss Moone a good lady?'

'She is very good,' said Garvey. 'She is good to me and she is good to Miss Moone. And isn't that good enough for anyone?'

He had a queer kind of curly smile on his face, the boy noticed, and suddenly knew that Garvey did not need to be told a word about Miss Moone, not one single word, no more than if he and not Eddie had been sitting in the tree, no more than if he had eyes like the boy in the Grimm's fairy-story who could see through ten layers of bandages and split stones open with the keenness of his glance.

AS GOOD A REASON AS ANY

EVELYN CONLON
Born in Rockcorry, Co. Monaghan, 1952, Evelyn Conlon has lived in
Australia and Asia and now lives in Dublin where she is active in the
women's rights movement. She has published one collection of short
stories, *My Head Is Opening*, and a novel.

I had you because of your father. It was because of where I came from. He took me (not just me, me and your sister and your two brothers) in after the divorce. It's not often you'll get a man like that. That was three years after the divorce. I had given the children one total year each of my life as well as the rest of it. I was ready for comfort. I had come from my grandmother whom I had seen crying only once when I handed her my child, her first great-grandchild. She said it wasn't fair. Once, someone coming on holidays asked her if she had a car so they could get a lift around. She wrote back no, but she had a washing machine. Once she went to her daughter's house where there was a dishwasher. She said, we do them in the new sink at home. I didn't want to betray dignity like that but there I was, divorced. My aunts and uncles had gone to Mr and Mrs competitions and laughed coyly when asked which room the wife took off her nylons in and how the husband cut his toenails, as if they were modern visionaries. Things had disimproved over the generations.

Your father wanted a child of his own. After the divorce I'd been sitting one day with my brother outside the hotel waiting for our grandfather. He'd said, there's a wedding. I could see that. He wanted me to look and approve. He left the car to get the paper or so he said but my self, that was vicious by now with goading, knew that he was going to look to see who was getting married. Your father was a relief after all that.

When I was first married they used to ask me how I was doing, then they changed it to how are you both. If I had the questionable advantages of marriage they weren't going to let me away with thinking that I was still me. Then they'd try to make me work up some sympathy for the next-door neighbours who were still single, just to test. All I could feel was envy. Your father said, when I met him three years after the divorce, that I'd taken the woman out of women with

my cynicism. I was flattered because he knew something of me, even
if he'd got it all wrong, and I smiled and fell for him.

We lived happily for some time, he bumbling around an area that
he hadn't ordinanced. He had been written into the script late. I would
meet my next-door neighbour, who was happy that year as well, in
the morning or the evening, and we would greet each other with large
smirks as if we were hiding some secret from the rest of the street.
Lovely day, isn't it. Beautiful. Big smile. Awful day. An evening for
the fire. Grin. Then your father began to look wistfully at your sister
and two brothers, ah but they're not mine. I'd feel for him the same
as I used to feel for my unmarried neighbours, but he was convinced.
His seed or nothing. I thought about pregnancy. I knew he didn't.
Because he had no children of his own. Then I remembered that my
husband hadn't thought about it either even after the experience of
the first, because he didn't have to have them. I got into a state then
because I'd always wanted to believe that some part of my husband
could be locked away like Oliver Plunkett's head, kept free of my
disappointment. I could fill up my despair hole with another child,
surely. Trouble with mothers is that they fall for everyone – all their
children that is, even the ones they haven't got. Yet. It's always yet
when they get to that stage. Being was all that my other children
wanted from me, doing didn't come high on their list. Motherhood
was threatening again.

I remembered being sick. Worse still I remembered being tired.
Not a whiff of energy left as the new generation collected all the
goodies that it could from me, so that it would have an easy growth
in the water I too provided. But being sick makes you appreciate little
things – health, bedroom slippers, spouses, lovers – things like that.
You forget that you wouldn't need bedroom slippers all day if you
weren't sick. I felt guilt about your poor father who hadn't a child of
his own, even though some days I knew that I was really a pedestrian-
crossing, skipped and trampled on heartlessly by offspring as they
moved to something else. Mothers are like that. Guilty, I mean. I
remembered one day that I'd looked out the window, for fifteen
minutes, and when I had landed back among my care, zoomed in like
superwoman, they had surrounded me with toy soldiers, all of them
pointing their guns at me. I was hurt.

I thought again about pregnancy – the effect it would have on my
body structure, you know the muscles inside and out, the womb, the
stance, the bladder (I was crossing my legs daintily already when I
coughed or laughed too much, what would another one do?), but most

of all my back. My poor poor back. But I had been excused from the gym class of the world by this time. I belonged to no team and your father had been good to me.

I dreamed a lot about women. They were whispering me on. They'd all had their babies. Some of them had been thrown out of their homes for it. Some of them had murdered their babies and themselves. Some of them had given the babies away but they were all still egging me on. Next morning they would fade into one woman, perhaps a stranger I'd seen on the bus one day, who had too many children and was expecting again. She lived in a new country where people now smiled encouragingly at their two children and asked them did they have a nice day at school and taught them to be positive about themselves before the money would run out. I had sniffed, disgusted at her. Get out of the hole. The war is over. But in all honesty, she couldn't.

I myself had been in parks with children, not talking to others with children. Creating allies might cause a war. But I had to leave myself with some beliefs. I even knew that I shouldn't trust men who were out all day, but I did.

My second son was going to dancing in the New Contemporary School that used to be my friend's kitchen before she got divorced and moved to a smaller house because of the poverty. I could have done with a bit less starvation and a holiday, but time was moving on. I swore that if I had a child, this time I would tell it the truth of where I was reared. In the end it was easy enough and what wasn't easy about it you don't need to know yet. You don't mind me telling you this . . .

OJUS

SHANE CONNAUGHTON
Born in Kingscourt, Co. Cavan, 1941, Shane Connaughton was
brought up in a police station on the Fermanagh border where his
father served as a Sergeant. He has acted – he trained with the Bristol
Old Vic – has written TV plays as well as the screenplay for the film
'My Left Foot', a widely-praised collection of short stories, *A Border
Station*, and one novel.

As often as he could he escaped from the barracks to roam the drumlin fields or sit with the farmers in hedge or house until the rain had stopped.

There was water everywhere. In the sky, in the lakes, in the light; running off the hills, off the trees, off the roofs and cornered into barrels; in the lime-bottomed well, in the village pump, in the rain gauge at the rear of the station, always in the air and constantly on tap in women's eyes and children's hearts.

'They're born with water in their veins instead of blood,' his father said. Bucketing rain they called 'A damp class of a day'.

In summer he watched George Conlon trying to machine the meadow land and being forced in the end to use a scythe. The swathes lay for weeks trying to dry in the skimpy winds between showers.

A constant net of drizzle hung from hill to hill, the people trapped as fish.

Their lives were moist, their words dry.

'That's a bad downpour.'

'I have me share of it.'

Words gurgled in their mouths like water going down a drain. It was a liquidy language, cranky, flat, sticky as strong tea.

'Why is Butlershill like a springin' cow?'

'Why?'

''Cos it's near Cavan.'

'I don't get it.'

'The bull did.'

In his innocence he had left himself wide open for a double punchline. Conlon tried to explain it to him.

'It's a bucolic joke with a sexual bent depending on geographical word-play. The cute hoors love someone like you. They've nothing better to do.'

They lived on dumpy hills rising out of water, along a political Border

miles from Dublin or Belfast. Their cut-off lives ran long and narrow
as a sheugh but their hearts were open to the boy and from morning
until dark he helped them from the ploughtime of the year to harvest
home.

'Give that lad a ponger of milk. He's earned it. Are you able for
another hunk of bread? Course he is! What'll you have on it?'

'Jam, please.'

'Which one?'

'Rhubarb and ginger, please. It's the best I've ever tasted.'

'Ah-ha, he's the little smiler can charm the missus.'

On the good days when the sun got lost above them he knew it
was the greenest country in the world. The golden light magnified the
green of grass and ivy, geraniums in window boxes, the glinty eyes
of basking pikes. On golden days bone of earth and rock screamed
green to the hidden marrow.

'That's an ojus day.'

'You have your share of it.'

His window and the light were out of joint. The sun could only just
sneak into his bedroom. It slithered over the sill, down the wall,
across the lino, beaming for a few moments into the empty fireplace.

Good days, bad days, being out was freedom from the damp within.
In the woods and lakes and hills was happiness. He couldn't bear the
thought of being sent away.

The first he heard of it was from George Conlon. They were working in a turnip field, following a horse-drawn slipe, when Conlon stood
up to light a fresh cigarette from the butt of the old.

'We'll miss you when you go.'

Puzzled, the boy stared at him. A mesh of drizzle gusted up from
behind a hedge, falling sticky on his face like prickly sweat. He hated
pulling and snedding turnips. A lumpy cold vegetable, his fingers were
the same colour as them – freezing blue. Their tufts of turquoise
leaves looked like fantastical wet ears and the sleeves of his cardigan
were soaked with touching them. The gungy earth clodded his boots
and the water in the shallow drills slurped through his laces.

'I'm not going. Tea won't be ready for ages yet.'

Conlon gasped the smoke into his lungs. Adjusting his brown hat
he looked at the boy.

'No. I mean when you go away to school.'

The part of the hat he held when putting it on and off was black
from use.

'I am at school sure.'

He could see from Conlon's eyes he regretted having spoken.

'Maybe your mammy hasn't told you yet. She doesn't like the beatings that go on where you are. You're going to a boarding school instead. That's what she told me anyway.'

Lifting the rope reins from the slipe he flapped them over the horse's back. 'Up there.'

The mare rumped along the required few yards, wet earth falling from its huge hooves.

Panic could stab at you anytime, anywhere. Even in a turnip field. In an attempt to keep dry he had a slit potato sack, like a cowl, over his head and back. Throwing it off he bolted across the drills, through a sodden pasture, into the farmyard and out the drive onto the road. He had never known such fear grip his heart. He couldn't imagine his mother wanting to send him away. She needed him. How could there be miles between them, especially at night? It would be like death. And what would be the point of life without his father? He was frightened of him, he hated him but he loved him too.

He loved him in the mornings when he turned round from shaving, cut-throat in hand, to wink at the boy and laugh when he tried winking back. He loved him when his father held his hand tight, giving him his strength. He loved him when they swam in Kilifanah lake, his father shouting, 'Isn't it grand to be alive?' He loved him when he told him stories of his own father, Black Jack and his uncle Red Mick.

'I saw the pair of them drag a dead horse up onto a cart. With nothing but their bare hands.'

He loved to see him saunter through the village in his dark blue uniform, high and handsome as a star. He loved him when he held his mother's hand and sang as best he could, 'In Pasadena where grass is green now . . .'

He wasn't going to go away to a boarding school. He would never leave Butlershill and all the people who fed him and let him sit at their open fires until night came down.

Running pell-mell, blind with fear, he came into the village. The tethered goat was crying on the green. He always stopped and spoke to it but now he cut straight past and up the hill to home.

Going by the forge the blacksmith shouted to him.

'How's she cuttin' gossun?'

He was in too much of a hurry and far too angry to reply.

He was so angry he didn't notice the car parked outside the station. Tearing round to the married quarters and without taking his mucky boots off, he hurried straight into the kitchen.

'I'm not going to be sent away and don't try, so I'm not.'

The kitchen was empty. Where on earth was his mother? He was
going to roar and shout and kick the furniture when he saw her. He
wasn't going to be sent away. She sometimes rested in the afternoon.
He ran down the hallway and crashed in through her bedroom door.

He could feel his dirty boots skittering to a halt and his face crumple
in amazement.

She was sitting on the bed, her vest and blouse pulled up over her
face so he couldn't see it. Her naked breasts and belly were exposed
and a man bent down towards her as if listening to something. The
man couldn't hear him and his mother couldn't see him. Her arms
crossed over her face held up her garments.

Her belly was white and round, her breasts bigger than he could
remember. The man turned and looked at him. It was Dr Langan with
a stethoscope hanging from his ears.

'Hello young man.'

His eyes were riveted on his mother's belly. It was round, round
as a moon. He was so shocked the world might have stopped turning.

His mother lowering her arms, smiled, embarrassed.

'I thought you were helping George Conlon, darling.'

Something of the utmost importance was happening but his brain
was in such a state he couldn't reason it out.

'Well young man, you're not going to be on your own much longer.
The baby is coming along very nicely indeed.'

That was it. A baby. His mother was going to have a baby. It was
in there in her moony belly, waiting to come out and take his place
whilst he was banished to a boarding school. The injustice of it was
so startling he couldn't move, ask a question, shout for justice or run
from the room and cry for mercy in a ditch.

'Go along, darling, there's some red lemonade in the meat safe. Dr
Langan will be going soon.'

Tears squeezed out his eyes and ran down the sides of his nose.

He walked out into the drizzle and stood dumbly staring at his feet.
A curlew speared along the hill behind the barracks, its fifing notes
drowning behind it in the rain.

Where was his father? He'd appeal to him. His mother wanted him
out of the way so she could enjoy the baby unperturbed. If they tried
to send him away he'd run into the demesne, climb the trees and live
there like a bird.

He went into the barracks, anger swelling his heart. His father was
in the day room with Guard Hegarty. They looked at him in huge

amused surprise as he began to rant and rave and stamp the wooden floor.

'I'm not going to no boarding school. I don't want no baby. I'm not leaving here. You want to get rid of me. I'm not going. I'm the big and only bab. I'm not going to be sent to school in Monaghan. I want Mammy. I want Mammy.'

His rage suddenly draining from him he sunk to the floor, tired and breathless.

His father and Hegarty were laughing. He felt a fool. As soon as he felt his father's hand on his head he lashed out with foot and fist trying to hit him. Their guffawing laughter tortured him.

'Begad, Sergeant, he must have got out the wrong side of the bed this morning, hah?'

His father swung him up onto the table and, standing in close to him, imprisoning him, blocked him so he couldn't kick out.

'Now look here, will you calm yourself for Heaven's sake? You're going away for your own good. The school in Monaghan is far better than the one here. Where you won't get thrashed and the teachers won't come in half-shot or hungover. And the baby when it comes will be the best thing ever happened to you. Mark my words. A baby brother? A baby sister? Man alive, you won't know yourself.'

His father's face was inches from him, his earnest eyes dancing, his lips now tight and serious, now smiling with conviction.

'Why didn't you or Mammy tell me?'

'We were going to, when we got round to it. Nothing we're going to do is going to be for anything but your own good. You know that, don't you? Hm?'

'I'm not going, I'm not going, I'm not going.'

Dr Langan tapping on the window, his father went out to talk to him.

Hegarty from deep in his trouser pocket handed him some coins.

'There's nothing like a bag of sweets to cure a fellah's heartache.'

He went out the main door, squeezing between his father and Langan who were sheltering from the rain.

They had planned the whole thing behind his back. He'd be sent away and when he came back there'd be someone else in his place, taking his food, stealing his kisses, sleeping by his mother's side. How could his parents betray him so?

He went into the demesne and sat on his hunkers against a tree, his mind grim and desperate.

He hated the baby already. Because he was afraid of it. It would definitely limit his mother's love and his father would be all strutting pride. His father wanted lots of children. His mother had locked her door against him but since he had been forced to sleep on his own, he knew his father was going into her and staying there for a good while before going back to his own bed. He sometimes lay awake listening to his mother's laugh. Laughter in the night burst out of mystery and was always followed by a deep secret silence.

The school he went to in the village he had to admit he didn't like. It had two teachers – a woman and a man. Being young he was in the woman's class but when she wanted children punished she sent them to the Principal's room. There in front of a wall-sized map of Ireland they were beaten without mercy. A cane was used – on hands, legs, back. Ears were twisted, hair pulled out in lumps. He had watched a friend being beaten until he sunk, crushed, to his knees. He had seen pools of urine on the seats, left there by frightened girls.

The boy was terrified. But why should a boarding school be any different? If he was beaten there he wouldn't have his mother to calm and soothe his wounds. They might as well send him away to jail.

Getting up he walked deeper into the wood. Round by the lake he met Lady Sarah Butler-Coote. She could tell straightaway he was unhappy.

'Oh, treasure, all alone? No chums? Do tell me what's the matter?'

Her old kind face and words turned him on like a tap and his fears came out in such a torrent of self-sorrow, a flock of ducks took fright and shot from the water, wheeling away above the trees.

'Oh my, oh my, oh my. I understand now. Hm. Boarding school? I do not approve of that at all. They sent me to one of those places too. The baby, though, that's golden news. It means you won't be alone in the world. Do you see? I wish I had a brother or sister. I wouldn't be all alone now. Rattling round the house like a pea in a biscuit tin. A baby? Oh yes, I approve of that. And so will you, my treasure, believe me you will.'

Her accent was rich and clear as music from a clarinet. He walked away, letting her words swirl round his head, testing them for sense, trying to defeat their purpose. She agreed with him about being sent away and if she was lonely why didn't she buy a husband? She didn't need a brother or sister at all. She loved animals, birds, fish, trees, children. None other came willingly near her. Her looks were legendary and deterred all comers. But surely her vast wealth could blind a desperate man?

When he arrived home, soaking wet, his mother scolded him for his sulking silence.

'You're a big boy now. You have to face up to things. I was a boarder, don't forget. With the nuns in Moyville Abbey. It'll cost money but we want you to have the best. And the day the baby is born, if all goes well, I'll send for you straightaway, kiss you and tell you I love you as much as ever before. Now that's a promise and you know I never break a promise, don't you?'

She was angry when he didn't respond.

'Do you know something? You're just like your father! The image of him in every way.'

Her words chilled him, tumbled his pride. He went to his room and sat on the bed for hours.

Events had hammered him into a corner and hard as he tried to escape over the following weeks, he couldn't. Everybody in the village and the surrounding farms knew about the baby and knew he was being sent away.

'I hear tell the stork's going to be landin' on the barracks chimney.'

'Boarding school? That's ojus altogether.'

Ojus was the most common adjective or adverb. It could be applied positively or negatively to any person, place or thing or stuck in front of any verb. It was a neutral word that could mean anything.

'We're going to miss you somethin' shockin'.'

He was going to miss them, that he knew. He couldn't think how he was going to manage to say goodbye.

His mother let him feel her stomach.

'It'll arrive in three or so months. If all goes well.'

'How do you mean, Mammy? It will go well, won't it?'

Without reply she went out and hung a line of clothes stretching the whole length of the garden.

He began to awaken early, and drawing the blinds, lie for hours looking out at the dark clinging to the trees and the pigeons and pheasants striding about the field in the growing dawn.

One morning he saw Tully, the rich publican and shop owner walking quickly past his window. Something must have happened. He was in such a hurry he wasn't even bothering to try and rouse the Guard who slept each night in the barracks dormitory.

The boy hopping out of bed had the hall door unbolted just as Tully knocked.

'You're a light sleeper, young fellah. Will you tell your daddy there's been a break-in at the lock-up shop out at Scotshouse

Cross. Ojus amount of damage and destruction done. You'll not forget will you?'

The lock-up shop was miles from the village and saved the people who lived in its vicinity having to journey for provisions. A shopboy worked in it during the day but at night it was empty.

Tully was the first man up in the morning and the last to go to bed. He thrived on work and worry. As long as he was moving he was making money. It was seven o'clock with a nippy breeze moving through swirls of cold mist. But Tully wore only his brown boots, trousers, braces and an open-necked shirt. He was a lonely bachelor. There was no one to keep him in bed. The boy wondered why he and Lady Sarah didn't get married. Two peas in a biscuit tin were better than one.

Later, he went down to his father and told him about the break-in.

'Well bad cess to them whoever it was. And Tully. Put the kettle on.'

The boy could see he was secretly pleased. This was crime. Not a murder maybe, but a mystery to be cracked. Someone to be trapped by evidence that had to be hunted out. It was what his father loved. His dream of course was murder.

'One good murder is worth a thousand bicycles without tail-lights. It's worth a hundred car crashes. A pub-full of after-hours drinkers doesn't compare. Murder is the only reason police exist.'

He watched his father shave, the cut-throat razor held delicately in his hand as a broken wing. He was humming, pleased with himself. The boy could smell the thick shaving lather from across the other side of the kitchen. It came squeezing out of its tube onto his father's hand like a green caterpillar.

'If it wasn't tinkers did the break-in, then I'm a Dutchman.'

'It might have been a travelling criminal, Daddy.' The boy knew the terms and enjoyed drawing his father out.

'As the Scotsman said, I have me doots. Tully said there was a lot of damage done, didn't he? That's the tinkers for you all right. Housebreaking with destruction – it's bred into them.'

'This can't be housebreaking, can it? A lock-up shop isn't a house, is it?'

'It's classified as such under the Larceny Act, 1916, Section 26.'

'How will you proceed with the investigation when you arrive at the scene of the crime?'

'Light the primus and do me a boiled egg and don't be annoying me. Oh cripes.'

A seed of blood pushed out from a nick on his lip and spread like red ink over his soapy mouth.

'Why is the primus stove made in Sweden, Daddy?'

'Do you want me to cut meself again? I don't know why! It's an impossible question. All I know about Sweden is two things. They're famous for hardy sailors. And they make primus stoves. Nothing else.'

'If there are any footprints at the scene will you take a cast of them?'

'You've reminded me, good boy. Go round to the dormitory and get the bag of plaster of Paris from the top of the wardrobe. I'll be needing it for certain.'

His father was happier than he had ever remembered him. Whistling, relaxed, calm. There were no epileptic roars in the night or moods in the day. He took his daily pill, spooned Milk of Magnesia if his stomach was upset and, after long rides round his sub-district, gulped his glass of barley water.

'Keep the bowels regular and God will look after the rest.'

He rode away from the Station, the bag of plaster of Paris buckled to the carrier by its thin, fraying, leather straps.

His mother calling from her bedroom sent him down to Reilly's for bread, butter and a box of matches. And the newspaper.

Reilly moved slowly behind the counter, letting the day seep gently into his bones. He was tall with handsome smiling looks and a quick temper which he used to poke conversation from all who went into him.

'What are you looking so happy about?'

'I'm being sent away to school.'

'Pity about you. Wasn't I sent to the same school meself?'

'Were you? What was it like?'

'Rough in them days. Not anymore from what I've heard.'

'Do they beat you?'

'Only if you shoot the teacher.'

The boy laughed.

'You'll have the time of your life. There'll be fellahs from all over the country, just like yourself. You won't want to know us when you come home on holidays. How is Mammy keeping?'

'Fine thank you.'

He went home knowing his days were numbered. There was no escape. He would have to obey.

Smoke was rising from the Station chimney. Through the day room window he could see Guard Hegarty down on one knee rattling at the fire with a poker.

In the kitchen he put the groceries on the dresser, spread the newspaper on the table and turned on the wireless. Jazz, all the way from New Orleans, blew round him like a hot wind. Standing at the table, listening, reading, he was content.

Thinking he heard his mother call he turned the wireless down. The door opening she staggered in, bent double, clutching her stomach, her face deathly pale.

'Oh no, oh no, oh please God no.'

The boy saw dark water breaking down her legs, then blood.

'Don't be frightened, darling. Get the doctor quick.'

In the day room Hegarty phoned for the doctor and when he raced back to the kitchen his mother was lying in the armchair, her stomach heaving, pain, panic, regret in her eyes.

His blood was running cold, his brain half dead. Low, on the wireless, a clarinet cried.

'A towel, darling.'

He got a towel and a glass of water. Holding her hand he looked at her. She was crying like a child and in her face was enough sorrow for the whole world.

'Please don't die Mammy.'

'Get one of the women.'

He ran to the nearest house and within seconds there was a flock of women running before him.

He hated himself. He had hated the baby and now this was happening. It was all his fault. Evil thoughts became evil deeds. Numb with heartache and guilt he knelt down on the roadside and prayed for his mother and for forgiveness. The occupants of a passing car looked out at him amazed.

Then on Guard Hegarty's three-speed bike he rode out to Scotshouse Cross to tell his father.

He rode like a fury, his leg and lungs aching. He didn't care if he crashed. At least he wouldn't have to face his father and see the bad news rooting in his eyes.

He was selfish. Kicking up such a fuss about going away to school! What did it matter? If God would spare his mother he would willingly go the whole way there crawling on his hands and knees.

He shot by the Orange Hall, the quarry, the Protestant church and a scatter of whitewashed houses with a barking dog at every gate. All the fields were pudding-basined hills flagged with ragwort. The pot-holed road was a rotten mouth, the hawthorn hedges on either side long thick lips red with lipstick. Reaching Tully's shop he flung the bike against the wall and went in.

He was aware of the destruction even as his father pierced him with his stare. Sugar crunched under foot. Big-bellied bags of flour were ripped open, their contents spewing. A box of butter was upended and walked on to a mash. The shop counter was littered with broken glass. A radio lay upside down, its back ripped off, the valves and workings kicked to pieces. Plaster of Paris dusted his father's trousers.

'Come quick. There's something wrong with Mammy.'

His father's face turned stone. His body went rigid, his fists tight. His eyes glazed over and for a few moments closed.

'Sacred heart.'

He went out, mounted his bicycle and methodically rode away.

To the boy it seemed as if his father had been half expecting the news. And knew how to steel himself to the moment. Perhaps it had happened before. Perhaps he was an only child because no other child had managed to make it from his mother's womb.

At the back of the shop, on muddy ground, was a large saucepan upside down as if covering something. On lifting it he saw a plaster of Paris cast. A footprint. The saucepan was to protect the plaster from rain or anyone accidentally treading on it.

The state of the shop was like his own state. Shattered. An alarm clock lying on a shelf began to clatter like a grasshopper, the hammer blurring between two bells. The glass was broken, the minute hand snapped. Abruptly it stopped. The world was a silent, chaotic place.

When he arrived home his mother was in bed, the doctor and his father with her. She was going to be all right. She was going to live. On the floor at the end of the bed was the foetus, wrapped in the *Irish Independent*. A death parcel. His own flesh and blood.

His father told him to dig a hole in the garden. He dug it beside a blackcurrant bush. He didn't want to dig it at the bottom of the garden because that's where they buried the contents of the Elsan lavatory. The ground there was sunken and spongy.

He saw his father coming carrying the parcel. His face was grim and grey as tallow. The corner of his lower lip was gripped in his teeth.

He took the shovel from the boy. Placing the parcel in the hole he began to fill in the clay. Gardening was his favourite pastime. He spent as many hours at it as on police duties. With a shovel in his hand and clay before him he had the grace that comes from power and rhythm.

Patting down the top of the piled clay with the back of the shovel, he turned away and stared at the hill rising from the swampy field on the far side of the garden hedge.

His back seemed to tremble, his shoulders shake. It was the first time the boy had seen him cry.

Going to him he clung round his waist and his father, dropping the shovel, held him tight. They stood as one crying bitter tears, his poor mother watching from her bedroom window.

'You're just like him,' she had said.

He knew his childhood was over. It would lie till Doomsday with his tiny dead brother or sister under the blackcurrant bush.

A week later they walked him to the railway station, where he would get the morning train to Monaghan. He would never have thought it possible but he was glad to be leaving. Since his mother's miscarriage the house was gloomy and dead.

Though it was before eight o'clock doors opened and people rapped on windows.

'Goodbye, we'll be thinking of you.'

'Good luck now.'

'God be with you, you ojus boy.'

To his delight and his father's amazement, as they neared the station, Tully hopped down from a lorry and, shaking the boy's hand, crinkled a pound note into it.

'We'll miss you, gossun, aye man surely.'

'Thank you Mr Tully, thank you very much indeed.'

When they had walked on his father muttered from the corner of his mouth – 'Wonders will never cease.'

'I always told you,' said his mother, 'Tully was a Christian man.'

Waiting for him on the platform was George Conlon. His parents protested when he handed the boy five pounds.

'Get away outa that, Sergeant, he earned every penny of it. And more.'

When they heard the train whistling in the distance his mother began to weep. He put his arms around her neck. She was powdery, perfumed, fresh as apples. He clung to her, dragging her scent down into his lungs, feeling for the last time the heat that warmed his soul.

As in a dream he stepped onto the train and felt outside himself as he waved goodbye.

The engine thundered away with him and just before they went into the deep cutting, he saw Harry, Conlon's twisted brother, waving to him from the turnip field. He would have had to set off very early to make that distance from the house.

There were still stars in the sky and a crescent moon hanging like an incense boat.

The night before when his mother was packing his suitcase, his father came into the room and gave him a plaster of Paris footprint.

'It's my own print. I did it as an experiment. You can show it to your class. I'm sure they'll find it interesting.'

It was an impression of the sole of his boot. The mark of the big seg on the heel was clear, as were the rows of studs. The plaster was the colour of salmon flesh. His father's foot was huge. Police feet. Clowns' feet.

Before he put his case on the rack, he took the footprint out and, leaning from the carriage window, as they crossed the Finn river, threw it in. He would never need reminding of his father's footprints.

A FAMILY OCCASION

EMMA COOKE

Born in Portarlington, Co. Laois, 1934, Emma Cooke raised a large family – nine children – before she began writing seriously. Her short stories have appeared widely in periodicals and anthologies, and she has published one collection, *Female Forms*, as well as two novels.

It was a Tuesday afternoon and the family was coming to tea. The parlour in 'Sunnyside' was fragrant, polished, waiting. Mrs Lee's chair stood, with its cushions nicely plumped, beside the wireless. In the fireplace a small flame licked its way around a sod of turf. The black marble clock on the mantelpiece coughed and struck three.

The Girls, Dodo and Polly, were home from England on their annual holiday. They had travelled from London on the previous Friday. They were upstairs getting ready. Dodo had filled the cut-glass vase on the bookshelf with roses and carnations. A posy of pansies, pinks and forget-me-nots stood on the pedestal table by the window.

Mrs Lee was in bed having her afternoon nap; dreaming that she was bringing the children on a picnic and that Polly and Dodo, who were unaccountably grown up, had taken Beattie away in the pram.

Lucy was in the kitchen counting the iced fancies that had been sent over from the confectionery. If Beattie brought all her brood, which of course she would, they were going to be short of a cake. She sighed and opened the box with the sponge sandwich in it. She cut a slice and added it to the plate of buns. She would do without her own slice. The act of self-sacrifice replaced her annoyance with a warm little glow. Now to start the potato cakes. She had just enough time.

At half past three Lucy untied her apron and put it away, looked into the small mirror beside the cupboard, patted her hair into place and went into the parlour. Her mother was already sitting down wearing the new black cardigan that The Girls had brought home.

Polly and Dodo appeared, elegant in pin-striped suits, tailored blouses and immaculate ties. Polly looked at the clock. 'Nearly time,' she said. She and Dodo lit cigarettes. Lucy took one as well. She only smoked when The Girls were home on holidays; by herself it felt wicked.

Mr Lee looked at them from his photograph on the mantelpiece. He had taken it himself – two years before he died. Now that she was

in her thirties the resemblance between himself and Dodo was very
pronounced.

Peg arrived before their cigarettes were finished. She swept in all
twitters and gaiety, her two children Barbara and Stanley, following
shyly behind her. Like The Girls, she had a neat figure, sallow skin,
dark glossy hair. But her style was softer. Her hair was permed and
today she wore a dress of navy blue and white striped material with
a little floppy bow at the neckline.

'My goodness. She's all dolled up, isn't she, Polly?' said Dodo.

'Chase me Charlie!'

'Look who's talking,' cried Peg, 'you're very swanky yourselves.'

Lucy watched them, thinking how close Peg and The Girls had
always been. She hoped that Beattie wouldn't be too late. Beattie was
so disorganised.

'How are Barbara and Stanley?' asked Polly.

The children hung their heads.

'Stanley, button your blazer,' said his mother.

'And Barbara has her school uniform on,' Lucy pointed out.

Barbara was brought forward to show The Girls her brown coat,
the special pleat in the front of her gym slip, the zip pocket, the cream
blouse.

She stood like a dummy, trying to hold onto the feeling of superiority
that her first year away from home had given her. But it drained away
under her aunts' scrutiny, leaving her as vulnerable as a snail without
a shell.

'How do you like Dublin?' Polly inquired.

'She loves it,' said her mother.

'Ever get lonely?'

Barbara shook her head.

'Good girl.'

'Are you fond of each other?' asked Dodo, who knew very little
about children. Barbara and Stanley nodded. The women turned away
from them with a sense of duty done, and began to talk all at once.

'Can we go and play?' Stanley called shrilly to his grandmother. Mrs
Lee nodded and they escaped to the garden.

The hands of the church clock stood at five past four. Beattie shoved
and pushed the children past the gate. They always wanted to stop
and look at the tombstones. Organ music pealed inside. A funeral
march. Mr Watson practising. Someone must be sick.

'We're late for Grannie, Barbara and Stanley will be there already,' said Beattie. She had a stitch in her side from rushing and the new corset. She was sorry now that she had left the baby with Mrs Green. She could have put Michael and Dickie up on the pram.

'Hurry, hurry, hurry!' she puffed. Mr Everard stood at the door of his shop. Hands behind his back, eyes half closed, not a speck on his white tennis shoes. Nothing to do except watch the world go by. Everyone except herself seemed to have time to spare.

'I want to see Barbara,' said Yvonne, who was the same age.

'Good,' said Beattie. Over the bridge and round the corner. They were nearly there. Surely the children had been a lot tidier when they left the house, thought Beattie. Sometimes she wished that she was like Peg, with only two. She wondered how she was going to last the afternoon in her corset. At least it might keep Dodo from noticing that she was pregnant again.

Last summer, when she was home, Dodo had called up one afternoon and sat through a complete ironing session; talking about England, and theatres and friends that she had made, while Beattie tried to fold sheets and dresses so that the torn parts would not show. Before she left she placed a brown paper parcel on the kitchen table, saying cryptically, 'I don't want to interfere.'

Beattie opened it as soon as Dodo had gone. It contained a book called 'Planned Parenthood'. Beattie had been annoyed at first. But then, knowing Dodo, she giggled at the funny side of it. She put the book on the top shelf of the wardrobe where Seamus would not find it. It was still there, gathering dust.

The children waited for her on the front step of 'Sunnyside'. The door was always on the latch and she pushed it open.

'Yoo-hoo!' she called.

An echoing call came from the parlour. She went in, the children straggling after.

'Ah! Beattie – at last!' said Mrs Lee.

'And all the chick-a-beatties,' added Polly and Dodo in unison.

'One, two, three, four, five –' counted Dodo.

'Six is with Mrs Green,' Beattie said quickly.

'– six, seven, all good children go to heaven.' Dodo crinkled her grey eyes.

'The whole family, Beattie. How lovely.' Auntie Jane, who wasn't really an aunt, was there because The Girls were home.

'Not quite, Auntie Jane,' Beattie said.

'Goodness me, I lose count,' said Auntie Jane, wafting lavender water with every gesture.

'I knew you were here, I smelt you through the door,' five-year-old Dickie told her triumphantly. The Girls smothered their laughter.

Beattie caught his arm. She could have murdered him. 'Tell Auntie Jane you're sorry,' she demanded.

Dickie looked at the carpet. 'Sorry,' he whispered. He wondered why it was rude of Auntie Jane to smell so pretty. He liked it. There was a short pause to let his apology register. Then Mrs Lee said, 'Barbara and Stanley are in the garden.'

The children tumbled out of the room. The Girls clapped their hands over their ears in mock dismay.

'Go easy!' Beattie yelled. 'Sorry, Mother,' she added automatically.

Lucy stood up. 'I think I'll put the kettle on,' she announced. 'Frank will be over from the shop soon.'

'Can I help?' asked Peg.

'Thank you, dear, but I know where everything is,' Lucy said apologetically.

So do we all, thought Beattie, sitting down on the sofa beside Auntie Jane. Everything in 'Sunnyside' had been kept in exactly the same place as far back as she could remember, down to the chocolate egg on the top shelf of the bookcase. It had been there since she was a little girl. A present from cousins in America. She remembered, when she was small, wishing and wishing that her mother would take off the cellophane wrapping and divide it up. Let them see what it tasted like. But she never did. It must be mouldy by now.

The women settled down to a comfortable chat about the things that had happened during the past year. Frank came from the shop and when he went back to sit in his office, Desmond, the younger brother, arrived.

'I suppose it's all gone,' he said when he came in.

'Every scrap,' said Polly.

'I'll go and squeeze the teapot.' Lucy bustled out to collect the pile of potato cakes that she had been keeping warm for him.

Desmond leaned back and rubbed his waistcoat after he had eaten six. 'Well that's more like it,' he said.

'Do you remember the day that we went on the picnic down the river and you gobbled up all the buns? You must have been about five years old,' Polly asked him.

'How many were there?' he prompted her.

'Twelve!'

'Oh my!' said Auntie Jane, her eyebrows nearly touching the brim of her hat.

Desmond guffawed – then, 'Do you remember the time that Frank gave Peg a carry on his motor bike and her knitted skirt caught in the wheel?' he said.

The memory convulsed the room.

Dodo took over. 'How about when Lucy fell down the grating in the church aisle?'

'I was going in to do the flowers for the Harvest Festival.'

'And Percy Ward had lifted the grating back to get down to the furnace.'

'The rector had to come and help pull her out.'

'Lucky she's well padded.'

The stories were told, one voice taking up the thread from another. Beattie shifted on the sofa. A bone from her corset was killing her. The room seemed very warm.

In the garden the children played their annual game of pelting each other with the small, unripe apples that had fallen off the trees. This year Barbara and Yvonne were the targets. They crouched in the greenhouse waiting for a chance to make a dash for the big laurel hedge.

'I'm getting a new coat,' whispered Yvonne as they peered out through the tomato plants.

'I'm learning ballet,' said Barbara.

'What's that?'

'Dancing, of course.'

'Oh!' They both tried to look nonchalant.

'Everyone learns –' Barbara was interrupted by a volley of ammunition from the enemy, who had decided to try a surprise attack.

'Come on!' They clasped hands and ran squealing through the doorway.

She was going to die. Here on Mother's sofa – after all they had done for her – in return for their tolerance – she was going to, at last, as they had always expected her to, commit a final, unforgivable breach of taste. Sweat drenched her armpits. She tried to smell it, distending her nostrils, her lungs aching for a whiff of some antidote to Auntie Jane's lavender.

'Do you really, Beattie? Imagine.' Auntie Jane was looking at her in amazement.

'Oh yes.' She bared her teeth at them, but nobody seemed to notice anything strange. What on earth were they talking about? The melodeon? It was quite true. She did lock herself into the kitchen and play it for half an hour after she had put the children to bed. Yes, if someone was still crying when she stopped she attended to them. She sat there nodding while the family recounted the details.

'Young people are marvellous nowadays,' gushed Auntie Jane.

A miscarriage would be worse than dying. Think of the mess. Poor Lucy would have to do all the work. But she couldn't have a miscarriage with Desmond still in the room. Mother would never allow it. If she was dying they'd have to send for Seamus – and the priest. They'd never think of the priest and Seamus would have a fit. She hoped Seamus wasn't drinking today. She'd have to make her last confession in her mother's parlour. Oh God!

'It's your own personal decision, Beatrice.' That's what her father had said. He had been a just man. He used to stop her on Sunday mornings when they met. Walking opposite directions to church. Both of them alone. Lucy was the only other churchgoer in 'Sunnyside' and she got up for eight o'clock. Seamus always went to last Mass.

'Good morning, Beatrice.'

'Good morning, Father.'

'Are you all well?'

'Yes, thank you.'

They might have been heads of state exchanging credentials. It often struck her as comical. But he wasn't a man for frivolity.

She felt dizzy. She wished that she was in her own house. She wished that they could afford to get their wireless fixed and then she wouldn't need the melodeon. Seamus had taught her to play it when they were courting. She wished –

Wails, reaching a crescendo as they approached the sitting room, halted the conversation.

'Oh dear!' Peg half rose to her feet. The Girls blew long spirals of cigarette smoke. Lucy got up anxiously.

'Some naughtiness, they're as wild as young goats,' said Mrs Lee, looking accusingly at Beattie. Desmond hid his grin behind a handkerchief as Lucy hurried from the room.

'I'll help her,' Beattie said. She wrenched herself out of her agony. The pains went through her heart as she stood up. But she made it to the door, only knocking a bowl of flowers to the ground on the way.

It was not the end of the world after all. Barbara's uniform was a bit muddy and Yvonne had a nasty scrape on her cheek.

'What were you doing in the hedge anyway?' asked Lucy, brushing away at Barbara's brown serge. Beattie had rushed upstairs muttering something incoherent.

'Playing,' they said vaguely.

Beattie came into the kitchen and took a sheet of brown paper from the pile in the left-hand cupboard.

'What's that for?' Lucy asked.

'A secret,' Beattie replied airily. She hurried out again and they heard her singing 'Ta-ra-ra-boom-de-ay' as she climbed the stairs.

'What's she doing?' asked the little girls.

'Goodness knows.' Lucy shook her head. There was never any accounting for poor Beattie.

In the bathroom Beattie wriggled out of her corset. It was a hideous pink thing with numerous laces and silver eyelets. If Seamus saw her in it he'd have a fit. She rolled it up in the brown paper and hurled it high onto the top shelf of the hot press; back behind the eiderdowns and winter curtains. A surprise for Lucy when she found it.

She stood in the middle of the bathroom floor and felt herself relax and expand, like a flower about to bloom. It was marvellous. Funny to think that she was a grown woman. She remembered the time when her chin was only a few inches higher than the rim of the bath. Sometimes the whole thing seemed preposterous – the children, babies, Seamus.

Funny how she had met Seamus. He had drifted into a social in the Parochial Hall. A stranger in town. Not knowing that he was trespassing. Masquerading under false colours at a Protestant dance. He had been sent to work in the region by the Turf Board. Everyone had been delighted to see a new young man turn up. When the rector's wife came over and introduced herself the truth dawned on him. He decided to bluff it out. It would make a good story for the lads.

Beattie had been standing near him at suppertime.

'Jesus!' The expression had surprised her. She had turned round to find Seamus standing staring at a sandwich as if it was about to explode.

'What's wrong?' she asked.

'What day is it?' he murmured.

She looked at the clock. It was after midnight. 'I suppose it's Friday,' she said.

Seamus looked at her in horror. 'And I'm eating meat,' he said. He often said later that the first thing that had attracted him to her was that she was such a good sport.

They danced together for the rest of the evening, the offending sandwich tucked away in Beattie's handbag. That was a joke that she had kept to herself. In the end it hadn't been funny at all.

A button like a little gum drop rolled down her dress and rested against her shoe. It was followed by another.

'Beattie,' a voice called anxiously, 'where are you?'

Beattie stooped and picked them up. Lucy would have a needle and thread. Dodo was outside on the landing.

'For heaven's sake, Beattie, what are you doing?'

Beattie held out her hand. 'Look!' she said.

Dodo peered at the buttons, then at Beattie's gaping dress, then at her flushed face.

'Oh Beattie,' she said, 'you're not –'

Beattie nodded her head. 'I am.'

'Honestly, you're hopeless.' Dodo looked at her with concern. 'I get worried about you,' she went on, 'when I come home and see you with all those children, and that man –' she broke off. 'Can't you do anything? Can't you be more careful?' she asked in a dry, matter of fact tone.

'No,' said Beattie, 'we're not allowed.' There was no point in going into all the details, but when she said it out like that, to her sister, it seemed ridiculous.

As they stared at each other Beattie felt a soft flutter in her stomach. It was the baby. The first time that she had felt it moving. She placed her hand protectively against her body. 'I'll be all right,' she said, 'keep your fingers crossed.'

'Wait,' ordered Dodo. She went into her bedroom and came out carrying a cardigan. 'Put that on, it will keep you covered.' She placed it gently across Beattie's shoulders.

They linked arms as they went downstairs. In the parlour everybody turned expectantly towards them.

'What's up?'

'We thought you were lost!' the family exclaimed.

'Beattie burst her buttons,' Dodo announced. And the way that she said it made it sound so comical that they all began to laugh.

THE LADY WITH THE RED SHOES

ITA DALY

Born in Drumshanbo, Co. Leitrim, 1944, Ita Daly has lived in Dublin since her teens and is a graduate of University College, Dublin. Her stories have been published in Ireland, Britain and the USA, and she has brought out one collection, *The Lady With The Red Shoes*, as well as four novels and two children's books.

The West of Ireland, as every schoolboy knows, is that part of the country to which Cromwell banished the heretical natives after he had successfully brought the nation to heel. Today, it is as impoverished and barren as ever it was, bleak and lonesome and cowering from the savagery of the Atlantic which batters its coastline with all the fury that it has gathered in over three thousand miles. But the West of Ireland can also be heartbreakingly beautiful; and on a fine April morning with the smell of gorse and clover filling the air and the bees showing the only evidence of industry in a landscape that is peopleless as far as the eye can see – on such a morning in the West of Ireland you can get a whiff of Paradise.

It is an irony which pleases me mightily that we as a family have such a strong attachment to the West. Our ancestors, you see, came over with Cromwell, foot soldiers who fought bravely and were rewarded generously and have never looked back since. And every Easter we leave Dublin and set out westwards where we spend a fortnight in McAndrews Hotel in North Mayo. It is a family tradition, started by my grandfather, and by now it has achieved a certain sacredness. Nothing is allowed to interfere with the ritual, and so when I married Judith one April day, some twenty-five years ago, it seemed quite natural that we should spend our honeymoon there. We have gone there every Easter since and if Judith has found it somewhat dull on occasion, she accepts gracefully a period of boredom in the knowledge that it gives me so much pleasure, while I in turn have been known to accompany her to Juan-les-Pins. An experience which, however, I have not been foolish enough to repeat.

McAndrews is one of the puzzles of the world. Built on the outskirts of Kilgory, looking down on the hamlet and on the sea, it dates back to the late nineteenth century. A large, square house, red-bricked and turreted, it is a reminder of the worst excesses of the Gothic revival, and every time I see its monstrous outline, lonely on the hill, my heart bounds and my pulse quickens. Nobody knows whether it was there before Kilgory and the village grew up around it or whether Kilgory was there first. But certainly it seems an odd place to have built a hotel, miles from a town, or a church, or even a beach. It is situated on a headland overlooking the Atlantic, but the cliffs are so steep and the sea so treacherous here that there is neither boating nor swimming available. Strange to build a hotel in such a place, stranger still that there have been enough eccentrics around to keep it in business for almost a century. My father, as a boy, used to arrive by train. The main line ran from Dublin to Westport and from there a branch line went to the hotel – not to Kilgory mark you, but to the actual hotel grounds. 'Any guests for McAndrews?' the porters used to shout as one disembarked at Westport and was ushered onto a toy train with its three or four first-class carriages, to be shunted along the fifteen miles and deposited a stone's throw from the grand front door of McAndrews with its noble stone balustrade.

The toy station is still there, although nowadays the guests arrive by motor. I am always glad when I see my Daimler disappearing into the cavernous garages, and most of the other guests seem to experience a similar sense of relief, for though they arrive in motor-cars, they continue thereafter on foot and the grounds and environs are delightfully free of petrol fumes. We are of a kind, McAndrews clientele, old-fashioned, odd perhaps; some would say snobbish. Well, if it is snobbish to exercise one's taste, then I admit that I am a snob. I do not like the bad manners, the insolence of shop assistants and taxi-drivers which passes for egalitarianism in this present age; I resent chummy overtures from waiters who sometimes appear to restrain themselves with difficulty from slapping one on the back. I am irritated by cocktail bars and at a loss in the midst of all that bright and fatuous chatter. I like peace and quiet and reserve in my fellow-man – decent reserve, which appears to be the *raison d'être* of McAndrews. I know most of my fellow-guests' names – like me they have been coming here since they were children – yet I can rest assured that when I meet any of them again in any part of the hotel, I shall be spared all social intercourse apart from a civil word of greeting. Such respect for dignity and personal privacy is hard to come by in commercial establishments these days.

This year, Judith was ill and did not accompany me. To say that she was ill is something of an exaggeration, for if she had been, I would certainly not have left her. But she was somewhat under the weather, and as her sister was in Dublin from London, she decided to stay there with her while I went to Mayo alone. In truth, I was somewhat relieved, for I am only too aware of how difficult it must be for Judith, gay and outgoing, to be married to a dry stick like myself all these years. I am glad when she gets an opportunity to enjoy herself and I had no doubt that Eleanor and she would be much happier without my inhibiting presence. Still, I was going to miss her, for like many solitary people I am very dependent on the company of those few whom I love.

But the magic of McAndrews began to re-assert itself as soon as I got down to breakfast the first morning and found Murphy, with his accustomed air of calm and dignity, presiding over the dining-room. Murphy has been head waiter here for over thirty years now, although I always see him more as a butler, a loyal family retainer, than as a smart *maître d'hôtel*. His concern for each guest is personal and his old face is suffused with genuine pleasure when he sees you again each year. He came forward to greet me now. 'Good morning, sir.'

'Good morning, Murphy. Nice to see you again.'

'And you, sir, always such a pleasure. I'm sorry Mrs Montgomery will not be with us this year, sir?'

'Afraid not.'

'Nevertheless, I hope you will have a pleasant stay. May I recommend the kippers this morning, sir? They are particularly good.'

Such exchanges would be the extent of my intercourse with the world for the next fortnight – formal, impersonal, remote, and totally predictable. I have always found it a healing process, part of the total McAndrews experience, helping one to relax, unbend, find one's soul again.

I quickly re-established my routine, falling into it with the ease and gratitude one feels on putting on again an old and much-worn jacket. Breakfasts were latish but hearty, then a walk as far as the village and back. Afterwards an hour or two spent in the library in the delightful company of Boswell, a man to be enjoyed only in leisured circumstances – I never read him in Dublin. Lunch and an afternoon in a deck-chair in the gardens, looking out to sea, dozing, dreaming, idling. After dinner another walk, this time more strenuous, perhaps two miles along the coast road and then back to McAndrews for a final glass of port followed by early bed with a good detective novel. The bliss of those days is hard to convey, particularly the afternoons, when it never seemed to rain. I would take my deck-chair and place it in a sheltered spot and sit, hour upon hour, and watch the Atlantic at its ceaseless labours. I'd watch as the light changed – from blue to green and from green to grey – until an occasional seagull would cut across my line of vision and I would raise my eyes and follow its soaring flight to the great vault of heaven. A couple of afternoons like that and things were back in perspective. The consciousness of one's encroaching age, the knowledge that one is regarded as a has-been, became less painful, and there, on the edge of the Atlantic, a peace began to make itself felt.

But then I have always been out of step with the world and even as a young man McAndrews was a retreat, a haven for me. However as I grow older and my unease increases, McAndrews becomes more precious. Here I can escape from all those aggressive young men with their extraordinary self-confidence and their scarlet-nailed women and their endless easy chatter. My son, Edward, who is married to a beautician – a profession which, I am assured, has some standing in this modern world – this son of mine tells me that my only problem is that I am a nasty old snob. This apparently puts me completely beyond the pale, and he views me as a pariah, almost as someone who should be put down. But we are all snobs of one variety or other, and what he really means is that my particular brand of snobbery has gone out of fashion. He has working-class friends and black friends, but no stupid friends; he would not dream of spending his holidays in such a bastion of privilege as McAndrews, but then neither would he think of going to the Costa Brava; he drinks pints of Guinness but abhors sweet wine. And he tells me that the difference between us is that he has discernment and that I am a snob.

The generation gap is what any modern sociologist would inelegantly and erroneously call it, for, as I have said, there has always been as big a gap between me and most of my own generation as there is between me and Edward's. It is a painful sensation, constantly feeling that the time is out of joint, although as I sit sipping sherry in McAndrews, in the pleasant expectation of a good dinner, I can laugh at my own foolishness and that of my son, and indeed, at the general idiocy of the human animal. This is what makes McAndrews so dear to me, but it is also what makes each leave-taking so difficult. I grow increasingly apprehensive before every return to the world, and as this holiday drew to a close and I finally sat waiting for dinner on the last evening, I was aware of my mounting nervousness and depression. I decided to console myself with that nectar of so many ageing men – a bottle of vintage claret. Now as I sought Murphy's advice, I ignored, with unaccustomed recklessness, both the price and the knowledge that if I drank the whole bottle, I would undoubtedly spend a sleepless night. There were worse things than insomnia.

By dinner-time the light had changed outside and a soft blue opacity was flooding in from the Atlantic through the great windows of the dining-room. This is the Irish twilight, most beautiful of times and that part of the day I missed most during those few years I spent in West Africa as a young man. It is a time that induces a half-wilful melancholia – helped no doubt by the glass in one's hand – and in McAndrews they respect this mood, for the curtains are never drawn nor the lights switched on until darkness finally descends. As I moved through the flickering pools of yellow light – for there were many diners already present and many candles lit – I was struck again by the solemnity of the room. Years and years of ritual have given it a churchlike quiet, a hint of the ceremony and seriousness with which eating is invested by both guests and staff. I took my usual seat against the wall, facing out towards the sea, and as Murphy murmured, priest-like, over the wine, we were both startled by a raised and discordant voice. 'Waiter, come here please.'

Together we turned towards the voice, both acutely conscious of the solecism that had been committed in referring to Murphy as 'Waiter'. The offender was sitting about six feet away at a small table in the middle of the room. It was an unpopular table, unprotected, marooned under the main chandelier, seldom occupied except when the hotel was very busy. I guessed now that some underling, flustered by the novelty of the situation, had forgotten himself to such an extent as to usher this person to it without first consulting Murphy. And the arrival of this new diner *was* a novelty. She was not a resident, which was odd in itself, for McAndrews has never been the sort of place to seek out a casual trade; then she was alone, unescorted, a sight which was not only odd, but simply not done: ladies, one feels, do not dine alone in public. But the most striking thing of all about our newcomer was her appearance. She was in her fifties, maybe sixty, with hair and dress matching, both of an indeterminate pink. She wore spectacles which were decorated with some kind of stones along the wings. These shone and sparkled as she moved her head, but no more brightly than her teeth, which were of an amazing and American brightness. She flashed them up at Murphy now, and as he shied away from their brilliance, I could see that for once he was discomposed. But Murphy is a gentleman and within seconds he had himself again in hand. Stiffening his back, he bowed slightly in the direction of the teeth. 'Madam?' he enquired, with dignity.

'Could I have a double Scotch on the rocks, and I'd like a look at the menu.' Her voice had that familiarity which so many aspects of American life have for Europeans who have never even crossed the Atlantic. I don't think I have ever met an American, but I have a great fondness for their television thrillers, and I immediately identified the voice as a New York voice, tough New York, like so many of my favourite villains. Proud of my detective work, I sat back to listen.

The whisky had appeared with that speed to which we McAndrews guests are accustomed, and if Murphy disapproved of this solitary diner, his training was too perfect to even suggest it. He hovered beside her now, solicitously, as she studied the menu, and as she turned it over and turned it back again I noticed her face grow tight and apprehensive. I should say here that McAndrews does not have a menu in the usual commercial sense of that word. Mrs Byrne, who has been cooking there for the past thirty years, is an artist, and it would offend her artistic sensibility, and indeed equally displease the guests, if she were asked to produce the commonplace, vast à la carte vulgarity that one finds in so many dining places today. For festive occasions she will prepare a classic dish in the French tradition, and otherwise she keeps us all happy cooking simple but superb dishes using the local fish and meat and the vegetables which grow a couple of hundred yards away. She is a wonder certainly, but I can perfectly understand that one used to the meaningless internationalism of the modern menu might find Mrs Byrne's hand-written and modest proposals something of a puzzle. One would look in vain for the tired Entrecôte Chasseur or the ubiquitous Sole Bonne Femme in this dining-room and be somewhat at a loss when faced with the humble, boiled silverside of beef followed by stewed damsons with ginger.

I could see that this was precisely the position in which our lady diner now found herself. She toyed with the piece of paper and looked up helplessly at Murphy. Murphy coughed encouragingly behind a genteel hand and began, 'Perhaps, Madam, I could recommend tonight the –'. But she gathered her shoulders together and threw back her head. 'No, you could not, waiter. I know exactly what I want.' Her voice had taken on an added stridency. 'I want a fillet mignon with a green salad. Surely a place like this can produce that – huh?'

'It is not on the menu, Madam, but certainly if that is what you require, we can arrange it.' I thought I noticed a hint of disapproval in Murphy's silky tones.

'Yeah, that's what I want. Nothing to start and I want the steak medium-rare, and I mean medium-rare. All you Irish overcook meat.'

I thought for a moment that Murphy was going to lose control, that years of training and polish would at last begin to give way before this latest onslaught of rudeness, but again he recovered himself. For a second he paused over his order and then looked up again and said, still politely, 'And to drink, Madam, would you like something?' The lady looked at him, genuinely puzzled as she held up her whisky glass. 'I've gotten it already – remember?' It was now Murphy's turn to look puzzled and I could see him struggling mentally before the implication of her remark became clear to him. This extraordinary person intended to drink whisky with her fillet mignon!

As I watched my fellow-diner I wondered how on earth she had ever found her way to McAndrews. It was not a fashionable spot, not the sort of place that attracted tourists. There was a hideous motel only ten miles away, much smarter than McAndrews, flashing neon lights, full of Americans, supplying what they called an ensemble for the gratification of their guests. Surely this woman would have been much more at home in such a place? But as I studied her, I began to realize that this strange creature was actually impressed by McAndrews. I was sure now that she hadn't accidentally happened upon it as I had at first surmised, but that for some unknown reason she had chosen it deliberately. And I saw too that her apparent rudeness was no more than awkwardness, an effort to hide her awe and inexperience in such surroundings. My daughter-in-law – the beautician – when she visited me here once, gave a display of genuine rudeness, authentic because it was based on contempt, for Murphy, for me, for our kind of world. She shouted at Murphy because she saw him as an inefficient old fogey. But he didn't impinge at all on her world and was only a nuisance to her because he did not mix her cocktail in the correct proportions. This woman, however, was different, although I saw that Murphy didn't think so – indeed whereas he was prepared to make excuses for Helen, as one of the family, I could tell that he had put up with as much as he was going to from an outsider. As the waiter placed the steak in front of her, Murphy approached, disapproval in every line of his stately person. 'Medium-rare, as you required,' he said, and even I, sitting some distance away, drew back from the sting of his contempt.

Other guests were taking notice now, attracted perhaps by Murphy's slightly raised voice, a unique occurrence in this dining-room. I could feel a current of mild disapproval beginning to circulate and I saw that the lady was noticing something too. She was looking discomfited but bravely she took up her knife and fork and tucked in her chin. I was beginning to admire her pluck.

Decency demanded that I leave her some privacy to eat so reluctantly I looked away. Soon, I was glad to see, the other guests lost interest in her, and when after a safe interval I glanced back at her table, she had finished her meal and was wiping her mouth with an air of well-being and relaxation. It must have been a satisfactory fillet mignon. When Murphy brought the menu again, she actually smiled at him. 'No, no,' she said waving it away, 'nothing more for me. We women have to watch our figures – eh?' And as she glanced at him archly, I thought for an awful moment that she was going to dig him in the ribs. Murphy looked at her coldly, making no effort to return her smile. 'Very well, Madam.' The words hung between them and as she sensed his unfriendliness, indeed hostility, the smile, still awkward upon her lips, became transfixed in an ugly grimace. 'I guess you'd better bring me another Scotch.' Defeat was now beginning to edge out defiance in her voice. She grasped her drink when it arrived, and gulped it, as a drowning man gulps air. This seemed to steady her somewhat and taking another, slower sip, she drew out a cigarette from her bag and lit it. It was then that she discovered, just as Murphy was passing on his way towards my table, that there was no ashtray. 'Excuse me,' she sounded embarrassed, 'could you bring me an ashtray please?' Murphy turned slowly in his tracks. He looked at her in silence for fully five seconds. 'I am sorry, Madam,' – and it seemed to me now that the whole dining-room was listening to his even, slightly heightened tones – 'I am sorry, but our guests do not smoke in the dining-room.' In essence this is true, it being accepted among the guests that tobacco is not used in here – a measure of their consideration for each other as smoke fumes might lessen someone's enjoyment of an excellent meal. I thoroughly approve of this unwritten rule – it seems to me to be eminently civilised – but I know well that on occasion, people, newcomers for example, have smoked in McAndrews dining-room, and Murphy, though perhaps disapproving, has never demurred. I looked at him now in amazement and maybe he caught my expression of surprise, for he added, 'Coffee is served in the blue sitting-room, Madam, there are ashtrays there. However, if you'd prefer it, I can –' The woman stood up abruptly, almost colliding with Murphy. Her face and neck were flooded with an ugly red colour and she seemed to be trying to push him away. 'No, not at all, I'll have the coffee,' and she blundered blindly towards the door. It seemed a long, long journey.

I finished my cheese and followed her thoughtfully into the sitting-room. All evening something had been niggling me, something about that voice. I have a very sensitive ear I believe – I am rather proud of it – and although, as I had noticed, this woman spoke with an American accent, there was some underlying non-American quality about it. Something familiar but different about those vowels and th's. Now as I sat and lit my cigar, I realized what it was – it was so obvious that I had missed it until now. Her voice, of course, was a local voice, a North Mayo voice with that thick and doughy consistency that I was hearing around me since I had come down. It had become American-ised, almost completely so, but to my ear its origins were clear. I could swear that that woman had been born within ten miles of this very hotel.

We both sipped our coffee, the tinkle of coffee spoons falling between us. I watched her as she sat alone, isolated and tiny in the deep recess of the bay window, looking out at the darkening gardens. Beyond, there were still some streaks of light coming from the sea, and I knew that down below on the rocks the village children would be gathering their final bundles of seaweed before heading off home to bed. The seaweed is sold to the local factory where it is turned into fertilizer of some kind and the people here collect it assiduously, sometimes whole families working together, barefooted, for the salt water rots shoe-leather. Even the little ones often have hard and calloused feet, sometimes with ugly cuts. Life is still hard in the West of Ireland. I looked across at my lady – *her* feet were encased in red high-heeled shoes with large platform soles. Her face, as she gazed out unseeing, was sad now, sad and crumpled-looking. I recalled again her voice, and as we sat there, drinking our coffee, I suddenly knew without any shadow of doubt what she was doing there. I knew *her* intimately – her life was spread out in front of me. I could see her as a little girl, living nearby in some miserable cottage. Maybe, when I was out walking as a child with my Mama, I had even passed her, not noticing the tattered little girl who stood in wonder, staring at us. McAndrews must have been a symbol to her, a world of wealth and comfort, right there on the doorstep of her own poverty-stricken existence. Perhaps she had even worked in the hotel as a maid, waiting to save her fare to America, land of opportunity. And in America, had she been lonely, frightened by that alien place, so differ-ent from her own Mayo? Had she wept herself to sleep many nights, sick for a breath of home? But she had got on, sent money back, and always, all those years, she had kept her dream intact: one day she

would return home to Kilgory, a rich American lady, and she would
go into McAndrews Hotel, not as a maid this time but as a guest. She
would order a fine dinner and impress everyone with her clothes and
her accent and her wealth.

She sat now, a rejected doll in her pink dress and red shoes, for
tonight she had seen that dream disintegrate like candy-floss. I wanted
to go to her, to tell her, explain to her that it didn't matter any more
– the world itself was disintegrating. She should realise that places
like McAndrews weren't important any longer, people only laughed
at them now. She had no need to be saddened, for she, and all those
other little Irish girls who had spent their days washing other people's
floors and cooking other people's meals, they would inherit the earth.
The wheel had come round full circle.

Of course I didn't approach her. I finished my coffee and went
straight to bed thinking how the world is changing, my world, her
world. Soon McAndrews itself will be gone. But for me, this landscape
has been caught forever – caught and defined by its heroine, the lady
with the red shoes. Of course, you, on reading this, are going to see
me as a sentimental old codger, making up romantic stories about
strangers, because I am lonely and have nothing better to do. But I
know what I know.

FIVE NOTES AFTER A VISIT

ANNE DEVLIN

Born in Belfast, 1951, Anne Devlin lives in England. She has written for the stage and TV – in 1984 she won the Samuel Beckett Award for TV Drama and in 1986 was co-winner of the George Devine Award. She has published one collection of short stories, *The Way-Paver*.

Monday 9 January 1984

I begin to write.

The first note:

'You were born in Belfast?' The security man at the airport said.

'Yes.'

'What is the purpose of your visit there?'

To be with my lover. Well, I didn't say that.

I had written 'research' on the card he was holding in his hand. I remind him of this.

'I would like *you* to answer the questions,' he says.

'I am doing research.'

'Who is your employer?'

'Self.' I stick to my answers on the card.

'Oh! The idle rich,' he says.

'I live on a grant.'

I might have expected this. It happens every time I cross the water. But I will never get used to it.

'Who is paying for your ticket?'

'I am.'

'What a pity.' He smiles. 'And what have you been doing in England all this time?'

'Living.' Trying.

'There was a bomb in Oxford Street yesterday. Some of your countrymen.'

Two feet away some passengers with English accents are saying goodbye to their relatives. A small boy holding his mother's hand is smiling. Two feet between the British and the Irish in the airport lounge; I return the child's smile. Two feet and seven hundred years.

'He's a small man doing a small job!' Stewart says, when he meets me at the other side. 'Forget about him.' I won't. 'Now don't be cross with me. But you could save yourself a lot of trouble if you'd only write British under nationality.'

'I think –' I start to say, but don't finish: next time I'll write 'don't know'.

I come back like a visitor. I always do. And I'm treated like one. On the Black Mountain road from the airport it is getting dark, when the taxi driver says:

'Do you see that orange glow down there? Just beyond the motorway?'

'Yes.'

'Those are the lights of the "Kesh".'

Like a football stadium to the uninitiated.

'And just up there ahead of us,' he points to a crown of white lights on Divis ridge. 'That's the police observatory station. That's where they keep the computer.'

'Is it?'

'I had to do a run up there once. But I never got past the gates.'

We plunge down Hannastown Hill in the dark towards the lights of a large housing estate.

If I don't speak in this taxi, perhaps he'll think I'm English.

'What road is this?' Stewart asks, as we pass my parents' house. His father is a shipyard worker.

SINN FEIN IS THE POLITICAL WING OF
THE PROVISIONAL IRA

is painted on the gable.

WESTMINSTER IS THE POLITICAL WING OF
THE BRITISH ARMY

'This is Andersonstown,' the taxi driver says.

There is barbed wire on the flower beds in my father's garden. A foot patrol trampled his crocuses last spring. Tomorrow I'll go and tell them I've come home. But not yet. Stewart isn't keen.

'They won't approve of me,' he says. 'I've been married once before. They'll persuade you to go back to England.'

'They won't!' I insist. But I have the same old fear. His first wife lives in East Belfast.

Tuesday 10 January 1984

The second note:

I am looking at the bus that will take me to my mother. Through the gates I can see the others waiting too. I hear myself say: 'Mother, I've come back!'; and I hear her ask me, 'Why?'

I have let him lure me from my undug basement garden in an English town; one egg in the fridge and the dregs of milk; my solitude wrapped around me like a blanket for those six years until he came – and presented me with the only kind of miracle I ever really believed in.

I hear her ask me, 'Why?'

I remember the summer months, our breakfasts at lunch-time in my garden, our evening meals on the raft, my bed. When term began again, he said: 'I've got a job in Belfast. Will you come and live with me?'

'Oh, I can't go back,' I said. 'I can't – live without you,' I tell him at the airport when I arrive.

I hear her ask me why?

My house is empty and the blinds are down. The letters slip into the hall unseen. The tanks will still turn on to the Whiteladies Road out of the Territorial Army Barracks and past the BBC. And the black cab driver will drive someone else from the station. 'Where to?' Blackboy Hill.

A For Sale notice stands in the uncut grass . . .

I hear her ask me why? I turn away from the stop.

Wednesday 1 February 1984

I have not kept an account of the days in between because I am too tired after work to write. And anyway I go to bed with him at night.

The third note:

It is the third day of the third week of my visit. I am working in the library.

'On the 1st of January 1957 the Bishop of Down and Conner's Relief Fund for Hungarian Refugees amounted to £19,375 0s 6d. Further contributions in a daily newspaper for that morning include: Sleamish Dancing Club, £5; Bon Secours Convent, Falls Road, £10; The John Boscoe Society for the Prevention of Communism, £25; A sinner, Anonymous –'

'Love?'

'£5. Three months later, in April of the same year, the Lord Mayor of Belfast welcomed the first 500 refugees. It was the only issue on which the people of Belfast East and West agreed.'

'Love.'

He is standing at my table.

'Oh, I'm sorry, I didn't see you.'

'Love. My wife's just rung. I'll have to go and see her. She was crying on the phone. She wants to discuss us getting back together. If only you knew how angry this makes me!'

'Will you tell her about me?'

Below the library window, voices reach me from the street. The students are assembling for a march. They shoulder a black coffin: RIP EDUCATION is chalked in on the side.

Maggie. Maggie. Maggie.

Out! Out! Out!

Police in bullet-proof jackets flank the thin demonstration through the square. The wind tosses the voices back and forth; I catch only an odd phrase here and there: 'Our comrades in England . . . The trade union movement in this country . . .'

'We have to keep a low profile for a while,' he said.

'And don't answer the phone in case it's her.'

When I was young I think, watching the demonstration pass, I must have been without fear. I make a resolution: I will go there after dark.

Thursday 2 February 1984

The Feast of the Purification. And James Joyce's birthday.

I always remember it.

This is the fourth note:

He is scraping barnacles off the mussels when I come back after midnight. 'Where were you?' he asks.

'I went to see my mother.'

'How was it?'

'She asked the usual questions. Did I still go to Mass? She said she'd pray for me.'

'Did you tell her about me?'

'I talked about my research: The Flight of the Hungarian Refugees to Belfast in '57. Can't think why. She said when I was leaving: keep your business to yourself. She was talking about you.'

'My wife cried when I told her. She thinks it's a phase I'm going through – and I'll get over it.'

There are pink and red carnations in a jug on the table, the man-next-door's music is coming through the walls. A trumpet. Beethoven. I'm getting good at that.

'He's obsessive,' Stewart says. 'He's played that piece since ten o'clock.' At the table I make a mistake: I push my soup away, I'm not as hungry as I thought.

'Go back! Go back to England, then! You said you *could* live with me!'

'I am trying.'

When I wake the smell of garlic reaches me from the bottom of the stairs. It was the mussel soup he lifted off the table. 'Go back! Go back to England! You're not anybody's prisoner!'

'I am trying!'

Mussel shells, garlic, onion, tomato paste, tomatoes and some wine, he threw into the kitchen. But the garlic hangs over everything this morning; and the phone is ringing in a room downstairs.

In some places, he said last night, amid the broken crockery, before a marriage they smash the dishes, they break the plates to frighten off the ghosts. Perhaps this is necessary after all.

When he wakes, I whisper: 'Love, I'll stay.'

'I've found you again,' he says.

The phone is still ringing in a room downstairs. It is 2.30 in the afternoon.

'Send your Fenian girlfriend back where she belongs, or we'll give her the works and then you!'

He is staring at the clock.

'I wonder how they knew?' he says.

'The estate agent has been writing to me from England. It was too much trouble to explain the difficulty of it. The postman would notice a Catholic name in this street. The sorters in the Post Office, too. Or maybe it was the man collecting for the football pools –'

'Football pools?'

'The other night a man came to the door, he asked me to pick four teams or eight, I can't remember now. Then he asked me to sign it.'

'You should have given my name.'

'I did. But I don't know anything about football. And I think I gave myself away when –'

'What?'

'I picked Liverpool! Or it could have happened at the launderette when I left the washing in. They asked: "What name?" And I forgot. Or it could have been the taxi I got last night from here to –'

'I suppose they would have found out some time.'

He is sitting on the bed.

'Could it have been – your wife?'

He looks hurt: 'I never told her that!' he says. 'I suppose they would have found out some time. I think I'd better call the police.'

I get up quickly: 'Do you mind if I get dressed and bathe and make the bed before you do?'

'Why?'

'Because they'll come round and look at everything.'

I am packing a large suitcase in the attic where we sleep when he comes upstairs.

'The police say that anyone who really meant a threat wouldn't ring you up beforehand. They're not coming round.'

'Listen. I want you to take me to the airport. And I want you to pack a bag as well.'

'I'm teaching tomorrow,' he says. 'Please leave something behind, love. That black dress of yours. The one I like you in.'

It is still hanging in the wardrobe. I leave my scent in the bathroom and on his pillow.

'It's just so that I know you'll come back.'

At 3.40 we are ready to leave the house. The street is empty when we open the door. The curtains are drawn.

'We're a bit late,' he tells the driver. 'Can you get us to the airport in half an hour?'

In the car he kisses me and says: 'No one has ever held my hand so tightly before.'

'What will you do?' I ask, as I'm getting on the plane.

'I'll have to give three months' notice.'

'Do it.'

'Teaching jobs are hard to come by,' he says, looking around.

'Whatever this place is – it's my home.'

5.45. Heathrow. Without him I walk from the plane. Who are they watching now? Him or me? Suddenly, a man steps out in front of me. Oh, Jesus!

'Have you any means of identification? What is the purpose of your visit . . . ?

Friday 3 February 1984

The fifth note:

A bell is ringing. I go cautiously to the door. I have slept with all the lights on. I see a man through the glass. He is wearing a combat jacket. This is England, I remind myself. The milkman is smiling at me.

'I saw your lights,' he says.

I tell him I've come back and will he please leave one pint every other day.

He tells me his son's in Northern Ireland in the Army.

'No jobs,' he shouts, walking down the path. 'Were you on holiday?'

'No. I was working.'

The bottles clink in the crate.

'It's well for some.'

He is angry, I begin to think, because I do not drive a milkfloat.

I am shopping again for one. At closing time I go out to the supermarket. It is just getting dark. There are two hundred people gathered in the road outside the shopping precinct. A busker is playing a love song. The police are turning away at the entrance the ones who haven't noticed.

'What is it?' I ask a young woman who is waiting at a stop.

'A bomb scare. It's the third one this week.'

I should think before I speak.

'There were fourteen people killed in London, in a bomb in a store.'

I am hoping she hasn't noticed. Some of your countrymen?

Then she says:

'Doesn't matter what nationality you are, dear, we all suffer the same.'

The busker is playing a love song. I am shopping again for one.

Noday. Nodate 1984

I keep myself awake all night so I am ready when they come.

A COUNTRY DANCE

MARY DORCEY
Born in Co. Dublin, Mary Dorcey is a founder member of many of Ireland's women's rights groups. She has written poetry and short stories, and published one collection of the latter, *A Noise From The Woodshed*, which won the 1990 Rooney Award for Irish Literature.

On the arm of your chair, your hand for a moment is still; the skin smooth and brown against the faded red velvet. I touch it lightly with mine. 'Maybe what she needs is more time,' I say.

The air is dense with cigarette smoke, my eyes are tired. You stare past me and begin again to fidget with a silver bracelet on your wrist. I make my tone persuasive: 'Time to regain her identity, a sense of independence, and . . .'

The words are swept from me in a sudden upswell of sound as last orders are called. The climax of the night, and so much left unsaid, undone. Every man in the room is on his feet, shoving for place at the bar, the voices bluff, seductive, as they work for one last round.

'Here, John, two large ones . . .'

'Pat, good man, four more pints . . .'

You ignore them, your gaze holding mine, your attention caught once more by the hope of her name.

'What did you say about independence?'

'I said you need it, need to cultivate it,' something perverse in me all at once, wanting to disappoint you. Your eyes drop, slide to the fireplace where the coal burns with a dim red glow.

'Ah, I thought it was Maeve you meant.'

And what matters after all which way I put it? In these stories aren't all the characters interchangeable? The lights are turned up full now, the evening over. And you as much in the dark as when we started. If I had used less tact; if I had said straight out what everyone thinks, would it have made a difference? I twist the stub of my last cigarette into the glass ashtray. No, whatever I say you will hear what you choose. Your misery safely walled beyond the reach of logic, however much you may plead with me to advise, console. If you were not fully certain of this, would you have asked me here tonight?

'Time, ladies and gents, please – have you no homes to go to?' The barman turns, the great wash of his belly, supported just clear of the crotch, tilts towards us. He swipes a greasy cloth across the tabletop, forcing us to lift our drinks: 'Come on now, girls.'

I take another sip of my whiskey and replace the glass emphatically on the cardboard coaster. You clasp your pint to your chest, swilling the dregs in languid circles.

'I don't think I can bear it much longer.'

I look at you, your dark eyes have grown sullen with pain, under the clear skin of your cheek a nerve twitches. Years ago, I would have believed you. Believed your hurt unlooked for – believed even in your will to escape it. Now, too many nights like this one have altered me. Too many nights spent in comforting others, watching while each word of sympathy is hoarded as a grain of salt to nourish the wound. On the blackness of the window I watch beads of rain glance brilliant as diamonds, each one falling distinct, separate, then merging – drawn together in swift streams to the ground. Why try to impose reason? Let you have your grand passion, the first taste of self-torment – never so sweet or keen again.

'Look, will you have another drink?' I say in a last attempt to cheer you. 'They might give us one yet.'

Instantly your face brightens. 'Thanks, but you've bought enough,' you say, and add lightly as if you'd just thought of it, 'Did you see someone has left a pint over there – will I get it?'

Without waiting for a reply, you slide your narrow hips in their scarlet jeans between our table and the bar. You reach for the pint of Harp and a half-finished cocktail. The barman swings round. 'Have you got twenty Marlboros?' you ask to distract him. While he roots on a shelf above the till, you slip the drinks over to me and turn back with a smile. Seeing it, placated, he tosses the cigarettes in the air, beating you to the catch. 'What has such a nice looking girl alone at this hour?' he asks, his voice oiled, insistent. You stand and say nothing. Your smile ransom enough. 'Go home to your bed,' he says, and throws the pack along the wet counter.

'Jesus, the things you have to do around here for a drink.' You fling yourself down on the seat beside me, close so that our knees and shoulders touch.

'You don't have to,' I say.

'Is that right?' you answer and raise one sceptical eyebrow. You pick up the cocktail glass and hold it to your nose. 'Is it gin or what?'

'I don't know and I certainly don't want it.'

Fishing a slice of stale lemon from the clouded liquid, you knock it back and reach for the Harp.

'Easy on,' I say, 'you'll be pissed at this rate.'

You take no notice, your head thrown back, drinking with total concentration. I watch Pat, the young barboy, guide customers to the door. A big woman, her pink dress stretched tight across her thighs, is hanging on his arm. She tells him what a fine looking lad he is, and laughs something caressingly in his ear.

'Ah, wouldn't I love to, Molly, but what would Peter have to say?' Slapping her flanks with the flat of his hand, he winks across at me, and slams the door behind her. Outside, in the car park, someone is singing in a drunken baritone: 'Strangers in the night, exchanging glances, wondering in the night . . .'

'At this stage of the evening,' I say, 'everyone is wondering.'

'About what?' you ask. You run your fingers idly through your long hair, puzzled but incurious.

'Nothing,' I reply. 'A silly joke – just the crowd outside singing.'

You have noticed no singing, much less the words that accompany it. Your gaze is fixed resolutely on the uncleared tables – you have spotted one more in the corner. It's obvious now that you have no intention of going home sober, but we cannot sit here all night and I do not want Paddy to catch you lifting leftovers.

'Well, if you want to stay on,' I say smiling at you, as though it were the very thing I wanted myself, 'why don't we finish what we have in comfort, next door?' I look towards the hallway and an unmarked wooden door on the far side. You are on your feet at once, gathering our glasses, not caring where we go so long as there is a drink at the end of it.

A thin Persian carpet covers the floor of the residents' lounge. On the dim papered walls hang red, satin-shaded lamps with frayed gold fringing, and three framed prints – hunting scenes – men and animals confused in the dark oils. A few of the regulars have drawn armchairs up to the fire. Pipe tobacco and the scent of cloves from their hot whiskeys hang together in the air. A man is kneeling over the coal bucket, struggling to open the tongs. He has the red face and shrunken thighs of the habitual toper. 'What the bloody fuck is wrong with this yoke anyway?' he says.

'Here, let me,' leaving him the tongs, you lift the bucket and empty half its contents into the grate. You rattle the poker through the bars, shifting the live coals from front to back. Dust crackles. After a moment, shoots of yellow flame break from the new untouched black.

'Nothing like a good fire,' the man announces, rubbing together his blue-veined hands. 'I always like to build up a good fucking fire.'

His eyes follow the line of your flank, taut and curved as you bend
to the hearth. His tongue slides over his bottom lip. 'Always like to
build up a good fire,' he repeats as though it were something witty.

He looks towards me, suddenly conscious of my presence and gives
a deferential nod. 'Excuse the language,' he calls over. He has placed
me then as protector, older sister. And why not after all? Is it not the
role I have adopted since that first day I met you in Grafton Street,
walking blinded by tears, after one of your quarrels? Did I not even
then, that first moment laying eyes on you, want to protect you, from
Maeve – from yourself – from that reckless vulnerability of yours,
that touched some hidden nerve in me? But it was not protection you
wanted, it was empathy. You wanted me to look on, with everyone
else, impassive, while you tormented yourself struggling to retain a
love that had already slipped into obligation. Though you would not
see it – you would see nothing but your own desire. Night after night,
following her, watching; your wide, innocent eyes stiff with pain, while
she ignored you or flirted with someone else. Waiting because at the
end of the evening she might turn, and on an impulse of guilt ask you
to go home with her.

'The last one, I think, do you want it?' You hand me an almost full
pint of Guinness – brown, sluggish, the froth gone from it. I accept
with a wry smile, why not – nothing worse than being empty-handed
among drunks, and you clearly will not be hurried.

'Are they residents?' you ask with vague curiosity, looking towards
the threesome on the opposite side of the fire.

'No, just regulars,' I say, and none more regular than Peg Maguire.
Peg who is here every night with one man or another, drinking herself
into amiability. A woman with three children who might be widowed
or separated – no one asks. With her blonde hair piled above her
head, lipstick a little smudged at the corners, her white coat drawn
tight about her as though she were just on the point of departure, Peg
– shrewd, jaunty – always careful to maintain the outward show. 'But
you know country hotels: once the front door is shut you could stay
forever.' I should not have said that, of course, it encourages you.
You will have to stay over with me now, I suppose, you are long past
driving.

I take a deep draught of the bitter stout, letting it slip quickly down
my throat, and to keep this first lightness of mood, I ask you about
the college. You are bored, dismissive. Second year is worse than
first, you tell me – the life drawing is hopeless, you have only one
male model and he wears a G-string; afraid of getting it on in front of

women. 'Anyway, I haven't been there for a week – too stoned,' you add as if that exonerated you. Tossing your head back to sweep the hair from your face. For which of us, I wonder, do you present this elaborate disdain.

'You'll come to a sorry end,' I warn you. 'All this dope and sex at nineteen destroys the appetite.' I have made you smile, a slow, lilting smile, that draws your lips from white, perfect teeth.

'Is that what happened to you?' you ask.

'Perhaps it is. I would say I have decayed into wisdom. A forty-hour week and a regular lover – no unfulfilled lust masquerading as romance.'

'Don't tell me you are not romantic about Jan,' you look at me intently, your eyes at once teasing and solemn, 'when anyone can see you're mad about her.'

'That's one way of putting it, I suppose. At least the feeling is mutual so there is no aggravation.'

'And what about Liz?' you ask. 'Was it not very hard on her?'

'Oh, Liz had other interests,' I say. 'There was no heartache there.'

I have shocked you. You want fervour and longing, not this glib detachment. Should I tell you I am posing, or am I? Is there anything I cherish more than my independence? You lean forward, the cigarette at your mouth, gripped between thumb and forefinger, urging some story of need or rejection.

'You know, it is possible for people to care for each other without tearing their souls out,' I hear my voice, deliberately unemotional. 'All this strife and yearning is a myth invented to take our minds off the mess around us. Happiness distracts no one.' And what is it that impels me to disillusion you? Is it only that this intensity of yours so clearly hurts no one but yourself? With impatience you fan the trail of blue smoke from your face and cut me short.

'Ah, you are always so cynical. You would think thirty is middle age the way you go on. Anyway it's different for you. You have your work – something you really care about. It's all different.'

And so, maybe it is. What answer could I give you that would not be twisting the knife?

You stare into the fire, blazing now. The flames bouncing up the chimney throw great splashes of light about the room. Dance on the red brown of your hair. You have finished your cigarette. Your hands in your lap are curiously still – palms upturned. My own lean, fidgeting. I look about the room, at the rubber plant in the corner, the gilt-framed mirror above the mantelpiece – from it my eyes stare back at me, to

my surprise still bright and sharp; a gleaming blue. I notice the faint
tracing of lines at the corners. First signs. Give up the fags for good
next week – get a few early nights. I look towards you. Your lips are
at the rim of your glass, sipping at it, stretching it out. Do you dread
going home so much?

'You can stay over with me, you know. Jan is in town – you can
have her bed. Maybe you would come jogging in the morning – do
you good.'

Roused for a moment, you regard me slowly, from shoulders to
thigh, appraising me. 'Aw, I'm not in your shape,' you say. 'I wouldn't
last more than a mile.'

'Well, you can walk while I run,' I answer, but your gaze has slipped
back to the fire, watching the leap of the flames as if they held some
private message. We sit in silence, lulled by the heat and alcohol until
I break it to ask – 'What are you thinking?' Foolish question, as though
you would tell me. But you do, holding my eyes to yours, you answer
slowly: 'I was wondering if I might ring Maeve – she could be . . .'

'At this hour? You are incorrigible.' I do not try to hide my irritation.
'I thought you said you were going to keep away for a week . . .'

You begin to smile again. For a moment I wonder if you are playing
with me. Then your face shuts, suddenly, as though a light had been
switched off. 'You are right, of course. I'd forgotten.'

And why should I strain to follow these moods? If it were not that
you look so forlorn, huddled in your chair, like an animal shut out in
the rain.

'You are inconsolable, aren't you?' I say, hoping to tease you out
of it. 'Tell me, have you not, even for five minutes, been attracted to
another woman?'

You turn away abruptly, as though I had struck you, and ask over-
loudly, 'Do you think we can get something to take away?'

'Is it a drink you want?' one of Peg's friends calls over. He has been
listening to us for some time, his gaze flickering between us like a
snake's tongue. 'I'll get you a drink,' he offers.

'It's all right thanks,' I say quickly.

'No, no, I insist. Name your poison, girls.' His speech is slurred.
Conscious of it he repeats each sentence. 'Pat will give us a bottle –
no trouble.' He hauls himself up from his chair, clutching the mantelpiece. Peg grabs at his arm.

'Pat has gone off hours ago – don't bother yourself.'

'No bother. Got to get these lassies a drink. Can't send them home
thirsty.' He rolls a watering eye at us.

'And what would you know about thirst – you've never been dry long enough to have one.' Peg is an old friend and wants no trouble with me. 'Sit down, Frank, and don't be annoying the girls.'

'Who's annoying anyone, Peg Maguire – certainly not you – not if you were the last bloody woman on earth.'

We have set them bickering between themselves now. Time to go. But you are edgy, persistent. 'Is there really no chance of another drink?' you ask Peg. She lowers her voice and gives you a conspiratorial look.

'What is it you want – would a six-pack do? If you come with us to the Mountain View, I'll get you something there. They've a disco with late closing.'

'The very thing,' Frank roars. 'A disco tit. Let's all go. Two such lovely young women need . . .' he staggers to his feet once more and begins to sing, 'I could have danced all night – I could have danced all night and still have begged for more. I could have spread my wings,' he wheels his arms in a jagged circle almost knocking Peg's glass, 'and done a thousand things, I'd never done . . .'

'Will you for God's sake hold on to yourself,' Peg snaps furiously, and pushes him forward.

'Are you right then, girls,' she nods towards us. 'I'll give you the lift down and you can walk back. It's only ten minutes.'

Well, that has done it. There will be no stopping you now. We will not get home till you are soused. And why should I try to deter you? Have I anything better to offer? All the tired virtues. Useless. I should be exasperated by you, dragging me all over the country as if a pint of stout were the holy grail. But something about you halts me. As you move to the door, something exaggerated in you – the turn of your shoulders, your head thrown back as though pulling from harness. Defiance and vulnerability in every line. Something more than youth. Something more than me as I was before I learned – and who was it who finally taught me? – the hard-won pleasures of realism and self-sufficiency. Yet if I had the power to bestow them on you, this very instant, would I want to?

In the unlit carpark we find Peg's Fiat and pile in – Frank pulling me towards his knee: 'If you were the only girl in the world and I was the only boy.' Rain slashes at the windscreen, one wiper stuck halfway across it. Peg seems to drive by ear. Wet fir trees arching over us make a black tunnel of the road. The road to God knows where. I recognise none of it, letting myself be carried forward – lapsing into the heedless collective will. All needs converging in the simple drive for one more drink. 'Nothing else would matter in the world today . . .' Frank's whiskey breath encircles us. We reach tall, silver gates, pass them, and sluice through rain-filled craters in the drive, the wind snapping at our wheels. A furious night – clouds blown as fast as leaves across the sky. Lights ahead – the tall Georgian house bright in welcome. Braking almost on the front steps, Peg jumps out, leaving the door wide: 'I'll put in a word for you.' We follow, our faces lowered from the rain. In the hallway with the bouncer, her blonde head bent to his ear, she is confidential, explaining that we want only a takeaway – no admission. Solemn as a mother entrusting her daughters. Then she turns back to the car and her boys waiting outside. She throws a wicked grin at me over her shoulder – why? – 'Enjoy yourselves, girls,' and she is off.

Out of the night – into a frenzy of light and sound. We push through the black swing doors. Red and purple light, great shafts of it, beat against the walls and floor. The music hammers through my chest, shivering my arms. A man and woman, locked together, move in a tight circle at the centre of the room. In the corner, beside a giant speaker, two girls on stiletto heels dance an old-fashioned jive. We push through the wall of shoulders at the bar, country boys shy of dancing. 'Two large bottles of stout,' I order. The barman reaches for pint glasses and shoves them under the draught tap. 'Bottles – to take away,' I call across to him. But it is useless, he has already moved to the far end of the counter to measure out whiskey.

'We will just have to drink them here,' you say, putting your mouth close to my ear so that I feel the warmth of your breath. So be it – at least we are in from the rain for a while.

We choose a corner table, as far from the speakers as possible, but still I have to shout to make you hear me.

'It's easier if you whisper,' you say, bringing your lips to my ear once more, in demonstration.

'You are used to these places, I suppose.' It is years since I have sat like this. Though so little has altered. The lights and music more violent maybe, the rest unchanging. Nobody really wants to be here, it seems. Young women dressed for romance display themselves – bringing their own glamour. The men stand banded in council, shoulders raised as a barrier, until they have drunk enough. The faces are bored or angry. Each one resenting his need, grudging submission to this ritual fever.

You finish half your pint at one go and offer the glass to me. I down the remainder and together we start on the next, laughing. A rotating light on the ceiling spins a rainbow of colours; blue, red, gold, each thrust devouring the last. Smoke hangs in heavy green clouds about us. As though it were the fumes of marijuana, I breathe it deep into my lungs and feel suddenly a burst of dizzy gaiety . . . the absurdity of it all – that we should be here. And back to me come memories of years ago – adolescence, when it might have been the scene of passion, or was it even then absurd? The pace slows and three couples move to the centre of the floor. 'I don't want to talk about it – how you broke my heart.' The voice of Rod Stewart rasps through the speakers in an old song. But a favourite of yours. We have danced to it once before – in the early hours at Clare's party two weeks ago, when Maeve had left without you. You stand beside me now and in pantomine stretch your hand. 'Will you dance with me?' You walk ahead onto the floor. Under the spotlight your white shirt is luminous – your eyes seem black. You rest your hands on your hips, at the centre of the room, waiting.

'If you stay here just a little bit longer – if you stay here – won't you listen to my heart . . .' We step into each other's arms. Our cheeks touch. I smell the scent of your shirt – the darkness of your hair. Your limbs are easy, assured against mine. Your hands familiar, hold me just below the waist. We turn the floor, elaborately slow, in one movement, as though continuing something interrupted. The music lapping thigh and shoulder. 'The stars in the sky don't mean nothing to you – they're a mirror.' Round we swing, round; closer in each widening circle. Lost to our private rhythm. The foolish words beating time in my blood.

I open my eyes. The music has stopped. Behind you I see a man standing, his eyes riveted to our bodies, his jaw dropped wide as though it had been punched. In his maddened stare I see reflected what I have refused to recognise through all these weeks. Comfort, sympathy, a protective sister – who have I been deceiving? I see it now in his eyes. Familiar at once in its stark simplicity. Making one movement of past and future. I yield myself to it; humbled, self-mocking. Quick as a struck match.

As if I had spoken aloud, with a light pressure of my hand, you return to consciousness and walk from the floor.

I follow, my skin suddenly cold. I want as quickly as possible to be gone from the spotlight. I have remembered where we are: a Friday night country dance, surrounded by drunken males who have never before seen two women dance in each other's arms. All about the room they are standing still, watching. As we cross the empty space to our table no one moves. I notice for the first time Brid Keane from the post office: she is leaning against the wall, arms folded, her face contorted in a look of such disgust, it seems for a moment that she must be putting it on.

'Let's get out of here – as soon as you've finished your drink,' I whisper.

'What – do you want another drink?' Your voice rises high above the music that has begun again. I stare at you in amazement – is it possible that you haven't noticed, that you don't yet know what we've done? Can you be so naïve or so drunk that you haven't realised whose territory we are on?

And then someone moves from the table behind and pushes into the seat opposite us. Squat, red-faced, his hair oiled across his forehead. He props an elbow on the table, and juts his head forward, struggling to focus his eyes. His pink nylon shirt is open, a white tie knotted about the neck.

'Fucking lesbians,' he says at last. 'Are you bent or what?' The breath gusting into my face is sour with whiskey. We look towards the dancers writhing under a strobe light and ignore him.

'Did you not hear me?' he asks, shoving his face so close to me, I see the sweat glisten on his upper lip. 'I said are you bent – queers?' He drives his elbow against mine so that the stout spills over my glass.

A familiar anger rips through me, making my legs tremble. I press my nails into the palm of my hand and say nothing. I will not satisfy him so easily.

'What were you saying about the music?' I throw you a smile.

'I asked you a question,' he says. 'Will you give me a bloody answer?' He runs the words together as though speed were his only hope of completing them.

'I said it's lousy,' you reply, 'about ten years out of date.'

He looks from me to you and back again with baffled irritation and his voice grows querulous. He asks: 'Look, would one of you lesbians give me a dance.'

A friend has joined him now, leaning over the back of your chair, a grin on his lips sly and lascivious.

'Will you not answer me,' the first one shouts. 'Or are you fucking deaf?'

Drawing my shoulders up, I turn and for the first time look directly into his eyes. 'No,' I say with warning deliberation, 'we are not deaf, yes, we are lesbians and no, we will not give you a dance.'

He stares at us stupefied, then falls back into his seat, breath hissing from his chest as though a lung had burst. 'Jesus, fucking Christ.'

You give a whoop of laughter, your eyes wide with delight. It seems you find him hugely amusing. Then you're on your feet and across the room in search of the toilet or God knows another drink.

I have my back turned to him when I feel the pink-sleeved arm nudging mine again. 'Hey, blondie – you've gorgeous hair,' he says, giving an ugly snigger. 'Did anyone ever tell you that?' It is a moment before I recognise the smell of singed hair. I reach my hand to the back of my head and a cigarette burns my fingertips. With a cry of pain, I grab hold of the oily lock across his forehead and wrench hard enough to pull it from the roots. He stretches his arm to catch hold of mine but I tear with all my force. 'You fucking cunt!' he screams.

Suddenly someone catches hold of us from behind and pulls us roughly apart. It's the bouncer – a big red-haired man in a grey suit. When he sees my face he steps back aghast. He had plainly not expected a woman.

'I don't know what you two want,' his voice is cold, contemptuous, 'but whatever it is you can settle it between you – outside.' He drops the hand on my shoulder, wheels round and walks back to his post at the door. At the sight of him my opponent is instantly subdued. He shrinks back into his seat as though he had been whipped, then slowly collapses onto the table, head in his arms.

You return carrying another drink. I wait until you are sitting down to whisper: 'We have to get out of here, Cathy – they're half savage. That one just tried to set fire to my hair.'

'The little creep!' you exclaim, your eyes sparking with indignation.

'Oh, he's easily handled – but the rest of them, look.'

At the bar a group of six or seven are standing in a circle drinking. Big farm boys in tweed jackets – older than the others and more sober. Their gaze has not left us, I know, since we walked off the dance floor, yet they have made no move. This very calm is what frightens me. In their tense vigilance, I feel an aggression infinitely more threatening than the bluster of the two next us. Hunters letting the hounds play before closing in?

'I think they might be planning something,' I say, and, as if in response to some prearranged signal, one of them breaks from the group and slowly makes his way to our table.

His pale, thin face stares into mine, he makes a deep bow and stretches out his hand. 'Would one of you ladies care to dance?'

I shake my head wearily. 'No, thanks.'

He gives a scornful shrug of the shoulders and walks back to his companions. A moment later another one sets out. When he reaches us, he drops to one knee before you and for the benefit of those watching, loudly repeats the request. When you refuse him he retreats with the same show of disdain.

'They can keep this going all night,' I say, 'building the pressure. With their mad egotism anything is better than being ignored.' And I know also what I do not say, that we have to put up with it. They have us cornered. Under all the theatrics lies the clear threat that if we dare to leave, they can follow, and once outside, alone in the dark, they will have no need for these elaborate games.

'What can we do?' you ask, twisting a strand of hair about your finger, your eyes attentive at last.

'I'll go off for a few minutes. Maybe if we separate, if they lose sight of us, they might get distracted.'

Five minutes later, pushing my way through the crowd to our table, I find you chatting with the one in the pink shirt and his mate, smoking and sharing their beer like old drinking pals. How can you be so unconcerned? I feel a sudden furious irritation. But you look up at me and smile warningly. 'Humour them,' I read in the movement of your lips. And you may be right. They have turned penitent now, ingratiating: 'We never meant to insult you, honest, love. We only wanted to be friendly.' His head lolling back and forth, he stabs a finger to his chest: 'I'm Mick, and this is me mate, Gerry.'

All right then, let us try patience. At least while we are seen talking to these two the others will hold off.

'You know, blondie, I think you're something really special,' with the deadly earnest of the drunk, Mick addresses me. 'I noticed you the second you walked in. I said to Gerry – didn't I Gerry? Blondie, would you not give it a try with me? I know you're into women – your mate explained – and that's all right with me – honest – that's cool, you know what I mean? But you never know till you try, do you? Might change your life. Give us a chance, love.' He careens on through his monologue, long past noticing whether I answer or not. On the opposite side I hear Gerry, working on you with heavy flattery, admiring your eyes (glistening now – with drink or anger – dark as berries), praising the deep red of your lips – parted at the rim of your glass. And you are laughing into his face and drinking his beer. Your throat thrown back as you swallow, strong and naked.

Mick has collapsed, his head on the table drooping against my arm. 'Just one night,' he mutters into my sleeve, 'that's all I'm asking – just one night. Do yourself a favour.' His words seep through my brain, echoing weirdly, like water dripping in a cave. Drumming in monotonous background to the movements of your hands and face. Half turned from me, I do not hear what you answer Gerry, but I catch your tone; languorous, abstracted, I watch you draw in the spilt froth on the table. Your eyes lowered, the lashes black along your cheek, one finger traces the line of a half moon. Behind you I see the same group watching from the bar; patient, predatory. My blood pounds – fear and longing compete in my veins.

And then all at once, the music stops. Everyone stands to attention, silent. The disc-jockey is making an announcement: the offer of a bottle of whiskey, a raffle, the buying of tickets – gripping them as the music and dance never could. This is our moment, with Gerry moving to the bar to buy cigarettes and Mick almost asleep, slumped backwards, his mouth dropped open. I grasp your hand beneath the table, squeezing it so that you may feel the urgency and no one else, and look towards the green exit sign. We are across the floor, stealthy and cautious as prisoners stepping between the lights of an armed camp. At the door at last, 'Fucking whoores – you needn't trouble yourselves to come back,' the bouncer restraining fury in the slam of the swing doors behind us.

And we are out.

Out in the wet darkness. The wind beating escape at our backs. I catch your hand. 'Run and don't stop.' Our feet scatter the black puddles, soaking our shins. The fir trees flapping at our sides beckon, opening our path to the gates. So much further now. The moon will not help – hidden from us by sheets of cloud – withholding its light. We run blind, my heart knocking at my ribs; following the track only by the sting of gravel through my thin soles. 'Come on – faster.' The gates spring towards us out of nowhere – caught in a yellow shaft of brightness. A car rounds the bend behind us, the water flung hissing from its tyres. We dodge under the trees, the drenched boughs smacking my cheek. The headlights are on us, devouring the path up to and beyond the open gates. The window rolled down, I hear the drunken chanting – like the baying of hounds: 'We're here because we're queer because we're here because we're . . .' 'Great fucking crack, lads . . .' Gone. Past us. Pitched forward in the delirium of the chase – seeing nothing to left or right. A trail of cigarette smoke in the air.

'All right – we can go on now,' you say, laughing – drawing me out from cover. 'Do you think it was them?'

'Yes, or worse. We had better be gone before the next lot.'

We run on again, through the wide gates to the main road. The alcohol is washing through me now, spinning my head. My heart is beating faster than ever, though the fear has left me. You are beginning to tire. 'We are almost there,' I urge you, marvelling that you can still stand, let alone run. The rain darts in the gutter, the leaves slithering under our feet. Jumping a pool I slip towards you. Your arm outflung steadies me. You're laughing again – the long looping kind you do not want to stop. 'You're worse than I am,' you say.

The moon all at once throws open the night before us, scattering in sequins on the tarred road, silver on the hanging trees. I see the house massed and still in its light.

'We are home,' I say.

You slow your pace and let go of my hand. Your eyes under the white gleam of the moon are darker than ever – secretive.

'Are you laughing at me?' I ask, to capture your attention.

'I'm not – really,' you answer, surprised.

I lift the latch of the gate, softly so as to wake no one. How am I to keep this? To keep us from slipping back into the everyday: the lighted, walled indoors – all the managed, separating things. And what is it I fear to lose? Any more than my desire – dreaming yours? Any more than a drunken joy in escape?

The cat comes through a gap in the hedge, whipping my shins with her tail. I lift her to me and she gives a low, rough cry.

'She's been waiting for you,' you tell me.

I turn the key in the kitchen door. You step inside and stand by the window, the moonlight falling like a pool of water about your feet. I gaze at your shoes for no reason; at the pale, wet leather, muddied now.

'Well, that looked bad for a moment,' I say, putting my arm round you, not knowing whether it is you or myself I am consoling. 'Were you not frightened at all?'

'Oh yes, I was,' you answer, leaning into me, pulling me close. 'Yes.'

And so, I have been right. So much more than comfort. I slide my lips down your cheek, still hesitant, measuring your answer. And you lift your open mouth to meet mine. I have imagined nothing, then. Everything. All this long night has been a preparation – an appeal.

You untie the belt of my raincoat. I feel your hands, still cold from the night rain, along my sides: 'I'm freezing. Are you?'

'Yes.'

'Are there beds anywhere in this house?'

'We might find one.'

You laugh. I take your hand and silently, as though fearful of waking someone, we cross the hall together and climb the wooden staircase.

The room is dark but for a shaft of moonlight which falls across the double bed, with its silver and wine red quilt, that waits at the centre of the floor. I light a candle by the window. You sit on the cane chair and unlace your sneakers, slowly, knot by knot. Then stand and drop your clothes – red jeans and white shirt – in a ring about them. I turn back the sheets and step towards you. Downstairs the phone sounds, cracking the darkness like a floodlight. It rings and rings and will not stop. 'I had better answer it,' I say and move to the door.

'Who was it?' When I return, you are sitting propped against the pillow, easy as though you spent every night here. I cannot tell you that it was Jan, feeling amorous, wanting to chat, imagining me alone.

'Jan . . .' I begin, but you do not wait to hear. Reaching your hand behind my head you pull my mouth towards you. I feel, but do not hear the words you speak against my lips.

The rain drives at the window, shivering the curtains. The wind blown up from the sea sings in the stretched cables. Your body strains to mine, each movement at once a repetition and discovery. Your mouth, greedy and sweet, sucks the breath from my lungs. I draw back from your face, your long dark hair and look in your eyes: you are laughing again – a flame at the still black centre. Your tongue seals my eyelids shut. Your hands, travelling over me, startle the skin as if they would draw it like a cover from muscle and bone. We move – bound in one breath – muscle, skin and bone. I kiss you from forehead to thigh. Kiss the fine secret skin beneath your breast, the hard curve of your belly.

The wind moans through the slates of the roof. The house shifts. Beneath us the sea crashes on the stones of the shore. Your voice comes clear above them beating against mine, high above the wind and rain. Spilling from the still centre – wave after wave. And then, a sudden break; a moment's straining back as though the sea were to check for one instant – resisting – before its final drop to land. But the sea does not.

You lie quiet above me. I taste the salt of tears on my tongue.

'Are you crying? What is it?'

'No, I'm not,' you answer gently, your head turned from me. Maybe so. I close my arms about you, stroking the silk of your back, finding no words. But it does not matter. Already you have moved beyond me into sleep. I lie still. Clouds have covered the moon, blackening the window of sky. I cannot see your face. Your body is heavy on mine, your breath on my cheek. I soothe myself with its rhythm. The rain has ceased. I hear once more the small night sounds of the house: the creak of wood in floorboards and rafters, the purr of the refrigerator. Then suddenly there comes a loud crash – the noise of cup or plate breaking on the kitchen's tiled floor. My breath stops – you do not stir. I hear the squeal of a window swung on its hinge. A dull thud. Footsteps?

Before my eyes a face rises: mottled cheeks, beads of sweat along the lip. A wild fear possesses me that he or his friends have followed us, come here to this house in search of us. I slide gently from under you. I creep to the door and stand listening for a moment, breath held, before opening it. Silence . . . Nothing but the hum of the 'fridge. And then . . . a soft, triumphal cry. Of course – the cat. How well I know that call. Elsie has caught a rat or bird and brought it home through the window. In the morning there will be a trail of blood and feathers on the carpet. Time enough to deal with it tomorrow.

I go back to bed. Lifting the sheet I press near to your warmth, my belly fitting exactly in the well of your back. I breathe the strange, new scent of you. A shudder goes through my limbs. I reach my hand and gently gather the weight of your breast. I feel the pulsing through the fine veins beneath the surface. You stir, sighing, and press your thighs against mine. You murmur something from sleep – a word, or name. Someone's name.

My arms slacken. I taste your tears, again, on my lips. In the morning what will we say to each other? Drunk as you were it will be easy to forget, to pretend the whole thing an accident. No need then to prepare an attitude – for Maeve (when she calls, as she will, as before, thanking me for taking care of you), for Jan – for ourselves. The night is fading at the window. The bare branch of the sycamore knocks on the wall behind us. Words echo in my mind, the words of the song we danced to, foolish, mocking: 'The stars in the sky mean nothing to you – they're a mirror.' And to me? What was it I said this evening about romantic illusion? I reach out my hand for the candlestick on the table. As I lift it, the flame flares golden. My movement has woken you. You regard me, for an instant, startled. How childish you look, your forehead smooth, your eyes washed clear. Was it only your hurt that set a cord between us – that lent you the outline of maturity? 'I thought I heard a noise downstairs,' you say.

'Yes, but it was nothing,' I kiss your eyes shut. 'Only the cat with a bird,' I answer as you move into sleep, your cheek at my shoulder. 'Nothing.'

Far out to sea, a gull cries against the coming of light. For a little longer night holds us beyond the grasp of speech. I lean and blow the candle out.

FATGIRL TERRESTRIAL

ANNE ENRIGHT

Anne Enright was born in Dublin, 1962, where she is a Producer/ Director in RTE. She studied at Trinity College, Dublin and the University of East Anglia, and made her writing debut with her short story collection, *The Portable Virgin*, which won the 1991 Rooney Award for Irish Literature.

Why could she never find herself a public man? A man to walk down the street with, a man who would tend to the barbecue and flirt lightly with her friends. The fact that she was fat might have something to do with it (though she had no trouble scoring); the fact that she was fat and so felt herself to be odd; the fact that she was fat and so felt herself to be beyond the pale – free. Because every man she found was perfect at the time, perfect within her four walls or his, but, without exception, they all fell apart when she put them on display. Perhaps she was not sufficiently odd. Maybe there was an insubordinate streak of the ordinary in her, a thin woman trying to get out.

Successful women are supposed to be fat, she decided early on. If they are trim and look like mistresses then the board room is a minefield. She developed a motherly laugh. She developed a viciousness that made people mutter 'Fat bitch' and 'No wonder she's so neurotic – would you look at the size of her,' as their assignments came in on time.

She liked sleeping with men. It changed them. They were always surprised by her body – fat being a novelty they would never have thought to pursue. They became nostalgic in her bed for first loves that had been reared on bread and dripping, for soft, Victorian thighs and garter belts that made a dent. They protested that sexuality was all to do with flesh – they were tired of being told to lust after skin and bone. Even so, their young wives were thin and expensive-looking. Bridget had noticed over the years that fat girls were expected to be cheaper and often went halves on dates. She didn't mind. She had plenty of money.

The men from work were not public men. They had nine-to-five faces and girlfriends who worked out. She could feel herself inflating when they walked into the room.

Nevertheless she confused them by her indifference and by the lack of conspiracy in her smile. Good-looking ones were the worst. They

wanted Bridget to fall in love and bother them in the canteen with
Significant and Resentful Looks. They avoided her ostentatiously and
became helpful, formal and efficient.

One of the great sadnesses of Bridget's life was the fact that it all
looked so sleek. Underneath the hard and friendly manner of a fatgirl
who made it against the odds was the commonplace sickness of a
woman who wanted a serious man. It was in public that the nausea
hit – because there was a whole rake of oddities that Bridget did risk
herself with. Men with sweaty eyes who liked to hold her hand walking
down a street and were dying to meet her friends.

Her friends had a taste in wired, artistic-looking types who liked to
talk about themselves; men who could make an impression. Joan was
addicted to the married variety and could not shake it, Maggie was
interested in sex for its own sake, and Sunniva was pure class. Bridget
adored and respected all three. She loved a good laugh and the privacy
of their nights out. She was nearly jealous of their men, even though
she knew that they were private disasters. These socially easy and
uniformly handsome beasts used Maggie, Sunniva and Joan like bust-
up sofas or wore them down with snideness and superficiality. There
were tearful confessions of violence or infidelity. But when they all
went out for the night no one had a bad time. Even their shirts were
witty and they insisted on buying all the drinks.

Bridget divided her disasters into sections and phases. There were
the fanatics, who had a tight, neurotic smell and undiluted eyes. They
talked about death all the time or were severely political. There were
the outright freaks: bizarre, hairy or double-jointed men who played
the saw on the streets or trained to be anaesthetists; men who hated
themselves so badly they might injure themselves if left on their own
in a room. Some respite was provided by the silent brigade: patriarchal
countrymen or foreigners, with rings of perspiration under the arms
of their shirts and mothers who ascended bodily into heaven. There
were the endearingly stupid. Men with beautiful smiles, who felt up
Joan, or Maggie or even Sunniva under various tables and made
obscene suggestions with cheerful tenacity and loping Woody Allen
eyes.

Bridget made all the more usual and banal mistakes though they
never lasted long: alcoholics, virgins, latent homosexuals, 'artists',
whores, seminarian types, and one man who never spoke at all, who
was mortified by the sound of female laughter.

The disaster was that Bridget loved them all. She loved them for
wanting to hold her hand walking down a street, even though she was

fat. She loved them because she knew that she was odd, despite the motherly laugh, the linen suits and the way she said 'Oh my aching feet!' to the person she sat down next to on the bus.

The life of an optimist is a lonely one. Bridget collected seashells and bits of blue glass in walks along the beach. Once a week she visited her elderly mother who had a medical pragmatism about sex. If Bridget did not find a husband soon then her insides would wither away and have to be removed. Of course when your daughter is thirty-five and a professional woman one doesn't enquire too deeply into her affairs, but in her mother's eyes Bridget was too fat for casual sex. She was, however, with her apartment, her job, and her motherly laugh, a Fine Catch. So there was a chance that some lonely and sensible man would save her womb from ossification in the grateful boredom of the marriage bed.

Bridget's mother believed in the marriage bed. When she was not talking about unmentionable diseases she was busy flirting with her dead husband. Bridget's dreams after these visits became infested with her father's eyes. She remembered the day that the world fell apart and her mother's secret store of cosmetics was found. He made one of his only visits into the shops in town with the bag in his hand, went into the make-up counter in Switzers and demanded an estimate of prices from the assistant in her startling white coat. He fined the total from her mother's housekeeping money, with interest. At his funeral, Bridget's mother was plastered so thick with make-up that the mourners took her for some secret mistress, grinned with pride for the dead man and looked the other way.

Bridget was doing her best. She made a conscientious search for the lonely and sensible man. She sat in café windows and watched young and old pass by. She looked at their backs and asked 'Is that a sensible bottom? Can you tell by their taste in socks?' But she knew as she examined them in supermarkets or in traffic jams that she was a hopeless case. Any number of men with nine-to-five minds could provoke her into a faint stir of heat – but it was the ones that twitched who turned her inside out. These she would follow and catch with an audacity that made them feel needed. She would bring them back and empty them out all over her flat. She made them tea, folded them into her, wiped away their hurts and talked them dry – until they were so wet-eyed in love with her that her breasts began to swell. She held their taste in her mouth through the day and laughed all over the office. She started to speak their language.

All would be well until they grew suspicious of this interior life.

They had to find out why she wanted them and who she was. They stood outside her office at six o'clock and asked to meet her friends. They claimed her, laughed abnormally and let their jealousy show.

Even her friends were settling down, and their evenings out took on an alien air. Joan's latest married man was on the brink of leaving his wife and moving in, with his green eyes and excellent tailor. Maggie decided that sex was nothing without procreation and had a child by some Casanova who reformed on the spot and started to dote. Sunniva decided at last on a quiet civil servant who was a dedicated cook, read three books a week and adored her. Bridget, meanwhile, met a small travel agent with dog-brown eyes whom she thought might do.

She was initially attracted by a sign in his window which read 'Have a Boring Holiday Instead. Do Absolutely Nothing in Kinsale. Gourmet Food.'

She appeared to him in her most attractive persona, very slow and very witty and he appeared to her as light and hungry. The matter was soon resolved.

For some reason she did not despise the travel agent. There was something secret about his body, as though it were invisibly tattooed and wild beneath his suit. It made his business clothes seem like some kind of perversion – as though the tweed were a step more dangerous than latex, and she undressed him with care. He was perfectly presentable, willing, witty, he had a good singing voice, and the charming face of a sexual child. Just when Bridget thought she had found it at last – the exciting, ordinary man – the travel agent showed her his collection of dolls.

The travel agent was a witch. He insisted that the word was 'warlock' but she couldn't see him in a sky-blue cloak scattered with stars. He believed in everything that was going, and a little bit more: astrology, herbs, zombie voodoo, Nietzsche, shamans, omens, some Buddhism and the fact that Bridget had been a water-buffalo and a Creole Madame in previous lives.

He talked to her about animal spirits and shape-changing with a ferocity that clashed with his lemon-yellow tie, and they followed discussions about telepathy and childhood with arguments about whether the bill should go on his expenses or hers. She gave him a key to her flat and he would turn up in the middle of the night with the strangest smells on his skin.

Bridget lived in an apartment block with a failing popular singer upstairs, two widows on either side, and someone who worked in TV below. She changed lightbulbs for the widows and they watered her potted plants. She met the failing popular singer in the hall with glitter on her cheeks, and listened to her sobbing through the ceiling all night. The TV person was rarely there and she did her crying in the mornings. Bridget and the widows never cried. As her affair with the travel agent progressed, a flicker came into the widows' eyes and they started to borrow more cups of sugar. Slowly the apartment filled up with feathers, beads, small sweaty pieces of paper with mysterious and banal phrases leaking in the creases and the occasional mask. Bridget believed. Why shouldn't she? She believed because the travel agent said that it didn't matter whether she believed or not. All these facts were indifferent to her, as the animals are, and they spoke a different language. As the travel agent said, when you are talking about Power the word 'true' had about the same weight as the word 'orange'. She started worrying about flights of crows, and wrote small hexes to put under his pillow.

The travel agent spent late nights grinding out his philosophies, trying to make her afraid of the dark. He started at hawk shadows on the walls and said that her body was a landscape of mist with a creature in it he could not meet. He begged her to howl and grunt, and the widows' hands started to tremble with admiration as she filled their cups with borrowed flour.

In point of fact, Bridget did feel herself to be under a spell. He flipped her body on the bed like a cake in a pan, he sang messages onto her answering machine. At inappropriate moments she would see him smile at the door, and when she looked, he wasn't there.

There must have been one particular morning when Bridget first neglected to take her shower. It was probably a morning in spring, which was always her most anxious time. Spring made her think of summer and her inability to wear shorts. The crocuses and the daffodils started pushing their way into her mind, like the sound of a party to which she had not been invited. The thin light made her pant going up the stairs and left a turbid scum on all her windows. It was the time when she forgot to like her fat. It was the time when she most distrusted the fact that she was odd.

She asked the travel agent to marry her and he rolled over onto his back in the bed, stared into the dark and said yes. This was shortly before he noticed that dust was gathering in the shower head and her

potted plants were all starting to die. As for the smell, he didn't seem
to mind.

There were other creaks and groans on her way to a final halt.
Bridget was bright as a button at work in the same dress all week,
although she changed hats from day to day. The hats were needed to
hide the beehive of tangles she got from writhing on her back underneath the travel agent, which she somehow wasn't interested in comb-
ing away. There were wrinkled noses and whispered complaints, but
her bosses were all men, so none of them took her aside for a few
words. Besides, Bridget had started to lose weight.

Maggie, Joan and Sunniva knew a crisis when they saw one, although
it was three weeks before they invaded, cut Bridget's hair short,
made her a meal and ran the bath. They all got splendidly pissed and
made plans for the wedding, which for Bridget's sake, and the state
she was in, would have to be fast or not at all. Joan said not at all, but
Bridget said Yes at all costs. Sunniva agreed and made a pact with
Bridget to 'pull herself together'. Maggie demanded that she get pregnant to make the union meaningful and all of them asked 'My God
Bridget, what IS he like?' 'He's a bit odd,' she answered. 'He's magic,'
and they laughed until four o'clock in the morning.

Bridget realised the need for secrecy. Both her lapses and her man
must be kept secret from the rest of the world. Her smell without
water settled down and she chose a musky perfume to compliment it
and make it more modern. She made the effort to dress and moved
without complaint to the backwaters of the firm. Her short hair
explained the new smallness of her face.

The travel agent seemed to be avoiding her except in the hours of
darkness. He said that he loved her. He slit his finger and left a small
bowl of blood beside her bed. There was a feather in the bowl.

One day she caught sight of him on the street and the ease with which
he walked and talked was a minor miracle. He was wearing a shirt
with thick blue-and-white stripes and an all-white collar. He had a blue
paisley tie. His blue-grey jacket was slung over his shoulder by the
maker's tag. (Unfortunately he was wearing brown shoes, but she
took that as an exterior sign.) There were two men walking beside
him in similar suits, one in navy blue, one in grey. They were bigger
than him, but their bodies were sloppy. All their attention was devoted
to what he was saying and they laughed a lot. She was hopelessly in
love with that man.

Maggie, Sunniva and Joan took care of arrangements while she took to her bed with the shadow of a hawk now real on the wall and wolf howls in the middle of the night. When things were very bad she went back to her fat laugh and her slow, witty talk. She pretended to listen a lot. Her days were spent in prescribed sets of movements, and when she erred – if, for example, she put her shoes on before her blouse – then she was made to suffer badly. She got cramps and side-stitches, shadows flitted and tormented her. Sometimes when she sat still there was music in the room that made her want to cry.

At night she dreamt of all the men she had loved, who queued by her bedside, and laid red, dark bunches of grapes in her lap.

Bridget got married in an ivory satin dress with a bouquet of freesias and the wedding march thundering down the aisle. Maggie, Joan and Sunniva cried their eyes out while her mother concentrated on the invisible knitting in her lap. Joe (for that was the travel agent's name) unveiled fifty-three relatives of impeccable respectability. Several nuns were in evidence, their hair unveiled and neatly styled. The women wore huge and expensive dresses in various sheens of acrylic, with splattered prints and enormous shoulder pads. They rustled and sagged in the church benches, sighing for their youth and the Day They Had Done It. The men were all backslappers, continually checked in their talk by the echoes from the vaulted roof, and they turned around in their seats, mouthing vigorous reminders of stag nights and holes of golf to each other, with jovial incomprehensibility.

Bridget trembled violently as she entered the church, after being held for ten minutes for photographs in the freezing cold of the porch. Her arms were purple and poked out of her dress like chicken legs. She clutched at the uncle delegated to give her away, as his chin went double with the formal effort of the long walk. Her progress was met with the traditional indulgence and good humour, and there was a great sigh from the bride's side when they saw how thin, how marvellous she looked. Joe waited for her in front of a Victorian Gothic altar, dapper in his morning suit, hands folded neatly, fingernails manicured and buffed to a slight shine.

She had a violent sexual tic when she felt the wool of his sleeve. What was under his suit? A bleeding sign slashed into his belly? A word on his breast? Or nothing at all? He smiled and so did she.

The priest was a malaria victim back from the missions who got her name wrong twice, though not at the vital moments. His sermon drifted back to the savannah as he lifted his eyes to the ceiling and talked to the simple black souls he saw there. He advised Joe against taking two wives.

When it came to the exchange of rings, Bridget was solid again. She could feel the ground under her feet and she didn't get his name wrong. Her hands, she noticed, as he placed the ring, were thin and expensive-looking.

At the reception Joe was the life and soul. Maggie, Sunniva and Joan could hardly contain their enthusiasm as they flirted with him beyond the call of duty. They were shy of expressing their surprise to Bridget, who was shrouded with the new privacy of a married woman, even to her friends. Of course she had married a normal man. How could they have expected a disaster?

Maggie got maudlin and cried as she said over and over 'I always knew you were beautiful. I always knew.'

Bridget wasn't used to looking so well. She danced with all of Joe's uncles and three of them made a fumble as they let her go. She got too much attention.

Her sixteen-year-old cousin tried to seduce Sunniva's civil servant and there was a tight little scene in the ladies' toilet. In the corner, the mother of the bride had three brandies, gave a polite rendition of 'Goodnight Irene' and told anyone who would listen about the horrors of a life spent with a mean man.

Through it all, Joe kept his eye on her, smiled and lusted sedately. They met amongst the dancers and he said 'How are you? All right?' and squeezed her hand like a brave girl.

'Wait until he gets you home Oho ye Boya!' said one of the uncles and Joe's teeth glittered as he smiled.

The D. J. hustled them into a ring to sing 'Congratulations'. He said 'Only virgins leave at nine o'clock, but a little birdie told me that they wanted to go.' Joe singed him with a look.

The bouquet was thrown and it landed in the chandelier, which would not stop swinging.

Joan whispered 'Don't forget the garter,' and Bridget felt a burning sensation on her thigh.

They were forced to run the gauntlet and Bridget was bruised by her mother as she attempted and missed a first and last kiss. Outside, the street was on fire with reflected neon that lit her dress in red, then blue. 'Jesus Christ, this is it,' said Bridget as she ripped off her veil and pinned it to the car aerial. The toilet paper flapped and everybody cheered as Bridget was driven into the thin, wet night by her public man.

A FAMILY AND A FUTURE

DERMOT HEALY
Born in Finnea, Co. Westmeath, 1947, Dermot Healy has published
a novel and one collection of short stories, *Banished Misfortune*. In
1980 he was the winning director in the All-Ireland Drama Festival
with his production of *Waiting for Godot*.

I never saw them go out that way in their cars by night. The new Ford Consuls, perhaps a Morris Minor. Volkswagens were always popular round that recalcitrant time. I can only imagine the secrets the night holds, the vulnerability of the isolated sex-object, the daring curiosity of those frightened, frustrated men and always the rumours of decadent tragedy. Perhaps those frightened, sharp-suited men would be walking up the road throwing nervous glances to the left and right of them. Or more assuredly, I'd say, in the heat of drink and summer they would drive bravely out to that beautiful place, where the Erne breaks sparkingly asunder between the forests, play the horn going past the cottage and collect her at her innocent, prearranged places.

For this is real pornography, to imagine the habits of June rather than describe them with authenticity, those quick flitting affairs where Sheelin thundered. Or the beat of visionary passion across an ancient cemetery overrun with shadows, for illicit lovers have always favoured as their first jousting place the quiet of the grave.

June was three years older than myself. She lived with an ailing though resilient mother, cantankerous, shoddy, quick-witted from dealing aggressively with shy people and successful farmers. June's father had been carried off by a fever from drinking contaminated water. Thus she took on the feeding of the few cattle that remained, carrying buckets of water from a spring well a mile away, dousing her socks, since the nearby well had never been cleared up or limestoned after the poisoning. She looked after the chopping of timber from the multitudinous forest of the Lord, facilitated dispassionately and excitedly the emissions of her neighbourly brethren.

From the locality she extended her doings to the town.

What had been mere sensual caprice became decadent business overnight.

I never then saw her in a pub or encountered her on the way to the Cathedral.

Befitting a hard worker, her body was strong but fat. She was not in the least goodlooking. But, because of the dark lashes, June's brown eyes confirmed that traditional estimation of beauty by the Gaelic bards of the area . . . You, the highest nut in the place. Tanned from wandering the fields after lost cattle she would wander through the market on fair day, watched by the treacherous eyes of the stall-holders, in ribbons and patched skirt, huge hips akimbo. The Louis heels of her pink shoes worn sideways because of the edge of her walk, dots of mud on the back of her seamed nylons. The street-corner folk would hail her as she passed. She might loiter by the winter Amusements, a little astray among the jargon of lights and fortune-telling, in those days when the giddy voice of Buddy Holly filled the side streets with 'I guess it doesn't matter any more'. But she was always attracted to the rifle range. Cold-blooded curses helped her aim. Her brown eyes squinted down and steadied on the centre of life, on the yellow thin heart of a crow, on the marked cap of a jester.

I was never attracted to her but we always spoke. Like Hallo, and How is the crack, and How is it going.

But I did see her father's polka-dotted tie that held up her worn knickers.

I was sick, about thirteen and on the back of a bike travelling along the edge of the railway lines. Sweeney dropped the bike when he saw June chasing a Red Devon cow across a field, from east to west, and the two of them fell together among the coltsfoot and daffodils, stripped in the frost and she masturbated him and then me, and there was something virulent about his satisfaction, something slow and remorselessly painful about mine.

It was her desire and detachment, my desire of love. And then Sweeney mounted her some time later and she called to him, for a minute Stop, stop, you're hurting, but he didn't and then she fainted. Her brown face keeled over in the frost, her father's tie round her ankles, and a look of horrified petulance on his face, he stood under a leafless oak, his brown cock unbloodied but fading. He would I think have buried her there had she not come to. But what did I say or do in those moments? Nursed her head in my lap, called to her, sung to her? Was I not at that moment as much to blame for her misfortune? But Sweeney returned with water and aspirins from a nearby house, she drank as I coaxed her, her eyes swam and steadied and then she thanked us, once more restored, she set off to capture the beast she had been following. And Sweeney shouted after her, I'm sorry June, and many's the time after they were lovers. For years too I was afflicted by this scene, in my dream I would, too, be about to come, and try to restrain for fear of hurting her, wake painfully in the dark, sperm like acid on my thighs. No, she never went into a pub for she never reached the peak of adult debauchery. Hers will always be the brink, the joyous, disparate moments of adolescence. Till none of the country folk bothered her, till she became the shag, the ride, the jaunt of the town. Eventually the police took a hand and barred her from the precincts, from her nocturnal clambering into parked buses at the depot, doors opened by skilled mechanics, from stretching under an impatient, married man in the waiting-room of the railway station. Thus those cars would be leaving town to pick up June, single or in groups, in the hubbub of careless laughter to spread her juices across the warm leather upholstery.

It was around this time that Benny met her, I think. He had been hired out to a farm in Dundalk for five years previous, and one full lush May he returned for the cancerous death of his last parent. Benny had a red freckled face, wore hunting caps, was a loner. He took her to the pictures, her first normal romance began. She was under great distress, as it was her first time in the cinema and they moved twice till she was immaculately placed one row behind the four-pennies. It was not short-sightedness but enthusiasm. Over his shoulder she stole timorous, enquiring glances at Maureen O'Hara, as the square filled up with wounded soldiers from the Civil War. Benny was to linger on a further three years in Dundalk, but that December he returned again to his deserted house, they cut trees together in the Christmas tree wood and sold them in the snowed-up market place, two shillings apiece, a week before the festival. Pheasants were taken with a shot of blood and feathers from the cloudy skies above Sheelin and presented by him to June's house for the seasonal dinner. Which he attended, the wily gossiping stranger, with a bottle of Jameson and orange.

But that was the first Christmas. The second or third he never came. June had mothered a child. By a solicitor, a priest, by myself, does it matter? That summer, too, her mother made it to the bath in time to vomit up a three-foot tapeworm. The old lady's skin and bone retreated under the shock. The release of the worm and birth of the child occurred within a week of each other. June grew thin again, her mother fattened. They grew more friendly, dependent upon each other. That year too, during these trying times, when they were burning the gorse and the furze, a fire swept the hill behind the house.

And the two sick ladies fought the flames, shouting encouragement
to each other, retreated successfully, covered in ash, their blouses
scorched, their arms thrown around each other, laughing, and stood
together that evening holding up the newly washed child to look at
the smoking field.

Neighbours came and mended their own fences and kept their coun-
sel to themselves.

The drama of that fiery evening was that it led to a reunion between
Benny and June and the dry-skinned baby. He came and repaired
the scorched sheds, replaced the burnt rafter, renailed the twisted
galvanize and played with the child in the cool kitchen, braved the
mad, wandering talk of the mother. From the window you could see
the water breaking out there like it was hitting water-coloured rocks.
Sails skimmed through the trees, boat engines roared, and behind, a
less formidable beauty, endowed darkly and modern among the pines,
with wooden seats and toilets for viewing the lake, a black modern
café with chain motifs on a cleared rise.

Soon the tourists would be arriving. 'To paint a dark corner darker,'
the old lady said. 'Think of who sired him that built yon.' She held the
bowl of soup at arm's length, licking her wrists and fists, grey brown-
tinged hair, deep-blue flowered nightcoat, fluffy shoes, yellow night-
dress peeking out at her strained neck, awkward movements. 'The
architect, the gobshite, came in here to explain, all airs and graces. Then
he started a fucking dirge. We told him where to get off.'

June was on the grass, on all fours, scrambling away from the child
and Benny smoked by the window.

They married, herself and Benny, the following April. And the next
time I saw them was at a dance at the opening of that café, where as
yet only light drinks were being served, given by the local GAA. I was
mesmerized after a day's drinking, and in drunken fashion attended to
their every need, needing heroes myself, but at some point I got into
an argument and was set upon by a couple of bastards from the town.
They ripped at my face with fingers like spurs, broken glass tore at
my throat. I heard the band breaking down, heels grated against my
teeth. Lying there babbling and crying on the floor while the fight
went on over my head. June came and hauled me free and Benny
swung out left, right and centre. They caught Benny's eye a fearful
blow and all I can remember is an Indian doctor in the hospital complaining of having had enough of attending to drunks in the middle of
the night. But a nurse stitched my scalp back onto my head and my
head back onto my body.

As for Benny, he was taken away to the Eye and Ear Hospital in Dublin where he was ably attended to and where I called on him. We shared few words, because only fighting brought out the intimacy in us. My life then for a number of years was spent in aggravating silly details. Benny returned to Dundalk to complete a final year and June took on other lovers, she mothered another child. With his money saved Benny returned a year later in spring for good. Shrunken reeds had washed up, carquet, light brown, two ducks flying together, the dark blowing in. Cars were parked on the entrance to the café, which was now a magnificent hotel, with C & W stickers on them. The little Pleasure House of the Lord of the Estate had been renewed by the Minister of Lands with new bright pebble-dash, and renamed. Going up a new lane seemed miles, coming back mere yards.

I was out at the Point after an endless day's fishing without a catch, curlews screaming in the background, cormorants fanning themselves in heraldic postures at the top of the castle. Benny and I stood together chatting. But aloof, too, from each other, for things change; sometimes you are only an observer, at other times you are involved intimately in other people's lives, but now as a mere recorder of events and personages, the shock of alienation arrived on me, yet deeper than that the ultimate intimacy of disparate lives.

Benny said that June's house was a well-seasoned, weathered cottage. His own deserted one had grown accustomed to rats; the dead people that had lived in the house, his parents, could often be heard arguing at night by passers-by. He only went up there by daylight to fodder the cattle. The hum of taped music drifted down from the hotel.

'They have everything at their fingertips above,' he said pointing. 'Take your money, boy, from whatever angle it's coming from.'

He pulled out his pipe and knocked it off a stone. A cormorant flew by, its coarse black wings aflutter, beak like silver in the spring sun that set now without the lake catching its reflection. For it was far west of the pines. Some people neglect their experiences by holding them at arm's length, at verbal distance. Not so Benny, his generosity of spirit was personal, abrupt. Behind us, June's three kids were playing, only one of whom I think resembled him. They were all beautifully turned out, like out of a bandbox, not a hair out of place. The eldest had straight black hair, gypsy-like, and seemed to reflect humorously on things. The youngest had fair curly locks, talked of TV programmes, wide astonished eyes, blue. The four-year-old had undistinguished auburn hair, colourless skin. She stood between us,

intent upon the fishing and saying and interrupting all the beautiful
encouraging things for life that a child can tell or repel.

The waves were heavy and cold as rock. Feeling was dispersed by
the heart, intestines and lungs. Like embryos, sluggishly, drops of
water broke away from under the ice and flowed, ice-covered. He,
Benny, didn't turn round to look at the cars as I did. He gossiped
away, cruel, erratic, interested in the beyond. As if he knew the
laundered space of each guilty psyche, and how each family renews
itself for the future. For though, over the past few months, myself
and Benny may have dispensed with familiarity, except for the cheerful
courtesies, all's well. For you see they had his house scourged for
years, those amiable frightened men, but now seemingly all's settled.
June has given him joy and sustenance, and she maintains an aura of
doubtful reserve, and I don't see her any more.

THE LAST TIME

DESMOND HOGAN
Born in Ballinasloe, Co. Galway, 1951, Desmond Hogan's first stories
were published when he was seventeen. His first collection, *The Dia-
monds at the Bottom of the Sea*, won the John Llewellyn Rhys Memorial
Prize in 1980 and was followed in 1981 by a second collection, *The
Children of Lir*. He has also written three novels and a play.

The last time I saw him was in Ballinasloe station, 1953, his long figure hugged into a coat too big for him. Autumn was imminent; the sky grey, baleful. A few trees had become grey too; God, my heart ached. The tennis court beyond, silent now, the river close, half-shrouded in fog. And there he was, Jamesy, tired, knotted, the doctor's son who took me out to the pictures once, courted me in the narrow timber seats as horns played in a melodramatic forties film.

Jamesy had half the look of a mongol, half the look of an autistic child, blond hair parted like waves of water reeds, face salmon-colour, long, the shade and colour of autumnal drought. His father had a big white house on the perimeter of town – doors and windows painted as fresh as crocuses and lawns gloomy and yet blanched with perpetually new-mown grass.

In my girlhood I observed Jamesy as I walked with nuns and other orphans by his garden. I was an orphan in the local convent, our play-fields stretching by the river at the back of elegant houses where we watched the nice children of town, bankers' children, doctors' children, playing. Maria Mulcahy was my name. My mother, I was told in later years, was a Jean Harlow type prostitute from the local terraces. I, however, had hair of red which I admired in the mirror in the empty, virginal-smelling bathroom of the convent hall where we sat with children of doctors and bankers who had to pay three pence into the convent film show to watch people like Joan Crawford marry in bliss.

Jamesy was my first love, a distant love.

In his garden he'd be cutting hedges or reading books, a face on him like an interested hedgehog. The books were big and solemn-looking – like himself. Books like *War and Peace*, I later discovered.

Jamesy was the bright boy, though his father wanted him to do dentistry.

He was a problem child, it was well known. When I was seventeen

I was sent to a draper's house to be a maid, and there I gathered information about Jamesy. The day he began singing 'Bye Bye Black-bird' in the church, saying afterwards he was singing it about his grandmother who'd taken a boat one day, sailed down the river until the boat crashed over a weir and the woman drowned. Another day he was found having run away, sleeping on a red bench by the river where later we wrote our names, sleeping with a pet fox, for foxes were abundant that year.

Jamesy and I met first in the fair green. I was wheeling a child and in a check shirt he was holding a rabbit. The green was spacious, like a desert. *Duel in the Sun* was showing in town and the feeling between us was one of summer and space, the grass rich and twisted like an old nun's hair.

He smiled crookedly.

I addressed him.

'I know you!' I was blatant, tough. He laughed.

'You're from the convent.'

'Have a sweet!'

'I don't eat them. I'm watching my figure!'

'Hold the child!'

I lifted the baby out, rested her in his arms, took out a rug and sat down. Together we watched the day slip, the sun steadying. I talked about the convent and he spoke about *War and Peace* and an uncle who'd died in the Civil War, torn apart by horses, his arms tied to their hooves.

'He was buried with the poppies,' Jamesy said. And as though to remind us, there were sprays of poppies on the fair green, distant, distrustful.

'What age are you?'

'Seventeen! Do you see my rabbit?'

He gave it to me to hold. Dumb-bells, he called it. There was a fall of hair over his forehead and by bold impulse I took it and shook it fast.

There was a smile on his face like a pleased sheep. 'I'll meet you again,' I said as I left, pushing off the pram as though it held billycans rather than a baby.

There he was that summer, standing on the bridge by the prom, sitting on a park bench or pawing a jaded copy of Turgenev's *Fathers and Sons*.

He began lending me books and under the pillow I'd read Zola's *Nana* or a novel by Marie Corelli, or maybe poetry by Tennyson.

There was always a moon that summer – or a very red sunset. Yet I rarely met him, just saw him. Our relationship was blindly educational, little else. There at the bridge, a central point, beside which both of us paused, at different times, peripherally. There was me, the pram, and he in a shirt that hung like a king's cloak, or on cold days – as such there often were – in a jumper which made him look like a polar bear.

'I hear you've got a good voice,' he told me one day.

'Who told you?'

'I heard.'

'Well, I'll sing you a song.' I sang. 'Somewhere over the Rainbow', which I'd learnt at the convent.

Again we were in the green. In the middle of singing the song I realised my brashness and also my years of loneliness, destitution, at the hands of nuns who barked and crowded about the statue of the Infant Jesus of Prague in the convent courtyard like seals on a rock. They hadn't been bad, the nuns. Neither had the other children been so bad. But God, what loneliness there'd been. There'd been one particular tree there, open like a complaint, where I spent a lot of time surveying the river and the reeds, waiting for pirates or for some beautiful lady straight out of a Veronica Lake movie to come sailing up the river. I began weeping in the green that day, weeping loudly. There was his face which I'll never forget. Jamesy's face changed from blank idiocy, local precociousness, to a sort of wild understanding.

He took my hand.

I leaned against his jumper; it was a fawn colour.

I clumsily clung to the fawn and he took me and I was aware of strands of hair, bleached by sun.

The Protestant church chimed five and I reckoned I should move, pushing the child ahead of me. The face of Jamesy Murphy became more intense that summer, his pink colour changing to brown. He looked like a pirate in one of the convent film shows, tanned, ravaged.

Yet our meetings were just as few – and as autumn denuded the last of the cherry-coloured leaves from a particular housefront on the other side of town Jamesy and I would meet by the river in the park – briefly, each day touching a new part of one another. An ankle, a finger, an ear lobe, something as ridiculous as that. I always had a child with me so it made things difficult.

Always too I had to hurry, often racing past closing shops.

There were Christmas trees outside a shop one day I noticed, so I decided Christmas was coming. Christmas was so unreal now, an

event remembered from convent school, huge Christmas pudding and
nuns crying. Always on Christmas Day nuns broke down crying,
recalling perhaps a lost love or some broken-hearted mother in an
Irish kitchen.

Jamesy was spending a year between finishing at school and his
father goading him to do dentistry, reading books by Joyce now and
Chekhov, and quoting to me one day – overlooking a garden of withered
dahlias – Nijinsky's diaries. I took books from him about writers in
exile from their countries, holding under my pillow novels by obscure
Americans.

There were high clouds against a low sky that winter and the gro-
tesque shapes of the Virgin in the alcove of the church, but against
that monstrosity the romance was complete I reckon, an occasional
mad moon, Lili Marlene on radio – memories of a war that had only
grazed childhood – a peacock feather on an ascendancy-type lady's
hat.

'Do you see the way that woman's looking at us,' Jamesy said one
day. Yes, she was looking at him as though he were a monster.
His reputation was complete: a boy who was spoilt, daft, and an
embarrassment to his parents. And there was I, a servant girl, talking
to him. When she'd passed we embraced – lightly – and I went home,
arranging to see him at the pictures the following night.

Always our meetings had occurred when I brushed past Jamesy
with the pram. This was our first night out, seeing that Christmas
was coming and that bells were tinkling on radio; we'd decided we'd
be bold. I'd sneak out at eight o'clock, having pretended to go to bed.
What really enticed me to ask Jamesy to bring me to the pictures was
the fact that he was wearing a new Aran sweater and that I heard the
film was partly set in Marrakesh, a place that had haunted me ever
since I had read a book about where a heroine and two heroes met
their fatal end in that city.

So things went as planned until the moment when Jamesy and I
were in one another's arms when the woman for whom I worked came
in, hauled me off. Next day I was brought before Sister Ignatius. She
sat like a robot in the Spanish Inquisition. I was removed from the
house in town and told I had to stay in the convent.

In time a job washing floors was found for me in Athlone, a neigh-
bouring town to which I got a train every morning. The town was a
drab one, replete with spires.

I scrubbed floors, my head wedged under heavy tables: sometimes
I wept. There were Sacred Heart pictures to throw light on my pre-

dicament but even they were of no avail to me; religion was gone in a convent hush. Jamesy now was lost; looking out of a window I'd think of him but like the music of Glenn Miller he was past. His hair, his face, his madness I'd hardly touched, merely fondled like a floating ballerina.

It had been a mute performance – like a circus clown. There'd been something I wanted of Jamesy which I'd never reached; I couldn't put words or emotions to it but now from a desk in London, staring into a Battersea dawn, I see it was a womanly feeling. I wanted love.

'Maria, you haven't cleaned the lavatory.' So with a martyred air I cleaned the lavatory and my mind dwelt on Jamesy's pimples, ones he had for a week in September.

The mornings were drab and grey. I'd been working a year in Athlone, mind disconnected from body, when I learned Jamesy was studying dentistry in Dublin. There was a world of difference between us, a partition as deep as war and peace. Then one morning I saw him. I had a scarf on and a slight breeze was blowing and it was the aftermath of a sullen summer and he was returning to Dublin. He didn't look behind. He stared – almost at the tracks – like a fisherman at the sea.

I wanted to say something but my clothes were too drab; not the nice dresses of two years before, dresses I'd resurrected from nowhere with patterns of sea-lions or some such thing on them.

'Jamesy Murphy, you're dead,' I said – my head reeled.

'Jamesy Murphy, you're dead.'

I travelled on the same train with him as far as Athlone. He went on to Dublin. We were in different carriages.

I suppose I decided that morning to take my things and move, so in a boat full of fat women bent on paradise I left Ireland.

I was nineteen and in love. In London through the auspices of the Sisters of Mercy in Camden Town I found work in an hotel where my red hair looked ravishing, sported over a blue uniform.

In time I met my mate, a handsome handy building contractor from Tipperary, whom I married – in the pleased absence of relatives – and with whom I lived in Clapham, raising children, he getting a hundred pounds a week, working seven days a week. My hair I carefully tended and wore heavy check shirts. We never went back to Ireland. In fact, we've never gone back to Ireland since I left, but occasionally, wheeling a child into the Battersea fun-fair, I was reminded of Jamesy, a particular strand of hair blowing across his face. Where was he? Where was the hurt and that face and the sensitivity? London was flooding with dark people and there at the beginning of the sixties I'd cross Chelsea Bridge, walk my children up by Cheyne Walk, sometimes waiting to watch a candle lighting. Gradually it became more real to me that I loved him, that we were active within a certain sacrifice. Both of us had been bare and destitute when we met. The two of us had warded off total calamity, total loss. 'Jamesy!' His picture swooned; he was like a ravaged corpse in my head and the area between us opened; in Chelsea library I began reading books by Russian authors. I began loving him again. A snatch of Glenn Miller fell across the faded memory of colours in the rain, lights of the October fair week in Ballinasloe, Ireland.

The world was exploding with young people – protests against nuclear bombs were daily reported – but in me the nuclear area of the town where I'd worked returned to me.

Jamesy and I had been the marchers, Jamesy and I had been the protest! 'I like your face,' Jamesy once said to me. 'It looks like you could blow it away with a puff.'

In Chelsea library I smoked cigarettes though I wasn't supposed to, I read Chekhov's biography and Turgenev's biography – my husband minding the children – and tried to decipher an area of loss, a morning by the station, summer gone.

I never reached him; I just entertained him like as a child in an orphanage in the West of Ireland I had held a picture of Claudette Colbert under my pillow to remind me of glamour. The gulf between me and Jamesy narrows daily. I address him in a page of a novel, in a chip shop alone at night or here now, writing to you, I say something I never said before, something I've never written before.

I touch upon truth.

THE DOG

PETER HOLLYWOOD

Peter Hollywood was born in Newry, Co. Down, 1959. A graduate of Queen's University, Belfast, he has published one collection of short stories, *Jane Alley*.

1.

The old man walked the dog out of the back yard and along through the side streets and the back streets and out of the town and up onto and across the mountain and down again and into the town at the other end and across it through the less traffic-heavy streets – it having not yet occurred to him the advantage of getting the dog used to noise and uproar, himself still nervous and particular about handling the dog, though it was as yet only a couple of days after the first month's mind, and what he had taken upon himself did need the experience and skill that, though the son might have had, he certainly lacked – and back into the back yard, where he returned the dog to the large shed that he had built into half of what had already been a tiny yard and which he had designed to absorb any restlessness the dog might experience, he and Sweeney, who was an artist, building it as wide and as long as room, and the old woman, permitted, intending for what space they did thereby create to mop up (he had somehow imagined it) the excess energy that he knew would resist confinement.

After all that, the old man could not help but be tired.

When he had made sure the dog was settled, he came in through the kitchen and into the little back scullery and found Logan lounging in one of the two armchairs. So Logan had come down off the mountain too then, and into the town and through the back streets – it being the likes of Logan – and the less heavy-trafficked streets and into the back yard, already in the know enough to take the sight of the empty shed to mean the old man was out, and up to and in through the back door, without knocking, no doubt.

He sat up now at his return, and grinned. He affected familiarity that had no intimacy, as some people, priests and doctors, the old man would have said, affect intimacy that lacks all familiarity. Logan's was the worst of the two.

'And how are you, friend? Or rather,' and here he laughed, 'how's the dog? Aye, that's more to the point seeing as I'll be having a wee bundle riding on it when you get it to the city.'

'I'd slit her throat this minute if I thought she was going to do you any good; and what's more, you can shift yourself and be on your way.'

Logan's grin remained, but even in the dim light – or was it a bright lightlessness of the little back room? – the old man could see the whole face change behind it. He thought the old woman, who was sitting at the scullery table, looked mortified. Logan came from her side of the family and Logan knew, as he knew everything that was to his advantage, that she herself, caught alone in the house, would never have the heart to turn him away.

The old man waited patiently. But he was tired.

'It's high time I went anyway,' Logan said.

The old man went back into the kitchen and put the kettle on. It did not need much heating. The old woman had it ready for him. It was only a couple of days after the first month's mind, but the old woman was used to the dog, she knew when to expect the two of them back.

He was waiting for Logan to take his leave of the aunt and for the front door to bang shut. But he was tired and forgot that Logan would be taking the back way.

'Right then,' Logan attempted as a means of getting past the old man. He would quite easily have ignored Logan only it was necessary to warn him to leave the dog alone on the way out.

'Have no fear,' Logan called back in from the yard, though in a lower voice than usual, as if afraid of disturbing the animal – though the old man knew that this was part of Logan's finely measured and tuned unobtrusiveness, refined almost to the point of instinctiveness. 'I wouldn't go near the dog for all the tea . . .' But by that time he was out of earshot.

He took down the bag of sugar and the old woman told him to use the bowl; he had to open a fresh bottle of milk, and the old woman told him to pour it into a jug – in case we have visitors – he poured the two of them a cup of tea and said, 'What did he want?' in a tone that indicated that both of them expected the question, that in a sense it was already there, posed in the half-light, asked even before the old man had entered and answered almost even before that: 'Nothing.' She got up to fill the sugar bowl, and put the milk bottle into the fridge.

Thirty years: the old man knew when she was lying; not by any betrayal of tone in her voice, or expression on her face, but by the register almost of an age-old weariness, as if the lie pondered the immensity of the thirty years and conceded there and then, gave up any presumption of verisimilitude, as if the almost palpable air of the little house, coloured in and filled out by the dusk of the warehouse-out-the-back's gable end, gave a minute, sceptical snigger that thrilled a stir through the whole house, which not even the draught excluders could deal with. To lie then was futile and the old woman, knowing that, probably meant that the whatever it was Logan had wanted must not have been very important. In any case the old man was dog-tired.

The dusk that was the evening thickened into the dark that was the night. The dusk that was the tone of the little two-up/two-down, sat as always, and almost visibly glowed inside the dark that was the night. The dark that was his dead son edged and hemmed in what little space was left the old man to dream in. The luminous Virgin Mary glowed, and the luminous hands of the clock glowed and after racing against the dog all night he woke up even more tired than when he had gone to bed.

2.

Sweeney was an artist; that is he had spent all his life, like the old man, working on the coal boats, first as a stoker shovelling coal into the glowing heart of the boat, then later as a docker, taking loads of coal and timber off the boats and heaping them into yards and Old Man Wordy's horsecarts and finally into lorries, towards the end.

About a month before the old man's son died, Sweeney got word or rather confirmation of his own death. The doctor identified the crab that was eating the insides out of him. But, of course, he had suspected and then expected as much and had joked with the doctor. 'It's a dog's life anyway.' And disease made the doctor familiar and intimate. 'You've got nobody to look out for you. I'll notify the priory for you if you like.' Sweeney deferred. 'No, it's all right,' he assured the doctor. 'I'll see to things myself.'

He lay in bed then at night and quietly listened as if audience to his own body, as it casually killed itself. He had suspected of course, had begun to catch some sickly sweet smell from off himself. He lay, hothouse to the silent, flameless burning of decay, and the aroma coming off him like smoke. He lay apart, removed, and watched as the treacherous meat shovelled him remorselessly onto the coals.

At night, too, the flora burst through his skin, and flowered and bloomed like wallpaper and sometimes he swooned in the poppy fumes and strangled in the vines and purple flowers and sometimes he lay down like an altar bedecked and watched as the little white sore elevated and changed quietly, casually, ignorant of all danger, into body and meat, and himself powerless, unable to warn it.

But by day he was calm. His only torment, then, was not whom to tell, but when, how or was it really, why? He knew the only ones to tell were the old man and woman. For the month then he weighed the question, wondering why he should burden them, until the news reached them of the son's death in the car accident and he decided to keep his own troubles to himself, at least for a little longer.

Sweeney was an artist because within the month he had soon mastered the art of knowing when to call at the house so as to get the old man in. Also, Sweeney knew without ever having to be told, that while coming up the back yard one should never stop to look in at the dog, should never talk to it or try to touch at it through the wire – a mistake that everyone else made, the milkman, the binman, the coalman; not that they made it a second time. The old man, no matter where he was in the house, was always suddenly on hand to bawl at them to leave the animal alone, 'It's not a fucking pet.'

When such a thing happened when Sweeney was in the house, he immediately began to wonder. He was sitting in the scullery and the old man suddenly leapt from his seat and ran out to chase some of the nextdoor kids out of the yard. The old woman came in out of the kitchen. She had her hands bundled into her apron. Her hair was grey, but plentiful, bunned up about her head. She shook her head. 'I don't know,' she said. 'You need the patience of a saint to put up with him and that dog.' Sweeney avoided her eyes, he did not want to contemplate full on the whole vista of implication that spread out beyond the few words the woman ever came out with.

'Sure, I'd be the same myself. Just think of how much a dog like that costs.'

'I know how much it costs to keep it,' she remarked grimly but humorously.

'And if it does cost so much wouldn't he be better off getting somebody who knows about such things to look after it for him?' Sweeney knew that some of her son's friends from the racing business had offered if not to buy it at least to help train it. Sweeney didn't know what to say; but the old woman was not one to put him on the spot, that wasn't the way with her. Without further ado, and also at the sound of the old man returning, grumbling to himself, she went back past him into the kitchen. She had made sure that Sweeney was fully aware of the change that was becoming obvious in his old friend.

She wasn't to know that the man had his own problems to worry about.

3.

Some of the dead followed the old woman home from the church. It had happened once before, the time she had the pain in the chest; but ever since her son's death, it was happening more regularly. Not that she minded; she let them enter and they quietly drifted upon the overall dimness, transparent, pale, but never interfering with her. The first time it happened after the death, she had carefully examined each face, in case one of them should be either her son, or a saint she might recognise. Disappointed in both these, she quickly got to ignoring them altogether. Her problems were with the living.

Logan terrified her; Sweeney worried her; but her husband, it was, who would be the death of her.

Logan, she thought, she hated. It was sinful she knew, but at least lying to herself that she didn't hate him would not be one of her sins. She hated him because she had lied to her husband; she had deliberately allowed what she had said about Logan wanting nothing to sound like a lie, to assuage the old man's suspicion. The dog had seen to it that the old man's temper was never now but on edge; he was ready to bark at anyone, to snap anyone's head off – including, she would think sadly, her own. If she had told him the truth about Logan, she feared there might have been violence. As it was she was surprised the old man had not at least badmouthed Logan out of the house. Logan she hated, but only because he made her hate her own shame, her own inability to stand up to him and his sly evocations of the past, the family, the ethics of tradition. None of the dead that followed her home were family. They knew better, she thought wryly.

Sweeney, she knew, was ill. Somewhere in the back of her mind she also knew it was cancer; but since Sweeney had as yet said nothing, she held her own tongue. But she had begun already to pray for his soul.

After what had been a lull or ceasefire, a couple of bombs in the town indicated that things were about to start up again. The old woman started to worry then. Logan hadn't re-appeared to take away the gun. But the greater worry was the thought of the old man walking the dog up in the mountains. Mountains had ambushes and booby traps and landmines.

Then one day he came in and she almost mistook him for one of the dead; only the dead are never out of breath. That made her mind up to have it out with the old man. Her tack was never obvious.

'How am I to cope? The dog's already eating half our pensions; prices aren't getting any lower, and you're certainly not getting any younger. Look at you.'

She realised her tongue was running away with her, that she had started and was afraid to finish, afraid to hear her old husband shouting and cursing at her. But there was a genuine tremor of anger in her voice, and the old man heard it. He tried to palliate it.

'We can get rid of that bloody TV set for a start, for all the rubbish that's on it.'

'It's not enough.' She was calm now. She had seen the fear, in his eyes, she could hear the panic in his voice.

'You can't ask me to sell it,' he said, but not pleading, not anxious. She was about to insist that he did, about to deliver her final blow, when suddenly she realised that the old man had not stopped talking, when she suddenly realised that she had begun to listen. And the old man's words were loose and clumsy, as he struggled against the wordlessness of the experience to try and tell his wife about something that seemed magic, holy almost. He told about the arrow-like lithe length of the dog's darting across the field, and how it was there and back again before he had stopped seeing it in mid-flight, a second's timelessness of stillness and speeding suspension, hindlegs and forefeet meeting almost, immaculate, motionless. And the old woman saw the elevated circle, and her mind told her it was life and death together, and the dog was swallowing its own tail and disappearing into nothing. It was divine; and it was killing her husband.

4.

Sweeney might not have realised it, but it was the morning after the raid that he got the idea, when they told him about it; and not long after that, that he got the conviction.

First there was the strident roar of motors, braking sharply out of high speeds, then the sounds of shoutings, orders, answers, and bootsteps, finally there was the thumping on the doors.

And it was something in the way the old woman let the shriek out of her that told the old man. This wasn't the street's first raid, but it was the first time he had ever heard the likes from the old woman.

It's imponderable the depth his soul fell away to, and his very mind almost losing balance and tilting in after it, when he suddenly realised that here he was trapped, about to be raided and some illegal cache in his house. He lay for a moment in stupor. Then he shook himself: 'Jesus Christ, woman.' The fury, the resentment almost of the words levered him out of the bed, 'Jesus Christ. How! How!'

Then he collected himself. 'Where? Where did he hide it?' But time and event were moiling past him like flood water and sluicing in under the bed and bouncing back off the wallpaper and drenching him in his own impotence, and his wife stared wide-eyed at him and couldn't speak. The thumping came to his door that was already hammering at his insides. If he spent any more time trying to get something sensible out of the woman they would have it off its hinges.

The first soldier almost knocked him down, was in and had all the lights on that he could find. The second soldier was about to similarly jostle him aside, when he saw the old man in front of him, looking as he was, like death heated up.

'How?' the old man asked him, forgetting himself. Then he started and corrected himself. 'There's just me and the old woman here –'

'Sorry Sir, just following orders,' the second one said, and he and a third hurried on in after the first. The old man watched in a daze; furniture shifted, carpet lifted, cupboards were gone through and left open-mouthed and speechless at such an invasion of privacy. When they came upon the old woman she gazed spectrally at them and through them and beyond them and remained heedless of their apologies, as if they were getting more and more embarrassed the more they realised there was just these two old mad people in the house. And the old man stalked them death-like about the house, and was perhaps making the three of them uneasy; verbal abuse and invective they were used to, but this grave-stricken silence started making them look at one another. One of them sniggered nervously. Another escaped out into the back yard, and there, lacking an outdoor light, he began to flash-torch the shadows. Only then did the old man gather his wits about him. He was suddenly out into the dark and the cold behind the soldier, and as the soldier started to approach the dog shed, he spoke.

'Don't go near the dog. Touch one hair of its head and I'll have you in court. That dog happens to be a champion.'

The soldier started and whirled round. The old man's eyes

glistened. Brushing past him he said 'Right then,' and rejoined the other two soldiers indoors.

The old woman was mumbling a novena by the time the soldiers left. At first furious, then frantic, then calmly, it took the old man some time before he got the woman around to tell him that Logan had hidden the damned thing in the dog shed, where he had loosened a brick in the wall.

The next day Sweeney swore he didn't know whether to laugh or cry.

5.

The disappearance of the dog coincided with Sweeney's killing himself.

In the days following the raid and leading up to this, the old man's fury and disdain remained; laughter had long since died inside him. He warned the wife to get rid of the gun within the next couple of days.

In the face of this the dead hastily decamped. The old woman remained shameful and silent, inattentive, even to Sweeney's quick deterioration.

Then one day she thought that Sweeney had lost his touch, for he called at the house, having just missed the old man who had left, with the dog, moments before. He had, however, come to help the old woman out of her predicament.

'Logan hasn't shown up, I suppose?' he asked.

'Not a sign of him; but if he doesn't come by tomorrow, the gun is for the canal.'

Sweeney then revealed his plan.

'Listen. I'll keep the gun for you, and if he turns up, send him round to my place.'

Something made the old woman agree to this.

That night, the old man dreamed about the dark that had quietly but consistently closed in about and dog-collared the little space left for him to dream in. Its circumference had thickened to such an extent that all that remained was a tiny, glowing centre.

Even in dreams his eyesight was bad, and even in dreams he no longer had the energy to close in upon the object, to struggle across the distance and expanse that separated them. That night he did struggle, and his dream body quickly cluttered and became choked; but within inches of the object, he saw that it was an old sixpence piece. The dog was emblazoned on one side. He reached forward to seize her, to make sure his son's head's imprint was on the reverse side when he suddenly woke up.

The luminous Virgin Mary glowed in the dark beside the luminously glowing hands of the clock.

The shed was empty the next morning. The dog was gone. He tore out the brick. The gun was gone. Logan. He was in the house, grabbing into his coat when the neighbours brought the news that Sweeney had done himself in the previous night.

There was no sign of the dog.

The old man walked along through the side streets and the back streets and out of the town and up onto and across the mountain and down again and into the town at the other end and across it through the less traffic-heavy streets and back into the back yard.

For about a week, he watched the old woman sweeping up the now wider yard each morning.

As far as she was concerned, she was sweeping up the little clusters of purple flowers that blew in there during the night and which she would go out to find there in the morning.

MR SOLOMON WEPT

NEIL JORDAN
Born in Sligo, 1951, Neil Jordan's one collection of short stories, *Night in Tunisia* (1976), won the Guardian Fiction Prize and in 1981 he received the Rooney Prize for Irish Literature. He has since published three novels and in recent years has gained a wide reputation as a film director.

The child had rolled pennies and the dodgem wheels had smoked for half a morning when Mr Solomon took time off to stand by the strand. He stood where he was accustomed to, on the lip of the cement path that seemed designed to run right to the sea but that crumbled suddenly and inexplicably into the sand. Mr Solomon smoked a cigarette there, holding it flatly between his lips, letting the smoke drift over his thin moustache into his nostrils. His eyes rested on the lumps of rough-cast concrete half-embedded in the sand. His breath came in with a soft, scraping sound.

The sea looked warm and lazy in midday. Down the beach a marquee was being erected. Mr Solomon looked at the people on the beach, the sunbathers and the men who were unwinding the marquee canvas. He wore a brown suit with narrow legs and wide lapels, his thin face looked like it was long-accustomed to viewing sunbathers, people on beaches. Mr Solomon then stopped looking at the people and looked at the sea. He took the cigarette from his mouth, inhaled and replaced it again. The sea looked dark blue to him, the colour of midnight rather than of midday. And though it looked flat and indolent and hot, its blueness was clear and sharp, a sharpness emphasised by the occasional flurry of white foam, the slight swell far out. Mr Solomon knew these to be white horses. But today they reminded him of lace, lace he imagined round a woman's throat, a swelling bosom underneath, covered in navy cloth. He had seen an advertisement for Sherry once with such a picture. He saw her just under the sea, just beneath the film of glassblue. If he lifted his eyes to the horizon again the sea became flat and indolent, and probably too hot for swimming.

Mr Solomon lifted his eyes and saw the flat sea and the flat yellow strand. He thought of the child he had left, something morose and forlorn about the way he pushed penny after penny into the metal slot. Then he looked down the strand and saw the large marquee pole being hoisted and only then realised that it was Race Day. And Mr

Solomon remembered the note again, he remembered the nights of surprised pain, the odd gradual feeling of deadness, how before it happened it had been unthinkable and how after it happened somehow anything other than it had become unthinkable. Now he dressed the boy, shopped, the boy sat in the change booth staring at the racing page while he drank in the Northern Star over lunchtime. He remembered how his wife had left him on Race day, one year ago. How he had come to Laytown three days before the races, to catch the crowds. How on the fourth day he had gone to the caravan behind the rifle-range and found it empty, a note on the flap table. Its message was hardly legible, though simple. Gone with Chas. Won't have to hate you any more. He remembered how he had wondered who Chas was, how he had sat on the unmade bed and stared at this note that over the length of the first night assumed the significance of a train ticket into a country he had never heard of. For he had long ceased to think of her with the words love or hate, he had worked, rolled his thin cigarettes, she had totted the books while he supervised the rent, those words were like the words school or god, part of a message that wasn't important any more, a land that was far away. And now he saw the note and thought of the world that had lived for her, thought of the second May, the May behind the one that woke first beside him in the cramped white caravan, that was sitting beside the singing kettle when he woke; this was Chas's May – but it mightn't have been Chas, it could have spelt Chad – and the thought that she existed gave him a feeling of surprised pain, surprise at the May he had never known of, surprise at the loss of what he had never possessed. But after three days the pained surprise had died and a new surprise asserted itself – a surprise at how easily the unthinkable became possible. He found it was easy to cook, to tot the books, to supervise the dodgem tracks and shooting-range all in one. The boy helped him, he watched the boy from behind the glass of the change booth emptying the slot-machines. When the races finished he stayed on, found the move to another holiday-spot too much bother and unnecessary anyway, since less money would do now. Even when the season ended he didn't move, he sat in the draughty amusement hall through winter and made more than enough to keep rolling his thin cigarettes. The rusted slot-machines became a focus for the local youths with sullen faces and greased hair and he found forgetting her almost as easy a task as that of living with her had been. She had been shrewish, he told himself as her memory grew dimmer, her hair had often remained unwashed for days, she would have soon, within the year, gone to fat. Thus he killed the memory of another her neatly, he forgot the nights at the Palais in Brighton, the evenings in the holiday pubs, her platinum hair and the rich dark of the bottled Guinness (a ladies' drink then) tilted towards her laughing mouth.

But he saw the marquee pole stagger upright and suddenly remembered her as if she had died and as if the day of the Laytown Races was her anniversary. He saw the white horses whip and the marquee canvas billow round the pole and thought suddenly of the dress she had called her one good dress with its sad lace frills and the bodice of blue satin that had more restitchings than original threads. A sense of grief came over him, a feeling of quiet sadness, not wholly unpleasing. He began to think of her as if she had died, he thought of the woman who had lived with him and who indeed had died. He imagined flowers for her, dark blood-red roses and felt bleak and clean as if in celebration of her imagined death he was somehow cleansing both him and his image of her.

He lit another cigarette and turned back on the cement path. He passed a family coming from an ice-cream van a little down it, the cones in their hands already sodden. Mr Solomon watched them pass him and felt he had a secret safe, totally safe from them. He felt as if there was a hidden flame inside him, consuming him, while the exterior remained the same as ever, the smoke still drifted over the same thin lip. He passed the green corrugated hall that served as a golf-club and remembered how each year they came through she had got him to pay green fees, how they had both made an afternoon's slow crawl over nine holes. How she had longed to be, someday, a proper member in a proper club. 'But we never settle down enough, do we, Jimmy, 'cept in winter, when it's too wet to play . . .'

Mr Solomon walked down the cement walk away from the beach and the rising marquee and felt his grief inside him like old port, hot and mellow. He came to the tarmac road and stood, staring at the tottering facade of the amusements and the dull concrete front of the Northern Star opposite. He wavered for one moment and then headed for the brass-studded door of the Northern Star, the mute lights and wood-and-brass fittings being like night to him at first until his eyes settled. He ordered a drink and gave the barman a sharp look before downing it.

'This one's for my wife,' he said.

'I didn't know you had one,' said the barman, who was always courteous.

'In memory of her. She died last year.'

'I'm sorry,' said the barman. 'Her anniversary?'

'Died on Race day,' began Mr Solomon but by this time the barman had headed off discreetly for a customer at the other end. He blinked once then finished his drink and began to feel very angry at the courteous barman. He felt the whiskey tickle down his throat, he felt something in him had been sullied by the bland courtesy, the discreet lights of the hotel bar. He left.

Outside the brightness blinded him as much as the darkness had before. Mr Solomon stared down the lean yellow street. It was packed with people and as he watched them, Mr Solomon began to feel for the first time a hatred towards them, *en masse*. He felt a malignant sameness in them. He felt they laughed, in their summer clothes. He felt they didn't know, in their summer clothes. He felt like a cog in the mechanism of holidays, of holiday towns, he felt somehow slave to their bright clothes and suntans. He no longer felt she had died, he felt something had killed her, that impersonal holiday gaiety had enslaved them both, had aged him, like a slow cancerous growth, had annihilated her. He felt his grief burning inside now, like a rough Irish whiskey. He crossed the street a little faster than he normally did, though his walk was still lethargic by the street's standards. He went into the pub with the black-and-white gabled roof.

That afternoon his tale competed with the banjo-playing tinker, with the crack of beer-glasses, with the story of the roadworker's son who returned and bought out three local publicans. Mr Solomon shouted it, wept it, crowed with it, nobody listened, his thin face acquired a weasel look, a sorry look, his eyes grew more glazed and his speech more blurred, the reason for his grief grew hazy and indeterminate. By half-past four he was just drunk, all he knew was there was something somewhere to feel sorry over, profoundly sorry, somewhere a pain, though the reason for it he could no longer fathom, nor why it should be his pain particularly. Why not that Meath farmer's, with the flushed face and the tweed suit, and at this Mr Solomon grew offensive, sloppily offensive and found himself removed.

He went through the hard daylight again into the dark of the amusement parlour. He heard a rustle in the left-hand corner and saw the boy starting up guiltily from the peepshow machine. Mr Solomon thought of the near-naked starlets in high-heels and out-of-date hairdos and got angry again. 'I told you never to go near that,' he rasped. The boy replied with a swift obscenity that shocked him silent. He could only stare, at his homemade cloth anorak, his hair clumsily quiffed, sticking out in places, his thin impenetrable face. At his son's face, new to him because he'd never seen it. He made to move towards him, only then realising how drunk he was. He saw the boy's hand draw back and an object fly from it. He raised his hand to protect his face and felt something strike his knuckles. He heard the coin ring off the cement floor and the boy's footsteps running towards the door. He ran after him drunkenly, shouting.

The boy ran towards the beach. Mr Solomon followed. He saw the horses thunder on the beach, distorted by his drunken run. He saw the line of sand they churned up, the sheets of spray they raised when they galloped in the tide. He saw the boy running for the marquee.

Mr Solomon could hear a brass band playing. He ran till he could run no longer and then he went forward in large clumsy steps, dragging the sand as he went. The sound of the reeds and trumpets grew clearer as he walked, repeated in one poignant phrase, right down the beach. Mr Solomon came to a crowd then, pressed round the marquee and began to push his way desperately through it. He felt people like a wall against him, forcing him out. He began to moan aloud, scrabbling at the people in front of him to force his way in. He imagined the boy at the centre of that crowd, playing a clear golden trumpet. He could see the precise curve of the trumpet's mouth, the pumping keys, the boy's expressionless eyes. He began to curse, trying to wedge himself between the bodies, there was something desperate and necessary beyond them.

He felt himself lifted then, carried a small distance off and thrown in the sand. He lifted his face and wept in the sand and saw the horses churning the sea-spray into a wide area down by the edge. He heard a loud cheer, somewhere behind him.

THE CHANGE

JOHN B. KEANE
Born in Listowel, Co. Kerry, 1928, John B. Keane is one of Ireland's
most successful and best-known playwrights. He has also published
many collections of short, humorous essays, an autobiography, a volume of poetry, two novels and a book of short stories, *Death Be Not
Proud.*

The village slept. It was always half asleep. Now, because there was a flaming sun in the June sky, it was really asleep. It consisted of one long street with maybe forty to fifty houses on either side. There were shops, far too many of them, and there were three decaying public houses, the doors of which were closed as if they were ashamed to admit people. No, that isn't quite true. The truth is that passing strangers upset the tenor of normal life. The locals only drank at night, always sparingly, and were therefore reluctant to accept habits that conflicted with their own.

In the centre of the roadway a mangy Alsatian bitch sunned herself inconsiderately and that was all the life there was. The day was Friday. I remember it well because my uncle, with whom I was staying, had cycled down to the pier earlier that morning for two fresh mackerel. Mackerel always taste better when they are cooked fresh.

Anyhow, the bitch lay stretched in the sun. From where I sat inside the window of my uncle's kitchen I could see the street from one end to the other. At nights when he didn't go to the pub that's what we would do; sit and watch the neighbours from the window. It was his place to comment and I would listen, dodging away to my room sometimes to write down something of exceptional merit. He was a great commentator but I never complimented him. He might stop if I did. It was hard, at times, to keep back the laughter although on rare occasions I was unable to smother it sufficiently and he would look at me suspiciously.

Behind me I could hear him in the kitchen. He made more noise than was strictly necessary.

'What way do you want it,' he called, 'boiled or fried?'

'Fried. Naturally.'

At the far end of the village a smart green sportscar came into view. Its occupants were a boy and a girl. One minute the car was at the end of the street and the next it was braking furiously to avoid collision with the Alsatian bitch.

'What's happening out there?' But he didn't wait for my reply.

He was standing beside me with the frying pan in his hand. The car had stopped and the driver climbed out to remove the obstacle.

'Come on. Come on. Get up outa that, you lazy hound.'

Slowly the bitch turned over on her side and scratched the ranges of twin tits which covered her belly. She rose painfully and without looking at the driver slunk to the pavement where she immediately lay down again.

By this time a number of people stood in the doorways of their houses. The squeal of brakes had penetrated the entire village and they had come to investigate. I followed my uncle to the doorway where we both stood silently watching the girl. She had eased herself from her seat and was now standing with hands on hips. She was tall and blonde. The tight-fitting red dress she wore clung to her body the way a label sticks to a bottle.

'Very nice. Very nice indeed,' my uncle said.

'I think,' the girl told the driver, 'I'll take off this dress. I feel clammy.'

'Suit yourself,' he replied. With that he returned to his seat and lit a cigarette. The red dress was buttoned right down the front.

'What's the name of this place?' she asked as she ripped the topmost button. From the way she said it we knew that she couldn't care less.

'Don't know,' the driver said. Then, as an afterthought, 'Don't care.'

She shrugged her slender shoulders and set to work on the other buttons, oblivious of the wide eyes and partly open mouths of the villagers. A door banged a few houses away but it was the only protest. When she reached the bottom buttons she was forced to stoop but she didn't grunt the way the village women did. Another shrug and the dress flowed from her to the ground.

Underneath she wore chequered shorts and a red bra, no more. The driver didn't even look when she asked him to hand her the sweater which was underneath her seat. Fumbling, his hand located the garment and he tossed it to her. He did make a comment however.

'Godsake hurry up,' he said with some irritation.

'Did you ever see such a heartless ruffian?' My uncle folded his arms and there was a dark look on his face. The girl stood for a moment or two shaking dust or motes or some such things from the sweater. Her whole body rippled at every movement. She started to pull the sweater over her head and then an astonishing thing happened.

Nobody was prepared for it and this is probably why no one ever spoke about it afterwards. Everybody thought about it afterwards. I'm pretty certain of that.

Quite accidentally, I'm sure of that too, while she was adjusting her neck and shoulders so that she could the better accommodate the sweater, one of her breasts popped out into the sunlight. There were gasps. More doors banged.

A woman's voice called, 'Hussy. Hussy.'

Obviously she didn't hear. It was a deliciously pink living thing, dun-nippled and vital.

'Do 'em good,' my uncle whispered. 'Give 'em something to think about.'

The sweater in place, the girl adjusted her close-cropped hair. It didn't need adjusting but girls always seem to adjust their hair when it least needs it.

She picked up the dress and with her fingers felt the bonnet of the car. It must have been hot because she took the fingers away quickly and covered the bonnet with the dress. She then sat on the bonnet and from nowhere produced a tube of lipstick. All the while the driver sat looking straight in front of him. He threw the cigarette away before it had burned to the halfway stage. Now he sat with folded arms and hooded eyes that saw nothing.

The girl, her lips glistening, neatly folded the dress, went round to the boot of the car, flicked a button and tucked in the dress. Closing the boot she looked up and down the street. Her eyes scanned the few remaining faces with interest. If she noticed any reaction she did not show it in the least. For an instant her eyes met those of my uncle. He winked almost imperceptibly but she must have noticed it because she permitted herself the faintest glimmer of a smile as she entered the car. She punched the driver playfully and to give him his due he caught her round the shoulders and planted a swift kiss on the side of her face. Gears growled throatily and the car leaped forward into sudden life. In an instant it was gone and I was old enough to know that it had gone forever.

Later when we had eaten our mackerel we went to drive in the cows for the evening milking. This was the part of the day I liked best. The morning and afternoon hours dragged slowly and lamely but as soon as the evening milking was done there was the prospect of some excitement. We could cycle down to the pier and watch the lobster boats arriving home or we could go to the pub and listen.

On that particular evening we decided on the pub. Earlier while we

were eating he had said that things would never be the same again.
'At least,' he confided, 'not for a hell of a long time anyway.' I had
pressed him for an explanation.

'Look,' he said, 'I don't know exactly how to put it but that girl we
saw changed things.'

'In what way?' I asked.

'Oh, damn,' he said, not unkindly, 'you have me addled. How do I
know in what way? Is this the thanks I get for cooking your mackerel?'

'Aren't you afraid I'll grow up in ignorance?' He was fond of saying
this when I failed to show interest in things he considered to be
important. But he didn't rise to it. Instead he said: 'Wait and see. Wait
and see, that's all.'

We went to the pub earlier than usual. He shaved before we left
the house which was unusual for him. Most men in the village shaved
only on Saturday nights or on the eve of holy days.

The pub was cool. There was a long wooden seat just inside the
door. We sat and he called for a pint of stout and a bottle of lemonade.
There were two other customers. One was a farmer's boy I knew by
sight and the other was the young assistant teacher in the local boys'
school.

'There was a lot of hay knocked today,' the publican said when he
had served the drinks and collected his money.

'There was indeed,' my uncle answered piously, 'and if this weather
holds there will be a lot more knocked tomorrow.'

I gathered from this that he was at the top of his form. He was
saying nothing out of the way. Nobody could possibly benefit from his
words. He would go on all night like this, relishing the utterly meaningless conversation.

The young teacher, who was not a native of the place, finished his
drink and called for another. There was an unmistakable belligerence
about him.

'A chip-carrier,' the uncle whispered, 'if ever I saw one.'

'What about the strip-tease act today?' the teacher ventured. When
no one answered him he went to the window and looked out.

'Nothing ever happens here,' he pouted.

'True for you,' said the uncle.

He joined the teacher at the window. The three of us looked out
into the street.

'Deserted,' the teacher said.

'Terrible,' from the uncle.

A couple came sauntering up the street.

'Here's up Flatface,' the teacher complained. Flatface was the name given to Mrs O'Brien. She had the largest number of children in the village. She wasn't an attractive woman. Neither was her husband an attractive man. But tonight Mrs O'Brien looked different. She wore make-up and her hair was freshly washed and combed.

'That's a change,' my uncle said.

'He'll have her pregnant again,' the teacher protested.

Other couples appeared on the street, husbands and wives who were never seen out together. Some were linking arms. All the pairs walked ingratiatingly close to one another.

'What is this?' the teacher asked anxiously. 'What's happening?'

'Strange,' said the uncle.

Later when the pub closed we walked down the street together. At the doorway of the house next to ours a man and his wife were standing. She wore her Sundays and he leaned heavily on her shoulder.

'I know he's leaning on her,' said the uncle, 'but for him that's a lot.'

Two girls were sitting on the window ledge of the house at the other side.

'Come in for a cup of tea, Jack,' one said. My uncle hesitated.

'Ah, come on, Jack,' said the other, 'it's early yet.'

The young teacher stood at the other side of the street, legs crossed, back propped against the wall. He looked gangly, wretched and lost.

'Care for a drop of tea?' the uncle called across. Suddenly the teacher sprang into action. He checked first by looking up and down to confirm that it was really he who was being invited. Then fully assured he bounded across the roadway, a mad hunger for companionship in his eyes.

The uncle explained to the girls how he would have to see me safely indoors but promised he would be back in a matter of moments. He suggested that meanwhile they start the proceedings without him. Courteously, or rather gallantly, the teacher stood aside to allow the ladies first passage indoors. One giggled but covered her mouth in atonement when the other nudged her to stop. In our own house the uncle poured me a glass of milk and we sat at the table for a spell.

'See what I mean?' he said. 'I told you things would never be the same.'

I nodded that I fully understood.

'Was that why you shaved tonight?' I asked.

'No,' he answered, 'but I can see now it was a good job I did.'

THE STUDIOS

SAM KEERY
Born in Lisburn, Co. Antrim, 1929, Sam Keery worked for many years in Australia and now lives in London. He has published a novel which was highly commended in the 1984 David Higham Prize for Fiction, and one collection of short stories, *The Streets of Laredo*.

It had been a dispiriting day for John Quinn. For one thing, when they had sent him to Personnel for a medical the doctor had immediately evinced a marked antipathy for the Irish. When John replied, in answer to a question put without looking at him, that yes, he had been back to Northern Ireland in the past year, the doctor had remarked with a knowing smile to the bustling nurse and the row of impassive waiting men: 'There you are. Probably pay less tax if they come and go. Used to dodge National Service that way.'

'It was my father's funeral,' John exclaimed, but the small seedy doctor dressed in a frayed club blazer did not bother to look up at him.

Then, when with difficulty he got off a little early to eat a pork pie in Lyon's before rushing to the Maida Vale basement flat of Mr Malone Fitzhoward for his singing lesson, he was made to wait a while in the shabby hall before the elderly singing teacher appeared, a warm yeasty smell of bread and tea on his breath, still masticating faintly. John had first met Mr Fitzhoward at a musical event in the Ulster Hall in Belfast where John had sung a small solo part. Mr Fitzhoward had asked him gravely if he had ever thought of having his voice trained professionally and had ceremoniously presented him with his card in case he should ever come to London.

Mr Fitzhoward arranged John in a singing posture at a brass stand with his chin down and hands folded over the groin, shaking him here and there to loosen him. As he made these preparations Mr Fitzhoward spoke indignantly of the jealousy in the musical world that was preventing him receiving the recognition he deserved. It was absolutely disgraceful, he complained, the lengths to which people would go to keep the Fitzhoward Method from gaining wider acceptance. Little black books were stacked high on the baby grand piano. Bright red lettering on them said, 'The Fitzhoward Method'. One letter seemed slightly askew. John had bought a copy after his first lesson and had been disappointed to find that it was full of case his-tories and testimonials from grateful singers in Melbourne and Sydney and contained little actual description of the Method. When John had timidly mentioned this Mr Malone Fitzhoward had cried 'Hah' in a congratulatory tone, with a little shrewd smile as if to say how clever of John to have spotted that.

'Wouldn't they like to know,' he had exclaimed fervently and had darted at John a pleased look to indicate that he could see that John and he were certainly going to hit it off, 'oh wouldn't they just.'

'Would you believe,' he now said as John placed a school notebook on the lectern, 'that *Voice and Instrument* has returned my card. Some nonsense about the letters after my name. The lengths to which professional jealousy will go would be a revelation to you, dear boy.'

'MEE MAI MOW,' sang John in a small sweet tenor, 'MAH MOO MAI.'

Mr Fitzhoward pushed his glasses up on his forehead and listened intently with his eyes closed and his mouth open, joining in occasionally in a fruity baritone.

When he began to prepare new exercises, which was a sign that the lesson was over, John would have liked to remind him that they had started late. Mr Fitzhoward hummed and mouthed sounds like RAH-OH, DAH-OH, LAN-OH, studying John through narrowed eyes as if tailoring the sounds to fit him. Then he scribbled them in a large imposing hand across the pages of the notebook with the tone they were to be sung to.

Was John's local public library, he enquired, making difficulties about ordering *The Fitzhoward Method* for its shelves? John looked unhappily at the clock as he handed over his fee and admitted that he had not yet asked them.

'Oh, do, dear boy, do,' urged Mr Fitzhoward gravely, 'these people should be exposed.'

Barrow men were crying strawberries when he came up out of the tube at Paddington into the warm spring sun. He carried a little box to his bed-sitting room nearby and stood eating them pensively at the window, sighing occasionally, setting against his feeling of discouragement the luxury of the rich red juicy fruit. He often consoled himself with little solitary snacks of some delicacy or other: smoked salmon, a peach, fruit out of season.

His attic room had a view of roofs shimmering in the spring sunshine. The thought of all that life hidden from view, with its secret pleasures, impenetrable and aloof, evoked in him a confusion of homesickness and sensual longings. He suddenly recalled, without any reason, some note in the prim polite murmurs of Belfast girls that might none the less have promised, though perhaps falsely, the assuagement of desire. He was filled with tiredness and languor. He would have liked to sleep and he looked resentfully at the scattering of books on his little table: *Hugo's Italian Made Easy, Hugo's Italian Verbs Simplified, The Fitzhoward Method* and an old-fashioned tattered Italian dictionary. Copies of magazines to do with opera and the stage were lying about. His eye caught the little text that he had copied on to a card and hung on the wall. It was a sentence from an exercise in the Italian grammar taken from a writer called Machiavelli. *E meglio a fare e pentirse che non fare e pentirse.* It is better to do and be sorry than not to do and be sorry. It had attracted him and he had made a text of it somewhat self-consciously but defiantly and, as he had been when he first arrived, full of optimism. He turned from it to gaze out of the window again.

He gazed across the daunting roofscape and the vast London sky, thinking of Belfast, of its easy smallness, of the glimpses of hillside and mountain that, everywhere in that drab city, redeem the meanness of its dingy streets and soothe the spirit with images of permanence and serenity. *I to the hills will lift mine eyes from whence cometh my strength.* He had never known the meaning of that text hanging in the parlour at home till now in London, flat, vast, inescapable. He thought of the many times in London when he had been assailed by an intense impulse to try to escape.

There was the day he took a tube to Epping, thinking hopefully of a walk in Epping Forest. But when he got there he did not like to ask where the forest was so he walked briskly in any direction, keeping an eye open for the trees. He had come to a country road, a real country road, no doubt about it; it was winding, and it had fields on either side, some with cows. He told himself he was getting a bit of country air into his lungs. This, he told himself, is a far cry from Paddington. Any minute and the forest was bound to loom. He had walked and walked. Cars passed him and made him stand well in to the side of the road. All the fields were fenced and had stout gates. He tried standing at the gates, looking over them to let the peace of the country descend upon him but nothing happened of that sort. Every time he turned a bend in the road there was more road. The trees in the distance which he thought might be Epping Forest got no nearer. Wearily he had turned. Cut your losses, he had said to himself resignedly. No use being stubborn, he had decided. Live to fight another day, he put it to himself shrewdly.

As he now looked reflectively at the roofs and chimneys of the capital, he thought of the winding empty road, with the strong fences and the iron gates, that he had traversed in vain, searching for the cool forest. He thought also of when he had first come to London. Then too he had had an impulse to see the country. Why not simply walk till he reached it? he had thought. Get up early. Take a packed lunch. Follow the postal numbers. Plot a rough course north. Steer by the postal numbers on the street names. Save asking. How could you ask where the country was? What country? they would ask back. Any country. Fields. Trees. Winding roads. He had walked with a bold step, feeling young and blithe. He had glanced with disdain at the strange names on the buses which flew past him and which he had no need to know the meaning of, exulting in his cleverness at following the postal numbers. But then it had gone wrong. Long streets began leading into long streets with numbers lower than before. N12 seemed to be succeeded by N2. He began to get angry and bitter. He had felt like appealing to the passers-by to bear witness that it was neither right nor just. But, baffled and defeated, he had given up and turned back, relieved and almost thankful to be once more in the centre of the great web in which he sometimes feared that he was caught for ever.

There was a loud quick rapping at the door and the voice of the housekeeper's daughter Moira calling his name. He had been so sunk in reverie that he blinked at her as if he had been roused from sleep.

'Ah holy Janey,' Moira complained half-humorously in a broad Dublin accent, 'are you drunk or not right in the head or something?'

He had learnt that her brusque scoffing manner was partly a defence, which, out of gawkiness, she thought necessary to adopt in a lodging house full of men, but only partly, for there was indeed something in her nature that scorned and distrusted men. She was a girl of eighteen who could be very pretty when she made up her mind to it and decided it was worth the trouble, which was not always the mood she was in. The only aspect of her looks which did not alternate between prettiness and an almost wilful plainness was her eyes, which were always fine even when she seemed to try to spoil them with a sulky frown.

'Phyllis wants to know,' Moira went on, referring to her mother by her first name and rolling her eyes in a disclaiming way, 'will you go with us to the Crown in Kilburn? That one has been deafening me all day with great reports of that pub. There's a piana and a microphone and the people come forward to make eejits of themselves.'

She had let her shoulders slouch a little, as if not in the mood to straighten them against a slight stoop imparted perhaps by too much carrying around of children for her mother. Her mother had married very young and Moira and she were sometimes taken for sisters. The years of helping to rear her brothers and sisters had given her the right to call her mother by her Christian name.

'I have to go out,' John replied, knowing she would point out that he could come on to the pub later.

'A number sixteen bus,' she explained, 'as if you were setting out for the Galtimore Dance Hall, but,' – and her way of saying BUT in the Dublin accent always fascinated him; to imitate it, as he sometimes did softly to himself, he found it helped to think of, though not quite to say, BUSS, 'but, you be getting off two stops before.'

Her eye caught the books on the table.

'Still at the old Italian, eh,' she said with a scornful laugh and rolling her eyes again, giving him up as incorrigible.

One evening in the basement, when he had smiled at something disparaging that Phyllis said about Moira's passion for rock and roll dancing, Moira had turned on him in a fury. 'Would you look at Harry Secombe there. Think if you learn Italian you'll get singing like Harry Secombe. Think you're the grand fella. But you're not. You're just a poor bloody Paddy like the rest of the poor bloody Paddies.' And she had rushed from the room, leaving him to be mollified by Phyllis and Big Patsy Burke the landlord who sent a crony out for some bottles to make a convivial evening of it. They had persuaded John to sing, calling for order to let him be heard in the now crowded room, shushing Moira as she angrily chased shirt-tailed children back to bed. He had sung them a song from a film musical learnt in boyhood and now somewhat despised, thinking it might be to their taste: 'How are things in Glocamara?'. Their appreciative murmurs that there were no songs like the old songs made him feel guilty, especially when their sense of exile and separation seemed powerfully affected by the list of place names in such lines as 'through Killybeg, Kilkenny and Kildare'. So he had sung them a real Irish song, 'Eileen Aroon', which however had not had nearly the same effect.

> After the ball was o'er
> What made my heart so sore
> Oh it was parting from
> Eileen Aroon.

It had filled him with regret for the old times when he had sung it at small concerts and musical evenings back home. Mixed with this feeling was a curious excitement, which, as he made his way upstairs with the air of 'Eileen Aroon' still lingering in his head and met Moira near his room – to get away, so she said, from that bloody knees-up down there – manifested itself as desire. The same desire that came over him now as she stood near his rumpled bed and studied him with wide dark eyes as yet unmarred by her sulky frown.

'Away with you,' she said with a short hard laugh.

'But you did the other evening,' he pleaded, putting from his mind the recollection of his clumsiness and her cry of pain.

'A number sixteen bus,' she called over her shoulder, clattering down the stairs, 'Big Patsy is coming too.'

Big Patsy with his pale fat face that no amount of drink could put colour in; his thin slatternly wife always at her mother's; his charming but authoritative ways; all of which coupled with Phyllis's compliant nature and her still-buxom looks made certain things inevitable. But to Moira's dismay Big Patsy had assumed not only the privileges of a husband but also the duties of a father – and Moira had thought that she was done with heavy-handed fathers. She had risen up against a tyrannical father in Dublin and, in what seemed to John an epic feat of will for a young girl, had organised the flight of the family to London. Moira wanted no more fathers! Yet more and more often did Phyllis invoke Big Patsy's name in quarrels with her daughter. 'Patsy said you weren't to wear your hair like that . . . It won't be well for you if I tell Patsy what you spend on clothes.' Moira, suddenly aware perhaps that her only escape lay in early marriage and that the time between drudging for her mother's children and drudging for her own might well be short, had plunged into a hectic round of rock and roll dancing night after night. One evening she had come home late to find both Phyllis and Big Patsy waiting up for her. John had strained to hear the sharp scream of Moira at her mother, 'Did you not get enough in Dublin?', seemingly followed by a blow. Then there came one night a sharp reminder to John that he could not regard himself as a mere spectator of these domestic struggles. He heard Phyllis railing at Moira that it was nearly one o'clock in the morning. 'What an hour to come in. As well for you it was John Quinn you were with or Patsy would have skinned you.'

He could not pretend to be unaware that he was lingering in the presence of forces and strong wills that could shape his life into something other than his dreams. He looked in panic at the copy of *The Stage* lying open with pencil marks he had put round certain advertisements concerning auditions for the chorus of new productions. He knew quite well that he should flee.

He left the house in haste, carrying a rather elegant little attaché-case as if already in flight. From up the area steps came the bawling of a child and Moira's voice harshly chastising it. The sound made him quicken his steps and he jumped on a bus going to Oxford Circus, where he got off and walked down Regent Street to the place of his appointment. He glanced wistfully at the windows of the smart shops. He liked nice things and had very good taste. He stopped at a famous jeweller's and goldsmith's and studied with satisfaction the small gold cufflinks for which he was saving up to console himself for rebuffs and disappointments, like the early strawberries, like the elegant little leather case he was carrying.

He turned into Hanover Street, and entered a large establishment which displayed grand pianos on the ground floor. A bored man in a little pay booth indifferently consulted a booking ledger.

'Quinn. Eight o'clock. An hour. No piano. Just a stand. Number twenty-two. Six shillings.'

From the floor above came a faint medley of sounds muted by the ceiling. As he climbed the stairs the sounds grew clearer. Scales and exercises from a variety of instruments. Voices not only singing but declaiming. From behind the doors of all the studios, muffled but still audible in the corridor, could be heard practising their skills the many aspiring musicians, actors, actresses, public speakers, those doing elocution exercises in order to rid themselves of plebeian accents.

He was a little before time and the door of number twenty-two was not quite shut. He listened impatiently to two North Countrymen telling the same funny story over and over in loud cheerful voices, stopping abruptly now and then to talk in flat tired tones about timing and gesture. 'There was this fella bought his mother-in-law a blow-lamp.' The two would pick up again where they had left off, in rich ringing voices full of laughter.

When the two comedians had gone John opened the window to let out the fetid air, singing as he did so. For a little while he did some Fitzhoward exercises. Then he sang a little piece in Italian with a look of concentration and seriousness that did not entirely correspond with the liveliness of the tune. Then he leafed through the papers in his case and his hand strayed to a very worn song sheet on the front of which was the picture of a merry-looking fat man in a dinner jacket. Harry Secombe the famous singer, the one-time working-class lad who could sing in Italian for the delight of millions and the inspiration of singers like John. 'If I Ruled the World,' John sang in his light pleasant tenor voice which, in the small studio, sounded more powerful than it was. He closed his eyes and lifted his face upwards and made pledging gestures with his hands as he sang of the things he would do for love if he ruled the world.

Opposite the window of his studio was a smart restaurant and those diners with window tables sometimes glanced across in amusement. But not especially at John. They had a view into many of the studios and saw, as it were, a composite tableau of artistic ambition that might have been staged merely as a diversion for them as they wined and dined. But this was an aspect of which John, shedding melancholy and foreboding as he sang, was quite oblivious. In any case he felt that his dreams were of a humbler order than those he sensed in the babel of sound briefly escaping through the open windows of the studios into the evening air before being swallowed up in the unceasing hubbub of London. It was not that great city's acclaim that he dreamt of but of another, smaller city, Belfast, and not even all of that. To walk triumphantly through the small streets he had grown up in; to receive the admiration of the people of his childhood who would remain fixed in his mind as at a certain time; to achieve significance in his native place; these things were all that he asked; these were his modest dreams.

As his song reached its climax he felt a moment of pure happiness, *almost* certain that such a modest dream must surely, surely be fulfilled?

THE SENTIMENTALIST

MAEVE KELLY
Born in Dundalk, Co. Louth, 1930, Maeve Kelly has lived in Limerick for many years where she is prominent in the women's rights movement. She has published two novels and two volumes of short stories, *A Life of Her Own* and *Orange Horses*.

The Americans say that eccentricity is the norm in Ireland. I wish they were right. What after all is normality? Can it simply be equated with dullness? I ask the question because the only people I find interesting are those whom the dull people of my acquaintance call odd. And I am certain that behind my back I am called odd, with accompanying shakings of the head, which frequent shakings may account for the displacement of the few brains my charitable analysts possess. It does not worry me at all. But then I am not a lover of people. I find children irritating, the old irritable and the middle-aged merely opinionated. And the young are so incredibly gauche. It pains me to have to acknowledge their familiarity. I do not care for animals, except for cows, who combine supreme usefulness with a rustic kind of beauty. I do not consider myself a misanthropist, but on the whole I find women silly and demanding, and men stupid and aggressive. Most people are dishonest. Worse, their dishonesty is contagious so that even I am occasionally infected and I find myself accepting their outrageous statements out of a false sense of good manners. Besides, it is wearing to be in disagreement all the time, and I confess I am a little lazy, which is why I live by myself in this three-roomed cottage in the middle of Martin Leahy's farm. I rent the house very cheaply because it has none of the inconveniences of so-called civilised living. Its chief attraction for me is the lack of a roadway to my door and whenever my relations or acquaintances feel obliged to visit me they must do so on foot, along a muddy track of about three miles. I have an old ship's spyglass in my sitting room and I occasionally scan the horizon to make sure I am not caught unawares. I cannot understand my relatives' need to visit me. I am sure they do not enjoy it, but they seem to take it on themselves as a painful duty and I am too considerate to deprive them of their sense of responsibility.

One visitor I welcomed was my cousin Liza. We knew each other since we were young girls. Her father and mother committed suicide in a romantic pact in 1915. They were pacifists, living in England, and refused, they said, to be embroiled in the folly of war. So they left their only child to the care of my parents, who, I think, fulfilled their obligation admirably. They gave her, and us, as much affection as was necessary for our survival. Very quickly Liza became one of the family. We loved her English accent and tried our best to copy her, with laughable results. Even more laughable were her attempts at acquiring Gaelic, which we were then just beginning to learn. It was quite beyond me. I have no flair for languages. Since English has been imposed on us, for historical reasons, I accept it and consider it adequate for my needs, a vehicle for communicating thought. I concede that I may have lost something, subtleties of expression more in keeping with my cultural background, not to mention the heritage of tradition which is difficult to translate adequately. However, I have always been a pragmatist and I accept the reality of conquest. The new nationalist fervour associated with the revival of the language was boring to me. I despise passion, wasted emotions. But not so Liza. Typical of the convert, she threw herself totally into the Gaelic revival. She joined the Gaelic League, attended the Abbey plays and became a member of Cumann na mBan. I could not approve. It has always seemed to me that organised groups, military or civilian or religious, are death to the individual and therefore retard human development. It can be argued that for the apathetic mass such groups are necessary, but I believe that one strong-minded individual can achieve more on her own if she is prepared to sacrifice her life for her cause. I do not mean by that the futile sacrifice of death, which simply perpetuates myths and has no logical value. Martyrdom is the ultimate folly, the self-indulgence of the sentimental. I mean that one person, standing alone, against the convention of her times, must, if she applies herself, learn wisdom, fortitude and knowledge, and provide the vital link between the generations which must lead to the ennoblement of all womankind. I use the term loosely to include men.

Liza was impulsive and sentimental in that charming way of the English. She scurried around the countryside in those early years waving flags and crying slogans. It saddened me to see her in her ridiculous uniform, allowing the uniformly foolish ideas of her group to take over. I do not deny that the history of this country has been a tragic one, but the worst tragedy of all has been the number and variety of its saviours – most of them with foreign or English blood – which it has attracted. Liza saw herself as one of those saviours.

In the course of her missionary work she married a young man from

Waterford, a timid ordinary fellow whom she tried to indoctrinate. It was useless. She wept over his 'dreadful tolerance' as she called it. He admitted the savagery of men, the injustices his countrymen had suffered, but he constantly saw the other side, and constantly made allowances. 'I love him for it,' she told me. 'He is so gentle and kind, he can see no evil in anyone. I hate him for it too. He will not fight for anything. I know *you* won't fight, but somehow that is different. And father and mother were different too. They were committed and so are you. He is not committed to anything. He loves everyone.' It was shocking that he died, shot down at their front door by the Black and Tans, before her eyes, probably because of her reputation as a nationalist. To me, it had a poetic justice, but I did not tell her what I thought.

I hoped the futility of his death could cure her. But no. She kept his hat and coat on the hall stand, left the bullet holes in the door and walls and the blood-stained rug where he fell, and carried on. But she was not political, not ambitious, not scheming, and she was not a man. So there was no place for her among the new policy-makers born out of his blood and others like him. 'I cannot give up my dream now,' she said. 'Poor Willie died for it. My house, his house, will be a memorial to him. It will be the glory of Ireland.' Her grief and her innocence moved me. Against my better judgement I helped her to organise the house for students. It became the only summer school of its kind, open from April until September for young people from all over the world and from all over Ireland who came to imbibe the old Gaelic culture and learn the language. For fifty years she kept the school going. For fifty years she took only Irish produced food and wore only Irish made clothes. She allowed herself tea and coffee, confessing it a weakness, but grew her own vegetables and fruit. She refused on principle to eat oranges or bananas because, she said, they were the product of slave labour. She was always available for picket duty, ban the bomb, anti-apartheid, women's rights. When the farmers were imprisoned after their marches she picketed the jail and was booed by the town population. A city woman herself, she believed in the nobility of working the land and declared the farmers were the guardians of the country's traditions. Dedication of that sort is truly admirable, and how rarely one finds it. But oh, the folly of it all. The folly of living one's life for a useless dream.

Liza's house was in the centre of a spreading suburb. All around her walled gardens, hundreds of semi-detached homes sprouted the inevitable television aerials. The view of the river which she used to enjoy from her bedroom window became swallowed up in the new hollow block landscape. When at the age of seventy she closed her school, she was unprotected during the vulnerable months of fruiting and had to fight to keep her apples growing. Hordes of boys challenged each other to climb her walls and rob her orchard, encouraged to do so perhaps by the silliest of all aphorisms, 'Boys will be boys'. The bravery of these young fellows is typical of the spirit of our time. One old lady became a formidable enemy to be challenged and defeated. To the socialists she was a property owner, a *fíor Gael* crank to the Language Freedom Movement, a rock in the path of progress to the speculators who viewed her two acres with hungry eyes. Worst of all, she was an embarrassing reminder to the few old nationalist members of the government.

I visited her last Autumn when the paths were slippy with the rotting leaves of her chestnut trees and the stone house seemed to fade into the grey day. While we sat by the fire over tea I asked her would she not think of settling in the Gaeltacht now that her work in the school was over. 'I am Gall to them,' she said. Vinegary was not an adjective I would have applied to Liza and I suppose I looked bewildered. 'I mean Gall as opposed to Gael,' she sighed. 'Foreigner.'

'Well, I suppose you are,' I agreed.

'Not because I am half English,' she said a little tartly. '*You* might be even more foreign to them.'

I had to admit that I felt foreign whenever I visited such places. 'Don't you think they are a little chauvinist in their separatism lately?' I asked.

'You don't understand,' she said. 'I don't mean to be harsh, but really, Jo, have you ever felt deeply about anything? Have you no values at all? Don't you care what has happened to this country, or what is happening? What do you do with your life?'

'I think,' I said. 'What else is there to do?'

'You sit in that hut, reading and thinking. Is that a way to spend a life?'

'It's the only way for me,' I said.

'But such a waste,' she cried. 'Don't you feel you have wasted your life?'

It seemed a strange thing for her to say.

But although she is only six months younger than I, she always seems much younger and I tend to indulge her. I did not tell her about my book, my life's work, which will, I hope, put all those foreign male philosophers to shame. It is time we had an Irish philosopher who does not come out of Maynooth tarred with the Roman brush, and it is past time we had a woman philosopher. But I could not discuss that with Liza. I am too old now to start exchanging confidences. It makes my life somewhat lonely, especially at my age, but I recognise that as being part of the price I must pay for my independence. Liza always said I was a cynic, but that was because she was a sentimentalist and only saw her own truth.

Last Spring she visited me and accused me of deliberately torturing her by living in my isolated kingdom. 'It is cruel to expect me to walk that distance to see you. Some day I will not come, and I suppose you will not care.'

'But you know it is my only defence,' I protested. 'It's as good as a moat around a castle. Otherwise I would never have any peace. I am always glad to see you, Liza. But not too often. Not even you.'

'Oh you hard heart,' she sighed. 'I don't know why I bother with you.'

I could not reply. Silence on these occasions seems the best policy and is often more reproachful than words. And then she said, 'Forgive me, dear. What would I have done without you all these years? You so sensible, I with my foolish, foolish dreams. Such folly.'

I was horrified. Here was a threat to my own integrity. If Liza became a cynic anything was possible. I might end my days guarding her orchard with her.

'Gaelic Ireland is dead,' she announced, as if she just unveiled truth. 'I and others like me prop up its corpse and pretend we are keeping it alive.'

I was forced to lie. 'Nonsense,' I said. 'You know you have lived your life in the fullest sense, believing in what you did. And you were right.'

'My gods were all false,' she said. 'You knew it. I should have looked for political power. That's obvious to me now.'

'Politics would have destroyed you,' I said.

'I am destroyed anyway. They are going to knock down my house and build sixteen houses where I have kept my summer school.'

'Be precise.' I had to be stern in order to hide my fear. 'Whom do you mean by they?'

'The Corporation has compulsorily acquired my house. They are right of course. I am taking up far too much space. I am old. There are young people with children waiting for houses. Think of all the children who could grow up in my two acres.'

What could I do but fight for her, poor sentimental Liza. I left my book unfinished and marched with her, up and down the path in front of the house, armed with placards of protest. Of course we made wonderful headlines. The cub reporters made their names with us. 'Two indomitable eighty year olds fight for their home. A husband's young blood spilled here for Ireland. Is the Corporation the new oppressor?' I expected some salvos from the Socialist Magazine, but age, I suppose, still arouses pity, if not respect. Liza's old pupils rallied. She became the heroine of the day, the integrity of the past standing against the hollow men of the present. They flocked around her, middle-aged and young, grandparents and parents. There were some emotional scenes in the garden last summer when after the success of our campaign, a hundred or so of her pupils came to cheer her. She stood in the centre crying happily. 'You dear people, you dear wonderful people.'

I attended her funeral when she died a few weeks later. I owed her that much. It amused me to watch the performance, since it finally vindicated my life-style. Everyone spoke in Irish. I suppose they praised her work, her dedication. When I passed her house yesterday I saw the demolition notice on the wall. Beside it was a brass memorial plaque with an inscription in Irish. Fortunately I could not understand it. I have never had a flair for languages.

TROUSSEAU

RITA KELLY

Born in Ballinasloe, Co. Galway, 1953, Rita Kelly writes both in English and Irish and has won awards for her work in both languages. She has published one collection of English language short stories, *The Whispering Arch*.

Having identified the harsh intrusion, bell, blast – would she ever get used to it? – Frances heard a soft but persistent sound outside her window. She imagined the yellow leaves flattened against the tarmac and being shocked by the full drops coming rhythmically from the bared branches of the lime. She shivered a little, drawing her feet up from the cold extremities of the bed. Already there were feet upon the landing, Agnes and Veronica going to the kitchen. Then her desire to lie on became a desire for a hot cup of tea. But no. Quickly, put a foot on the waxed linoleum. How right her father had been. She had never found it easy to get up. And 6.30 am was simply extreme. There was Mass, and to feign sickness would only increase trouble and embarrassment, besides, one could not be sick every day. Not today especially, after Maggie's – Mother Margaret, of course – detailed plan of attack. Leave at 9.00 am. Madness. Oliver to drive. Thank goodness for that much.

Frances slipped on her underwear, cold clothes, trying not to feel the chill. Caught her rather meagre curves, an instant, in the mirror, and wished, yet again, for nearer normal proportions.

Mass was as usual, sleepy and distant. White chrysanthemums stood elegantly in brass vases. The atmosphere was drowsy with shoes smacking and stopping, wax, voices, wine, and the refined tang of flowers. Dawn began to break through the stained glass, limned in bleak colour. Frances felt more awake after Mass and looked eagerly to breakfast. The essence of kitchen wafted itself along the landings and corridors leading from the Chapel.

Sister Oliver read from Isaiah with admirable feeling, as was natural with her, labiodenting each phrase through a grate of cutlery and plinking china. Frances was not fully concentrated upon what was being read, rather she thought the idea of reading sensible, especially at breakfast, when scarcely anyone had the necessary energy for conversation. For a moment she allowed the remembered chaos of her natural home to intrude, but only for a moment, seven tones of voice, each with its own shade of impatience, half-wakeful cares and complaints, and the rending radio-voice competing with the entirety. Mother Margaret's eyes were upon her, but in a maternal way – yes, we're quite ready, aren't we – without saying a word. But the look was toned, or at least coloured, as if intended for a child or pet animal. Frances swallowed, tea and air, awkwardly.

Why was it taking her so long to settle, to feel comfortable with the community? Of course she could not feel one with them, she was as yet a postulant, and strangely it seemed such a reversion: before entering she felt less embarrassed, less choked with the nuns, had more real contact with them, perhaps. It was too early to be disillusioned and hardly late enough for objective evaluation. Basically, she must be a junior again, but with some difference, there ought to be more certainty now as an indefinite stretch of life is not just five years of boarding school. But somehow breakfast with thirty-six nuns in a refectory reverberating with Isaiah, Oliver, and unhomely china created anything but certainty.

'I'll meet you in the Blue Parlour at five to nine. And don't forget your gloves, dear . . . yes of course, but I always feel that a young lady is never quite dressed without her gloves!' Mother Margaret disappeared, leaving Frances to debate the possible existence of an insinuation in the glove remark.

Sister Oliver joined her on the stairs, at ease as usual, and affable. Frances felt that sense of certainty which she herself lacked, Oliver's very posture and carriage seemed assured. But this was a state she might appropriate to herself with time, perhaps she was glimpsing the process: move on, replace and be replaced.

'Well, Frances, are we all set?' Then with a change to the Margaret tone, mocking was it? 'Now dear, you must remember your gloves, a young lady . . .'

'Yes, I know. Does she think I'd appear otherwise?'

'Of course not. It has become so much a part of her. It will be interesting to notice your foibles after your silver jubilee.'

'And imitate them,' snapped Frances.

The slight raising of an eyebrow let Frances know that that remark was just a shade too impulsive.

'I didn't mean it that way, Oliver.'

Sister Oliver was fine enough in perception to know exactly what was meant, but she sympathised with the attempt to extract the sting and became jovial.

'Well, whatever about your gloves, I hope you have all your measurements. You hardly want Maggie taking a tape from the mystical depths of her bag, and set about assessing your vital statistics in the shop, do you?'

'Oh for God's sake, Oliver!'

'Would you like me to do it for you?'

'Now you are embarrassing me and you know it!' Bitch. Getting her own back. Why must I blush? She knows well that my figure agonises me.

Frances' perceptions were scarcely as fine, but in her own way she could grasp immediately the primaries of a situation.

'Very well, Frances my love, I shan't be an embarrassment to you. But you must allow me to help in your choice, I should hate to think that Mother Margaret's opinions were the only ones in matters such as these.'

'Look, Oliver, I'm quite capable of making my own decisions.'

'But are you?'

'Well . . . you know what I mean. I never saw such fuss, you'd swear I was going to buy a trousseau.'

'In a way one might say you were.'

'All right, if you must have the final word.'

'I only seem to have, Frances. I know what you are thinking.'

'I . . .'

'Yes? But really I'm not as insensitive as you may be inclined to think.'

'I didn't say that, Oliver. No, you're not the worst, but you are drawing me out, and you're so good at it. You penetrate all my defences.'

'Not quite, rather you delightfully expose yourself.'

'Well, I wish I didn't.'

'No, Frances, don't wish that, it is particularly refreshing among a group of ossified exteriorities. I'd better go. I'll see you, don't tell me, in the Blue Parlour at, let me see, five to nine.'

'Oliver, please don't make fun of me, not today.'

'I'll scarcely have time. I, too, must have some underwear and my supply has become rather scanty. Oh, don't look so surprised, I mean . . .'

'And pray, Sister, to whom does the pleasure of measuring you belong?'

'That, Frances, is a little premature in the asking.'

She was gone, leaving Frances with a tangle of conflicting thoughts and half-thoughts. But she too must prepare. She noticed from her window that the rain had stopped, leaving a sparkle on the lawns and smudged leaves. The air was damply fresh, the light wistful, it seemed to flicker between a loosening of more rain and a general clearing of sky.

Frances made way for Mother Margaret entering the Blue Parlour with her huge bag. Sister Oliver was there already, about to savour calmly the foibles of her Superior, feeling ready to be irritated in the extreme, but certainly not hoping for any surprise or fascination. Perhaps she, too, had begun to grasp the process of replacement. Senile Phillip upstairs, whose days were reduced to Eucharist in bed, meals and medicine. The final stage. Emaciated authority.

'You say we have enough petrol, Mary Oliver. It is best always to give the business to those we know. But we must be very particular about dear Frances. I'm told there is a sale at this place. What do they call it?'

'Give-'n'-Take.'

'Yes. Very demotic, isn't it? But I suppose economy has to come to that. Well, Frances, I see that you are quite ready, and you didn't forget your gloves.'

Frances was disgusted with herself for taking instant notice of the ironic comment in Oliver's eye.

'I've told Mary Veronica not to include us for lunch. I have a few little items to see to myself, and I think that we might stretch things just a fraction and have lunch out. *The Residential* was always reasonable, but the manageress would talk one's face off. Suppose we can't have it everyway, and when we think of what the good Lord suffered . . . Hope you enjoy your little trip, Frances, pity the weather, but what matter. Oh Mary Oliver, are you sure you checked the water?'

'Yes, Mother, quite sure.'

'You know how I am with these mechanical things.'

'Yes. I do.'

And there was a shade of impatience in Oliver's shaking of the car-keys.

Mother Margaret was settled into the front seat in a wilderness of rugs and cushions, while keeping a firm grip on her bag. The driver flicked her veil aside. Frances had the entire back seat to herself, chilled by the upholstery, and unable to free herself from the cool eyes fixed in the driving-mirror.

'You may start now, Mary Oliver. Are you all right back there, dear? Wrap yourself up well. Not too much choke, Mary Oliver, and the price of petrol. In the Name of the Father and of the Son and of the Holy Spirit. Amen.'

Frances got a sprinkle of holy water on her nose, forgot herself, and caught the eyes in the mirror showing a sophisticated and held intolerance for the religious observances.

The drowsy village gave on to the main thoroughfare. Forty miles of it. The known tree-clumps, villages, and scraggy bushes; the strings of stonewall rising and declining with the land, stacked up over the years, grey and continent. These things, through a wet patina, held no interest or freshness for Frances. She had seen it all before, and so often, and seeing it from the back of the convent car made no difference.

Sister Oliver drove with cool caution. She was so much in control of the process that her eyes could be divorced from it for inordinate periods, float disjunct, and be the only real portent of her interiority. Frances was disturbed by the dislocation: to her right, the back, shoulders and veil exuding a slight perfume, while just above, centred, of the scene and outside of it, those liquid eyes in secret commenting.

Conversation evaporated, or rather Mother Margaret's repetition of the niggling logistics had begun to tire even herself.

'I think we should say a decade of the Rosary.'

Beads were extracted. Oliver being saved the necessity, looked sympathy at Frances, who allowed herself to respond, knowing the drone of Maggie's voice, and that a decade meant at least five with caudae. It did. Each taking her turn against the tyres and slopping wipers.

'Hail, Holy Queen – Jesus, Mary and Joseph look out! I thought we were all killed – Mother of Mercy, Hail, our life, our sweetness and our hope – do be careful, Mary Oliver, for goodness sake. Wouldn't you think that man would keep over to his own side? Keep back you. Let him off, we're in no hurry thanks be to God.'

Frances fixed her gaze on the mirror, waiting, provoking almost. A too sudden release of the clutch seemed to escape Maggie's notice, and she resumed her claim for Eve's children: poor and banished.

The city, its irritant rash of outgrowth, was reached.

Mother Margaret, in keeping with her logistic capabilities, accentuated the problem of parking. The advance along the pathways involved a series of polite pushings. Frances was pushed off her two companions as they vied with each other in elbowing her forward.

The *Give-'n-Take* store was unmistakable in its brashness and blatant colour. Mother Margaret stopped an instant, incredulous of the extremity. None of them was impressed by the untempered display and the harsh music. People, their sex conspicuously indeterminate, held items of clothing to themselves, slipped in and out of shoes, quieted babies, tossed cellophane wrappers into disorder and talked loudly and incessantly.

'I suppose there is a Ladies' Department. Do you think we could see an assistant, Mary Oliver?'

'That won't be necessary, Mother, it is self-service.'

'I see. Well then we'd better get on with it. Frances dear, come with me. Hm. Self-service, is it? They're never without a term for vulgarity. Buying things all my life . . .'

'But Mother –'

'No objection now, I am well used to this. What have we here? Brassières. We may as well start here.'

They had moved to a counter laden with cellophane packages, bulging with stiff cups, pink violet, perky with pastel flowers. A young man, his shirt and tie were of a similar horticultural opulence, stood by. Sister Oliver kept a little to the rear, savouring the situation, yet ready to save Frances from exposure if necessary.

'Disgusting. What young lady would dream of wearing such unbecoming bits of blatancy? After all a brassière is a brassière. Young man, do you think we could have a girl to help us?'

'What kind of help do you want? My girls are rather tied-up at the moment. Want to buy a bra is it? Well?'

'I suppose you'll do, but I had much rather have a girl. You see I want to buy some brassières for this young lady. Now I don't want any of those awful flowery things you have here. Do you have anything in white?'

'What size?'

'What size, my dear?'

Frances blushed, bit her lip, and tried to keep the unavoidable answer as low as possible.

'You must be joking,' said the young man.

Mother Margaret, not quite appreciating the statistics of the situation, but finding a chance to assert herself, launched into the attack.

'Of course she's not joking, as you call it. And I'd thank you to keep such remarks to yourself. Now, either you serve me properly or I take my business elsewhere. My dear man, do you or do you not have white brassières, size – size? what did you say, my dear, your size was?'

Too much. Worse even than Frances had been dreading. Sister Oliver had no choice, and approached Mother Margaret in quiet but hurried tones of suggestion. Mother Margaret could not let such an unexpected opportunity go by, but while she asserted her authority and a faith in her own competence, Frances slipped quickly out of the store. Dazzled by anger and shame she started back to the car. It would probably be locked. Bumping off people, she wondered how she could stand about waiting. How awkward, how isolate. Yet anything was better than going back to the torture. Maggie would have her own back, no letters for a month, continual reference to it. What would happen now? And it didn't seem as if Oliver would be much help, she could have prevented the scene . . . Yet, how unexpected to find the back door of the car unlocked.

Frances sat in, breathless, crouched into a corner, flinging the rugs aside. Damn. A great joke, Oliver would make fun of her too. Maggie would lecture at length, contorted old fool. She felt a fear breaking through the vexation, a disgust, too, with the intruding flowery things which she dared not name. Their curious attraction was blunted by a dismissal, couldn't wear them anyway. There was no longer any point in fooling herself with cotton wool. The dark habit didn't hide her inadequacies, it hid nothing, not even the full pointed breast, the embarrassment, the bulge, that awful advertisement in the shop, bouncing – Christ! The picture mocked her in its confident display. It loosened hints of envy in her, evoked desire, and pushing a disturbing truth before her: that her firm advocation of the chaste made a virtue of her deficiency.

Numbed by such a confusion of feeling and half-realisation, she scarcely recognised the tall figure coming. Oliver. Alone. Frances held her breath, a message from Maggie to return, what else.

Sister Oliver unlocked her door, slipped in, placing some parcels beside her without saying anything. With deliberation she chose a parcel and handed it back to Frances.

'These, Frances, should last you for some time.'

'But Oliver, I also needed . . .'

'I know. I got them too. Hope you don't mind the liberty, but I couldn't suffer such treatment of you, and appear to subscribe to it.'

'Where is she? She'll kill me, I know.'

'Insensate old hag! Where do you think she is, in the manager's office giving him a definition of a gentleman and a course in economics. She will probably persuade him to take twopence off a nightshirt for her. Never misses a chance. The insensitivity of it.'

'Oh thank you, Oliver, thank you indeed. I thought that you had deserted me.'

'I felt you knew by now . . .'

'Yes, but –'

'Never mind. I went a little further in my purchasing. Here, Frances, something to take the sting out of the day.'

'For me? You're too kind.'

'Perhaps I am. Hope it fits.'

'Well if it doesn't the fault is mine maybe, I didn't take your kind suggestion, you wanted to measure me in private.'

Frances unwrapped a soft nightgown, blue, and decidedly feminine. Oliver awaited the response, but it was unspeakable.

'We'll pay for this, Frances. Maggie will do her best to . . . insensitive yes, unsuspicious no. But I feel you can take it.'

The eyes flashed into the mirror and Frances was disturbed by their intensity, their chill blue.

BEND SINISTER

ADRIAN KENNY
Born in Dublin, 1945, Adrian Kenny was educated at Gonzaga College
and University College, Dublin. He has published a novel, an autobiography and a collection of short stories, *Arcady*.

Dicky Corker, BA, was rather skilful with a brush. He dipped it in fine glue, twirled it while he worked and smeared the base of one large cup and the middle of a matching saucer. When he had set the two together he replaced the sticky pot and donned a subfusc gown. With immaculate fingers he then reached down his copy of M. Cicero's *Pro Archia, Poeta*.

With plump, square, entirely different fingers Mr Graf closed his book: it looked to be a big Bible.

'Attention. Now!' He was irritable and it was hard to blame him. Living in Ireland for almost six months, he had not yet been granted a coat of arms. 'I said Attention!'

With dustless and non-toxic chalk he wrote carefully on the blackboard: PAPAL AGGRESSION (PHASE 13). Then he returned to his rostrum, chose a piece of red chalk and underlined the statement.

'Now, what do we mean when we say?' – he pointed with red chalk to the board, with the white to a boy in front of him – 'Papal Aggression? Galwey?'

Pencil in limp fingers, red mouth slack and eyes half-shut, he was sketching naked women along the margin of his history notebook. Dusty girls were his forte. The HB 2 sloped sideways as he shaded in huge breasts and bellies . . . thighs were more troublesome.

Mr Graf's huge face bent and blushed as he repeated the name, 'Galwey,' the problem, 'The Pope!' Flaccid jowls, peculiar in a young man, swung and brushed his lapels. The boy looked up almost irritably. 'It's when the Pope interferes with you, sir.'

Other boys, notably Fogg, master sketcher of the nude, tittered.

'Very well!' Mr Graf hunched his shoulders as he advanced to the desk. The enormous body, doubly obese in orange tweed suit and clinker-built brogues, seemed to blot out all of the summer sun. Tufts of unshorn tweeding jutted out in silhouette as he raised a hand and roared.

'Look here, Galwey! Do you realise what I'm trying to do here? Do you?' He emphasised every word: 'I'm trying to give you the truth, the facts about this country of ours. I've gone through hell for these facts!' The Tennessee accent twanged madly with emotion. He pointed up towards God. 'I'm telling you things that are hidden from Protestant boys in this Republic. I know. I'm giving them to you and how do you thank me?' He snatched the notebook, glanced at it and then drove a fist against the pubescent ear. 'Get out! The Church of Ireland doesn't need people like you!' He almost shrieked. His two puffed cheeks swelled yet more and seemed to suck his little grey eyes in to the root of the great square nose. The spectacles he wore shifted and were caught on the sun as two elliptical glares. But the voice continued to bellow abuse after the wretch. The room was a small one, wainscotted in wood, and it echoed every blast. The boys lay low and peeped over one another's shoulders. Finally a little suck named Block arose.

'Sir.'

Mr Graf returned to his rostrum still snorting.

Block began to speak of Philip II, Innocent III, Mr de Valera and the Penal Laws. He droned on till Mr Graf's normal grey colouring returned. 'The Roman Catholics,' Block concluded, 'wouldn't pay more than £5 for any good horse . . .'

For the past fortnight history class had been spent in the study of papal arrogance. Mr Graf had included all: from Adrian's Bull of 1156 to 1922 and the papal nuncio's usurpation of the Under-Secretary's Lodge. Modern events had been examined more deeply, with copious examples drawn from Mr Graf's own experience.

'Good,' he said. He let the slight errors pass and ran fingers through his dank hair. 'This brings us to a rather interesting point – a point that may lead us to rather interesting conclusions.' He spoke more carefully: 'interesting' was dispersed into four lackadaisical syllables by the accent. Then he smiled. 'You see, boys, as Protestants you don't really understand the average RC obsession with horses . . . Now do you?' He invited questions, supplied interesting and startling facts. The more daring sat erect and asked for more. 'I could tell you things you would not believe . . . things I've seen at Roman Catholic races. Take Galway for instance . . .'

Block smiled, looked towards the door.

Mr Graf frowned. 'Galway races. Curious, isn't it, that it was the Romans who could afford to build a cathedral there. It was opened you know, just after the runners were declared for the next year's meeting. You didn't know that?'

The class had not.

'Of course not.' He spoke in a low voice, occasionally looking at the door or at his watch. He mentioned the Republic's army, the barracks in Athlone ('Curious the RC Cathedral is beside it . . .'), he digressed meaningfully to the Garda Siochana and their blue shirts, discussed the threat of Fenianism and agrarian unrest.

A bell rang. Pens were dropped.

'Silence!'

But class was over.

'Silence.' Mr Graf reluctantly stood. 'For tomorrow I want you to write me an essay . . .'

The door opened. A cynical-looking man entered. He padded across the room, Cicero in hand. Mr Graf stopped talking, swung a hand towards the blackboard, nodded once and wiped it clean. Mr Corker placed his text upon the table, murmured, 'Leroy, there's a very fancy letter for you in the staff-room, from Dublin Castle.' He smiled.

Mr Graf nodded gravely as he descended the rostrum. 'That should be from the Chief Herald. He's being awkward about that Bible Proper in my blazon . . .'

Galwey entered the room and crossed to his place, eyes downcast beneath silky lashes.

'*Quaeret quispiam, quid* . . .' growled Mr Corker. 'Start reading.' And Mr Graf reluctantly left his pupils.

'The Bible!' For the tenth time or so Leroy shouted the holy word into the telephone. 'A black Bible. Sable.' Perhaps the Chief Herald was hard of hearing. 'Yes, a Bible Sable on a stool. S. T. O. O. L. All Proper.' He began to describe in more detail this coveted coat of arms. Angrily he concluded, 'You suggest Mr Stoole had no right to carry such a blazon, sir?' The Herald's letter was waved impatiently as he spoke. 'Now look here, Mr Herald . . .' He turned his back to the staff-room and began to discuss his forbears.

The assembled masters sipped their morning coffee tepidly and chatted about the enemy. Mr Corker hovered on the rim of this circle ever eyeing the door. He was aged about forty, still handsome, with the feminine slovenliness common to mature bachelors. He sipped coffee, nibbled biscuits slowly, and occasionally bit his lip to hold back a snigger. Eventually a small round-shouldered master entered. His gown was dragging from his elbows and he wore little sandals over woolly socks. In one hand were crumbs of chalk, in the other a copy of *Peig*.

'Morning, Jack!' Dicky held out a cup of coffee. Other members of the staff gathered about, the tall overlooking the small. Some hairy, others bald and already in collapse, they gave a seedy impression like the crew of some tramp steamer still plying between ports of the British Isles.

Jack Leake, Irish master, spooned in his sugar and lit a cigarette. Mr Corker had already bent double as he raised cup to lips. Leake's saucer refused to yield and other masters stumbled away, choking with laughter.

'Oh,' said Dicky. He gasped like a poor swimmer and bent low again, beating his breast for air. Mr Leake tugged once more and removed one half of the cup. China and coffee splattered the carpet.

'Oh!'

'Hohhoh!'

'Wheeagh!'

The masters rolled from side to side of the room, shrieking and baying and bawling in hilarity. Jack snatched the gluebrush (for it was an old joke) and ran plover-like in circles. Dicky Corker seized a cricket ball, pressed it to his teeth as if to withdraw a firing pin and lobbed it in best grenadier style towards Jack.

'Wharoom!'

'Aargh!'

Of course the noise was a trifle curious but Leroy never looked around. 'I say it for the last time, I want Graf impaling Stoole, sir. And I mean to have it. I have a right to this. I will not be intimidated . . .'

Over fresh coffee Jack and Dicky discussed cricket and made their way to armchairs.

Leroy must have appreciated the silence. He lowered his voice and discussed Irish heraldry in whispers. For a man but half a year in Ireland he was incredibly familiar with the subject. This was only one of his interests. No clergyman died nor corncrake called but the newspaper was informed. Leroy P. Graf, Parson's School, Co. Offaly, was a familiar address to all concerned with rare birds or the Church of Ireland. His reasons for leaving the United States were not clear to many. There were sporadic rumours of military service, flat feet, defective vision. Leroy discouraged conversation on his life in the New World, mentioning only a certain Mr Stoole, his maternal grandfather, who had emigrated from Londonderry, about the turn of the century. Stoole had married late and had not lived to see his only daughter espouse a large Swede and give birth to Leroy.

'Goodbye!'

'Good news?' said Jack Leake. Dicky Corker looked up.

Mr Graf slammed the telephone a second time to make sure he had shaken off Dublin Castle. He approached the two older masters, blowing his nose with great care, stressing first the right nostril, then the left. 'Yes,' he said with some caution. 'I think I have them running. They tried to bluster and browbeat but I expect all that. The Chief Herald is obviously concealing something.' He smiled sideways and rubbed a thumb along a coarse lapel. 'I simply wish to impale the ancient Stoole coat of arms with my father's Graf coat of arms and . . .' he bent his head . . . 'include some words of Scripture. The Republic won't tolerate this apparently.' He was about to explain but, mercifully, the bell for classes then rang.

Little Jack Leake was thinking. His eyes were shut but his dry mouth moved with butterfly twitches of amusement. He was an unlikely friend for Mr Corker to have, different from him, apparently, in every way. He was short, Dicky was tall; he was baby-like in appearance but his pal had worldly-worn features. Mr Corker was sitting at a table in a hard wooden chair; Jack lay stretched in a mighty sofa. Along with Mr Graf they were the only resident bachelor masters; school had ended for the day and it was not yet time for prep. In the distance was the howl of boyish amusements.

Leroy sighed. He had changed his mind again about the motto suited to his family. Sheets of paper littered the table before himself and Mr Corker. Sketches of Bibles, swords and mailed fists were being examined.

'No. There's something about French mottoes I don't like.' Leroy was staring keenly at Mr Corker. 'There's a touch of frivolity . . .'

To help Leroy in his troubles Dicky had suggested a few slogans. At first attracted, now repelled, Leroy was impatiently fingering The Good Book.

'This is what I want. I feel it. Something –' he gave the word a sacred lisp, '– tells me it's what I need.'

In desperation Mr Corker took his pencil, sketched again the stool and the open Bible upon it. 'Why not have the motto on the open pages of the book? Like the crest in Oxford publications?'

The beauty of the idea did not immediately strike. Then Leroy described acres of bliss in the air and he bayed out thanks. 'Of course. Yes! Do you have a Latin edition of the Bible?' He asked this apologetically. 'It's not the sort of thing I like . . .' He patted the King James Version boldly.

'Perhaps this evening.' Mr Corker stood briskly. 'If you'd like to drop into my room, I could put Latin on whatever you chose.' Leroy arose with him, unbending his knees at equal pace. Then he put a hand on Dicky's arm. 'I appreciate this deeply, Mr Corker. I feel that in these times of loose morals and revolution and the defiance –' he lowered his head '– of God, we must stand firm on our tradition. You see what I'm getting at . . .'

Dicky nodded and waved his fingers hopelessly at the sun outside. 'I promised the boys I'd help them at cricket this afternoon. Mr Leake . . .' He looked around, saw with envy that Jack had slipped away and concluded '. . . has already gone down to the nets. The dandelions have arrived, too. Terrible.'

Leroy accepted the news stoically.

'It makes spin impossible. Next thing we know there'll be dock. And that's the end.' He edged by the wall towards the door. While Leroy grappled with this news and made remarks about the plagues of Egypt, he took off his gown, hung it carefully and hastened outside.

In a gown Jack was slight; without it and at night he was near invisible. As he stood under Mr Corker's window only the noise of his sniggering was perceptible. The scent of crushed wallflowers wafted about his snub nose. Rocking in wistaria two thrushes crooned themselves to sleep. It was after ten o'clock and the boys were in bed. Once as a boy while watching his father perform a funeral service, some old bicycle chain had been shovelled with the loose clay onto the coffin. Rev. Leake had been tickled by this and the service ended in a ghastly mixture of dirge and smothered giggles; little Jack had sloped away behind a mausoleum and very near vomited with laughter. Not until now had he been so amused. 'Ssh,' he said to himself. For he was withdrawing a starting-pistol from his pocket. He had found it in the games cupboard that afternoon and immediately realised its uses. It promised to be a magnificent joke, surpassing even the howl he had enjoyed that spring when Dicky had removed a wheel from the headmaster's motor car; then he had laughed so much that matron had to be summoned to give him sips of iced water.

He held four or five tiny shells in one fist and raised the pistol. 'I'm going to get you! Come out and die like a man! I'm gunning for you!' Poor man, he rarely stirred outside the walls of Parson's School except on business: twice a year he went to Dublin to buy raw linseed oil for the cricket bats; once a year he went on holidays to a Mayo rectory. His knowledge of the vulgar world was slight. 'Come out! Or I shoot!'

he bawled. Twice he fired the pistol. The report boomed on the walls and echoed about the warm garden. He roared, fired twice more and, hoarsely now, cried a last threat. 'By God, I'll kill you if it's the last thing I do.' All the birds were awake and were screeching. The pistol spat another tiny flame. Jack collapsed into a stream of laughter. He fired once more and ran to a little arbour where croquet mallets were stored. There he relieved himself fiercely and then galloped across the garden buttoning his trousers. All the lights were on now and boys were shouting excitedly. Jack did not delay. If he had he might have seen Dicky gaping out of his window. Leroy, however, had run into the corridor. In red slippers and dressing gown, Bible in hand, he drove his fist against the fire alarm and roared above the din.

'No surrender! Never. O Lord, Thou has smitten my enemy – Thou has broken the teeth of the ungodly!' It was his new motto.

'Howzatt!' Jack cried with vigour. Mr Corker replaced the off stump and grinned in his usual way.

Mr Leake was bowling a slow twister, Dicky was in the nets trying out a new bat. But light was slipping down slowly and still Leroy had not arrived.

'I'll try a few leg-breaks and finish then.' Jack rubbed the ball on his little bottom. He had removed most of his usual clothes. The shiny black waistcoat and jacket hung on the paling. His collar and tie were curled on the grass. Great white boots were visible at the ends of his trousers. He ran crabwise towards the popping crease. The ball slithered yards wide but somehow broke in behind Dicky's heel to dislodge a single bail.

'Oh. Beautiful!' Mr Corker wiped his eyes.

Modestly Jack drew stumps. 'It's that new dandelion spray. It brings up a lovely spin.' He walked towards his companion and helped him to remove the enormous and antique box he wore.

'A pity Leroy wasn't here to see it. Where on earth did he get to?'

Dicky looked a little irritable and said nothing. Mr Graf had promised to field balls that evening. Instead Mr Corker had to do all the running himself. His absence was certainly peculiar, for no keener cricketer now lived in all King's County. On one of his frequent visits to Belfast he had procured faultless white flannels. His bat was a model to the willow world, so Dicky had said. Something about the game, its stolid orthodoxy perhaps, had appealed to Leroy. He had read deeply on the subject and was an authority now on the rules. In recent weeks he had ploughed up and down the wicket, fielding balls and offering advice. True, his bowling was rather erratic and he was inclined to stand on the wrong side of the wicket: all minor points, Jack had assured him.

'I think it's shameful,' he said one evening as they returned from the nets. 'Really shameful the way this old game has been suppressed in the Republic. I could tell you things . . .' He had looked away from the bat as if it might conceal a microphone. 'Did you know that the IRA once dug up a crease in the Phoenix Park?' He made some more observations and cried 'We must stand firm on this!' Mr Leake, half asleep as usual after exercise, had murmured something about defensive batting.

'There aren't many of us left.' Leroy had gazed out at the red sun setting about his empire. 'I know what it means to be persecuted. I'm standing firm though.'

'And the thing to do then is stonewall. Stand right back on your crease, keep your left shoulder up.' Mr Leake had demonstrated what he meant: 'Head still, slide foot out to meet line of ball.'

It was still bright as the pair sat in the cool back room. It had been a hot evening; although it was early June both were perspiring. Jack sipped cider. Dicky sipped beer. In this alone their tastes differed. Both were rectors' sons. Together they had failed and re-sat their university examinations. Dicky had begun to teach immediately; after a short experiment with Divinity Jack had followed him. They had both been at Parson's School for a decade. It was small, elegant and very dull: they enjoyed it immensely.

'I simply cannot get over that dandelion spray,' said Mr Leake. He sipped an unusually large mouthful to show his surprise.

'If we sprayed it before next week's match we should be lucky.'

'That's the idea. You see, it doesn't give spin like an ordinary wet wicket. It's completely different. Even if we were batting first we'd have the advantage.'

They droned on and grew sleepier but merrier. They discussed holidays, past cricket, future cricket, the next year's work.

'Do you remember that year the corncrake nested at short square leg?' This caused great laughter and they drank a great deal more beer. The bird had been allowed to rear her brood, apparently, in the middle of the cricket field.

'But Percy! Do you remember how angry he used to be? HOW THE DEVIL CAN I CATCH A BALL WITH THAT CREATURE SQUAWKING?!'

They spluttered beer, cider, in laughter.

'If only Mr Graf had been here then!'

But Mr Graf at this moment, as Jack and Dicky unsteadily arose, was driving home through the warm dusk. He had not willingly missed the evening's cricket. Nothing but an interview with the Chief Herald himself could have prevented this. Leroy's patience was at its end. His motto from Psalms III had been rejected. He had offered an even pithier text from Revelation IV: this too had been dismissed. And now, that very evening, Dublin Castle had lied to his face, told him the Chief Herald was not there. He pushed his shoe deeper to the floor and the car sped down the main street of the village. For the first time since leaving the New World he was affected with nostalgia. Perhaps it was the sated chestnut trees hanging over the street which reminded him of the old home town. His memory filled with the scent of magnolia, the twang of preacher in pulpit, the whining noise of negroes at prayer and the reassuring thud of the good old hymns from Moody & Sankey.

'Hail cricket, manly British game!'

'Encore!' cried Jack.

Dicky stumbled slightly and continued to sing his rendering of James Love's little-known song. But he began to laugh and had to stop. As Jack bent to help him a car raced by. The colour was unmistakable.

'Leroy!' they both cried.

The car stopped further down the street. But Mr Graf had not paused for them. He hurried out and knocked on the door of the police barracks.

Sergeant MacGusty, less arthritic in the summer solstice, met him at the door. He was not surprised. At all hours Leroy visited him, discussing the peace, the state of the county, the latest reprisals of agrarian outrages. Unhappily married, both MacGusty and his wife had grown to love Leroy and they listened with awe as he drank their tea and told them of fresh atrocities.

'Jack!' wheezed Dicky. 'Let's do it again!' He lurched slightly, indeed imperceptibly, against his pal. Of course he had guessed soon after the starting-pistol prank just what had been done. But true friend, he had not squealed, not even when the headmaster and Mr Graf had put the whole school in detention.

'Bang!' squeaked Jack. His soft little face wrinkled up with tipsy glee.

But they had no gun.

'Oh damn!'

Dicky took a fountain pen from his pocket and shoving it inside his jacket barked, 'Stick 'em up!'

When they recovered from this joke they began to trot. Keeping under the trees the pair were soon out of the village. The school was on the outskirts, bounded by a high crumbling wall. There was a single entrance.

They hid, one by each gate-pier. The moon appeared, throwing the shadows of the ornamental pineapples fifty yards along the avenue. There was a halting splashing sound.

'Ssh.'

'Can't help it.' Leake was at it again. He relieved himself into the rhododendron and hurried back to shelter. They tied handkerchiefs about their mouths and turned their jackets up at the collars.

'Now!'

Leroy had not delayed long. He was tired and had stopped only to hear a summary of the day's events. A strange lorry had delivered something to the parish priest that afternoon: a serious but not conclusive piece of information.

'Halt!'

They ran, one to the bonnet, one to the boot. Neither was very steady on his legs but the car stopped. Dicky's accent was as bad as Jack's and carried slight conviction. 'Come on! Come on! This is a stick-up!'

Jack poked a Conway Stuart pen from within his shiny coat. 'Get out of the car!' Leroy turned pale and his jowls hung limp as he fumbled with the door handle.

'Quick! Quick! Come on, we mean business!'

But as the handle turned Jack began to titter. He stumbled backwards to cover the noise but fell spluttering to the ground. Dicky staggered to help him to his feet.

And that was quite enough for Leroy. He took his revolver from the dashboard and fired twice. Then he reversed. He did not pause to see if both were dead but sped down the dark scented road he had come on, back to the police station. Then he ran inside to alert Sergeant MacGusty.

WINDFALLS

MARY LELAND
Born in Cork, Mary Leland was a reporter with the *Cork Examiner* and later a Production Assistant in RTE. She is now a freelance journalist. She has published two novels and a collection of short stories, *The Little Galloway Girls*.

Every September there was this rush to save the best of the windfall apples. A brief gale would shower fruit not fully ripe but wearing patches of red against the dark green skin, tumbled and untidy among the vegetables, sometimes as far down the garden as the grass, where the children would squash them to sodden pulp as accidents in a game of football.

Some had to be cooked or eaten straight away. An apronful, gathered just because they were there in such bounty, would be tossed into the sink in the kitchen and enough peeled and stewed to last a week. A week of apple tarts, pancakes, flans, fritters, of stewed apples and custard, apples and muesli, apples to be eaten after chocolate for the school lunches. Ruth gave away as many as she could, always with the warning that they were just windfalls, to be used quickly, bruised fruit.

But even before picking the sturdier apples still on the branches, Ruth liked to select from the earthy litter those fruit worth keeping, the ones which with a little care might last so that the good fruit, soon to be stored in boxes in the loft, would not need to be disturbed quite so soon, but might even be left there until close to Christmas.

Ruth called this 'husbanding', a word of care and of comfort, and she loved the quiet hours it brought her in the loft, at the top of the garden, a still, warm, secret place, with a sharp dusty smell hinting at hidden corners. Of the children, Lottie was the one who liked it least. She was slow to like the dark, reluctant to pry, preferring the light to be switched on even though its weak illumination created more shadows than it dispelled.

Yet it was Lottie who had sought Ruth here, this long Sunday afternoon, and together in the companionable quiet they made beds for the apples, patting the straw in layers between the fruit, putting aside the damaged ones and throwing them instead into a plastic bag from which there would later be a further sorting.

As her hands worked among the harsh green or mottled yellow
skins, Lottie's little face was still. The calm of the loft, the peace of
the afternoon, made her voice quiet too, quiet and oddly careful. 'You
know, Mum,' she said, not asking a question, 'you know when Daddy
comes to take us out, you could come with us.'

Seeing Ruth's mouth open in protest, she went on, in a hurry to
get it said. 'I think that if you could come with us you would see that
me and Des, we don't fight at all now. And if you were with us, with
Daddy and Des and me, you would be able to learn not to fight with
Daddy either, wouldn't you?'

Silent, Ruth could only think again that she had not given a good
enough explanation. What *was* a good enough explanation? She had
tried to foresee the questions which would be asked, but in giving
simple reasons she had not thought about the simple response. She
certainly had not expected the sustained, although gentle, siege
against the separation which had been Lottie's reaction. Lottie's love
was not something that could be selective. Even now, as she divided
the windfalls, she mourned those which could not be saved for storing,
which would not be left nestling in the winter straw.

In this silence Lottie told her mother of the way in which she and
Des were learning to get along together, abandoning the bickering,
avoiding the teasing which started out as determined fun but ended
in yells and tears and shrieking slaps – these from Ruth, whose usually
sturdy emotional balance would be pitched to blazes by their resound-
ing squalls.

Yesterday both children had walked together down to Confession
in the village church, and on their way back had spent their pocket
money in the shop. Travelling slowly home again they talked without
fighting, and Lottie did not add what Ruth knew must have been the
case, that they had been munching all the way up. Both brother and
sister were still at the age where sweets soothed every quarrel and
distracted every consciousness of pain.

Sweets would be no good here. A quiver of despair hung over
Ruth's mind for a second. There was no nice way out of this, pallid
lies were not good enough for Lottie any more, if they ever had been.
Ruth hadn't tried to lie to either of them, she had tried to reduce the
element of fatalism, or of tragedy, or what might seem to them – what
she was terrified would actually be to them – tragedy in their own
stark terms.

She couldn't let the child go on like this, plotting, bravely planning
for other people's lives, perhaps consoling Des with little scenarios in

which Lottie would try to talk both parents back into living together. It wasn't that Des had been terribly distressed by what had happened, but he was puzzled. He was inclined to accept that adults knew best for themselves, if not always for him. But because he saw his father for hours at a time and perhaps twice in the week, he was not bereft. He was anxious, worried that his father was all right, and firm in his belief that things would turn out for the best for all of them, if only he knew that the best wouldn't cost him too much. But Lottie hungered for the heart in things; there were no distances for her, she understood loneliness, at eight years old she knew it when she saw it.

Ruth wondered how much she had not seen of what her children were feeling, or fearing. She began, now, with cautious consolation. 'Look, Lottie, I know how much you love your Daddy. No one wants that to change. And that doesn't mean that you can't love me – I know you love me, of course I know that. All Daddy wants, all *I* want from you, is that feeling, that you love both of us. But, Lottie, I have to tell you this one thing.'

When she stopped, the child looked gravely up at her. Ruth crumpled a wisp of straw in her hand, and held it out to the two small hands which had put, so carefully, another unmarked apple into its nest. The small fingers curled around fruit and straw, and the small face waited for the message which was to have no hope.

Ruth moved closer, her earnestness like a bridge between them. 'Look, my love, this is hard for you to understand. Some things *are* hard. But I must tell you this: you, Daddy and I will not be living together again. Not ever, never any more. You must stop trying for us. There is *nothing to try for!*' The fierce words clung to the dust around the two of them.

In Lottie's hands the apple glowed in scarlet streaks through the straw. With Ruth's words heavy on the air, she began to weep, the slow tears overrunning her eyes, down the soft white cheeks so pale in the gloom. But for her hand stroking the heavy globe of fruit, she did not move.

The hot rush of her own rare tears dimmed Ruth's view of the old chair in the corner, into which she huddled with the child crushed in her arms. 'Don't be sad, my little love, it will be all right, don't be lonely for him, don't be frightened, he knows all about it, he knows you love him . . .' her words groaned through the dimness. What had she done? She had never pretended that the separation was without sadness or without loss. The anger they had known about – all she had tried to do was soften it. Had she been wrong to try to put a layer of love, like straw around the apples, between the children and the bruising corners of their parents' disaster?

She let the sobs run down in their own time, talking, saying the same words over and over again, trying now to build up another kind of hope for Lottie and for Des. Ruth's own hope, in saying to the child that it would all come right, was not so much for that to happen in the way they wanted, but that they might never be inclined to guess in the future how much different it could all have been. A wild plea to be allowed cry longer throbbed in her throat as she set the child down, but she knew she couldn't do that, that her own losses had to be set against theirs, that her grief could not be slipped from her shoulders onto the bones of the children.

Together they worked again until they were finished and the garden outside was dark. The dog ran ahead of them to warn the shadows on the path, and from the windows of the house uneven beams slanted across the grass, sending their consolation of home, the place for them to be.

Later, when the children were in their separate beds and after all at peace, Ruth realised how impossible an understanding she had expected from them. How could they have accepted a story which held so much pain, uneasy suffering, such an interruption in their lives, but which was a story without a villain, with no-one to blame?

They needed someone to blame. But she had tried to protect the children's love; now she wondered if there had been no need to protect it, if maybe once they knew where the big blame lay they would still love their father just as much as before they knew this truth. The thought grew into a certainty, they would forgive him, even if they thought in such terms as there being anything to forgive.

As she moved through the rooms, tidying up, preparing the breakfast, the school sacks, the lunches, Ruth felt the weight of their lives in the sleeping house, her burden. She asked herself if they had ever recognised that in some new irrevocable way they were hers, for years to come. With the question came another: as certain as she was that these two would always love their father, would they love her, who most certainly had not forgiven?

Before she went to bed she took her customary stealthy peep into the rooms where the children lay asleep. The tide of her thoughts still lapped against the promontories of her talk with Lottie, and she was not surprised when she found the child not in her own bed, but asleep with Des. The children lay together for comfort, close but not touching, like the windfalls too easily bruised.

THE BREAK

BERNARD MacLAVERTY
Bernard MacLaverty was born in Belfast, 1942. A graduate of Queen's University, he now lives and writes full-time in Glasgow. He has written two novels which became highly successful films, and three volumes of short stories, *Secrets*, *A Time To Dance* and *The Great Profundo*.

The cardinal sat at his large walnut desk speaking slowly and distinctly. When he came to the end of a phrase he pressed the off-switch on the microphone and thought about what to say next as he stared in front of him. On the wall above the desk was an ikon he had bought in Thessaloniki – he afterwards discovered that he had paid too much for it. It had been hanging for some months before he noticed, his attention focused by a moment of rare idleness, that Christ had a woodworm hole in the pupil of his left eye. It was inconspicuous by its position, and rather than detracting from the impact, he felt the ikon was enhanced by the authenticity of this small defect. He set the microphone on the desk, pushed his fingers up into his white hair and remained like that for some time.

'New paragraph,' he said, picking up the microphone and switching it on with his thumb. 'Christians are sometimes accused of not being people of compassion – that the Rule is more important than the good which results from it.'

The phone rang on the desk making him jump. He switched off the recorder.

'Yes?'

'Eminence, your father's just arrived. Can you see him?'

'Well, can I?'

'You're free until the Ecumenical delegation at half four.'

'I think I need a break. Will you show him up to my sitting-room?' He made the sign of the cross and prayed, his hands joined, his index fingers pressed to his lips. At the end of his prayer he blessed himself again and stood up, stretching and flexing his aching back. He straightened his tossed hair in the mirror, flattening it with his hands, and went into the adjoining room to see if his father had managed the stairs.

The room was empty. He walked to the large bay window and looked down at the film of snow which had fallen the previous night.

A black irregular track had been melted up to the front door by people coming and going but the grass of the lawns was uniformly white. The tree trunks at the far side of the garden were half black, half white where the snow had shadowed them. The wind, he noticed, had been from the north. He shuddered at the scene, felt the cold radiate from the window panes and moved back into the room to brighten up the fire. With a smile he thought it would be nice to have the old man's stout ready for him. It poured well, almost too well, with a high mushroom-coloured head. He left the bottle with some still in it, beside the glass on the mantelpiece, and stood with his back to the fire, his hands extended behind him.

When he heard a one-knuckle knock he knew it was him.

'Come in,' he called. His father pushed the door open and peered round it. Seeing the cardinal alone he smiled.

'And how's his Eminence today?'

'Daddy, it's good to see you.'

The old man joined him at the fireplace and stood in the same position. He was much smaller than his son, reaching only to his shoulder. His clothes hung on him, most obviously at the neck where his buttoned shirt and knotted tie were loose as a horse-collar. The waistband of his trousers reached almost to his chest.

The old man said, 'That north wind is cold no matter what direction it's blowing from.' The cardinal smiled. That joke was no longer funny but the old man's persistence in using it was.

'Look, I have your stout already poured for you.'

'Oh that's powerful, powerful altogether.'

The old man sat down in the armchair rubbing his hands to warm them and the cardinal passed him the stout.

'Those stairs get worse every time I climb them. Why don't you top-brass clergy live in ordinary houses?'

'It's one of the drawbacks of the job. Have you put on a little weight since the last time?'

'No, no. I'll soon not be able to sink in the bath.'

'Are you taking the stout every day?'

'Just let anyone try and stop me.'

'What about food?'

'As much as ever. But still the weight drops off. I tell you, Frank, I'll not be around for too long.'

'Nonsense. You've another ten or twenty years in you.'

The old man looked at him without smiling. There was a considerable pause.

'You know and I know that that's not true. I feel it in my bones. Sit down, son, don't loom.'

'Have you been to see the doctor again?' The cardinal sat opposite him, plucking up the front of his soutane.

'No.' The old man took a drink from his glass and wiped away the slight moustache it left with the back of his hand. 'That's in good order, that stout.'

The cardinal smiled. 'One of the advantages of the job. When I order something from the town, people tend to send me the best.'

He thought his father seemed jumpy. The old man searched for things in his pockets but brought out nothing. He fidgeted in the chair, crossing and recrossing his legs.

'How did you get in today?' asked the cardinal.

'John dropped me off. He had to get some phosphate.'

'What's it like in the hills?'

'Deeper than here, I can tell you that.'

'Did you lose any?'

'It's too soon to tell, but I don't think so. They're hardy boyos, the blackface. I've seen them carrying six inches of snow on their backs all day. It's powerful the way they keep the heat in.' The old man fidgeted in his pockets again.

'Why will you not go back to the doctor?'

The old man snorted. 'He'd probably put me off the drink as well.'

'Cigarettes are bad for you, everybody knows that. It's been proved beyond any doubt.'

'I'm off them nearly six months now and I've my nails ate to the elbow. Especially with a bottle of stout. I don't know what to do with my hands.'

'Do you not feel any better for it?'

'Damn the bit. I still cough.' The old man sipped his Guinness and topped up his glass from the remainder in the bottle. The cardinal stared over his head at the fading light of the grey sky. He could well do without this Ecumenical delegation. Of late he was not sleeping well, with the result that he tended to feel tired during the day. At meetings his eyelids were like lead and he daren't close them because if he did the quiet rise and fall of voices and the unreasonable temperature at which they kept the rooms would lull him to sleep. It had happened twice, only for seconds, when he found himself jerking awake with a kind of snort and looking around to see if anyone had noticed. This afternoon he would much prefer to take to his bed and that was not like him. He should go and see a doctor himself, even though he knew no one could prescribe for weariness. He looked at his father's yellowed face. Several times the old man opened his mouth to speak but said nothing. He was sitting with his fingers threaded through each other, the backs of his hands resting on his thighs. The cardinal was aware that it was exactly how he himself sometimes sat. People said they were the spit of each other. He remembered as a small child the clenched hands of his father as he played a game with him. 'Here is the church, here is the steeple.' The thumbs parted, the hands turned over and the interlaced fingers waggled up at him. 'Open the doors and here are the people.' Now his father's hands lay as if the game was finished but they had not the energy to separate from each other. At last the old man broke the silence.

'I'm trying to put everything in order at home. You know – for the big day.' He smiled. 'I was going through all the papers and stuff I'd gathered over the years.' He pulled out a pair of glasses from his top pocket with pale flesh-coloured frames. The cardinal knew they were his mother's, plundered from her bits and pieces after she died.

'Why don't you get yourself a proper pair of glasses?'

'My sight is perfectly good – it's just that there's not much of it. I found this.' His father fumbled into his inside pocket and pulled out two sheets of paper. He hooked the legs of the spectacles behind his ears, briefly inspected the sheets and handed one to his son.

'Do you remember that?'

The cardinal saw his own neat handwriting from some thirty years ago. The letter was addressed to his mother and father from Rome. It was an ordinary enough letter which tried to describe his new study-bedroom – the dark-brightness of the room in the midday sun when the green shutters were closed. The letter turned to nostalgia and expressed a longing to be back on the farm in the hills. The cardinal looked up at his father.

'I don't recall writing this. I remember the room but not the letter.' His father stretched and handed him the second sheet.

'It was in the same envelope as this one.'

The cardinal unfolded the page from its creases.

Dear Daddy,
    Don't read this letter out. It is for you alone. I enclose another 'ordinary letter' for you to show Mammy because she will expect to see what I have said.
    I write to you because I want you to break it gradually to her

that I am not for the priesthood. It would be awful for her if I just
arrived through the door and said that I wasn't up to it. But that's
the truth of it.

These past two months I have prayed my knees numb asking for
guidance. I have black rings under my eyes from lack of sleep. To
have gone so far – five years of study and prayer – and still to be
unsure. I believe now that I can serve God in a better way, a
different way from the priesthood.

I know how much it means to her. Please be gentle in preparing
her.

'Yes, I remember this one.'

'I thought you might like to have it.'

'Yes thank you, I would.' The cardinal let the letter fall back into
its original folds and set it on the occasional table beside him.

'And did you prepare her?'

'Yes. Until I got your next letter.'

'What did she say?'

'She thought it was just me – doubting Thomas she called me.'

'It was a bad time. Every time I smell garlic I remember it.' He
knelt to poke the fire. 'Another bottle of stout?'

'It's so good I won't refuse you.' His father finished what was left
in the glass. The cardinal poured a new one and set it by the chair.
The old man stared vacantly at the far wall and the cardinal looked
out of the bay window. The sky was dark and heavy with snow. It
was just starting to fall again, large flakes floating down and curving
up when they came near to the glass.

'You'd better not leave it too late going home,' he said. The old
man opened his mouth to speak but stopped.

'What's wrong?'

'Nothing.' His father knuckled his left eye. 'Except . . .'

'Except what?'

'I suppose I showed that letter to you . . . for a purpose.'

'As if I didn't know.'

'I want to make a confession.' Seeing his son raise an eyebrow the
old man smiled. 'Not that kind of confession. A real one. And it's very
hard to say it.' The cardinal sat down.

'Well?'

The old man smiled a smile that stopped in the middle. Then he put
his head back to rest it on the white linen chair-back.

'I've lost the faith,' he said. The cardinal was silent. The snow kept up an irregular ticking at the window pane. 'I don't believe that there is a God.'

'Sorry, I'm not with you. Is it that . . . ?'

'Don't stop me. I've gone over this in my head for months now.' The cardinal nodded silently. 'I want to say it once and for all – and only to you. I have not believed for twenty-five years. But what could I do? A son who was looked up to by everyone around him – climbing through the ranks of the Church like nobody's business – the youngest-ever cardinal. How could I stop going to Mass, to the sacraments? How could I? I never told your mother because it would have killed her long before her time.'

'God rest her.'

'Frank, there is no God. Religion is a marvellous institution, full of great, good people – but it's founded on a lie. Not a deliberate lie – a mistake.'

'You're wrong. I *know* that God exists. Apart from what I feel in here,' the cardinal pointed to his chest, 'there are convincing proofs.'

'Proofs are no good for God. That's Euclid.' The old man was no longer looking at his son but staring obliquely down at the fire. 'I know in my bones that I'll not be around too long, Frank. I had to tell somebody because I would be a hypocrite if I took it to the grave with me. I am telling you because we're . . . because I . . . admire you.' The cardinal shook his head and looked down at his knees.

'Do you know what the amazing thing is?' said his father. 'I don't miss Him. You'd think that somebody who'd been reared like me would be lost. You know – the way they taught you to talk to Jesus as a friend – the way you felt you were being looked after – the way you were told it was the be-all and the end-all, and for that suddenly to stop and me not even miss it. That was a shock. I'll tell you this, Frank, when your mother died I missed her a thousand times more.'

'Yes, I'm sure you did.'

'To tell the God's honest truth I miss the cigarettes more.'

The cardinal smiled weakly. 'If this was a public debate . . .' He seemed to sag in his chair. His shoulders went down and his hands lay in his lap, palm upwards. The snow was getting heavier and finer and was hissing at the window. The old man looked over his shoulder at the fading light.

'I'd better think of going. I wonder where John's got to?'

'Did he say he'd pick you up here?'

'Yes.' The old man looked his son straight in the eye. 'I'm sorry,' he said, 'but I wanted to be honest with you because . . .' he looked into his empty glass, 'because I . . .'

'You can stay the night and we can talk.'

'There's not much more to be said.' The old man got up and stood at the window looking down. He looked so frail that his son imagined he could see through him. He remembered him at the celebration after his ordination in a hotel in Rome banging the table with a soup-spoon for order and then making a speech about having two sons, one who looked after the body's needs and the other who looked after the soul's. When he had finished, as always at functions, he sang 'She Moved thro' the Fair'. The old man looked at his watch.

'Where is he?' He put his hands in his jacket pockets, leaving his thumbs outside, and paced the alcove of the bay window.

'If I may stand Pascal's Wager on its head,' said the cardinal, 'if you do not believe and are as genuinely good a man as you are, then God will accept you. You will have won through even though you bet wrongly.'

The old man shrugged his shoulders without turning. 'The way I feel that's neither here nor there. But this talk has done me good. I hope it hasn't hurt you too much.'

'It must have been a great burden for you. Now you have just given it to me.' Seeing the concern in his father's face he added, 'But at least I have God to help me bear it. I will pray for you always.'

'It's not as black as I paint it. Over the years there was a kind of contentment. I had lost one thing but gained another. It concentrates the mind wonderfully knowing that this is all we can expect. A glass of stout tastes even better.' The old man took one hand out of his pocket and shaded his eyes, peering out into the snow. 'Ah there he is now. It must be bad, he has the headlights on.'

'Does John know all this?'

'No. You are the only one. But please don't worry. I'll continue as I've done up till now. I'll go to mass, receive the sacraments. It's hard to teach an old dog new tricks.'

'That's the farthest thing from my mind.'

The old man turned and came across the room. The cardinal still sat, his hands open. His father took him by the right hand and leaned down and kissed him with his lips on the cheekbone. The hand was light and dry as polystyrene, the lips like paper.

The cardinal had not cried since the death of his mother and even then he had waited until he was alone but now he could not stop the tears rising.

'I will see you again soon,' said his father. Then, noticing his son's brimming eyes, he said, 'Frank, if I'd known that I wouldn't have told you.'

'It's not because of that,' said the cardinal. 'Not that at all.'

After he had seen his father to the door and had a few words with his brother – mostly about the need for them to get home quickly before the roads became impassable – the cardinal went back to his office. He sat for a long time with his elbows on the desk and his head in his hands. He blessed himself slowly as if his right arm was weighted and said his prayer-before-work. He picked up the microphone and spoke.

'The Church has a public and a private face. The Church of Authority and the Church of Compassion, the Church of Rules and the Church of Forgiveness. What the public face lacks is empathy. This was not so with Jesus. We who are within the Church must strive to narrow the gap that exists between . . . them. We know that . . .' His voice trailed away and he switched off the microphone. Then, with an effort that made him groan, he slid from the chair to kneel on the floor. The cushioned Rexine of the chair-seat hissed slowly back to its original shape. He joined his hands in prayer so that the knuckles formed a platform for his chin. When the words would not come he lowered his hands, and his interlocked fingers were ready to waggle up at him as in the childish game. He parted his hands and laid them flat on the chair.

In the car with John the old man sat forward in his seat watching the brightness of the snow slanting in the headlights.

'Did you do what you had to do?' he asked.

'Aye – it's all in the back,' said John. 'What do I smell?'

'Stout.'

'The odour of sanctity.'

The windscreen wipers, on intermittent, purred and slapped. In front of them the road was white except for two yellow-dark ruts.

'That snow's thick.'

'It'll get worse as we climb,' said John.

'Just follow the tracks of the boyo that's gone before and we'll be all right.'

From then on there was silence as John drove slowly and with great care up into the mountains.

THE ATHEIST

SEÁN MacMATHÚNA

Séan MacMathúna was born in Tralee, Co. Kerry, 1936. A graduate
of University College, Cork, he writes both in Irish and English. His
first collection of short stories, widely acclaimed, was in the former
language, and he followed it in 1987 with his only English-language
collection, *The Atheist*.

The day after she was buried the cork blew off her elderberry wine. It was only then he knew she was dead and that he would never see her again. The bird had not flown. She hadn't even been snatched. She had been torn through the bars of the cage, leaving some blood and a fine down lingering in the air. It was this fine down that drifted through his mind now, eternally heavy, deathlessly cold. He stood in a bay window somewhere on planet earth, which was but a stone twirling in the sunbeams, and he wanted to shout out her name loud enough for it to ring out for all time, he wanted the whole universe to know how much he wanted her. But he didn't. For he knew he might as well talk to a rocking horse. He watched the curtains being sucked out into the garden by the gale. He looked up at the sky. Nothing except cloud chasing cloud, and somewhere above them the moon and all the stars. All dead. There were no other worlds. There were no more dimensions. There was merely what is. No could be's, should be's, might be's, maybe's. Just the reality of the indicative, and the nightmare of subjunctives. There was merely Time and if you were in it, you were of it. And at any given time there was only one micro second and we were all, all five billion of us, biting on it together. And as we bit, each one of us journeyed towards our eternity and the road flying from under us.

He cursed intelligence, culture, education and insight. These things had deprived him of the comfort of a God, and the solace of a happy eternity united with loved ones. But in a way he was proud that he felt like this, for such loneliness was dearly bought and paid for in Ireland. She would have felt the same if it had been he who had died, for she too was a lonely disbeliever.

He had envied the others at the graveside, the weeping relatives and friends, as the sods thumped down on her coffin. Their show of emotion went with their religion. He remained erect, whitefaced, and fierce throughout it all. Dry-eyed atheism. If she could hear he would beg her forgiveness for the awful funeral and tell her that it wasn't his fault. They, that is both his and her relatives, wouldn't hear of cremation. Her brothers would attack him. It was taken out of his hands and was a traditional funeral: priests, splashing of holy water, full requiem mass. Some woman sang *Lacrimosa Dies Illa*, she would have liked that. But the rest of it was sordid, and the display of religiosity and piety especially from her side of the family was sickening. How had so fine a mind as hers escaped from that dunghill called the extended family? Yes, forgive him all the bowing and scraping. For the last few days he was as a man tumbling through another's dream. But what was the point in talking to her, for he knew that a few seconds after the head-on collision on the Killshaskin Road the billion, billion cells of information that was Emer de Brún, flickered out one by one, all the poetry, laughter, plans, music, memories of her father, taste of blackberries, smell of fuchsia in the Gaeltacht, joy of dawn, the know-how for making plum puddings stay alight, the feeling of cool windowpanes with the rain streaming on the outside, the warmth of a kiss from the man she loved – all gone. And he had paid the priest. It was ironic that the only contact she ever had with priests since she became an independent teenager was at her death. Fr O'Herlihy had gently suggested that now he might reconsider his ways and start coming to church. He gave him a most emphatic no. As she would have done. It was a bitter cross to carry – to carry in Ireland – the cross of Godlessness. But carry it he would through dungeon, fire and sword.

Suddenly the movement in the scullery brought him back to reality. The symphony of rattles, scrapings, and poundings that was titled 'Life must go on' carried all over the house. Then silence. Then the footsteps of Julia, her mother, slow and heavy up the hallway, then the pause, then the rattle, the knob and the creak of the door. He didn't turn but he felt eyes peering at him, as if someone had parted the curtains in another world and gazed at the miracle of a man standing alone at his bay window.

'You can't go on like this.' The voice was taut but quiet, telling of the effort of resignation. 'You'll have to eat, even a little.'

He didn't turn, nor did he reply. He felt totally indifferent to her and to his own bad manners. She coughed, then paused before saying: 'If you don't eat we'll be running another body into the ground. 'Tis what she would have liked – that you should eat something, even a small bit.' She was only here a few days, he thought, and already she knew that to mention her was the way to get him to act. He teetered for a moment, then sighed and turned and said almost inaudibly: 'Whatever you say.' They went to the kitchen. The meal she had prepared was prawn provencale. It had always been their favourite meal together. Now, to eat it without her seemed thoughtless. He would have preferred something more neutral like a hamburger. He ate a forkful and nibbled at a piece of bread. She sat opposite him and watched him eat. Then as if she felt it was the right time she said quietly: 'I know how you feel about the mass cards. It is a pity, but that's the way it is. Remember it's love and sorrow that makes people go to pay a priest for a mass card. You'll have to read them, there are 54 in all. They are mostly from people who couldn't attend the funeral. They will have to be answered. I've a list of the people who sent wreaths. They must all be acknowledged.' He went on chewing. He found himself wondering why they had been so attracted to each other. It had, he thought, been their agreement on so many things. That and her face. It was full of sensuality and energy, very impressive. She had been a rebel. God had been one of the early casualties. They had spent many of their first meetings sharing their hatred of Irish Catholicism. They had a huge long litany which was almost inexhaustable: scapulars, rosaries, confessions, communions, indulgences, prohibitions, aspirations, sins, masses, bowings, bells, candles, scrapings, *mea culpas, mea maxima culpas,* mortal sins, hell, priests, nuns, holy hours, processions, shamrocks, holy wells, churchings, god boxes, three Hail Marys for Holy purity, the rhythm method, etcetera. Where religion had come from had engaged endless hours of speculation. He always quoted the chapter and verse of atheism: it was fear that first made gods in the world, and the religion that followed was nothing but submission to mystery. It was the sum of scruples that impeded the free exercise of our faculties. She always gave as an example the belief in the west of Ireland about acne. If you had acne watch for a falling star. As the star fell wipe your face. All eruptions would vanish. If they didn't it was because you were not quick enough.

Julia's voice came from another world. 'Flanagan is cutting a stone, it will be black pearl granite. It's dear but it's the least we can do for the girl. I didn't like the limestone. Flanagan has a machine in from America that can cut a picture of the crucifixion on the granite, all on its own, for an extra hundred pounds. It would have taken an old stonemason a month to do it and he wouldn't do it half as good.' He stopped chewing and looked at her. Her eyes were polished from recent crying. Any minute she could start again. She was brave and it had been her only daughter. He leaned towards her and said gently but firmly: 'No crucifixions, no crosses, just her name: Emer de Brún, 1953–1985 and the words:

> *Sunset and evening star,*
> *And one clear call for me!*
> *And may there be no moaning of the bar,*
> *When I put out to sea.'*

She looked down at the ground and fought off the tears. 'What in the honour of God does that mean? What bar? Whose bar?'

He told her they were favourite lines of Emer's from Tennyson.

'And who around here is going to know that for God's sake?'

'I will and that's enough,' he said.

She got up from the table and busied herself about the sink. Idleness she knew brought the wrong kind of emotion. He felt that there was quite a lot of unnecessary splashing. She stopped and looked out into the garden above the counter.

'It was a shameful thing that both of you never darkened the door of a church.'

'What would we go in for?'

'To pray for your immortal souls of course.'

'We might as well play hornpipes to a couple of signposts.'

'It was a mistake not to. She knows it now.'

'How dare you say that about her. How dare you,' he shouted in anger. Terrifying images from his childhood suddenly erupted in his mind. The face of a cruel God with a curling lip saying to the soul of a sinner a few seconds after death: 'Depart from me you cursed, into the everlasting flames of hell.' He could protect her while on earth but he was helpless against a divine maniac, a hell packer.

'You shouldn't talk like that about her, she never harmed a hair of anyone's head.'

But the woman was not to be intimidated.

'I'll say what I like about her. It was I who brought her into the light of day, nursed her, loved her, spoiled her. She is as much mine as yours. But she belongs to neither now. She is God's. What'll she say to Him when He asks her why she never even baptised that poor child up in the bed?'

She splashed more water around defiantly. He just stopped himself in time from telling her to leave. But what was the point of a religious argument. It was the same all over Ireland. Men without hope for the good things of this world clung to the promise of the next. Superstition was part of their quotidian. And each day as Ireland grew poorer the beasts of Lough Derg slithered eastward more and more. It was his duty as a member of the minute educated classes to raise the standards of reason and to clash with the forces of evil. But Julia saw some advantage in his failure to reply and she pressed it.

'And no first communion. The day that every child in the parish is leppin' with joy you took the child to the Zoo in Dublin. She'll answer to the Lord for that I'll tell you. Monkeys instead of the grace of God.'

He leaped up from the table.

'Enough is enough. That's it. I'm going to ask you to leave this house now Julia – this minute.'

She looked suddenly crushed and she sat down at the table.

'Yes, yes,' she gulped as she fought back the tears, 'I want to leave too. But I can't.' She looked about the kitchen. 'It's this place, her cups, her saucers, it's all I've got that reminds me of her. And all her clothes in the wardrobe.' She pulled a handkerchief out of her sleeve and dabbed her eyes. 'My advice to you is to get rid of all her clothes – anything that reminds you of her that you don't need. Give them to the poor.'

'Certainly not,' he said. 'I like being reminded of her.'

'You should heed what the old people say about these things. Get rid of her clothes, shoes, perfume, otherwise they'll drive you mad. The old people have wisdom as old as the fields.'

He began to understand Julia better each time she opened her mouth. She wasn't a person anymore, just a mobile parish-lore unit that consulted the *is* of the moment with the *should* of local tradition and matched them up willy-nilly.

'Everything stays as it is.'

'Have it your own way then.'

'I will.' He would just, especially the light blue frock with the Helen-of-Troy sleeves that revealed chinks of skin made golden in the Mediterranean sun. Suddenly she was splashing again; that meant she was about to have another go at him.

'You're going to have to think about what you're going to do. I mean you and the child.'

He detested the peasant way of referring to a young boy as a boy but a young girl as a child, even though she was seven. It offended.

'We'll manage quite well thank you,' he said.

'Well, I'm sorry but you're not managing too well at the moment. The child is out of her mind with loneliness.'

'We'll both have to get over it.'

'It's not going to be easy for her. She needs a woman.'

He glanced across at her sharply. 'Meaning?' he said testily.

She grabbed a tea towel and wrapped it round her wet fingers. 'Would you not think of letting the child back to Ballinamawnach with me for a few months. She will get the care and loving attention of six women. It would be good for her. Women need women in times like this. A man is no good.' There was pleading in her voice.

He looked at her for a long time just to make sure she was serious. Such an act would be to condemn the girl to the world of the pishogue, magic, the attitudes of the culturally deprived, hobgoblins, a world of enslavement for women, a world of slyness and rascally brutality for men. 'No!' He said firmly. 'We will adjust in good time. Róisín has the resources of her mother. She is intelligent and adaptable.'

'She is only seven years old. She wouldn't even know the meaning of these words. Give her at least a month in Ballinamawnach.'

Yes, and she'd come back with miraculous medals sewn into her clothes. It would be like 'taking the soup' in reverse. He arose from the table and thanked her for the meal. He said he was going up to tell Róisín her usual story. Julia reminded him that she was in his bed, refusing to go into her own. Then she turned back to the dishes.

It was a four-poster that had gone for a bargain at the auction of furniture of the last of the Bingham-Woods at Killscorna House. He peeped at her from the doorway, clutching her teddy fiercely, white-faced and so alone in the big expanse of bed. Her eyes were large and puzzled. It occurred to him that he had hardly seen her in the past few days – since the trouble – she was still in shock. He pushed open the door and beamed at her as he moved up to the bed. 'Hi, honey,' he said, 'come into my heart and pick sugar. Any kiss for Dally?' He leaned over and pecked her on the cheek.

'Hallo, Dally,' she said without a trace of warmth. She clutched her teddy all the more and he thought he noticed an imperceptible move away from him into the pillows. He searched his mind for the small talk that is the essential currency of getting through to children. He was always uneasy when alone in her presence, never having mastered the subtlety of the child's imagination.

'You look lovely in your pyjamas, you know that, just lovely. Do you remember where you got them first?' Suddenly he realised his mistake. Emer had pounced on the psychedelic floral pattern in Sacramento last summer. It had been a sunny carnival of McDonalds, Disneyland, the ice-cream parlours. Now, damn, he had done it as he watched her eyes cloud over and then precipitate into a mist of tears.

'Where is Mommy? I want Mommy, what have they done with her? They said she's sick. I'm afraid Dally – I want her.'

He almost reeled. He looked open-mouthed at the hurt innocence of her eyes. Jesus Christ in heaven, had nobody told the child her mother was dead. Now what am I going to do? He walked to the window to think as fast as he could but all he could think of was how swift the night approached from Cloon Wood. It was late autumn. The house shivered. He walked back to the bed and looked down at the quietly weeping child. She was the sole issue of atheists. And atheism was merely to bite the bitter truth. Out, out, hobgoblins! He cleared his throat. 'Róisín, pet, Mommy is no longer with us.'

The child tried to focus on his face, tried to wring meaning out of his words but failed. 'What do you mean? What do you mean?' she whispered aghast. 'I want Mommy to tuck me in.' She almost wailed the last words.

He gulped and looked around the room. He knew it was brutal. But children had to have teeth pulled, the quicker the better.

'You remember Shaska, the dog?'

There was the faintest flicker of recognition. 'Yes, Shaska was a nice dog.'

'That's right, he was a nice dog, but he died, and we buried him in the garden, in the ground. Shaska is no longer with us.' He waited for that to sink in. He was sure it wasn't too obtuse. The child hugged her teddy all the more fiercely and backed farther into the large pillows, away from him.

'Is Mommy under the ground?' She looked at him as if he were a ghost. She was a bright child, he thought, she got the message, thank God for that.

'Yes,' he said simply.

'Will I ever see her again?'

He paused as he mastered all his strength. 'No,' then quietly, 'never again.'

She looked up slowly at him, her tears gone, with an open uncomprehending expression on her face. It was at this precise moment that he saw for the first time the resemblance between her and her mother. Emer had sort of looked like that at times, such as when he tried to explain to her how he made bridges that wouldn't fall down.

'Why never again? What did I do?' She cried again quietly: 'What did I do wrong? Why won't you let me see her Dally, please Dally, just once?'

He needed his wife badly now, even more than the child. What would he say? Words were summoned to his lips, each more useless than the next. Words from a brave world. Words from the world of storm-trooping humanity. But the world of a seven-year-old was equally valid.

'Róisín, little apple, Dally is going to look after you. We are alone but we are together – we're going to be happy.'

'Mommy,' the child said dumbly. 'Just Mommy, I don't want you, Dally.'

'It's going to be all right, Cherry. I'm going to look after you.' He picked her out of the pillows and put his arms around her, hugging her tightly. She began to wail for her mother all the more, her body bundled into tautness. Then the wail turned to sobs which made her body convulse in his embrace. He became frightened. He had never seen her like this before. The sobs became gasps. He thought she was having a fit. He ran for the door, opened it, and shouted: 'Julia!' But she was there outside the door, waiting. She took her from him. He noticed how the child relaxed and clung to her granny.

'I told you she needed women. Now go and take a walk and leave her to me.'

He moved downstairs and out into the garden. He was shaken by this first encounter with his daughter. It made him feel helpless. He wondered if he was about to become a wreck. Without Emer would he revert to irresponsible bachelor drinking with the boys and going to discos. He shuddered. His memory of those days was a mindless *carpe diem* of pints of stout and sexual exploits. He looked about the garden. It was almost dark, but he could make out her half-built rockery, her fountain, her vegetable patch, all hers; he began to realise that his life had been mostly hers and that without her it would automatically collapse. He was in dread of not being able to cope. He was trapped in this garden, trapped in the half-realised plans of someone now gone. Torment took control and steered him across the road and up on Shanahan's field. He could no longer see the cattle but he was close enough to them to hear their heavy breath shake the dew off the grass. He hoped that distance from the house would give him peace. He decided that if he could walk to the end of Shanahan's field without thinking of her once it would be the beginning of independence. After ten successful steps he felt it reminded him of the ruined church of St Fachtna, where it was commonly believed that if you could walk around it three times without once thinking of a woman you would be assured of eternal salvation. Everybody tried it but most gave up honestly after a few steps. The few who achieved it were accused of being homosexual, for which they would be damned all the more. Emer had dismissed it as a typical expression of ecclesiastical chauvinism. Damn, that did it, he had thought of her. He stopped in the middle of the field and turned round. In the distance a light shone from the upstairs window. Somebody drew the curtain, nearby a cow belched. He was afraid. Now he knew he was afraid they'd get the child. He was afraid he wouldn't be man enough on his own. He decided then to march back and take control of his own house, to establish his own word as the only law. However, before he would march back he would march forward a little more because he needed time to think. Soon he found himself at the edge of Cloon Wood. He ventured in till his eyes grew accustomed to the total dark. He leaned his back against a tree and peered at the distant window through the twigs. He moved deeper in and then he turned to look again. Nothing. It was a beginning.

Later he wandered into the kitchen and sat beside the big range. Julia was knitting beside the table. No word passed between them. After a while she coughed and said, 'Wouldn't you think of taking off your shoes – they're sodden – leave them there near the range – they'll be dry in the morning.'

She couldn't keep it in, he thought. Years of fighting damp, of outmanoeuvering draughts, of sitting in the shade in summer – all punctuated with cups of tea – had dulled her mind to all other sensibilities.

'They're sodden and I'm glad of it,' he said, and he spread his feet in front of him in order to observe the water trickle onto the floor.

'That's all very fine now. But you might have a cold tomorrow, where would you be then? A chill is the beginning of the end of us all. That's what happened to Jack, God rest him.'

He thought of her husband, a silent man who had spent his time on this earth walking about the haggard with bucketfuls of this, that and the other.

'I thought he died of cancer.' There was the smallest trace of malice in his words. She almost dropped the knitting.

'None of our family ever died of cancer. He got cancer all right but it was pneumonia that got him in the end.' She said it with a certain note of triumph. You had to be careful how you lived in Ireland but you had to be even more careful that you didn't die of the wrong disease. She continued to knit. Click, clack, went the needles, never dropping a stitch. He listened to the sparring needles in a bemused fashion until it occurred to him that something was wrong. Suddenly he knew what it was. The clock, the big two-hundred year old Dublin regulator was stopped. It had been an extravagant purchase of Emer's in the early days. She had always kept it wound up.

'The clock is stopped,' he said. She didn't look up at him but continued to knit. He got up and walked to the corner where it stood, mute as a milestone. As he reached for the key, she said, 'Would you not think it would be a great honour to the dead to let the clock hold its peace for a month?' He thought about it. Killing the clock, gramophone, and radio for a month was a commonplace practice. But it was superstition and had he and Emer not fought superstition as ruthlessly as Julia had fought damp and chills? Anyway, it had a grand generous tick and tock which had punctuated the happiest years of his life. He wound it up slowly. Then he had to move the hands and realised his mistake as the clock chimed all the way up to 10.00 p.m. It chimed all over the house, in each chime a message he daren't interpret. Then it settled down to its tick, tock. He sat beside the range again fearing he could do nothing right. His feet were freezing but he couldn't take his shoes off now, it would be a defeat, in spite of the fact that everything she said made sense. He glanced at her out of the corner of his eye. Did he imagine she had a self-satisfied look about her? He was sure of it. She'd have to go that was all – he'd manage quite well without her. He would master basic cooking in a few days – laundry and things like that would not be too difficult he decided. Beyond that there was little else to housework. Still, he'd have to go back to work the following day because the bridge over the new by-pass was reaching a critical stage and the subcontractors were beginning to give hassle. Maybe he'd let her stay a few days, maybe even a week. His feet were so cold he had to get up and stamp the floor. He walked to the clevy and took down a bottle of Crested Ten.

'Would you like a drink?' he said as a truce gesture.

'A solitary drop of that stuff has never dampened a tooth in my head and never will till the day I go under.'

'OK,' he said as he poured himself a very large whiskey. He tossed it all back neat in rare abandon, winced and then waited for it to expand within. It did, and he exhaled in gratitude.

'I've heard it said many a time that a man in the grip of fresh sorrow would be better off to go dry at least until he is on his old mettle again,' she said blinking between stitches. You're as dry as an old limeburner's boot yourself he said to himself as he topped up his glass again.

'All my life I've watched men drink their way through farms and fields.'

'For Christ's sake, Julia, give me a break. You're playing the tune the old black cow died of.'

'That's all very well to say that today,' she said, 'but where will it all end? That's what I'd like to know. Where will it all end?'

Emer, girl, he said to himself, you were a sparkling trout out of the genetic cesspool – the others were all perch and pike. All your brothers and your mother are fatheads. They all live and you die – another proof that God does not exist.

'Look what happened to Paky Connor,' she said.

'Who's Paky Connor?' he asked in desperation.

'He was a second, no a third cousin of my own dear Jack, God rest him. He was going out with a no-good hussy of a girl who left him down. It was the luck of God that she did for if she had married him there would be no end to the calamity. She was a stupid ignorant gligeen who wouldn't know B from a bull's foot or C from a chest of drawers. Anyway, he took to the drink until he got himself and the farm into such a state that one night they had to tie him to a chair until the van called for him.'

'What van, for God's sake?'

She put her knitting down on her lap and looked at him as if he were a tramp who called to the back door. 'The van from the mental asylum of course. He's in there to this day and I'll tell you one thing for sure, he's living a very dry life.' She resumed her knitting. 'The brothers signed him in and I'll tell you one thing for sure, if they ever sign him out, 'tis out in a box he'll come.'

He looked at her openmouthed. 'And I suppose the brothers are looking after the farm.'

'Yes,' she said, 'it's as green as holly and not a buachalán or a weed in sight.'

He poured himself another whiskey. 'That man was just suffering from a nervous breakdown, it's disgraceful that he should spend all his life in the asylum.'

'Well, that's one name for it, but we call it going insane. Thanks be to God for mental asylums or the countryside wouldn't be safe for a body.'

'Jesus, sweet Jesus,' was all he said. What a paradox was Ireland he mused. His job called for a mastery of the most up-to-date computer technology, but at night he'd have to come home to this bronze age view of life. What a pity machines couldn't change people. He knew that in the year 2085 things would be just the same. Tools and machines might change but they would never lick the bronze age. He got up and corked the bottle and put it back in the clevy.

'Well I'm going to bed,' he said. 'I'll have a peep in at Róisín and see how she's doing. I might tell her that story if she's awake.'

Julia became as alert as a cat, dropped her knitting and said in a threatening tone: 'Wouldn't you be advised by one in the know and leave well alone?'

'How do you mean?'

'She's satisfied now, she's in her own bed. If you go in now you'll start the whole thing again.' He resented her tone and the implication of her control. If he left her away with this she'd have him wandering around the place with buckets, same as she had her unfortunate husband.

'I'll see you, good night,' he said and trudged up the stairs.

The night light burned beside her bed and she lay between the sheets clutching her teddy and sucking her thumb. Her eyes darted towards him but no flicker of joy appeared as it used before. He moved quietly up to her bed and bent down over her. Her eyes were focussed somewhere in the dark part of the room.

'How about a little kiss for Dally?' he said as he nudged her teddy.

She continued to suck for a minute without looking at him. All of a sudden she raised herself up on her elbow and said accusingly to him: 'Daddy, you told me a lie.'

'Why don't you call me Dally, as you used to?'

''Cause, Gran said that was wrong, only babies say Dally, it's Daddy.'

He felt like rushing downstairs and throwing Julia out into the garden for good.

'Call me Dally. Now what lie did I tell you?'

'You said Mommy was like Shaska in the ground.'

He sat down beside her gently, hardly daring to ask her what she meant. 'I'm afraid she is, pet. That's the way it is and we must put up with it.'

She backed away from him, a hurt look crossing her face. 'She is not, she is not. She is in heaven with Holy God and all the holy angels.' She presented him with the left side of her jaw in defiance. The thumb popped in for three more sucks then out again. 'And if anybody goes near me or hits me she'll send an angel down to stop him.' The thumb was jammed back for refuel.

He never knew how to react quickly when taken by surprise – it was a failing. He began to stammer, then stopped himself and asked coldly: 'Who told you this nonsense?'

'Gran,' she said defiantly but her mouth quivered with lack of conviction. Then she continued but there was pleading in her tone as tears began to spring at the corners of her eyes. 'She is up there now and she is looking down at the two of us and she is laughing – and one day Gran and me and you will die and we'll go up to her – and we'll have a great time. Isn't that true Daddy, please Daddy?' Her little face quivered shades of hope, loss, and shaky defiance. Her thumb went in and she looked up expectantly at him. He looked at her but he hadn't the courage to hold her eye. He took her hand in his, it was as limp as a sock. 'The fact is,' he said, 'the fact is,' but he didn't know what the fact was, except that he was tired and would have to put an end to this once and for all. 'The fact is, I'll have to close the window because you'll get cold.' He got up and crossed the room and looked out onto the garden. There was nothing to be seen except a moth which banged against the windowpane to escape the autumn chill. 'The window is shut already,' the child said. 'And so it is,' he said and came back slowly and sat down with a sigh beside her.

'Look, we've got to be brave about this, you and me,' he took her hand again but she pre-empted any strategy by starting to cry out loud. He had no defence against tears. Once only Emer had to resort to them and he conceded the universe. As for a crying child he usually handed it over to a woman. But he wasn't going for Julia again. He took her in his arms and this time she did not resist. But she continued to cry and sob. 'Sure Mommy isn't out in the cold ground?' she pleaded.

He hadn't considered that aspect of it, it could be upsetting for a child. Anyway Mommy was nowhere.

'Mommy is not out in the cold ground.'

'And she is not where Shaska is?'

'No.'

He could feel her relaxing in his arms. She was soft, cuddly and yielding. She put her thumb in her mouth and sucked on this new confirmation. After a while she asked only just a little tearfully: 'She is in heaven with Holy God?'

Heaven was a mere metaphor for the dark eternity of non-existence. Children above all needed metaphors. Santa Claus was one,

so were witches. He had never questioned stories about witches and
magic before, why heaven now. A witch was a metaphor for the forces
of hazard. We were all victims of hazard.

'Yes,' he said almost inaudibly, 'she is in heaven.' He was an atheist
who felt he had just committed mortal sin.

'Why didn't you tell me that before? Gran was right.'

'Call me Dally,' he said simply.

'And is heaven full of angels?'

'Yes.'

'And will they look after me if I cut my knee?'

'Yes.'

'And is Mommy laughing?'

'Yes.' He felt like a thieving dog. What had he stolen? He had stolen
away truth and put in its place a lie, hoping that it would not be
discovered. It was the same as stealing his wife away from life and
putting in her place some rags and bones. He felt he was stuffing the
effigy of Emer de Brún in the name of peace. The crying had stopped
now. She sucked peacefully beside him.

'What dress is she wearing?'

'What do you mean?'

'In heaven. Now.'

'She's wearing a new dress. It's pink and long and sways as she
walks.' He had bought it for her fifty billion years ago way out in the
Crab Nebula and she would wear it for all eternity and it would always
blow gently about her legs in the cosmic breeze. The child was asleep.
And religion was born. Only five days gone and already philosophy
had caved in at the knees. They had vanquished. Heaven had arrived.
Hell would follow in its own good time. They had vanquished because
he was not strong. It was this more than anything else made him cry,
slowly at first just the way a mist becomes rain. Then he cried freely
and all the coldness of the last few days turned hot and flowed with
ease down his cheek. It was good to cry. It was warm. It was warm
also to think of her in heaven and not in the cold ground. She had a
favourite proverb for calamity. 'If the skies were to fall we'd catch
larks.' Well the skies had fallen, and he had caught a lark – a lark from
the clear air: now he knew where religion came from. From children.
All the great philosophers had been wrong. Spëngler, Schleiermacher,
Remach, Murray, Ellis. It was to appease the child. At least he had
borne that much from the fray.

He held her in his arms and looked out the window. There was but
one star shining. It shone like a cat's eye from under a bed. It was an

evening for oneness, one star, one man, one child, one lost love, one lark from the clear air. And one faith. Faith in the goodness of man and no more. He felt himself repeat her favourite lines.

> *Twilight and evening bell*
> *And after that the dark*
> *And may there be no sadness of farewell*
> *When I embark.*

IN THE DARK

AIDAN MATHEWS

Aidan Mathews was born in Dublin, 1956. A graduate of University College, Dublin, he won the Patrick Kavanagh Award for poetry in 1976 and the Listowel Drama Award in 1984. Now a Drama Producer in RTE, he has published a novel and two collections of short stories, *Adventures in a Bathyscope* and *Lipstick on the Host*.

The lights had gone out all over the O Muirithe household, and Harry and Joan were obliged to talk to one another. At the end of a difficult day, this was the last straw. Indeed, it was the short one. After all, they had been married for twenty-seven years, and were naturally speechless.

'The bastards,' said Harry. 'The bloody bastards. They said eight o'clock. They swore it.'

'I know,' said Joan. 'I know they did.'

'Zone B. No risk after eight. You can't believe daylight out of them.'

'It's only ten past.'

'I tell you this,' said Harry. 'The next house we buy, it's going to be . . .'

'Within spitting distance of a hospital,' said Joan.

'Within spitting distance,' said Harry. 'So near, so close you can hear the doctors putting in stitches, and the static on the set in the television lounge of the geriatric ward.'

(Harry had been to visit his father once when the old man became prematurely senile and had spent was it four years in just such an institution, rambling on about the toy-train in the park and the baby wallabies in the zoo sticking their heads out of their mothers' pouches; but it was the static on the set which had always angered his son to the point where he had walked away in a pet. This, by the way, is a digression, the first of four, and you are quite at liberty to ignore them utterly. For my own part, I shall play fair, and indicate each one by the use of the parentheses.)

'. . . of the geriatric ward.'

'And the nurses at their tea-break,' said Joan.

'And the nurses at their tea-break,' said Harry. 'Scraping out the last bit of strawberry yoghurt.'

'Next year,' said Joan.

'Next year,' Harry said.

There was a long silence. The battery clock on the mantelpiece ticked, as battery clocks do; and the curtains stirred, but only slightly.

'I could light a fire.'

But that was typical of Joan: trying to look on the bright side.

'I wouldn't bother.'

'Not for the heat. For the light. It'd be nice for Johnny and Avril.'

'You wouldn't see your nose under the stairs. You'd crack your skull open.'

Joan was hurt by this. Not that she noticed. She was as used to being hurt as to being fifty.

'I would have missed my bus if I'd stayed to set it,' she said. 'I had to be out by eight.'

'Am I complaining? Have I uttered a single syllable of recrimination? You shouldn't have to set it. Let Johnny set it.'

'You try asking Johnny to set it. Set it, my foot. Johnny wouldn't even know how to roll a newspaper.'

'Don't ask him. Tell him. Order him. Asking gets you nowhere. Telling gets you nowhere. This world is about the boot. Get the boot in. Look, where are those other candles? These two are useless. They're wobbly. They'd set the whole place on fire. You have to soften the bottom ends first. Soften the bottom end of one of them with the flame off the other. Then you sort of wedge it into the saucer till the wax hardens again. Are you with me?'

'I'm not a fool,' Joan said. 'Don't talk to me as if I were a fool.'

'I'm not saying you're a fool. I'm not suggesting you're a fool. I'd never have thought of going to the church. I thought the candles were electric nowadays. At least they were the last time I was there. So you did well. I hand it to you.'

'Now you're patronising me,' Joan said. 'Please don't patronise me.'

Harry had meant well. He had meant well and he had been misunderstood. It was the story of his life. The story of his life could be summed up in the one word 'misunderstanding'. But he would be patient. He would not retaliate. 'Have you taken your Melleril?' he asked gently. 'Or did you forget again?' And then, before Joan could answer, he was noisily rummaging among the remaining candles.

'Here,' he said. 'What about this one?'

'What one?'

'Here. Where's your hand? That one.'

Joan smelled it.

'Harry, it's that awful scented kind. I can't stand them.'

'But it'll give us more light. And we need more light. Those piddly ones are for shrines.'

'The shrine of St Jude,' Joan said, which was, all considered, an excellent riposte; that is, if you know your saints, and Harry didn't. But it was still worth saying, and I personally regard it as a high point in the story. Harry lit a match. It struck the third time round, lighting their faces in a quite uncomplimentary fashion, and filling the room with their shadows.

'Harry, that scented smell makes me sick,' said Joan.

'Well, I'm not just going to squat here in total darkness. I've been working since I woke up. Surely to Christ I can . . .'

'I've been working too,' said Joan. 'Ever since I came in from work I've been working. I did the washing by hand. I went out again, to get the candles. In the rain.'

'Violins,' said Harry softly. 'Violins.'

'This is just hell. They never strike when it's summer. They do it when it gets dark.'

Harry had moved quietly out of the small circle of light in which she was sitting. He knew perfectly well why he was doing it too, but it was not revenge. It was a matter of principle. He still felt misunderstood.

'Harry? Harry? Where are you?'

'Nigeria,' he said. 'Where do you think I am?'

'Are you sure you're all right?'

Harry managed a small wheeze. He even tried to prolong it, but his lungs were clear. In any event, it achieved the desired effect.

'Are you breathless?'

'A bit. A bit breathless. It'll pass.'

'Sit down, Harry. Sit down and hold your head in your hands.'

(Harry's father had died on a ventilator, and Harry had persuaded Joan that the ailment was hereditary. He had almost persuaded himself. Ventolin inhalers were scattered strategically round about the whole house, and they served to inhibit outbreaks of marital discord. After all, Harry might not be here tomorrow, and words spoken in wrath might well be regretted. It was still only five years since her husband had taken the bus from the funeral parlour to add to the pathos of his father's removal, and had sat staring at 'Charley's Angels' without uttering a sentence, letting the barbecue chicken grow cold on his lap: Joan had forgotten none of this, and was easily panicked.)

'. . . and hold your head in your hands.'

'I am holding my head in my hands.'

'When do you think we'll have light, Harry?'

'When we reach the end of the tunnel. And not before.'

'This is hell.'

There was a long silence. The battery clock on the mantelpiece was still ticking; and the curtains stirred, but only slightly.

'What we need,' Harry decided, 'is someone like Mussolini. Benito would have known what to do. Line up the ring-leaders. Shoot 'em down. Finito. That's the only thing that would bring these fellows to their senses. Make them tighten their belts. Both barrels. No bloody strikes in those days.'

Joan was relieved. Harry hadn't wheezed once.

'I wouldn't mind if they were paid badly,' she said.

'Yes, sirree,' Harry said. 'There's a lot to be said for a man like Mussolini.'

'You're just cross because you're missing your programme.'

'I was waiting for that,' said Harry.

'I don't know why you race home to watch that eejit.'

'I don't race anywhere. I haven't the energy. I work too hard.'

'And he's not even funny,' said Joan.

'My God, if I had to choose between Benny Hill and . . . and Mother Teresa, I know who I'd plump for.'

'Just bottoms and sniggers,' she said. 'And the two of you sitting there, tittering. You're as bad as Johnny.'

'I've made up my mind,' said Harry, who hadn't. 'I *am* going to smoke.'

'You can't, Harry. Not now. Not after three weeks.'

'I can't have a hot meal,' Harry said. 'I can't watch Benny Hill. I can't have a normal conversation about normal things. The least I can do is smoke myself silly.'

'You mustn't give in.'

'Give me one good reason.'

'You'll live longer.'

'Jesus Christ,' said Harry with a ferocity which almost surprised him. 'That's the best bloody reason for taking them up.'

Noise in the hallway startled Joan.

'Harry, stop it, they're coming. And make an effort for me. Don't call her Shelley. Please. It's very unkind.'

But Harry was not about to lower his voice.

'Well, I liked Shelley. She was good for Johnny. Besides, she was a doctor. This one's a nurse. Next time round, I suppose he'll be dating the porter.'

Johnny's voice called out from the darkness of the doorway.

'Dr and Mrs Livingstone, I presume?'

Then Avril's, more timidly.

'Hello, Mr O Moorithe.'

'Shelley,' Harry said.

'Avril,' she replied. The girl was obviously dense: there wasn't a hint of malice in her voice.

'Force of habit,' Harry said to the darkness. 'Mea culpa.'

'Don't mind my Pater, Avril,' Johnny said. 'His nerves are shot. He's off the fags.'

But Avril ignored him. Shelley would have shown more spunk.

'Hi, Mrs O Moorithe.'

'Hello, love. Mind where you stand. I have a tray on the floor somewhere.'

'I can't stand the way she says it,' Harry said to Johnny in an audible undertone. 'O Moorithe. Can you not get her to pronounce it the right way? Shelley never had any difficulty, but then Shelley . . .'

'It has to do with the way you part your lips,' Johnny said. 'I'll work on it later.'

(Johnny was not ordinarily insolent; indeed, he lacked a capacity to do otherwise than dislike his father, a circumstance which chose him for this fiction, since in fiction the facts must fit that fabulous domain we poormouth as the ordinary world. But he'd been studying late in the National Library, and Avril had arrived to collect him at least an hour after the agreed time. He had pretended irritation, feeling little if any; so Avril had told him that, later in the evening, she would dress in her nurse's uniform and allow him to spank her across his lap with a rolled-up newspaper. He had had an erection ever since, and feared no one, not even his father.)

'Isn't this a gas?' said Avril to Joan. 'I bet there'll be tons of babies in nine months time.'

'Don't be putting ideas in his head,' Joan said. But she liked Avril; it was a feminine thought and, besides, the girl worked, or had once worked, in the neo-natal unit.

There was a long silence. The battery clock could not prevent itself ticking gently and gingerly; and the curtains stirred in the lightest of breezes.

'You could have set a fire,' said Johnny.

'You could have set one,' said Joan. The darkness made her confident.

'Missed your programme, Dad?'

But Harry ignored him.

'I tell you this for nothing, Avril. I don't know how you feel, but I was saying to Johnny's mother that Mussolini had the right idea.'

'What was that?' said Avril.

'My father is about to deliver himself of a political apophthegm,' said Johnny. 'Stand well clear.'

'Johnny's father is just being difficult,' said Joan.

'What is that dreadful smell?' said Johnny, sniffing the darkness.

'I think it's lovely,' Avril said. 'I think it's churchy, sort of.'

'Bring in the troops,' Harry said. 'Pick four men at random. You, you, you, you. Out to the factory gates. Bayonet practice. Now that's my kind of crash course in industrial relations.'

'More crash than course,' said Johnny.

But Avril disagreed.

'I think it's a wonderful idea, Mr O Moorithe. After all, the working classes are getting ideas above their station. They think they can hold the country up to ransom.'

'How right you are, Avril,' Harry said warmly. 'How right you are.'

'But wouldn't it be a better idea to cut off their arms and legs first?'

(Avril was no more impudent than Johnny. I have known her a long time and have always found her to be easily cowed and crestfallen, with a complex of sorts about her skin, which is so fair it tans badly even with minimal exposure on the sunbed in the solarium. But that very afternoon she had been taking a quite handsome patient's blood pressure in the Admission Ward, and the back of his hand had grazed against the watch strap which she wore on her left breast. It was only a moment, a matter of seconds. But it had been deliberate. Of that she was sure. And the surety solaced her.)

'Well,' said Harry, managing another slight wheeze. 'That puts me in my place, doesn't it?'

The silence lengthened like a strip of chewing-gum between a child's fingers. The battery clock went on ticking with a desperate self-consciousness, like a man breaking wind in company; and the curtains twitched, but only just.

'I'll put . . . the kettle on,' said Joan.

'Momma,' Johnny said. 'No electricity. Ergo, no tea.'

'I wasn't thinking. I must be . . . tired.'

'We should be going,' Avril said. She was sorry now.

'And let the two of you get back to . . . to . . .' said Johnny, whose erection was beginning to subside.

'We were just chatting,' said Harry.

'We were . . . reminiscing,' Joan said.

'That's the great thing about power cuts,' said Harry. 'They give you time to talk. You're not just sitting like a zombie in front of the goggle box. And when you go to bed, you can't even remember what you were watching. No, your mother and I were talking. Looking back. There's so much to look back at. And to look forward to, of course.'

'We were remembering your blanket, Johnny. Johnny had a blanket, Avril. He was only a toddler at the time. People kept showering him with toys, you know the sort of cuddly bears people buy. But he couldn't be bothered with any of them. All he wanted was his dirty old blanket. He wouldn't sleep without it. He even took it to Montessori in his satchel.'

'And the games he used to play,' said Harry. 'With his marbles and his toy soldiers. He'd line them up at one end of the room and aim at them with his marble from the other end. You should have seen the skirting board. Chips here, chips there, chips everywhere. Great years. The best years. We were looking back . . . at it all.'

'You can spend hours . . . looking back,' said Joan.

'Ages. A lifetime.'

'We didn't even notice it was getting . . .'

'Dark all around us.'

'We were so engrossed,' Joan said.

Johnny was furious. Furious, yet contrite too. His erection had collapsed.

'Well,' he said, 'we don't want to break up the party. Or is it a seance?' Blankets and marbles. How could they do this to him? And what chance was there now of Avril's stretching herself across his lap in her nurse's uniform? Bugger all. She would want to talk about his childhood.

'Tell him off, Mrs O Moorithe,' Avril said. 'He needs a good clip on his ear.'

'Your predecessor set a high standard when it came to that sort of thing,' Harry said.

'Pater,' said Johnny, 'missing Benny Hill is no excuse for rudeness.'

'Do you watch Benny Hill, Mr O Moorithe?' said Avril.

'Who,' he replied, 'is Benny Hill?'

'Oh, you'd love him. He's a panic. A bit saucy, but he makes you laugh. Johnny says he's a dirty old man, but I like him.'

Harry decided Avril was all right. But Johnny's despair had deepened.

'What are we doing here, standing in the darkness?' he said.

'Power cuts make you queer,' his mother said.

'Andiamo,' Johnny decided. 'Avril Airlines announce a flight departure.'

'Where are you off to?' Harry said. He wanted Avril to go on talking about Benny Hill. In a strange way, he found it rather arousing.

'We're off to *The Seventh Heaven*,' Johnny said.

'I'd go there like a shot if I knew where to find it,' said Harry.

'I should have rang my folks,' Avril said.

'Ring from the club.'

'Stay a bit,' Harry said. 'It's early. Please.'

'Sure what's your hurry?' Joan said.

The truth is, Harry was a little afraid of being left alone with Joan. Why had she started all that nonsense about blankets and cuddly toys? And Joan was a little more than afraid of being left alone with Harry. By now, the ice-cubes would have melted in the freezer, and Harry hated his whiskey without at least three ice-cubes.

'There'll be lights any minute now,' said Harry. 'You'll see. You could even watch that programme you were talking about.'

But Johnny stood his ground.

'Adieu, farewell, remember us.'

'I suppose I'd better . . .' Avril said.

'Do stay,' said Joan. And she prayed for the lights to come on; she prayed against the darkness which was so bewildering.

'A firm and final Ciao,' Johnny said. It delighted him to hear his parents begging. Openly begging. His erection began to stir again.

'Wear your safety belts,' his father said, giving up and giving in.

'We'll take every precaution,' Johnny said. He could get a newspaper at the corner shop. Unless it was closed because of the power cut. Anyhow, there were dozens of newsagents along the route to the club.

'See you,' said Avril, who had seen neither of them.

'That's right,' Johnny said. 'We'll see you in a different light in future.'

And the two of them left, just like that.

When the hall door slammed shut, there was a short silence. I am not going to talk about the battery clock or the curtains because that point has been well and truly established, and you can imagine it for yourself. After all, we are in this together.

'So,' said Joan.

'Well?'

'Hmm?'

'Nothing,' said Harry.

'Nice child.'

'I should have rang.'

'Who?' said Joan.

'Rang. It's wrong. It should be rung.'

'What?'

'Never mind.'

He had not thought of the whiskey or the ice-cubes yet. Perhaps there was still time.

'She's very confident,' Joan said.

'I like her.'

'That's a bit of a U-turn.'

'She's very . . . feminine.'

Joan was thunderstruck. Harry had always doted on Shelley, though he tended to mistake her surname and call her Winters instead of Brennan.

'Is there a full moon tonight?' she asked him.

Harry came clean. One tends to do that in the darkness.

'I liked what she said about Benny Hill. It was natural.'

'I think we're all going mad,' Joan said.

But Harry had made up his mind, the way Joan made up her face: slowly and deliberately.

'Yes,' he said. 'She's more natural than Shelley.'

It was more than a decision. It was a conviction. Harry felt he owed himself a drink. A double, at that. And why not? Who was there to see? So he edged along the sofa in the general direction of the kitchen.

'Damn it, damn it, Harry, look at that! You've knocked the candle! It must have dripped wax all over the carpet.'

'So what?' said Harry. 'It'll come off.'

'It'll come off? All on its ownie own, I suppose?'

'Would you ever calm down?' Harry shouted.

'It won't just "come off",' Joan sobbed. 'I'll get it off. On my hands and knees, that's how.'

'Isn't there a pill you could take?' said Harry. He had just remembered that the freezer would be off and the ice-cubes melted. What was a whiskey without an ice-cube? A gin without a tonic, that was what.

'And it stinks the whole house,' Joan said. She was weeping now. It was so bloody typical. She made the effort for strangers. For her own husband it was a different matter. All hell broke loose once the hall door heaved to.

'Blankets,' Harry spat. 'What in Christ's name were you doing talking about blankets?'

'You were worse,' she wept. 'You were worse with your marbles.'

'Eight o'clock,' Harry said between clenched teeth. 'Eight o'clock. The bastards. They said eight o'clock we'd be out of danger.'

'I know,' Joan shouted at him. 'I know.'

'Mussolini was right. Shoot every last manjack. To hell with them. To hell with the whole lot of them.'

And the lights came on. Delicate white lace curtains blew in the air of the open window; and from the kitchen, above the hum of the peach-coloured fridge, Harry and Joan could hear the fragile sound of the battery clock, with a noise like matchsticks breaking. For a brief moment, husband and wife looked at each other: the man with the stained moustache and the tiny crack in the lens of his spectacles; the woman in her housecoat with needle and thread stuck into the linen lapel, and the bright, brown hair with grey at its roots. For as long as the moment lasted, they longed for the darkness. But it passed, as all unendurable things must. Light was one thing, illumination another. That was a word to be kept strictly for Christmas.

'Well, glory be,' said Joan.

'The power of prayer,' said Harry.

'Just like that.'

'All's well that ends well.'

'I'd better go round the house,' said Joan anxiously. 'I left lights on all over the place.'

'May light perpetual shine upon us!' said Harry. It would only take an hour or so for the cubes to congeal again. 'What time is it?'

'Ten to nine,' said Joan.

'Goodo. I'll get the last ten minutes of Benny Hill. And there's Dallas at ten. Is it tonight is Dallas night?'

'Don't you know well it is?'

'We're set so. Crisis averted.'

'Right as rain.'

'Right as rain,' Harry agreed.

'High and dry,' said Joan, as she turned off the overhead light and one of the side-lamps.

'High and dry,' Harry repeated. 'Or is it home and dry? I'm always getting the two of them mixed up.'

Joan banged the window shut, and the curtains stood stock-still. Harry was pressing the buttons on the television remote control. The noise of the stations swelled above the sound of the battery clock.

PLACE: BELFAST
TIME: 1984
SCENE: THE ONLY PUB

JOHN MORROW
Born in Belfast, 1930, John Morrow left school when he was fourteen and worked in various jobs. He now works for the Northern Ireland Arts Council. He has published two novels and two short story collections, *Northern Myths* and *Sects*.

'. . . Listen to that, would ye. Must be the sweetest sound in the world – "Faith of Our Fathers" on the Uillean pipes. Jas', wouldn't you wonder how they keep time hoppin' along on one leg like that. Did you see the TV cameras when they were marchin' past at the City Hall? Roun' them like flies . . . Oh it's bin one great day an' no mistake . . . Eh? . . . Whadda ya mean "for some"? Look, you, for yer own good, keep yer lip buttoned. All right among yer own mates, but you niver know who's listenin' . . . Yis, yis, we all know whose cousin it is got the Grand Central Hotel. An' doesn't he deserve it? . . . No, not the cousin – but you must admit he came in handy with the oul' plenary absolution after many a sticky one – if you could catch him sober, like . . . No, I mean that wee man in the black shirt up on that rostrum the day. See him . . . all their daddies. Sure doesn't he deserve anything he can grab afore the big vultures from the South git in on it. Remember, if it wasn't for him there'd be no United Ireland, an' no pickin's an no nothin' an' well you know it. Just look at him the day, that time he came down off the rostrum to set fire to the bonfire of dirty books, an' all the TV boys got roun' him, eh? Knew ivery manjack by his first name – "Hank" this an' "Auberon" that an', "How's yer father, Fritz?" Oh that wee man has the measure of them all. Brains over brawn, y'see; niver pulled a trigger or fused a bomb in his life. The oul' grey matter, that's what counts; the oul' school-master touch . . . An' yit, an' yit, wi' all that, still one of the boys. Did I tell you what he says to me at the inspection this morning? . . . Well, down the ranks he comes with that oul' cocky dander of his – yid hardly notice the club fut now – down he comes an' stops right in front of me wi' all the big brass behin' him. "Well, Mickey," says he, "how's yer hammer hangin'?" . . . Jas', you wanna seen the Bishop's face! Looked like he was gonna drop a litter on the spot! Ah, he's the boy, right enough. Niver changes. No side with him – as far as his own's concerned anyway. I knew him from the start – aye, an'

well before that, when he was livin' with his Da an' school-masterin'
. . . What's that? Look, I toul you to watch yer mouth. If talk like that
gits back you'll be in the shit when they start givin' out the pensions.
Because he didn't smoke or drink or run after weemin doesn't say
. . . Ah well, if yer gonta pull a man down for givin' the Priest a bit
of a han' at Parish dances – seein' that dirty buggers like you behaved
yerselves! An' what about the good work he done for the gee-ah-ah,
eh? Huntin' roun' the soccer pitches and rugby grouns ivery Saturday
lookin' for fellas moonlightin' at the foreign games. What were you
doin' for Ireland then? I'll tell ye – two years hard chokey for non-
payment of maintenance to yer wife an' seven sprogs. If you hadn't
gatecrashed that jailbreak . . . Look, any time . . . Fist, gun, knife or
boot – I'm yer man . . . An' I'm no arse-licker. I'm just sayin' that if
it hadn't bin for him we'd still be runnin' roun' the streets lookin' to
draw a bead on a stray Peeler. Brains, y'see. What's that word he
used to use . . . aye – "orchestration". Like that first time when he
started what he called "The Bishop's Game". D'you mind that? Had
oul' Bishop O'Loot runnin' roun' with the head-staggers . . . ended
up in a Jesuit funny farm down in Dingle. Eh? What was "The Bishop's
Game", he says! Where the hell were you? The Bishop's Game, son,
is what's known as "tactics". Them was the oul' "No-go" days, y'see,
so if you wanted to knock aff a sodger you had to go outside the
ghetto, which was a very dodgy caper, I can tell ye. An' even if you did
manage it, the squeals of the clergy an' the do-gooders was terrible.
"Adverse Propaganda" he called it, an' as soon as he took command
the first thing he done was to ban all maverick operations. "If you're
gonta do it," says he, "the thing is to git as much moral sanction for
it as possible." An' the way he showed us was "The Bishop's Game".
"Checkmate in ten moves," he used to say, tickin' them off on his
fingers:

Move one:	blow up any Prod pub on a Saturday night;
Move two:	angry Prods blow up a Taig pub the next Saturday night;
Move three:	joint approach to the Bishop by a cross-section of the ghetto community led by the cousin – if sober – complainin' about lack of protection by the security forces;
Move four:	Bishop makes appeal via the media regarding protecting his innocent flock from vindictive Prods. The Green Tories jump on bandwagon and ask

	questions in the House;
Move five:	Army forced to move into ghetto by politicians eager for a sign that the community is turning away from the gunmen;

Allow at least a week to lapse, then –

Move six:	approach to the Bishop by the same cross-section, led by the cousin, this time complaining about Army harassment at road checks, the terrible indignity of the body-search and its traumatic effect on a proud people;
Move seven:	the Bishop, his poor oul' head birlin' by this time, appeals for an end to Army harassment;
Move eight:	we follow up with the threat that if the foresaid harassment does not cease we, as the protectors of the people, will be forced to take action;
Move nine:	shoot a sodger at a road check – or two if you're lucky;
Move ten:	the "Troops Out" Lobby at Westminster howls that they shouldn't'a'bin there in the first place. Politicians pressured. The Army withdraws from the ghetto an' Bob's yer Uncle! You've blown up a Prod pub, shot a sodger, made the Army look like a load of Boy Scouts, an' somehow it's all somebody else's fault! So you can start again at Move One . . .

That, son, is what you call "tactics", as laid down by the wee man. God, we pulled the oul' "Bishop's Game" time outa number. An' that was only one of his dodges. Sure that last time, the time that eejit up in Derry put the bomb under the wrong school bus, sure everybody was ready to throw in the towel. The clergy squealin', the Yanks squealin' . . . even the cousin refused to wave the wand that time . . . 'coorse you can see his point, like, half the kids bein' our own sort. The culchie that done it said he didn't think it mattered, seein' they were goin' to a state school an' weren't confirmed anyway. But it didn't wash. Jasus, the ruction was terrible – talk about "adverse propaganda"! An' yit, because of that wee man's tactics, no more than a week later the tables were couped, the Brits were givin' notice of intention to withdraw, an' a United Ireland was on the way. The Jackpot! How? . . . I'll tell ye how . . . A coupla days after the bombin'

the Prods decide to do a tit-for-tat – but this time, instead of the usual
pub bomb, they're gonta put the lid on the wee man himself. So, over
they comes this day, three of them in a clapped-out Mini, without
even botherin' their arses findin' out where he'll be. Up to the house,
kick in the door, an' the only one in is the wife – the three kids are
playin' in the back garden next door. What? In the name of God do
you know anything! 'Coorse he had a wife before this one. Wasn't I
with him when he first got houl of her, at a Freedom Fighters' confer-
ence in Algiers in 1969. An Englishwoman – oh real marley-in-the-
mouth uppercrust – but a holy terror for the bombin' an' killin'. I heard
tell her oul' fella was a millionaire. Maybe that's why the wee man
took up with her, thinkin' maybe there'd be a few bob in it. Couldn't
'a bin anything else . . . Jasus, she was one hard-lookin' ticket! They
say her oul' fella spent a fortune gittin' her hare-lip fixed. All I can say
is he must have took the wrong turnin' an' ended up in Smithfield
instead of Harley Street. I'm tellin' ye – a bake that would turn milk.
Even oul "Sheep" O'Keefe could hardly face it. D'you mind "Sheep"?
From over the border in Armagh. Aye, the very one – would have
mounted a tired horse! Anyroad, him an' me was hidin' out at the wee
man's place one time, an' after a coupla weeks "Sheep" was in such
a bad way with his engine that it was either me or hur. He says himself
it was touch an' go. Anyhow, he went at her, as the Poet Laureate
would say, "Like a frog up a pump". That last kid was Sheep's. The
wee man knew it, but he didn't give a damn. Him an' hur had been
hammerin' hell outa each other for years, mostly over the dogs. Aye,
dogs – she was a breeder, y'see; had the garden wired in an' all.
Alsatians an' Doberman Pinschers, great slaverin' brutes of things
would'a ate the kebs aff ye. I swear to ma Christ she treated them
better than the kids, up to her eyes in muck an' shit from mornin' till
night. When them Prods broke in they couldn't have known whether
it was man, woman or dirty chil' they were shootin' at – an' couldn't
have cared less, like. Left her spoutin' like a colander on the mat.
Anyroad, up we comes ten minutes later, the wee man, Buxy Hoy
an' me, an' there's the Prods still tryin' to git their motor started!
Shows you their wit, like – comin' on a hit job in a Leyland Mini! Buxy,
he blows the head off one an' the other two takes to their heels. Into
the house we goes an' there's yer woman, corpsed face down on the
mat an' the bloody dogs howlin' like banshees out the back. Well, the
wee man just stan's there lookin' for a minute. Then he reaches out
with his fut an' turns her over. A wild, wild sight, I'm tellin' ye. Then
he turns to me with that oul' sly grin of his, y'know, an' he says:

"Well, Mickey," says he, "they didn't half fix her lip." Laugh! – Jas',
Buxy an' me nearly bust a gut. I tell ye, he didn't give a curse about
her, one way or the other. But the worse was, y'see, he knew damn
well nobody else would either. When she was with the Arabs she'd
bin up till her neck in a coupla airplane hi-jackin's. The Jews had bin
after her for years over some school bombin's in Israel. Y'see what I
mean? – here's him hopin' the Prods'll do somethin' drastic in revenge
for the school bus, like blowin' up a load of nuns, an' all they do is
somethin' the NSPCC would give them a medal for . . . Aye, nuns
. . . Ah well, you an' me mightn't, but he used to say that nuns rank
almost equal with kids on the propaganda scale – especially with Prods,
funnily enough, ever since Ingrid Bergman in "Going My Way". Anyroad, yer woman on the mat was no nun an' we were still up shit
creek if we couldn't come up with somethin' sharpish. God! you could
almost hear that wee man's brainbox creakin' . . . 'coorse, Buxy an'
me, we comes up with the obvious answer, same as you would yerself:
shoot the kids. There was still time enough for it to be blamed on the
Prods – an' the woman next door whose garden they were playin' in
was one of ours, so no problem there. OK, only three agin a busload,
but better than nothin'. But that's the difference, y'see – the obvious
– that's what has you an' me still common five-eights an' him cock of
the walk the day. Nothin' "obvious" about his way of thinkin' – an',
y'see, he knew his Brits inside out. All them years school-masterin'
he'd studied them. He knew what comes top on their propaganda
scale – an', above all, he knew what week it was. Well, he just stan's
there, lookin' down at yer woman, scratchin' his oul head an' sayin'
nothin'. Then, like lightnin', he swings roun', points his finger at me
an' says:
"Shoot the dogs!"
'Boys, you talk about historical moments! 'Coorse I niver realised
it then. I thought it was just that their howlin' was gittin' on his wick,
so I goes straight out an' sprayed the full magazine of the oul' Mauser
roun' the garden. But afterwards, before he sent Buxy an' me off to
phone up all the TV men an' newspapers, he toul' us what week it
was . . . Crufts!! . . . The doggie show . . . The one week of the
year when London is jammed with dog-lovers, the papers full of doggy
pictures! Well, yis all know what happened. A hunnerd thousand dog-
lovers from all over England, led by Peter Hain, marches on Downing
Street under the Tri-colour; Merlyn Rees pelted with hot turds; the
Government ready to topple; black-edged newspapers; Leyland shop
stewards declare a four week mourning strike; special Capital Punish-

ment Bill forced through Parliament in time to hang the two Prods
who were supposed to have done it; and – the jackpot – a declaration
of intent to withdraw in 1984!

'Ah, here we are, lads, the Big Day. A Nation Once Again. Less
than a quarter of a million Prods left, an' most of them restricted to
East Belfast; the last trainload of Jews went out a week ago; an'
there's not a black bake to be seen the length an' breadth of Ireland.
An' all due to that wee man's tactics. Here – there's him an' hur now
. . . turn that sound up – the King an' Queen of Ireland! What d'you
say? Aye – well, nobody's perfect, an' his blind spot just happens to
be weemin. Christ, you could drive a bus through that gap in her
champers! I think even the boul "Sheep" would have to put a bag over
that one.'

LOOKING

ÉILIS NÍ DHUIBHNE
Born in Dublin, 1954, Éilis Ní Dhuibhne has worked as a civil servant, librarian, archivist, lecturer, and folklore collector. She has published a novel and two collections of short stories, *Blood and Water* and *Eating Women Is Not Recommended*.

The television set broke down on Saturday night. No warning had been given. They were sitting there in the white armchairs when suddenly the picture fizzled away to a small circular rainbow, and then to a blank. The voices remained, persistent jets of bright frivolous argument shooting into the room. But, even though the programme had been a 'talk show' they didn't continue to listen to it. It seemed unnatural to listen to television.

The breakdown would prove significant, Margaret immediately divined. Indeed, it would blight the weekend. In the first place, Edward would become depressed at the thought of one more item in his ever-disintegrating flat having failed him. He would take it as a personal blow struck by a life which he considered to be waging a constant vendetta against him. He would feel, as he usually felt when these catastrophes occurred, that life was surely gaining ground and that the next blow would be its supreme trump. He would feel all this, and Margaret would know it, but he would tell her nothing and turn away from her. In short, he would be grumpy and that would be enough to spoil her weekend anyway.

But in the second place, she would be left physically alone and bored. Their principal shared activity was television watching. 'Dallas' and 'The Late Late Show' on Saturday night, 'The Sunday Night Feature Film' on Sundays. He supplied a running commentary as they watched. Her grandfather used to do that, she recalled, long ago in her parents' kitchen, drumming his feet against the tiles at the same time. She had hated it then and tried to freeze the old man into silence.

Now she listened and laughed at Edward, not from any motivation of politeness but because she enjoyed his patter and the sound of his voice. How much better it was than the sound of his fingers drumming against the typewriter in the study, while she sat at the kitchen table and tried to work. Typing was his other weekend activity, and one which he naturally engaged in alone.

He fiddled with the knobs on the television set for what seemed to her a very long time before accepting that the thing was simply broken, a fact which had seemed very obvious to Margaret from the outset. He suggested, in the tones of a broken man who is grinning and bearing it, that they play Scrabble and she gladly acquiesced. She was the weaker player of the two. From a sense of superiority and altruism, she played a considerate game, spreading long words across the board in order to make it accessible. He played ruthlessly. In other games, card games or dice games, he usually let her win. Perhaps he thought it was important to prove oneself at Scrabble. No, it was impossible! It might have been because of the broken television set. Anyway, he used as many triple-word scores as possible, and won by a large margin, something which pleased Margaret a little since it might make him happy, and annoyed her because she liked to win games. Then she worried. He was always so ruthless and victorious, in important things, while she was always pluralistic and defeated. Was it the difference between masculinity and femininity or activity and passivity or simply between him and her? Whatever it was, she wished the gap were narrower. She ought to win sometimes, at something, she felt.

They had survived Saturday night without television. That was a victory for both of them. At eleven, the Scrabble game was over, and they went to bed. He read 'The Song of Roland' in Old French. She turned off her lamp and fell asleep.

Early in the morning, she heard his voice murmuring beside her, like the far-off whirr of a lawnmower. Vaguely conscious of a hot projection of sun streaming through a gap in the curtains, she switched back into sub-consciousness. Her dream was suffused with light and sweat. A seaside scene flashed across her eyes. She knew it to be Brighton. She walked along a wide green park close to the water. Cotton-clad crowds milled through it, sporting sunglasses which glittered harshly and hid their souls. At the end of the park a fairground loomed: merry-go-round, ferris wheel, swings. She moved in the direction of the swings but a hand pulled her away. A white hotel, cruel and cold as only white seaside hotels can be, jutted up in front of her. A voice said: 'It's time to change.' She was pulled along towards the white concrete, filled with bleakness and despair. She still walked by the water. It wasn't green or grey or blue, but as clear as glass. She could see right down to the bottom. People were swimming underwater; men in dark suits and hats, women in coloured frocks and high-heeled shoes. One person rode a bicycle, up and down, round and round, under the water. All the people moved like fishes with blank faces and invisible strokes and they were silent as fishes. There was no noise in the dream now at all.

She awoke, properly this time. Sunlight still poured onto the foot of the bed, and the room was hot and sticky.

'Oh, you turned on the heater?'

She could see its red glow.

'I told you that an hour ago. It was so very cold. I've saved you from freezing.' His face was pale and the crow's feet around his eyes seemed to have multiplied during the night. He sniffed. A cold. She had anticipated it.

'How are you this morning?'

She leaned over and ruffled his hair. It was dark grey and soft. She loved it. Morning was her happiest time, no matter what.

'I don't know.' He lay back and directed his attention to the ceiling. His pyjamas were blue. 'I think I want to lie in bed today, and read.'

'Poor darling!'

She crawled down to the end of the bed and jumped out. The room was so narrow that there was no space at the sides. It had been built for a single bed. These were bachelor apartments. Most of the people in them were not bachelors, however, but spinsters, a fact which reflected something, something statistical, Margaret sometimes thought, not without a wince.

The living room was cold after the stuffy bedroom. The green carpet selfishly sucked in the sun. But, in the kitchen, it bounced back from the chromium-plated cooker and kettle, and danced on the walls. She stuck two pieces of bread in the toaster and began to sing. She felt like a housewife. Especially like a housewife she had seen in a film a week before. It had been a silly film, a badly disguised fantasy, in which all the women were married and thin and beautiful. They spent their mornings making toast and pouring out orange juice in sunlit kitchens, their afternoons playing tennis and complaining about their boredom. Well, they had plenty to complain about, she was sure of that. But at least they had the sun. That was a realistic detail. She remembered American kitchens herself, and they had always been filled with sun and sparkling orange juice first thing in the morning. In Ireland, sun didn't often happen, but today was an exception, and moreover, they had orange juice.

She opened a tin and mixed it with water, and then turned to the stove to make porridge. Edward always had porridge when she came to make it. It was a ritual, one of her privileges and duties. She couldn't eat it, but liked to see it boil. Today, as always, she stood and gazed into the hissing beige mess, enjoying the tiny eruptions and listening to the explosive sounds: plut, plut, plut plut! Or was it plap plap, plap plap? A fine distinction in sound existed, she knew, between different brands of oatmeal, but she had never been able to decide what the precise sound of any particular brand was.

Plop! The morning papers dropped through the letterbox. What a luxurious noise, the utter confirmation of the Sabbath! In answer, the sound of Edward springing out of bed came to her ears. She stopped staring at the porridge, reluctantly, and began to tinker with cups and plates on the table. He looked into the kitchen, his head sticking out of the dark pyjamas, pale and smiling.

'I'll get up, after all,' he said, rather cheerfully. She said: 'Ah!' and continued to play with the cups. He had not put on his spectacles. She had fallen in love with him in his spectacles, and he never attracted her without them.

They read as they ate, and went on reading for an hour or more afterwards. It was a silent period during which only the crackle of folding newspaper broke the vacuum of the flat. Sometimes, on Sunday mornings, he talked, and pointed out interesting snippets of news. Not today. Perhaps his cold exhausted his spare energy. She did not talk at all. She never did, unless he began. At other times, she might have resented this silence and suffered. Today, she accepted it as an inevitable contribution to the mood of the weekend. As it happened, her mind was silent, too, and held only blank, white impressions.

After lunch, Edward retired to bed, looking relieved to escape into the small stuffy room. Tired of cooking and of washing up without any encouragement, she sat down in an armchair again and opened a book. The sun had crept around to the corner of the flat, and there was only one sickly yellow line dividing the carpet, at an oblique angle. It had an old autumnal quality, even though it was spring. She felt a slight nausea. The day was slipping away, barren as autumn. Unbearable.

'I think I'll go for a walk,' she told Edward. He was sitting up, reading P. G. Wodehouse with apparent glee. He looked hurt, as she had known he would, but he said: 'All right.' She went outside. The air was morning-like, not at all what it had been in the flat. Instead of walking, she took her bicycle, and cycled down the road towards Blackrock. The sea spread out below her, navy blue and vital. It was a cold day, despite the sun, and when she looked back at the Dublin

Mountains they were capped with snow. April was filled with incongruities, usually expected but still stimulating when they occurred. As she cycled, she grew warm, and approaching Dun Laoghaire she could not remember what cold was.

The motion of cycling freed her physically, and, as her blood began to circulate faster, her mind began to loosen. The air raced past her and through her: it seemed to penetrate her brain and tease it into activity. It pushed her hair against her face and into her eyes, and she was happy to have hair and be thus made aware of it.

The route she had chosen for her cycle was a lively one. From Blackrock to Dalkey, hundreds of people jogged. It was National Milk Run Day, and they jogged for charity, tripping along the footpaths in small groups. At Seapoint, canoes rode the white-tipped waves, with a tender appealing movement, and a swimmer walked down the slip into the sea – she would freeze to death if she got in.

At Dun Laoghaire, sailboats bobbed around in the bay, and at Dalkey people rode on surfboards with sails, looking like large coloured bats. It was the town of Dun Laoghaire which gave greatest cause for wonder, however. Like an anthill, it teemed with people. They walked up and down the promenade, up and down the pier, up and down the main street. They talked a little, and shouted at children, and ate oranges and chocolate. They spent long, long periods standing in queues waiting to buy ice-cream. Many of them did not walk, or talk, or eat, but simply stared. They stared at the waves, at the boats, at the mailboat which was moored and would remain so for hours. They gazed at the lighthouse and at shops, and some of them even stared at Margaret, as she cycled, quickly, past.

Near the railway station, a large crowd had gathered to peer over the wall at the railway line, where workmen operated a large and noisy but by no means unusual machine. What is this life if, full of care, we have no time to stand and stare, far-off children's voices chanted from Margaret's past. The children had not had time to stare. But in Dun Laoghaire, everyone had too much time. They were for the most part doing nothing else. Margaret was staring herself, even as she moved past different scenes. The long finger of the pier pointed at the truth: she had been staring for years, at herself and at life and especially at Edward weaving an elaborate passage through her existence while being nevertheless in staunch command of his own. No bell-jar pinned her to a barren patch of reality. Edward made few explicit demands, he used no padlocks. But she stood and stared like a big-eyed cow and never mooed. That was why she fantasised sometimes about cycling down to the end of Dun Laoghaire Pier and going on cycling down to the bottom of the sea.

The meaning of her life had been plain to her from the moment she woke up this morning, if not before. She had so often conjured up the image of her dramatic end, in the freezing cold water. She had even imagined the gasps for breath, the horror of the realisation that she would not surface, the fear of slimy eels and mackerel which scavenged always in the bay. She was a coward and would not take the final step, not now and probably never, but she would deserve it and be forced to it if she did not stop staring ineptly at foreign surfaces. The air whipped past her and into her, but she needed to be a part of that air, to be a dynamic collection of atoms in continual interaction with the world, if she were to be saved.

She cycled faster and faster, and reflected very vaguely in a deep part of her belly that perhaps she would be knocked down by a car. But when she found herself swerving towards one, just at the large grey wall of Longford Terrace, she braked so hard that she jumped off the saddle and her breath was rammed into a hard ball in her chest. Faster and faster she cycled, thinking of herself lying in a hospital bed, in a ward with brown linoleum on the floor and pink dusty curtains on the windows. Her mother and father would be there waiting anxiously for the moment when her eyes would open. They would, at last, and she would peer up and see their old wrinkled faces. Edward's would not be there: he had said he would never visit her in hospital if she became ill, and stressed the point that she should not visit him either, if he did, something which he considered much more probable and imminent. Or would he perhaps be there? She did not know exactly which ending she would choose to this incident if she were God plotting it in a grubby little notebook in the sky above Blackrock. Or even if she were herself.

She pondered the sequel to his being present at her hospital bed or not present, as she locked her bicycle to the downpipe outside his hall door. She let herself into the flat. He was not in the living room. When she looked into his bedroom, he was lying asleep in semi-darkness. The paperback Wodehouse was upside-down on the counterpane. She smiled over the end of the bed and crawled up beside him. He wasn't snoring. He never did snore. It was, she considered, closing her eyes and tucking herself in against his large warm body, an advantage not to be under-estimated.

HEAT

GILLMAN NOONAN
Gillman Noonan was born in Kanturk, Co. Cork, 1937. A graduate of University College, Cork, he spent many years working in various European countries. He won the 1975 Writers' Week in Listowel Short Story Competition and has published two collections, *A Sexual Relationship* and *Friends and Occasional Lovers*.

Under its grid the cobalt's luminous energy appeared to rise up and enter his blood, chilling him with a power as cold and distant as the stars. Mick O'Dwyer had beckoned him in to the sterilising room as he passed by, and there it was beneath his feet in its bed of water like some creature of the deep frozen forever in the blue gleam of its signal. So silent was it among the boxes of syringes, so far from the rap and roar of the factory, that Danny had a picture of them, Mick and himself, as insiders, people who had slipped behind the wheel and din of life and stood now, alert and still, in the eye of its monstrous power.

What would happen if he fell in? 'Not much,' Mick had said, adding with a smile, 'if you didn't swim around for too long.' And now in the dark bedroom Danny saw himself diving into the blue pool as into the true element of his spirit that had remained hidden from him, locked away as though he had no right or competence to enter it, diving down and then rising to shiver into being again like a character in Dr Who, to stand at the window alive with the cobalt's ghostly light, the kids below running screaming into their homes. But the colour changed to the dirty copper flowing from the first spluttering hose they had trained on the fire.

He thought: I should have let it burn, the factory, instead of sounding the alarm and grabbing the extinguisher. The small tongues of flame were darting greedily among the broken cartons. In a minute the stacks of cardboard boxes would have gone up. The breeze whistling through the open warehouse doors would have carried the flame into the factory itself, engulfing the partitions and causing the bags of polypropylene to melt and fuse. People would have thrown down their earphones and run for the exits. But he had rushed for the alarm shouting 'Fire! Fire!' and later, standing hot and embarrassed in the assembly room while Mr Gully commended him for his swift action, Danny realised that even as his hand had reached for the small hammer to break the glass of the alarm he had been moved by the presence of the cobalt, moved almost in a religious way as if, only a few minutes earlier, he had been allowed a peep into the tabernacle of power, and now the factory was no longer just walls and a roof and lines of machinery but a precious edifice built around a magic stone.

The thought mocked him while he listened to Mr Gully uttering grim warnings about smoking on the premises. He felt tricked by the righteous words, the slick bull-necked tirade that masked a dumb ritual, no less than he had been deceived by the mysterious veil of blue masking a dumb isotope harnessed to a gauge. Once before Mr Gully had praised him openly for the tidiness of his work place. Across from him stood Smithy and Donaldson with smirks on them. And there was Dympna in the front row smiling and pleased as punch. Her fella. Man of the hour.

In the street below boys played at commandos shooting from the unlit hallways. The power had failed after tea and it was a novelty with only candles and lamps flickering in the houses. His mother had brought him up a candle but he had blown it out.

He thought of Dympna, their walk (was the pier in darkness too?), their two drinks in Walters. His body tensed as if preparing for another ordeal. She would be tender in the shadow of the pier wall. Later, on one of the red stools in the lounge she would sit erect with her knees together and sip her vodka and lime. They prided themselves on not being part of the singalong mob. But there were limits to individuality. 'Thirty quid!' she had exclaimed when he said he had signed on for a philosophy course. The card he had picked up in a pub was soiled and wrinkled. She held it by a corner as if afraid of contamination. 'Probably a rip-off,' she said. 'What's it all for anyway?'

And that was the point, because he had expected to be told all about philosophy, to dip into the wisdom of ages, whereas the tutor only dwelt on how the mind worked, what parts of it take over at certain times, what happens when we daydream or lose ourselves in anger. He made them do exercises sitting very still, just taking in what they saw and heard without thinking too much about it, being aware of themselves, the weight of the body on the chair, the clothes on the body, seeing and hearing at the same time what was within and without but with no immediate search for 'meaning'.

Meaning, Danny had thought, was what it was all about. Still it was important to him to be there between a housewife and a young farmer who said he had come to the course because he was bored with pulling cabbages. Hadn't he come for the same reason? And the farmer was out in the fields all day not stuck behind a machine!

'But where does it get you?' Dympna went on. 'Isn't it only aping the college boys?' She believed in focusing attention on what was within range. Danny was a bit of a dreamer, 'as soft as an egg inside but as complicated,' as she expressed it to his sister. It was what had attracted her to him – their first night out he never once mentioned football or discos – but was also, she soon realised, the fatal chink in her knight's armour. Or rather, the armour of his job and life that should be bearing down on the obstacles in his path was proving to have a thousand chinks through each of which Danny was tempted to peep, ambition meanwhile whistling past his ears. At twenty-six it was a bit late for dreaming.

'Truth waits in us all,' the tutor told the group. 'And it is now we have to reach for it, not yesterday which has passed or tomorrow which may never come. We are all intellectuals.' He even rhymed it, saying, 'We can fly to knowledge without ever going to college.' Danny regretted not having had that on his tongue when Dympna came out with her sneer about the college boys. Still, if she had asked, 'What *is* this knowledge?' he would have had no answer. He had ceased to talk about it. They went for their walks and discussed other things. But it upset him that he had started a search which she showed no desire to share. As a creature awakens from some state of instinct to a canny awareness of itself as a solitary being, he was asking himself the crucial question: Why Dympna? Why not another? Why anyone right now? He was growing away from her, from their cosy plans, their account with the Dublin Savings Bank (target: £1,000 down for the mortgage, saving £20 a week), their budgeted two drinks in Walters, a few more on a Saturday night.

A lorry roared by and shook the house. He hoped the power failure would last. In the lull of traffic that followed, his father's voice below took up the receding hum. The candlelight had played on his face as on an image graven and timeless. Through half-closed eyes Danny had flipped in a time loop in which *he* was his father as a young man looking out upon life from a kitchen full of the same sounds and shadows, a place disturbed only by human thought and sinew. He would have sat before such a man with features full of strong resignation, burlier perhaps (to judge by an old photo of his grandfather) with fiery whiskers, telling of his action, proudly repeating Mr Gully's words.

'What . . . do . . . you . . . think . . . is . . . at . . . stake?' Mr Gully had spaced his words with dramatic effect. 'Two hundred jobs

and one fag end, that's what's at stake. If it hadn't been for the swift
action of Danny McGee here . . .' At the end, after preaching his
favourite gospel of cleanliness in toilet, canteen and locker room ('We
have a party of visitors today and I was appalled at the matches and
papers strewn about'), he reverted to jobs, all jobs, 'in these times of
want and insecurity' calling them 'gold, pure gold.'

Danny sat at his machine, numbed and empty, grateful only that
with the noise there was no need for him to speak to anyone. If 'truth',
he thought savagely, as the tutor said, was the quarry, then what he
had been praised for was mere chance.

The syringes travelled up the elevator from the hopper and into the
drums where they were vibrated around with a great noise until finally
dropping into their polythene bags. Occasionally they bunched in the
rails and seemed to quiver with impatience until he freed them. Thus
at times he had waited, quivering, to be off work to meet Dympna.
Down the line more product was moving, vibrating, dropping. Nimble
fingers were scooping up the bags from the conveyor and putting
them into cartons. Blue ear phones, yellow (Dympna's were yellow
with a black stripe), red, each mind a hush and hiss and a hum and
again a hush and a hiss, and scratchy voices from far away. One came
to him from over his shoulder.

'What's your . . . ?' It belonged to one of the party of American
Chinese visiting the plant. Danny turned and shook his head. 'No
speak American chink,' he said with his lips. 'Fuck off.' The visitor
beamed and repeated his question, putting his mouth close to Danny's
ear. His breath was sweet and heavy from wine.

'What's your hourly rate?'

'About 80,000,' Danny shouted. He provided other facts. A dud
syringe was blown out by the air jet and struck the little man in the
face. Great fun. The slit of his eyes sealed up in a smile.

'Good,' he said, patting Danny on the shoulder and trotting after
the group. Danny did not look in Dympna's direction but he knew that
she was watching him. She liked to see him talking to people, being
involved. At such moments he hated her most. She loved to guide his
nose into some close and smelly conceit of himself. As if one day he
could believe in it and turn it into something strong and fine. He
shouldn't be such a loner, she urged. Even in the canteen she noticed
him frequently sitting apart from the others (what *he* had noticed on
his first day was that the women all tended to crowd together in one
corner) or joking with the men he had worked with in dispatch before
being trained as an 'operative' complete with white coat and ear

phones. He should be sitting with the technicians and fitters and learning from them, learning perhaps about the huge injection moulders to which he might move on. Her own brother Dan had started in his kind of job ('Routine really, just knowing how to service your machine, isn't that right?') before going on to become an electrician.

What Danny could not explain was that he was losing his feel for the simplest forms of communication. When he sat with his old mates from dispatch he would hang on their words as if searching for clues to the sense of normal human fellowship he had once enjoyed. Often in the canteen he experienced rather than heard the noise, the bursts of laughter, break around him, and then he was afraid to utter the simplest words and attended to those of others as if he were a foreigner in his own country picking up the idiom and slang of his fellow workers. Or he would be tempted to say too much, words would spill from him, a story badly told or what his brother was up to. He might lose the thread entirely or bungle the point, and then his mates (especially Smithy) would look at him as if indeed he was a foreigner trying to get his tongue around the language.

One evening, reading a library book about a man who studied ducks and lived with them, Danny startled his mother by saying that she had been 'imprinted' on him. He elaborated. The idea seemed to explain a lot. He argued that he – and maybe all working class people – had never learned to think at all but had the thoughts of the higher-ups, the experts and poshies, imprinted on them. They had been fed with ideas about themselves as he fed his machine with syringes. Then through the door he heard his mother wondering aloud to his father whether 'knocking about with that communist Billy Caffrey' was good for him. Perhaps Father Nolan should have a word. Disgusted, Danny took to wearing ear phones in the home. He took down from the wall the photo of him that had appeared in a company brochure looking resplendently white and clean and efficient at his machine. His father drew him aside and said, 'Look, son, if the job is getting you down, all that noise and everything, well, look for something else. Maybe what you need to do is get out in the open. I heard from Matt Twomey there may be a job going up in Larkin's yard . . .' Which of course started a row with Dympna who thought that his father's concern would simply turn him back into a labourer. What he needed was 'to cop himself on' and not go around pretending he was 'a bloody genius or something.'

Danny ignored them. He bought a diary and wrote down what he saw. In the mornings before work he recorded his dreams. On their walks he would talk about them and Dympna listened, suppressing her impatience. 'Real' thought appeared to him in one dream as a dark shambling thing lagging far behind on the road where his body raced along. He hadn't lost his head – at least when he put his hand up to touch it it was still there – but it was manned only by the everyday brain maintaining essential services like feet and elbows, breathing and bowel movements. The shape wasn't something threatening, some horror in the subconscious waiting to pounce. When he tried to will it as such, slowing down, tempting it to overtake, it hid behind a tree like a shy monster. And the next morning it still followed him around the factory! (At this point Dympna suggested he should take a week's holiday.) He felt it lurking in places, waiting to uncoil like a Jack-in-the-box from every carton of product he slit open.

When he did take a week off the sun blazed as if, in league with the others, it approved of his getting out and away from his obsessions. He messed about with his brother's skiff and went for rides through the Wicklow hills on his old Honda. His favourite place became a narrow grassy ledge high up on the Scalp. There he sat and scribbled things in his diary. He tried to express what he felt but the words fell dry and lifeless like dust upon the page.

He even made a list of other jobs he could take up. Lighthouse keeper was one that appealed but on enquiry he found that he was over-age and under-educated. There was forestry work but again his background was unsatisfactory and anyway he couldn't tell one tree from the next.

'You are trees,' he said, lying on his back and addressing the greenery above his head. 'Hello, trees.' He patted the warm rock beside him. 'Hello, rock. We both crazy things.' In large letters he wrote down: I'M GOING CRAZY ON THE SCALP. This was a great joke and he hooted with laughter. For a while he seriously considered taking out his share of the money from the bank and just bumming around the place. But what would that solve? When he stood up things went black for a moment and he had the sensation of falling through space. Shaken, he lost his nerve for the descent and climbed over the ridge and down by the golf course and the artificial ski slope. Sitting in the plush lounge of the hotel he imagined that the set of clubs beside him were his. He started an eye flirt with a young barmaid and she and her mates began to giggle at him. Then he was back at his machine again and everyone was saying what a lovely tan he had, as if he'd been abroad.

'Jimmy!' a woman called in the street below. 'You come in here this minute, you young pup!'

All around in the dark street people were waiting for the light to come on, their voices hushed. Danny had a picture of caves and then of molten steel bursting like gold from a gap in the wall and flowing among the streets, the people emerging from the houses to stand and gaze at it, their faces bright and glowing. In the factory the syringes were golden pens dropping into silver bags and he scooped them up, scattering them among the children.

In the afternoon he had sat lost in thought ('circling thoughts', the tutor would have said) and when he looked up it was to see Smithy leafing through the diary he had placed beside him on the table. 'What's this?' he read aloud. 'I'm twenty-six and know nothing. But I'm a good robot. That's one truth.' For a few seconds, his heart pounding, Danny held back, hoping that Smithy would toss the book back on the table. But with a triumphant glance at the others, he read on: 'Walters – all the men staring at the box like at mass waiting for the consecration.' Then: 'I'm going crazy on the Scalp.' Amid laughter Smithy said, 'That's a queer fuckin' place to be going crazy.' Danny reached across and tried to snatch the book but Smithy jerked it up. A chair was upturned and then the table as Danny lunged. Smithy caught him with a side swipe that sent him flying and Danny reached for a chair but when he swung it around it connected with the phones on the wall beside him. By order of the management the numbers on them had been removed to discourage incoming calls, and now as if something had popped in Danny's brain, this became the real object of his fury. 'As if we were bloody nameless creatures,' he cried, striking at them again. Ignoring Smithy entirely he turned towards where the buns were displayed in a vending machine as though intent on settling a score with them, and perhaps with the awful soup dispensers as well . . . And there was Mr Gully in the doorway, staring in astonishment at his golden boy.

'I suppose in one sense it's quite an achievement,' he said later in his office. Danny stood before him, pale and tight-lipped. 'In the morning I commend you for saving the factory from being burnt down, in the afternoon I have to reprimand you for trying to wreck it with a chair. What was it all about?'

'A personal matter.'

'Personal matters are to be dealt with after work, is that clear?'

The door-bell rang. That would be Dympna. Danny got up and lit the candle. What would he tell her about the fight? The truth? That suddenly appeared enormous, entirely outside their world. But he saw that she would approve of his action as she understood it. The kind of head-on anger he had displayed in the canteen was healthy. Indeed before the tea break was over he felt he had achieved quite another standing with the younger men. Smithy had offered his hand, returning the diary. Danny the firebrand. With a little effort he might even become their spokesman, get management to put the numbers back on the telephones, achieve something tangible that would improve conditions. It was as if the whole plane of his concern had shifted from the personal to the social, his sullen longing for some unattainable truth within himself transformed within minutes into the kind of anger the world understood. He might strike out again in future but it would be for other reasons, loud plausible ones, and Dympna would be proud of him. But would he ever again swing a chair at what had been for one brilliant moment the real and mighty enemy that was yet as elusive as the air, the real one glimpsed in a crowd, in a bit of depersonalised plastic, that was one's own pitted against gratitude for what was less than life, scarcely more than insult?

The candle flame rose tall and sleek, flattened. He thought of a long black wave ever-breaking with a few bright blue flecks of phosphorescence. On the ceiling his head and shoulders hulked ten feet tall. He closed a huge hand over the light flex and it slid down and away, moving nothing. The house shook as another lorry thundered past. When the noise had faded a cry was heard, a sharp angry aaah! that died on the air yet echoed in the minds of people sitting in their shadowy rooms. A fight somewhere in the small warren of redbrick houses? They waited for the shouts, the breaking glass, but there was nothing.

The bedroom door opened and Danny's mother looked in. Danny stood with his back to her, holding his wrist.

'Did you call, Danny?' she said.

'No.'

'Dympna is below.'

When he said nothing she approached and took his hand in hers, turning it over. The skin across the palm was taut and shiny, a rising silver weal that caught the gentle candlelight.

'Jesus, child,' she said after a moment's wonder, 'what have you done to yourself? Water, come on, quick, into water with it!'

HENRY DIED

KATE CRUISE O'BRIEN
Kate Cruise O'Brien was born in Dublin, 1948. A graduate of Trinity College, Dublin, she has published a novel and a collection of short stories, *A Gift Horse*.

HENRY DIED. University students are rarely able to cope with universals and death is the most embarrassing universal. I was shocked, and I was embarrassed.

I was sitting on the steps of the college chapel, eating apples in the sun and watching people emerge from the front gate into the enclosed cobbled front square. I was counting smiles as opposed to stumbles. Some people who emerged from the dark hall, hopefully called gate, stumbled, some smiled. I was sure it was significant and was trying to make up my mind why. Then I saw my most recent boyfriend smilingly stumble out of the front gate and I picked up my newspaper. I dislike watching people approaching from a long distance or I dislike acknowledging their approach from a long distance. A greeting smile wanes somewhat after five minutes and yet one cannot cease smiling. It seems impolite. My concern over this was superfluous as he immediately crossed the square in the opposite direction. Having ascertained this, I returned to my newspaper. Then I saw Henry's picture. It was familiar to me. Peter, his best friend, had taken it the term before. There was Henry with his long pointed nose, his myopic eyes concealed by round rimless glasses and his curly hair surmounting a heading on the front page of one of Dublin's less restrained evening papers: 'TCD student takes own life.'

There is a rhyme:

'Mary's the one who never liked angel stories,
But Mary's the one who has died.'

I always thought it was inept. It is easier to mourn the gay than it is to mourn the morose. One can write inept rhymes, one can remember their funniness with a suitable catch of the breath. The morose, who do not become life, become death even less. One should not even say that they 'were somehow marked out for death.' Though one does say it. The morose are usually morose through the disparity between their expectations and their reality. They are glum because life is mistreating them and they are misjudged. This however is supposed to be a comment on poor Henry who had taken his own life and it could be said that Henry had been marked out for death. He had, after all, marked death out for himself. He must have contemplated it. He achieved it, I read, with gas and sleeping pills. He had sealed up his windows and door with 'Fixit – the self-adhesive that really sticks', locked the door, taken six sleeping pills and turned on the gas. 'He died holding a letter from his fiancée, Miss Jennifer Carter, terminating their engagement.'

Miss Jennifer Carter at that moment jumped across into the sun from the dark hallway of Front Gate. She yelled at me across the busy quiet square, 'Sarah, you bitch, I've been searching for you everywhere.' I smiled and waved as she bounced across the intervening space. I was never embarrassed by Jennifer's approach. We always smiled and waved and shouted in ironic acknowledgement of the difficulty of that situation, and of our enjoyment of our exhibitionism.

She reached me and grasped my shoulder. She was giggling and breathless. 'I'm pissed, don't be cross, Sarah, it's such fun.' She always apologised for what she hoped I would be shocked by. She liked to regard me as her strict mentor from time to time. It added interest to two mild glasses of shandy.

I handed her the paper. She read the column, handed the paper back to me and sat down beside me. She picked up an apple and began to eat it in large bites, munching and swallowing it quickly.

'I've known that, Sarah. They rang, Henry's parents rang last night and told me.'

'Well why didn't you tell me?'

She fiddled with a corner of her eyelash (false) and looked across the square.

'Because I didn't know what to say. I don't know how to deal with this.'

'You don't have to say anything, not to me, anyway, but when you do, don't pretend it was your fault or that you have to feel guilty. All right, you're sorry. You were engaged to him. You once thought you were in love with him and you'll have to see people blaming you because you discovered you weren't. You might make that easier for yourself if you rushed around saying it was your fault and that you felt guilty. People would pity you. It would be bad for you, though, and untrue. You might get to believe it, and no one, no one is responsible for taking their own lives but themselves. Don't dramatise it, Jenny, it's a supreme situation for self-dramatisation and you mustn't do it because this time self-dramatisation is dangerous.'

She had watched me carefully throughout this speech. 'You're dramatising, you're acting the wise friend, the knowing confidante. And I don't know why you're so defensive about my guilt.' And then she grasped my wrist and began to laugh, hiccupping pieces of half-chewed apple out of her mouth. She coughed then and choked, and I withdrew her grasp from my wrist and thumped her back until she stopped choking. She looked at me again.

'I could have cried then, laughing to tears, but I won't, I promise. Let's go away from here.' And so we went.

Despite my homily, I began to realise the next morning why Jennifer hadn't told me until she had to. I did not at all know how to deal with this situation and I was very tempted to pretend it had not happened. But I had gone out with Henry's best friend the term before and I loved Jennifer. Since I could not pretend with them, I could not pretend with anyone, for acting over something as large as this would have to be an uninterrupted business.

Jennifer, I saw, when I arrived in the coffee bar, was definitely dressed for a part, which I noted commenced with everyone else's knowledge of Henry's death, not with her own. She was wearing a very dashing black floppy hat, with a veil which half-covered her face, a brown and white checked coat, and a black dress.

I looked at her as I sat down on the bench beside her. She was smoking a cigarette with difficulty because of the veil, and also because her fingers were shaking.

'Why are you wearing that thing?' I asked, nodding at the hat.

'Isn't it gorgeous! I think I look mysterious and dangerous.' She lifted the veil a little and peered out at me. 'And a little, little bit tragic?'

'No,' I said.

'No, I didn't think so either, really.' She opened her handbag and took out a pair of dark glasses. She then lifted the veil and put them on and lowered it again.

'More mysterious, more dangerous, Sarah?'

'Yes,' I said. Then I paused. 'Jennifer, what did you say to Henry's parents?'

'Oh, I was quite terse really, you know, "Yes, no, how, when?"'

'Were they nice about it?'

'Well,' she said, or drawled with consideration. She is accurate and careful in her assessment of behaviour. 'It was his mother, and she was really very nice to me. And it was a bit difficult for her because I was so terse. So she said I should come to the funeral, which is tomorrow, and then she said something at the end like "You mustn't blame yourself, my dear, and you must let your feelings go, have a good cry." The main idea was that underneath my tough exterior there's a heart of pure molten gold, that I was pretending not to care when I did really.'

'Do you?'

'I don't care,' she said. 'I didn't depend on him any more, and if someone is dead, and one doesn't see them dying, and one didn't depend on them, how can one care?'

She took off her glasses and I saw that the skin around her eyes was puckered and red. Above her eyes she wore her usual rather strange make-up. Wispy black lines were drawn out in a radius from a black socket line. From her eyes to her eyebrows her skin was painted a light blue-white. The veins of her eyelids showed through the paint.

'Have you been crying?'

'A bit, but it's more or less acting to myself really, and worry because I'm frightened of meeting people.'

'You mustn't, love. The people who matter will know you well enough not to blame you.'

'Do you really think they shouldn't blame me?' It was a question I didn't want to answer.

'Are you coming to this lecture?' I asked. She pulled her long hair. Her hair was inclined to be very wavy and grew unevenly. It was one of her permanent and irregular attractions, for it stood out around her head like a jagged brown and yellow cloud in blurring bars of colour. Jennifer put a yellow end of hair in her mouth and sucked it. 'No,' she said, out of the other side of her mouth.

'Will you be all right?' We allowed ourselves to look after each other, for although we were aware of the occasional excess of our concern, or because of our awareness of it, we were never embarrassed by our own sentimentality. It was like talking to oneself to cheer oneself up.

'Yes, love,' she put a hand on my shoulder. 'Run along, Sarah, and I'll be a big brave girl, big certainly.' She giggled. She was tall with very big bones, but not fat. Her figure was a constant source of worry to her and again, as in the case of her hair, in not conforming to the skeleton standard of conventional beauty, it held an attraction of its own.

I went out of the coffee bar and walked along a line of low Elizabethan rubrics towards my lecture, which was in an ugly, but not obtrusive building in the square behind. As I turned the corner I saw Peter coming towards me. Peter and I together had formed, for a short while, a foil for Henry and Jennifer. Or, as Jennifer said, 'I got you and Peter together, love, to mitigate the boredom, the ghastly, intolerable boredom.'

'Sarah, I want to talk to you,' said Peter.

'Yes, I'm going to a lecture, but I don't have to go. I think we should talk. I mean –' I stumbled on the cobbles and, as Peter put out a hand to help me, I bent my head. I am incapable of exchanging looks with men I care for.

'Come for a walk,' said Peter. 'Around College Park.' We walked into College Park, where young men in track suits were training by running slowly around the periphery of the shorn grass. We both sat down on a bench and, for a time, sat still. Peter watched the runners and I watched the trees which grew around the sides of the park. They were large elms. The sun shone through them, dappling the long grass at the side of the track. I could see two friends of mine lying side by side, their heads against the bole of a tree. The man was tickling the girl's neck with a twig.

'How does Jenny feel now?' asked Peter. He turned his head towards me. I thought that I had forgotten how big his nose was and his chin.

'How do you mean "How does she feel"?' The young man had abandoned his twig and now gently eased his arm under the girl's neck.

'About Henry.' The girl settled her head against the man's shoulder and I could see her two white feet twisting.

'Sorry, but not guilty. She shouldn't, you know, feel guilty. Henry never tried to help himself whenever she broke it off. He just ran around after her and asked for more.'

'You are a bitch, Sarah. I mean that.' Peter bent over towards me. His eyes, which were big and blue, opened widely. The muscles at one side of his nose contracted and the corresponding side of his mouth lifted. He achieved a sneer. He had large features, big eyes, a large crooked nose and a long chin. His cheeks were fleshless. Until I met Peter I never believed that there was such a thing as a gaunt face. His was gaunt. When he smiled his face did not relax, it tautened, and the skin around his eyes wrinkled. His whole face was used in his smile, and when he sneered now I felt a little sick.

'I liked Henry, he did Jenny good, he made her grow up a lot.' I lied, and then was afraid that Peter knew that I was lying and would despise me for betraying the integrity of my own feelings, and then I thought that I was not betraying my integrity, for my first feeling was of wanting Peter. I knew that was a lie, for if I had to change myself to please Peter, wanting Peter was an illusion, but I knew I wanted Peter. These thoughts made themselves felt in an unhappy confusion which resolved itself in uneasiness and a sudden desire to cry and run away, to go home and wait until Henry had been forgotten.

'Yes, Henry did help Jenny, and he really loved her. She just used him. She kept the engagement going until Trinity Ball because she wanted a partner, and she kept herself amused in the meanwhile by having constant rows with him. I went through it, Sarah. I sat up with him each night after their constant quarrels. And I know what he felt like because I've been through that too.' As he spoke, he lowered his voice. I suppose he thought that I would be moved. But I was too much at his emotional mercy to pity him now for his past and vague sufferings. Also because I felt *I* was to be pitied I was sure *his* self-pity was insincere. I did not, of course, say this to him. Because I act so constantly I hate catching other people out in their little acts.

'You don't know what Jennifer felt like.'

'Why don't you tell me?'

'She acts, you know. The quarrels weren't real to her, they just alleviated the boredom.'

'Boredom?' asked Peter. His face seemed to fall away from his eyes now and he swept his hair back from his face dramatically, but ineffectually.

'Is that all it meant to her?'

'No, it isn't at all all it meant to her. It was just extra.'

'Extra?' He was really quite funny with his one-word interjections. Peter truly has an expression that represents to me all the things that I associate with the word quizzical. He can look attractive, questioning and amused all at the same time. I feel then like a young and intelligent child who has been so clever that her schoolmaster almost loves her. The expression was there now and, in response, I was clever.

'She loved his love, you see. It was the one thing in Henry she felt above all others, and by quarrelling she could see it working.'

'There were, eh' – the 'eh' sounded silly – 'other ways of seeing love work?' I was disappointed in him and I deteriorated. Back to amateur Freud, the bane of my young life, when I couldn't be ill without my clever elder sister telling me that it was only my unconscious.

'She didn't trust those ways.' I felt uncomfortable. I couldn't say sex. Not to somebody I'd been to bed with.

'She felt that those ways were the only reason Henry wanted her, and she kept on having to remind him they weren't.'

'That's nonsense.'

'I know,' I said, and was pleased that Peter should think it was nonsense. I like people knowing I'm being trite when I am being trite.

'Well, if you know, don't try and justify her. She just wanted to manipulate Henry, and she did, out of existence. A great power game.' I felt very shaky. Peter said the last sentence with a pause after each word and I felt a terrible impulse to giggle, and once I started to giggle I knew that I would be unable to stop. I decided to pretend to cry instead and curiously, once I let the hiccupping motion which was in my stomach out, I was crying.

'Don't do that, Sarah.' He patted my shoulder from behind. Not caressingly. Just trying to stop me. 'Don't get yourself torn up by this, don't make yourself believe that Jennifer was justified and then get upset because you can't convince yourself, and you can't feel sorry for Jennifer and Harry at once.' Peter saying Harry made me cry again. Because of the late-night coffee sessions they had together, their camaraderie, their being funny together. At last I did feel sorry and, more than that, unhappy, that Henry was dead.

'Don't, Sarah, I can't leave you like this. Here.' He gave me a large, dirty handkerchief and I mopped my face with it. I refrained from blowing my nose, though I wanted to. 'Look, if you face the fact that your defence is useless to Jenny and you, you'll be a lot better off. The most important thing now is that Henry is dead and he died because Jennifer was too occupied with her frivolities to see that his feelings for her were entirely serious. That must have been terrible. Feeling so much and never getting a response that wasn't calculated, for effect.'

I blew my nose. I decided that it was, after all, childlike and endearing to blow the nose. 'I know that, Peter.'

'Well, don't defend her then.'

'It is nothing to do with defending her. Jennifer acts. That's Jennifer. It was a terrible accident.'

'All right, she acts, but she should have gone somewhere else to

act. She should have seen that Henry wasn't acting. It was not seeing
that's unforgivable, and if she refuses to see her guilt that's even more
unforgivable.' I was pulling a button on my coat, and as I tightened
my hand the thread broke and it fell to the ground. Peter picked it up
and gave it to me.

'Didn't you see that, Sarah?'

'Yes, I suppose I did.' I had, of course. It is easier not to realise
something one does not want to realise alone. When someone one
respects realises it for one it is unhappily inescapable. Now I had been
forced to face her guilt, which was considerable, and appalling to me
because she did not seem to have recognised it at all. I had tried to
avoid thinking about her guilt because I did not want to be separate
from her. To disapprove of her without her approval.

We got up to go by common, but mute consent. We had nothing
else to say to each other and I needed to see Jennifer.

As we approached the coffee bar I saw Jennifer peering out of the
window. Her hat had slipped back on her head and the veil of the hat
was now covering, not her eyes, but her hair. I did not tell Peter I
could see her, although I knew he had seen her and though I knew
he knew I had seen her.

'Thank you for the walk,' I said. I wouldn't have said that if I could
have thought of anything else to say, or if I could have borne silence.
Silence was embarrassing between us now. We were neither companionable nor uninterested.

'What are you thanking me for?' asked Peter.

'For nothing, obviously, if you can ask that.'

'How do you mean "if you can ask that"?' Now that Henry was
dead, the only subject on which we could talk with any ease at all was
his death. Every other subject would be affected by that fact. Because
any other subject would be an escape from the embarrasment of
Henry's death, which was much less embarrassing than the escape.
At least that was what I felt Peter felt. What I knew was that the
escape was from the sudden absence of intimacy between us, which
left us with no knowledge of how to deal with each other. I felt regret
for this, but I wanted the ending to be over.

Jennifer came out of the coffee bar. Her veil was back over her
eyes.

'I must go, Sarah. I'll see you sometime.' The sometime meant he
wouldn't see me. Then he looked at Jennifer as she came up and
smiled, or grinned. For the smile was concentrated towards one end
of his mouth and his nose wrinkled.

'What a hat, Jennifer, are you by any chance Miss Garbo wanting to be alone?'

'I vant to be alowne,' said Jennifer.

Peter laughed, waved and left us. I both admired and despised him for his manner with Jennifer. I admired him because I hate scenes and I dislike coolness, and I despised him because he ought to have addressed his complaints about Jennifer to Jennifer. I knew that in the same situation I would have behaved in the same way. Unfortunately for me, I always hope that my men will have greater integrity than I have myself. Integrity is a quality that I admire because I find it so hard to possess it. I would rather be liked than to sit in judgement because I would rather be protected than be the protector.

'Let's go to the park,' said Jennifer. She grabbed my arm and I clung to it.

'Thank God for you, Jenny.'

She lowered her glasses and looked at me. 'Was it that bad?'

'Worse.'

'Is it over?'

'I can't think of any way it wouldn't be.'

The park was empty now. The lovers had gone and whitish clouds had come over the sun. They were low clouds, for one of them raked the top of the trees and began to look like mist, fading from cloud to thick air to air.

'What did Peter say?'

'Nothing much.'

'Did he say anything about me?' A small piece of cloudy mist seemed to be caught in a branch of the tree. The two ends of it moved slowly apart and together, embracing the branch and then letting it go.

'I'm not going to the funeral.'

'Why not?'

'Because there'll be all those people knowing it was my fault.'

'Knowing?'

'You know it was, don't you, Sarah? I've been thinking about it. I know it was my fault because I've enough knowledge of psychology to know that that's why I'm afraid of people thinking it was. But I don't know it for any other reason. I mean I don't feel guilty.'

I was released from blaming Jennifer because as soon as she knew it was her fault, I didn't have to know for her. It was a shared, not a separating emotion. But I still didn't see what the trouble was.

She sat on the grass, which was moist, for the mist was gradually thickening and dampening. She dug little holes in the grass with her bare fingers. 'Sarah,' she said, and her voice was very high, 'I don't feel anything at all. I know everything and I don't feel anything, and I know everything because I've been informed. I do really want to feel something.'

And a line came into my head:

'Oh God, I believe. Help Thou my unbelief.'

AFTER THE MATCH

MARY O'DONNELL

Born in Co. Monaghan, 1954, Mary O'Donnell is a graduate of
St Patrick's College, Maynooth. She has worked as a translator at
Heidelberg University and as Drama Critic for *The Sunday Tribune*.
She won the William Allingham Short Story Award in 1989 and the
Writers' Week in Listowel Short Story Competition in 1990. She has
published one novel, a volume of poetry, and a short story collection,
Strong Pagans.

They burst into the reception hall at Old Woodleigh, fists raised in triumph, the growing *waaahh* sound which had been audible from a distance now deepening, distorting their faces as they fell *en masse* through the double doors. The opposition had been trounced in a stunning display of muscle and airborne muck at the Leinster Schools Rugby Final.

Helen stood with Doreen and Katy, the wives of two other Bellemont teachers. *Waaahhh* . . . The women shifted uncomfortably, taking pointedly casual sips from their drinks as they watched the boys close in around the two trainers. Helen studied Adam's face. He was in seventh heaven. This was the moment when all the extra time spent training the young beasts – the late nights, the pep-talks and sessions which had intensified during the last, vital weeks – suddenly added up. She was pleased for him, the happy glow on his face some sort of pay off.

'Isn't it marvellous for them!' Doreen giggled over her G and T, adjusting a frothy pink blouse at the neck as the tangle of cheering bodies suddenly shifted in their direction.

'Absolutely!' Katy agreed. 'You must both be thrilled skinny.'

'Oh it's great to see them win. As a mother I know just what it means to the boys,' Doreen said, eyes shining with pleasure.

'Aren't you thrilled, Helen?' said Katy again, more for something to say than in true speculation.

'Delighted. Delighted,' said Helen, distracted by the whooping and back-slapping.

'Of course it's your first time so it'll seem very new,' said Doreen, conspiratorially. 'But when Adam has worked with Patrick and brought them through like this a few more times, you'll take it all in your stride. I know when Patrick started training I was so nervous you wouldn't believe it. I mean you want them to win, you wish so desperately for everything to work out.'

'Well, it has anyway.' Helen was vague, uncertain of her humour.

Patrick and Adam were hoisted shoulder-high, good-humouredly tolerating the heaving and jostling. The parents of the players mingled with the group, not quite at the centre of the knot of bodies but near enough to be hugged and kissed by sons who were out of their minds with joy. One of the boys forced the cup, a well-dented trophy chased in silver and gold, into Adam's hands.

'Ah, lads, I can't balance!' he shouted, raising the cup unsteadily. They roared again and took off at a lumbering gallop around the hall.

'Easy now, lads!' Patrick called. Nobody heard. He was older than Adam, his face finely-lined, more assured.

Flustered helpers tried to seat the jubilant mob. Waiters and serving women signalled, ignored until a few of the parents and most of the teachers made their way to the dining area. The boys followed untidily. Helen groaned quietly as one of them started the school rallying song again. It was rapidly taken up as they filtered through. She was starving. The afternoon on the terraces at Lansdowne had been freezing, hail and wind whipping in under the stand till they were drenched. They were proper ninnies to have taken so much trouble with their appearances, she thought, observing the other women. Like fresh, dewy flowers, individually not so interesting, but as a group colourful and strangely expectant. Like girls at their first party. The older ones were muffled in furs and fine wool. Because it was a day which had promised victory, she'd had her hair plaited, and wore a new navy and green dress bought specially for the occasion. It had cost too much but she liked it and Adam would find the effect exotic and interesting among all the matrons.

'Womba, womba, womba,' the slow chant began. She tried to look benevolent and pleasant as she took her seat and watched the team and their followers crash their way down along the tables. 'Ing-gang-oolie-oolie-oolie-oolie,' they growled, reminding her of visiting rugby teams from New Zealand whose ritual dance was intended to intimidate the opponents. One of the boys grabbed a seat opposite her and sat down, panting.

'Jaysus!' he gasped, blinking in her direction, but she realised that he wasn't looking at her so much as drifting in and out of some hallucinatory and highly-pleasured dream. 'Ing-gang-goo.'

To her right a restless middle-aged man with lightly-tanned skin shifted continually in his seat.

'Hello, I'm Helen Kilroy.' She introduced herself easily, decided she'd best make an effort and be sociable. The bane of her life. Being

sociable. Making an effort for the sake of civility. He looked at her for
a moment, surprised at her presence, not expecting to be addressed.

'Oh. How d'you do? McElligot. Jim,' he mumbled, extending his
hand.

'You've a son on the team, right?'

'Wrong. Nephew,' he said curtly, looking over her shoulder and
waving at somebody.

'Good man Delaney! Knew you'd do it, ya bloody hound!' he
bellowed, taking a slug from a glass of wine. '*Chow-chow-chow*,' the
call went, its barking rhythm strengthening. Helen tried again. For
Adam's sake she must make an effort to be amenable.

'Oh yes, I remember the boy – Ciaran McElligot is your nephew.'

'Got it in one!' he said, before stopping suddenly. 'But . . . but . . .
my God, I've just realised who you are!' He sat back, absorbing her
from head to toe as if she were a vision.

'I do apologise Mrs Kilroy . . . Helen, that what you said? . . . The
way things are today, I don't know what's happening. Super isn't it,
you must be so proud of Adam, delighted with yourself, what?'

'*Womba, womba, womba.*' She wondered how to counter the flood
of hyperbole. How pleased did she have to be, how could she convey
her pleasure, that yes, it was wonderful?

To her left, Doreen chattered to somebody's father. She was cut
out for it, Helen thought, remembering the chocolate eclairs and
apple-tarts which Doreen had ferried to the team the evening before
every match. 'I really feel for them,' she was saying, staring wide-eyed
at the man. 'It's so hard for them in a boarding-school. I find they
really need something to remind them that we all care, that somebody
really, really cares.'

'Oh you're quite right, quite right,' the man replied politely.

The poor bugger was bored stiff. Helen peered pointedly over
Doreen's shoulder and into his eyes. He caught the look and in the
flicker of an instant almost responded, stifling a smile. She looked
away then. No joy there. *Homo domesticus* if ever she saw him.
Common-or-garden species. Widespread in the British Isles. Sheds
its inhibitions only during summer migration. Likes the company of its
own sex. Probably saves his charm for the rugby tours. Miles away
from solicitous wives. Still. Best not start messing. For Adam's sake.
Best behave and keep her talents for the home front or circles where
they wouldn't be misinterpreted. This was no place for wit and irony.
Or so much as a hint of sex. '*Yak-yak-yak-yak-yak-yak-yak*,' the boys
roared. '*Come on, Bellemont, win it back!*' The '*Waaahh*' sound rose

again as they finally settled down, plastic chairs scraping and hacking
on the wooden floor.

Adam and Patrick sat like young bulls, penned off at the top table,
surrounded by priests, the headmaster and various significant sup-
ports, including the priest who had once found her bathing naked with
Adam in the school swimming-pool. Adam had been raging afterwards.
Hadn't he told her not to strip, but no, she'd insisted, determined to
tease, and had even tried to rip his swimming-trunks off, just as
Goggle-face walked in. The thought of it made her suddenly splutter
with laughter. The McElligot man peered at her closely.

'God but it's a tremendous occasion,' he muttered to her, as if
testing her sanity.

'God but it is,' she replied glibly, giggling again in recollection of
the priest's bland face as she'd waded to the side of the pool in an
attempt to conceal her flesh. Word inevitably got around. A black
mark. A man who couldn't control his wife in certain situations was
open to question.

During the meal, people were absorbed in the post-mortem: the
earnest dissection of every moment of play, comparisons with
previous finals leading to disputes, jokes, noisy debate. She could
think of a million and one more interesting topics, even if it was
their special rugger day. Hadn't she shown interest in other people,
even in the brat sitting opposite, hadn't she tried a variety of
conversational options, from current affairs to UEFA and British
soccer hooligans, the Olympics? Of course it wasn't necessary to
say anything to that lot. She glared balefully at her soup. More a
matter of making the right sounds, little-woman chat. She listened
to Doreen.

'Well of course education is important, it's one of the most important things any parent can give a child!' she was saying with
vehemence.

'Quite. The wife and I like to take certain decisions too. All in all
some guidance is needed and the discipline which rugger adds is damn
well unbeatable,' the man beside her said.

'Discipline?' she cut in over Doreen's shoulder. 'What do you mean
by discipline?' she asked, putting on an interested face, hand curling
under her chin. The man looked extremely surprised.

'Aaaah! Discipline? Discipline's discipline any way you look at it: the
boys have to be ready to forge good careers, stand up for themselves,
go for it in a tough world, that type of thing . . .'

A waiter slid a plate of turkey and ham before her, then another slammed a heap of mashed potatoes and liquidised sprouts on top of the meat.

'You mean externalised discipline?' Helen asked, determined to be awkward.

'What? Beg pardon?'

'The ability to kow-tow to authority and suchlike – a bit like doing things without asking why?'

Doreen nodded her head in agreement and Helen was suddenly aware that she was listening intently.

'But what else is there?' Doreen asked.

The man started to hum and haw.

'Asking why isn't always such a bally great thing, young woman,' he commented, focusing thoughtfully at a point beyond her.

'You'd drive yourself crazy if you were constantly questioning things, Helen,' said Doreen.

'Is that so?' said Helen.

'Yes, and the long and the short of it for me is that they get such a lot out of the experience. It stands to them, makes . . .' she searched for the word, '. . . it makes men of those boys.'

'Well said, well said.' The man applauded quietly with manicured hands.

The meal was over. There was, she thought, little to say which would have made the slightest difference. She glanced along the length of the table, making no effort to conceal an expression of boredom. Katy was chirruping with some guy from the IRFU, Doreen was flirting with the disciplinarian, McElligot brayed joyfully over his wine, his nephew smiled like an imbecile and the muscular boy opposite, who told her he was a hooker and laughed, expecting her not to understand what the term meant, rocked backwards and forwards on his chair, spooning trifle into his flaccid mouth. Adam and Patrick sat in the sanctuary of the top table. Thank God Adam wasn't a yob, one of those aleckadoos. At least the whole thing was a game for him, a sport. Rugby was rugby was rugby and if people didn't know the difference between Phase One and Phase Two possession they could forget it. Nor for him the ribald tribalism that emanated from their opponents' dressing-rooms prior to every match as trainers bullied mercilessly and told the team they couldn't generate a pint of piss between them. That wasn't Adam's style. Instead, Patrick had been persuaded to adopt Adam's half-baked meditation techniques, picked up as a result of some cursory reading and a trip to Bangkok some years back. The Bellemont boys had been ribbed mercilessly, with

'Bellemont Boys Levitate' and 'A Try for the Maharishi' lashed across the evening papers. All the more satisfying to prove them wrong, Helen thought, to see Adam have his glory. She was nothing if not loyal.

McElligot wheeled back in his chair as the speeches began. He had reached the point of no return, and lit a cigar unsteadily. The place was noisy: boys and fathers shouted and catcalled across the room; wives and mothers smiled in complicity, the *waaaahhh* sound threatening to erupt again until the headmaster raised his right arm in a plea for silence.

'*Sieg heil!*' somebody shouted from the back of the room. The whole place exploded.

'Dear colleagues,' he finally began, 'Reverend Fathers, parents, staff and – of course – students.'

They yahooed long and loud. Tables were hammered, floors pounded with heavy feet.

There were at least five separate toasts and a few broken glasses. Helen's hands were sore from clapping. Nobody cared. This was Happyland. She knocked back her fifth glass of wine, face slightly numb, wanted to crawl into bed. Any long, wide, spacious area would do, somewhere she could wiggle her toes and open her bra. She helped herself to another drink. The red was good, fair dues to the priests. The headmaster was blathering on about history and the future, the importance of the Bellemont tradition and the splendid good fortune they'd had in their trainers.

'Hear, hear!' she called in a full, confident voice.

Doreen looked at her quizzically, then tittered.

'It's all right – I'm not pissed, just pissed off!' she whispered loudly. She waved at Adam. His attention was held by McElligot's nephew who was at that point unbuttoning his shirt. She tutted with impatience, as it came to her that her husband was as remote as he had ever been, perhaps as he had always been.

'But there are two people we especially want to mention, to whom gratitude is due for their unstinting support, without whom much of what we achieved today might not have been possible.'

He beamed down at them, his face radiating good intentions and assurance. There was a slight hush.

'Would Mrs Patrick Watson and Mrs Adam Kilroy care to stand and make themselves known?' he said good-humouredly.

Doreen stood up hesitantly, beckoning to Helen.

'It's us, stand up!' she hissed uneasily. People applauded halfheartedly. Helen stayed sitting, her face pounding as two smirking boys waltzed down the length of the hall carrying bouquets. '*Waaahhh*' came the sound again as they were jeered on their way. The smoke from McElligot's cigar was cutting the back of her throat. Someone slapped her on the shoulders from behind and told her she must be proud as punch, as the flowers were plonked at her place.

'Well done, well done indeed, my dear,' said McElligot.

'Congratulations! A wonderful day for Bellemont!' someone else called.

'Thank you,' she said with what dignity she could summon.

Flowers. She simpered bitterly to herself. '*Ing-gang-oolie-oolie-oolie . . .*' Flowers for those who selflessly support the great endeavour. For rugger-hugging ladies. Healthy activity ze old rugby, she muttered to herself. The city hotels were flooded with women on the rampage during internationals, desperate because they'd reached thirty and might be left on the shelf, hungry for Frenchmen, Welshmen, Scotsmen, any man who'd take them, willing to do or die for a life of leather balls and pungent socks. Good at the old rucking too, just like the lads in their own way, in for the kill. '*Womba, womba, womba.*' Doreen looked pleased with herself, poked her face into the flowers time and again, saying wasn't it lovely of them, so thoughtful to think of such a thing, sure they'd done nothing to deserve it.

'When you make the sandwiches and cakes, that's what you get,' Helen said loudly, then checked herself. Make an effort.

McElligot was reminiscing about his schooldays to nobody in particular.

'It's very nice of them all the same,' Doreen insisted.

Helen was about to contradict her but stopped. What was the point when Doreen was so humble? Flowers. She didn't want anything. Being rewarded wasn't the point. The point – she took a deep breath – was that everybody pretended that the women were necessary to the scene, and the truth was they weren't. Which was fine with her but, by God, they needn't expect her to feel grateful.

'I wonder why everybody goes through the motions of thanking us?' she asked.

'Oh they're not just the motions, Helen!' said Doreen quickly. 'It's well-meant, it's their way of saying something to us.'

'Yeah, like fuck off, girls!'

Doreen raised her eyebrows, her jaw falling open.

'Sorry, sorry Doreen,' said Helen. Oh Jesus, here we go again,

apologising when there's fuck-all to be sorry for. The McElligot man
cut in.

'They're saying thank you for putting up with this,' he said in a
wavering voice, his eyes moist and sentimental.

'Yip. It's a lot to put up with, isn't it?' said Helen.

'Ah now, ah now, it's not that bad.'

'It's very important, Helen,' said Doreen. 'That's how the system
works and it's very important for the boys.'

'Of course it is, of course it is,' Helen replied, folding her arms.

'There's no point resenting it, my dear,' said McElligot with surpris-
ing lucidity.

'I don't resent it,' she said lightly.

'But my dear lady, you've sat here all evening on sufferance. Mean
to say, what are you, some sort of feminist or something?' he spat
the question. She swallowed hard.

'Helen has her own ideas on everything,' said Doreen in jolly tones,
trying to smooth the atmosphere.

'I don't know how to answer you,' said Helen. Her face was
blotched, even her neck and chest felt hot. She caught a glimpse of
Adam. Nabbed by yet another adoring mother ingratiating herself for
a ray of his attention. Lapping it up. Both of them.

'Of course I'm a feminist,' she responded, not knowing whether it
was a lie or not. Weren't most of them ball-breakers anyway? McElligot raised his eyebrow in amusement.

'But I don't resent rugby. I just think it's given too much importance.' She was hamming it up. Sounding resentful.

'In what way, my dear?' he asked, taking a puff from the cigar, his
lips making a wet smacking sound as he inhaled. She could have
shoved it down his throat.

'To enhance careers. Old boys network, that kind of thing. It has
damn all to do with sport.'

'I see. But you're a feminist too – I don't meet too many of those
– thought all that kind of thing had faded out in the early eighties
really.'

'No.'

'Thought they were all lesbians too if you don't mind my saying so.
You're not one of those, are you?' he chortled.

She laughed, because otherwise she might have wept.

'Ah well, I'll leave you to it, my dear. The wife's over there waiting;
got to get home y'know. Nice meeting you, don't take it all so
seriously.'

He was gone, leaving a whiff of after-shave and cigar smoke in his wake. Reason and honesty didn't make for satisfaction when dealing with his sort. But neither did outrage. What he'd possibly expected. At her age she knew a few things. One of them was that most men would follow a ball or a pint across a roomful of naked sylphs, much like the joke said. The other was that women were always on the losing team, whichever way you looked at it. The trouble was, she couldn't figure out whether it was types like Doreen or types like herself who were the greatest fools. Doreen could sit back modestly, like an artless virgin, all self-effacement and wide eyes and got along grand. She, on the other hand, didn't even bother to conceal her feelings, or when she thought about it, to use her attractiveness. When she felt sour it showed. Men could sniff out womanish discontent and rebellion wherever it lurked. Doreen seemed spot on. For the umpteenth time she wondered why the hell it mattered what men thought about women. And then again maybe she'd been codding herself. Look at Doreen. A decent skin. A nice woman who worked hard at keeping Patrick happy, doing what she thought he wanted.

'*Womba, womba, womba.*' There it was again. The boys had formed a train and shuffled Maori-style around the two trainers. '*Ing-gang-oolie-oolie-oolie-oolie-oolie.*' Gathering her bag and jacket, the green one borrowed from her sister to match the dress, so that she'd look well on the day, she stared at Adam. He was like a god to the boys, even looked like one, a colossus, in command, the glow of victory on his smooth brow. Patrick was more avuncular, a sort of tribal chief. If this were the Amazon jungle, she thought, the rites of passage would be somewhat different. Circumcision with a piece of flint. A bit of vine-swinging. Ritual raping and pillaging instead of socialised aggression. A time for the elders to pass on the wisdom of their sex, the lore of centuries. They were getting their lore today, all right, messages in abundance. How to live. Entitlements. An inheritance.

She turned in disgruntlement to Doreen. 'How did Patrick enjoy Paris?'

'Had a ball, won all their matches – didn't Adam tell you?'

'He did. Just wondering how Patrick found it.'

Patrick had drunk himself footless one night, the gendarmes eventually prising him from a restaurant into which he'd staggered, wearing a balaclava, shouting something about *un petit hold-up*.

'It's all right Helen – I know what happened,' said Doreen.

'What?'

'He rang me up in the middle of the night singing the Can-Can.'

'Oh.'

'Count yourself lucky that at least Adam's no boozer,' she added. The tables were turned. But Helen didn't mind. It was common knowledge. She was used to it. Adam's French floozie. Adam's bonbon, sweetmeat or whatever. He'd told her himself, guilt-ridden, full of boyish remorse.

'Men,' she said grimly.

'Bastards.'

'Have you been drinking?' Helen asked, unaccustomed to Doreen's directness.

'Two G and T's. It's such a load of shit, isn't it?'

'Wish I'd never set foot in the place.'

It was a kind of truce, an acknowledgement of some essential baseline failure on both sides.

'Would you look at them!' Doreen spat in outright mockery.

'Boys will be boys as they say!'

'Chow-chow-chow.' In this setting, she didn't recognise Adam. This was what he escaped to, like all men in flight from women. He looked innocently past her, certain of his life, its correctness. Through it all, she did not exist.

'Are you staying, or d'you want a lift?' she called to Doreen. Let him find his own way home.

'I'll come: God knows where the carry-on'll end tonight.'

'Yak-yak-yak-yak-yak-yak-yak.'

'Your hair's gorgeous,' she said companionably.

'Oh, look the flowers –'

'Leave them,' said Helen irritably.

The crowd had dispersed slightly. The atmosphere was damp and beery, like a hotel after a hooley. Forlorn. She stood at the exit and searched for the car-keys. It was drizzling. Outside, daffodils wavered unsteadily. But the light was spring-like despite the needling cold. And the season was over. Her husband would gradually shed his inattention. He would be hers again in some limited way. He might want her, might learn that she was more than a sanctuary of peace. He might actually desire her. That was what mattered. It was why so many women turned out in force. Hanging on to men they loved in some quirky way. *'Yak-yak-yak-yak-yak-yak-yak,'* the sound faded as the two women hurried across the carpark. The main road was blocked with traffic.

'Will we go somewhere?' said Doreen, straightening her coat as she sat into the car.

'What? You mean not go home? Entertainment?'

'I wonder what Bad Bobs is like?'

'Full of men. Have you any money?'

'Cheque book,' said Doreen, opening a bottle of perfume and spraying both wrists.

'That'll do. Let's go,' said Helen, her expression set.

She fastened the seat-belt, listened for a moment to the distant *'Waaahhh'* sound and revved up. She was ready for anything.

KYRIE BOOM-BOOM-BOOM

BRIAN POWER
Brian Power was born in Dublin, 1930. A graduate of University College, Dublin, with a Master's Degree in Sociology from Boston University, he was ordained in 1958 and has been curate in various parishes in and around Dublin. He has published two collections of short stories, *A Land Not Sown* and *The Wild and Daring Sixties*.

I was fond of Gerry Winters.

It wasn't just that, as senior curate, I took a special interest in the raw young recruit. There was more to it than that. I could see that he enjoyed visiting my room, even if it was mainly for the purpose of pouring out his suppressed frustrations. Soon I began to look on him almost as a son – somebody to care about and help develop. In my forties I had often missed the wife I never had. In my fifties I missed the might-have-been children growing up and was ready to adopt – but never mind, all this has really nothing to do with Gerry Winters abandoning his vocation. Since I knew him I have become far too analytical altogether.

The departure of young Winters, I must admit, was as much a shock to me as to the rest of the parish. I knew the lad was unsettled, but I never expected him to leave. In the autumn of nineteen-sixty-nine it was the last thing I expected any priest, young or old, of my acquaintance to do. Like most island races we Irish tend to place our trust in the likelihood of gathering stormclouds bursting far out over the open sea. We were slow to accept the possibility that some of our own priests might abandon ship as readily as American or Continental clerics whose defections were at that time hitting the newspaper headlines.

Although I say it myself, for a man of my age I have kept fairly well in touch with developments in the Church. I have read practically all the documents of the Second Vatican Council, two booklets by Karl Rahner, Teilhard's 'Divin Milieu' and the first few pages of Lonergan's 'Insight into Insight', or whatever he calls that extraordinarily complex piece of clairvoyance – I didn't understand a word of it. I also began reading one or two paperbacks, by authors whose names I have happily forgotten, which I consigned to the flames at the first signs of heresy. Nevertheless, I was in a position to understand to some extent the background against which Gerry Winters' personal difficulties demanded to be viewed.

'It's an incredible situation, Father O'Flaherty,' he would explode, flinging his lithe young limbs into an armchair by my fireside and throwing his head back on the antimacassar. He always wore too much hair oil; Lily had to change the cover on that particular chair a couple of times a week. 'Here we are in St Gertrude's singing Latin hymns at Benediction since October began, only twenty people in the church, and half the population outside going stupid on drink, drugs, bingo and television. The most exasperating part of it, though, is the two-facedness of our parish structures. As I was going into the church tonight crowds of people were streaming into our hall to play bingo. I mean, why do we pretend? Why put bingo and Benediction at the same time and then moan about the vanishing congregations?'

'If we didn't provide bingo, somebody else would.' Although I am no great supporter of Church gambling, I always feel that in fairness to the Canon I have to put up a logical defence of his methods of administration. 'Besides, I defy you to get tuppence out of the faithful of St Gertrude's parish without resorting to some form of painless extraction.'

'But wouldn't it be better to let the debts mount up than to pull them down at such a terrible cost to the quality of life in the parish?'

That's just one example of the sort of thing Gerry got upset about. Everything we were doing in St Gertrude's, it transpired, was either irrelevant, outmoded, paternalistic or downright scandalous.

'And it's impossible to do anything about it,' he would cry, 'because there's absolutely no dialogue here whatsoever.'

His blue eyes would open wide like the eyes of a child seeing death for the first time. My heart would go out to him while I tried to induce him to laugh away his fears. Slipping a Beethoven symphony on the record player for soothing background music, I would encourage him to play a little golf, read a little P. G. Wodehouse, go to bed earlier instead of sitting up brooding over the contradictions in a life that was meant to be contradictory anyway. He always calmed down and eventually went away cheered by my interest and by Lily's exquisite jam tartlets which she never stopped baking once she realised they were so well appreciated by the nice young curate. You know, they're all the same, these young idealists. They try to live simply and end up living off other people without any sense of shame whatsoever. Nevertheless, as far as I was concerned, he was more than welcome. I even taught him to play chess and he soon developed into a worthy opponent whom I could just about manage to defeat.

Young Winters lived in the same presbytery as myself and Monty

Lowe. After the manner of the secular clergy each of us was responsible for managing his own financial affairs. The tradition in St Gertrude's presbytery is that each man lives completely independently of the rest. It's an enormous house, of course, but there are far fewer rooms than you would expect to find in it. Monty lives so independently, mostly on the middle floor, that you would hardly know he was in the parish at all only for seeing him on the altar on Sundays. His housekeeper, Felicity, a thin wraithlike creature who never speaks, has a kitchen in the basement and with silent devotion succeeds in spiriting all Monty's meals up to his dining-room without ever being spotted doing so by human eye. Monty himself is no wraith. Although I never see him, his presence above me is verified by bursts of Spanish music, the light laughter of well-filled guests, and curious bumping noises every morning and every night which I have identified as Monty doing his physical jerks. Altogether a sociable and sprightly fellow, Monty. The sort of chap it should be quite nice to know. In the sacristy, when we meet, he is courteous, debonair and absolutely non-committal about anything.

The ground floor of this mammoth structure is my territory, but Lily's kitchen is also situated in the basement. No fear of Lily's ministrations being ignored. Imperiously generous, fat and waddling, she is a different type of poltergeist by far from Felicity – the type who throws things around and creates confusion. Mops and brushes batter walls and wainscotings, the hoover drones its busy way up and down stairs, trays are dumped loudly on chairs and tables in the hall. Lily, thank God, works hard and believes in letting the whole world know it.

Gerry Winters, being the junior curate, was exiled on arrival to the upper regions. His kitchen, however, was also in the basement. As he never got an indoor housekeeper, this meant he had to undertake a considerable journey whenever he felt the urge to eat. I still believe Gerry might never have left if he had got somebody more permanent to look after him than the thrice-a-week octogenarian who tottered all the way up to his den and back down again with baskets full of literary litter. Unfortunately, he was odd about such things.

'The time has come,' he could declaim, 'when we must stop employing female slaves to wait upon our every whim.'

I never take this kind of thing in the young too seriously. I mean, the sheer absurdity of referring to Lily as a female slave, if that is what he intended . . . well, you should meet the redoubtable Lily. Besides, I never noticed Lily's jam tartlets sticking in Gerry's throat after she had spent the afternoon baking just to please him. As I said before, many young priests who are extremist in their determination to retain personal independence end up completely dependent on their more provident seniors. Mind you, I don't want to harp on this, I enjoyed the lad's company, but I feel I'm more than entitled to make the point. Employing female slaves indeed!

Our parish priest, of course, lives in a house to himself. A happy arrangement for all concerned. When the crisis came, things might have been smoothed out only for the Canon. Looked at objectively, I suppose Canon O'Shaughnessy is rather a bizarre institution. A parish priest of ninety-four can hardly be expected to be the most energetic of administrators.

'It's a downright scandal,' Gerry would insist. 'How can this sort of thing be justified?'

I would point out patiently that the world is full of even more scandalous and objectionable objects than Canon O'Shaughnessy and ask him which of the curates he thought would do a better job anyway. Inevitably he would indicate me, which was highly gratifying and probably true. Monty would take no more notice of parish affairs than the Canon does and Gerry would have emptied the church within two Sundays with his socio-theological lunacies.

In practice, the Canon's age and eccentricities never bothered me unduly. Having him as parish priest can be quite a convenience. Anything that's wrong or neglected in the parish is naturally attributed to his incompetence or bungling, and the fact that he is an openly avaricious little gentleman who has been saving assiduously for his old age for the past thirty years draws a great deal of sympathy from the populace towards his long-suffering and relatively deprived curates. Gerry, being a perfectionist, was incapable of perceiving any such compensations in the situation.

If Canon O'Shaughnessy had been an ill-mannered tyrant, things would not have been so bad. As matters stood, he was, and still is, the most urbane, genial and agreeable old swindler you could possibly meet in ecclesiastical or other circles. You couldn't even have the satisfaction of fighting with him. When Gerry approached him about changing the hours of confessions, modernising the sodalities, or co-ordinating social relief agencies in the parish, he would remove his rimless glasses, begin cleaning them with his handkerchief, and after an unbearably long pause would enquire eagerly, 'Eh? What was that you said?' When Gerry repeated his petition, the Canon would replace his spectacles and announce brightly, 'Ah, that's better. I can see better now. Tell me about that again, Father. Don't forget now.' And out of the sacristy he would go, to climb into his nineteen-fifty-eight car and zigzag down the road with his chin resting on the steering-wheel and his scrawny neck cocked to one side so that his better eye might pick out trespassing cyclists, dogs or policemen straying across his erratic line of progression. Strangely enough, he has never actually killed anybody – unless you'd count Monty's yip-yapper of a poodle which he mowed down several years ago in the church driveway and that was probably deliberate.

It wasn't, needless to say, the Canon's driving that bothered Gerry Winters. It was his total unawareness of, not to mention his indiffer-ence to, the problems of the parish. But there I go again, talking about 'problems'. It was Gerry who infected me that way. In my philosophy, once you branded something a problem, it became a problem. If you forgot about it, it usually went away.

Gerry's problem, unfortunately, didn't go away until he took it with him. The annoying thing is that it wouldn't be a problem at all these days. What a difference a few years can make in the development of the Church's outlook on so many things! What Gerry did seems very simple now. He said Mass in a small basement clubroom, only a hundred yards from the parish church. It was simple and crazy at the same time. Why he couldn't have walked as far as the church is beyond my comprehension.

It was Mrs Baggot, our church cleaner who is also employed two nights a week at the club, who brought the matter to my attention. Mrs Baggot spends half her life bringing things to people's attention. She may not be a very efficient cleaner in matters material, but in matters spiritual she will go to the ends of the earth to clean up the mess into which she believes the Church has fallen. The day she poured this latest scandal into my ears my reaction was one of pro-found dismay. Not so much because I believed it was wrong of Gerry to have offered Mass in a basement, but because I knew that if it got around he would be hauled from the Canon to the Bishop and God alone knew where else.

'Say nothing about this to anybody,' I told Mrs Baggot. 'You can depend on me to handle it.'

Her falcon eyes gleaming, she nodded and went straight next door to the parish priest. After watching helplessly as she rang the doorbell, I hurried upstairs to Gerry's den. He was squatting on his hunkers before a cassette tape recorder listening to what sounded like jungle liturgical chant.

'For God's sake!' I was surprised to find myself shouting, but it was the only way I could get a hearing in any case. 'Are you gone out of your mind? Do you know what country you're living in? You haven't the sense of survival of a lemming.'

He sat back on the tintawn floor covering. From the look of expectancy on his face I could see he had a good idea what I was talking about. Throwing a massive *Commentary on the Gospel According to John* off one of the chairs, I planted myself in its place.

'Mrs Baggot has been to see me. What's more, I'm afraid she's gone to the Canon now.'

His features assumed a betrayed expression.

'You mean you didn't try to stop her?'

That nettled me. I mean, the young fool surely didn't think he could go around saying subterranean Masses without having to face the consequences.

'My dear boy!' I was becoming, I must admit, a trifle pompous. 'The Church came out of the Catacombs many centuries ago. People like Mrs Baggot may once have delighted in persecuting the early Christians, but in these more civilised times they count themselves lucky to find an anachronistic eccentric like yourself to feed to the lions and aren't going to let themselves be robbed of their prey without a fight.'

'Kyrie boom-boom-boom,' commented the tape recorder, but Gerry cut it short and rose to his feet.

'You don't understand,' he cried. 'I simply offered Mass with a group of young youth leaders. It wasn't something I did on the spur of the moment, it was something that evolved quite naturally out of interpersonal communication on the meaning of the Eucharist.'

Something that evolved! He was right about one thing. I didn't understand. Strangely, though, I wanted to.

'Look here,' I said, 'it isn't the end of the world. I'll see the Canon and find out what he knows. If he's heard about it, I'm sure I'll be able to stop him taking any action. Only you'll have to promise there'll be no more of these mysterious religious happenings.'

Naturally, by the time I saw the Canon he knew everything. He seemed to know more than I did. He padded about his draughtproof carpeted sitting room like an aged panther injected with amphetamine.

'Incredible!' he exclaimed at every step. 'Communion under both species! Mass without an altar stone! A *woman* reading the Epistle! I'm making out a report for the Bishop at this very moment.' He nodded enthusiastically at a sheaf of papers in huge copperplate handwriting lying on his desk. 'I've asked Mrs Baggot to send the President and Secretary of the youth club to me tonight. A full enquiry must be instituted.'

In vain I argued that the whole affair was not particularly significant, that undue publicity might only perpetuate such liturgical deviations. The Canon didn't pretend to hear me.

'The Bishop will be deeply disturbed. At the last retreat he warned parish priests to exercise constant vigilance against insidious attacks upon the Faith. Yes, yes, he will be disturbed and dismayed.'

The prospect of the Bishop's distress seemed to delight the old boy no end. As I was leaving the room he called me back and hope stirred faintly inside me.

'What's this the young fooleen's name is? Waters? Winterson? Eh?'

'Gerard Winters,' I sighed and went home feeling like Judas, which was exactly what the old rogue intended.

Although I had to tell Gerry how the matter stood, I treated it as rather a joke. All that usually happened in such situations, I pointed out, was a personal inquisition by the Bishop, followed by transfer to a mountain parish, and somebody had to look after the mountains. I made Lily bake extra rations of jam tartlets, produced a bottle of brandy I had been keeping for special occasions which never came, and played Strauss instead of Beethoven on the record-player. As I chattered on and on, falling into a mood of benevolent reminiscence, Gerry seemed to relax. I remember telling him the absurd story of how I almost got a lectureship in Old English at Maynooth many years ago only for the machinations of an obscure Western prelate who wanted it for his nephew. Long after midnight, Gerry rose to go. To my surprise he put his hand on my shoulder, almost as if it was I who needed sympathy.

'Thank you,' he smiled, 'for all your kindness.'

I never saw him again. Next morning he was gone without trace. Yesterday, three years later, I received a letter with a London postmark.

'Tomorrow,' he wrote, 'I am to marry a very nice girl at Brook Green. I am teaching in a comprehensive school and am very happy.'

Naive as ever. For a long time I held the letter in my hand, pondering the strange coincidence that this very evening our new Bishop is to celebrate Mass in the new club premises with a guitar group providing the music. After due consideration I decided to tell the Canon the news about Gerry's wedding.

'What's that? Winterson? Winters was it? Married, is he? The little fooleen! He'll find no happiness in this world or in the next, you mark my words.'

If either Gerry or his bride dies of a heart attack at seventy, Canon O'Shaughnessy, should he be still alive and there's no apparent reason why he shouldn't be, will see it as the just sentence of an avenging God.

UNIVERSITAS

RONAN SHEEHAN
Born in Dublin, 1953, Ronan Sheehan was educated at Gonzaga College and University College, Dublin. He has published one novel and a collection of short stories, *Boy with an Injured Eye*.

I approve of the new Stillorgan Road which enables motorists to pass the University in twenty seconds. I approve of the road on Inishmore which enables motorists to cover the island in twenty minutes. I approve of the open-access system operated in the Belfield library which enables students to go through all the books in half an hour. I approve of the fifth bend on the road from Kilronan to Kilmurvey where I saw an American watch an islander add a rock to a limestone wall. The wall was supposed to separate his sheep from fields which were themselves limestone. The sheep wandered anyhow to Dun Aengus, which guards Aran against the sea, whose waves carried Aran's emigrants to America, from where tourists fly to Shannon and Galway, thence to the new airfield on Inishmore.

I'm a student who was once on Inishmore. I've been in different places at different times. Yet in a sense I'm always in the same place at all times, because I remain the same person. Different places at different times are wherever I am. It's not that nothing can go on without me, but that I can't go on without everything.

I fell in love at the first lecture I attended. She was sitting in a row beneath mine in Theatre L, her black hair falling across the collar of her sheepskin coat. When the lecture was over and she was out of sight part of me went with her, part of her stayed with me.

In the morning the University resembles a pier, an airport, a railway station. Hordes of people rush about. Everyone sees a rapid succession of random faces. Most of the faces were foreign to me but I recognized a few. Some were my friends' faces. One was her face. This became the only one that really interested me. The other faces mattered insofar as each could have been her face. Other times I would pretend that it was her face that I saw. Soon I had to re-think the whole question of faces.

The subject of one lecture was the short stories of Liam O'Flaherty. He emerged from the obscurity of Aran to become a successful writer in the 'thirties and 'forties. His themes are the sea, the land, animals, men. The source of his power as a writer is his direct apprehension of physical qualities like strength, weight, texture. He hasn't written anything for years. He vanished into a block of flats near that bend in the road where Leeson Street becomes Morehampton Road, which continues into the new Stillorgan Road. Perhaps he feels at home there. Perhaps he sees a rapid succession of random faces every day. He may imagine that these faces resemble the Aran faces described by nineteenth-century travellers. They saw faces whose expressions were abstract, suggesting an oriental stoicism.

I developed the habit of looking straight into her face when passing her on my way out of the lecture theatre. She always seemed bold and unafraid. I never managed to sustain these gazes of mine for very long. I discovered that she lived in Mount Merrion, just off the Stillorgan Road, at the opposite end to O'Flaherty's.

In the library I chanced upon a volume by John Ruskin, the Victorian writer. He compared the face of an angel in an Irish illuminated manuscript with the face of an angel from a contemporary piece of Italian sculpture. Both were beautiful but neither was perfect. The Italian angel was aware of its imperfection but the Irish angel reckoned that it was already perfect. The Irish angel would resent any suggestion that it was not perfect. Ruskin understood this angel to be symbolic of the political face of nineteenth-century Ireland. The Irish could not conceive of the possibility of their ever being in the wrong. Ruskin's personal opinion was that the Irish were generally right, but he admired the English ability to admit occasionally to mistakes. I share his admiration of this civil, self-effacing element in the English character, but surely Ruskin should have realised that sometimes people must keep a straight face, bold and unafraid like that beloved face, or abstract and stoical like the Aran islanders'?

I managed to attach myself to her. We used to watch her brother play rugby for the University. This always made me think of O'Flaherty's story 'The Wing Three-Quarter' which probably grew out of his experience of Blackrock College. The hero is jeered by the crowd for being a dandy and for funking tackles. He redeems himself by scoring the winning try. O'Flaherty brilliantly conveys the humiliation of his being smashed against hard cold ground, the glory of that last unconquerable sprint.

Her brother was a wonderful player. He had such depth of apprehension of his body and of the bodies surrounding him. He knew his own superiority. It was thrilling to see him frighten and humiliate his opponents before being knocked to the ground. He was like one of O'Flaherty's magnificent tinkers.

Yet there is only one tinker's face and that is unchanging.

Like O'Flaherty I am fascinated by hierarchies. I am fascinated by the faces which culminate in her face, by the forts of Aran which culminate in Dun Aengus, by those Ruskinian angels which culminate in the figure of Daniel O'Connell, The Liberator. I am fascinated by social hierarchies, like the top brass of the rugby club, whose members are hopelessly inadequate in any non-rugby social situation. They always make me think of clannish Aran men in their separate corner of a London public bar, or of me and her sitting together in the huge library in Belfield, or of the tinkers round their fire on the new Stillorgan Road, or of Americans huddled together in a bar in Kilronan. I am fascinated by the moment which transfigures all other moments. I am fascinated by my own eye which sees everything, by my eyelid which obliterates everything.

TIME PASSES

EDDIE STACK

Eddie Stack was born in Ennistymon, Co. Clare, 1951. An engineer by profession, he represented Ireland at the International Young Scientist Convention in 1969. He has lived in the USA since 1986 writing full time and has published one collection of short stories, *The West*.

We often threatened to take the Boat on those wintry mornings after Christmas while we waited for the dole office to open. Huddled in deep doorways, sheltering from the spray blown up from the river, we shook our heads in despair. We were sentenced to another year's penance in the wind and rain. Another year in a world of shuttered shops.

There would be no market until the Saturday before Saint Patrick's Day and it was common knowledge that some shopkeepers, bored and bothered by the stillness, would take to their beds for weeks at a time, only surfacing for the funerals that always followed the rain. There would be people in town for the funerals. The funerals, the Mass and the dole brought us together to complain and spend the government's money on cold porter. And the more we drank, the more pitiful our situation seemed – grown men being paid by the government to remain on the census sheets and being despised for doing so.

But yet we stayed. For some obscure patriotic reason we lingered on in that place where there was neither hope of work or lover. We passed the year threatening to leave for England and retelling tales we heard from the Lads. There was another world on the far side of the water and the Lads were in the thick of it. They were our heroes in those days. Altar boys who went to Camden Town wearing scapulars and came home with blue tattoos. Seven days a week they worked in the midst of rogues and ruffians, ripping up roads and pouring concrete so they could spend Christmas in Ireland.

They arrived the evening before Christmas Eve on a special train that brought them from the Mail Boat, and from early afternoon that seldom-seen station was the liveliest place in town. Stalls sold hot soup and toffee apples and two women from Barranna hawked naggins of poteen for half the price of shop whiskey. The school choir sang

carols and Father White collected money for a new church from a
dwindling congregation. For the first time in almost a year, laughter
and song drowned the sound of the roaring brown river and months
of gloom vanished like the night.

Hours before the train was due, groups of young people walked up
and down the windswept platform, cajoling with railway officials and
shouting false alarms. The more anxious preferred to wait in the
colder waiting room, or sit on icy grey platform benches. Cloaked in
scarves and shawls, country women crunched clove sweets because
they were too shy to smoke in public. Their husbands sucked pipes
and looked up and down the rusty track, conferred with railway
officials and reported home.

By four o'clock the gas lanterns were lit and hackney drivers
arrived, muffled in coats and scarves. These shrewd men noted what
parties were in attendance, what fares to expect, who to solicit and
who to avoid. They only left their warm cars when excitement peaked
and everyone swarmed to the platform, peering up the line and listening to the harassed rumblings of the approaching Steamer.

The Lads emerged from the dimly lit carriages to a rousing reception
of cheers, waves and back slaps. Pink faced and closely shaven they
looked angelic. Helpers and hackney drivers took their brown bulging
suitcases and Father White's choir sang 'Come All Ye Faithful.' We
all joined in. Parents shyly welcomed home their young with tears and
we sang louder and marched around the platform. Gloria, Gloria, it
was really Christmas.

But there was always someone or other who failed to return, even
though they had written to say they were coming. Bewildered relatives put a brave face on grief –

'They'll probably arrive for the New Year,' they said. We nodded
in agreement, even though we knew better.

The Lads passed their first night at home and were brought up to
date with the year's happenings, the weather, the state of the country,
church collections and other burdens the plain people had to bear. Old
and new news was exchanged until the travellers showed signs of
fatigue. Then they were urged to go to bed with a glass of hot punch
and a sprinkle of Knock water.

On Christmas Eve they came to town with their parents and drank
moderately in long-ago haunts while the old people did the shopping
and attended confessions. There was no end to their money on that

day, loans were offered freely and drinks were bought for everyone who wished them well, enquired about the sea crossing or asked –
'How're things beyond the Pond?'
And things beyond were always good.

By Saint Stephen's day all family dues and duties had been attended to and the Lads rambled to town after breakfast, packing the small bars and attracting hordes of hangers-on. It was a day of banging doors, thirsty Paddys criss-crossing town in shoals of blue suits. Bars steamed with sweat, smoke and after-shave lotion. Floors were littered with charred Swan matches, Senior Service cigarette ends and bronze thrupennybits, left for late night sweepers. Pubs hummed every time the Queen's face decorated the counter – no monarch had ever raised so many smiles in Ireland. And later when the Wrenboys descended on the town with flute, fiddle and tambourine, we jumped for joy. We had the best of all worlds then – the Queen's money and plenty music, in our own backyard.

As time passed, old acquaintances were renewed and the Lads trusted us with tales about the parish's forgotten sons and daughters. These secrets were imparted in the strictest confidence and later retold with the same sentiments.

Every second year Rufus Ryan, a man who had emigrated long before I was born, had another wife. Jim Flynn was either in or out of jail. One year we heard in detail why Pat Browne left the priesthood and took up the shovel. And why Mary Scully went on the game after a tempestuous marriage to a Welshman. Hatchet O'Day met her in a boarding house and she cried in his arms and begged him not to tell. But he did, and more.

The Lads began to wither as more time was spent in the pubs than at home. By the fifth day of Christmas the blue suits were creased and crumpled, white shirts were stout-stained and London socks left unchanged. In the mornings eyes were bloodshot and watery and the Lads resorted to drinking hot whiskey to line their stomachs. They were in topping form by the time faithful friends and professional listeners arrived.

Their stories and antics brought Kilburn closer to us. We quickly became familiar with the 'Tube' and knew the stops on the Circle Line, the Piccadilly and the Jubilee. We heard about their haunts and

habits. Wild sprees in Camden Town and dicey nights in the Gal-
tymore. Saturday sessions in the White Hart, Quirke Road Church
for Sunday's Irish papers.

Each year we discovered anew that there was little comparison
between life at home and in London. The Lads pointed out that we
had few comforts. No Soho. Or no Chinese caffs where waiters bowed
and took your coat. And bowed again when they served you unidenti-
fiable piles of food, at four shillings for two. We often had to sympath-
ise with them for bothering to return home at all, and they always
looked us in the eye and said –

'If it weren't for the aul lad and d'aul lady, I don't think I'd bother.'

And yet they spent little of their holiday at home. They preferred
instead to entertain us with stories about subbies from Roscommon,
granite hard gangers from Connemara and cute foremen from Cork.
All tough men who were respected for their crookedness and cruelty
to others.

As the days trickled away our heroes became slovenly, sometimes
unruly, often drunk. The sessions were lengthy, and sometimes in
the evenings a brother or sister might be dispatched to town in an
effort to coax them home for dinner. But they preferred to linger on in
the smoke-filled bars and chew dry turkey sandwiches at the counter,
turning around between mouthfuls to quip –

'You'll never go back, Scobie.'

They regularly fell asleep beside pub fires, waking unexpectedly to
startle us with songs from London juke boxes. Some got awkward
when they were refused more drink, publicans were insulted, glasses
were broken.

The last day or two of their holiday was spent at home with their
families and on the sixth of January they left again for London. Lonesome men with empty pockets and brave faces, seen off from the
station by weeping women and stone-eyed old men. There were no
hackney cars, no helpers, no stalls, no hymns. The green train rolled
into the rain and stole Christmas with it.

Ivy and holly were taken from the walls, the Crib and decorations
were stored away for another year and there was a hush in the
countryside. We heard the wind and the river again and felt the grey
drabness of January that paved the days for Lent. It was a lonely
period when even clocks refused to pass the time and their hands
lingered between hours for hours on end, or so it seemed. Again we

threatened to take the Boat, lonely for company and the spirit that had been whisked away from us. Weeks passed before we got into step with the year and then Christmas became a legend, one to be compared with previous ones.

But time passes, and when Christmas came around again the Lads dutifully returned home. They came every year until the government closed down the railway line, shuttered the station and sold the track to small farmers. Dublin turned its back on us and London slipped further and further away. Then the journey home became full of obstacles and hazards.

After a few Christmases the Lads gave up the ghost. When they did come home it was for family funerals and then they drank too much and cried too much. Angry tears for stolen years. In drink-stained whispers they promised to come home the following Christmas, for old time's sake.

But we rarely saw them again. There was nothing left to return to and the Lads moved on. Life had set its course and school friends drifted away without warning. Time tricked us and it became too late to change, too late to take the Boat, too late to wake up.

We are still on the census sheets and still drinking pints of cold porter for the government, when we meet for the dole, the Mass and the funerals. But there is little life in the public houses, now colder than the station waiting room. Only post mortems are held here in these ghost-ridden rooms where jackdaws block smokeless chimneys. And yet they are our only refuge. It is here we are forced to shelter before moving through the Winter.

Time passes, but memories linger.

THE BRIDE OF CHRIST

EITHNE STRONG
Born in Co. Limerick, 1923, Eithne Strong's stories have appeared in many periodicals and anthologies. She has published one collection, *Patterns*, and a number of volumes of poetry.

About three weeks gone now, the term. The students did not all have their uniforms yet. It took the tailor close on six weeks from the first measurement to get them all covered. Not that the measuring made very much difference to the final turn-out. Square long-sleeved garment to the waist. Navy serge. 'Blouse' it was called in the college prospectus. A shapeless overdress of the same material hung to the calves. In over twenty years the outline had not changed.

'Ugly,' assessed Sister Benignus in the silence of her cold detachment. 'But what does it matter what they wear? Marking time.'

She walked along by the wall where the September figs were ripening. Away on the far side beyond the trellised clematis they were at recreation. Games were compulsory. Sauntering groups were forbidden during recreation. The girls from Dingle were good at camogie; their rapid Irish urgent with the game came to her, their fluency of throaty aspiration, liquid diphthong and beautiful attenuation giving the tongue its living grace. Listening to them, richly vocal in the spontaneity of the playing-field, was one of the few things left that she liked. They could not see her through the screening clematis.

Outside of the class proper, English was allowed for only one half-hour in the day, the last one before evening silence and prayers. Accents from all over the country. But English as spoken by the Dingle girls was like a third language. What they wrote in it would be mostly correct, if stilted; this she knew for she had been given their papers to mark. But when they spoke it they made their own of it, in cadence and lilt and phraseology. It would have been scarcely intelligible to her own urbanised family, she sometimes thought.

Only now and then did she stop and face squarely towards the field; mostly she allowed the mixed noises from it to filter through her thinking while she walked, hands folded into deep sleeves, face well back in the recess of her veil.

'Clodhoppers, culchies,' most surely that would have been Julia's opinion of them. In her mind she could hear that particular daughter's voice, the most incisive in the family, 'God, what a life! How can girls *live* this way? It can't be called *living*. They don't know a thing . . . two, three years in this dump, wearing clothes like that – I wouldn't be seen dead in such a freakish get-up.'

'Well, they *are* fulfilling a function,' Sister Benignus parried, in the safety of the mental juxtaposition, with its emotional detachment from Julia, and purely for the sake of argument since her convictions concerning the matter were null. 'They are *good* girls. They will teach the rising young.'

'Good?' Julia was contemptuous. 'Do you mean good holy or good working?'

'It's a point,' answered her mother with an open-mindedness that this mental argument favoured. 'Considering it, I would say most likely both; most of them anyway. That is, when "holy" means observing the rituals of making the sign of the cross before class, before meals; gabbling some automatic noises called prayers; never, never missing Mass; never giving scandal by a, possibly quite sincere, love experiment; sticking to the required observances. Yes, this bunch of girls will probably answer all the holy requirements. *And* are likely to work more or less as is demanded of them; often desperate enough, trying to cover the quota for the Department inspectors. Imagination? Even if they have it they will scarcely have the courage to substantiate it. Imagination is dangerous to religiously established tenets and to be checked at first evidence.'

'But what life is it?'

'Depends how you see it. Contempt is arbitrary, and any life can be despised if we want to despise it. Is your sophistication more of an answer?'

'For me at present, no doubt about it; yes. You can have this lot any time.'

'In fact, I think,' Sister Benignus went on discursively, 'there are some among them a bit like yourself but without your heritage of freer thought; these won't answer to the acceptable standard, in all likelihood, but will shape a bit after their own fancy. Sooner or later they bump into the trouble of their own punishing guilt and the censure of the powers that be. Probably the greater bulk of them, the abiders, the holy ones if you like, will make the strongest teachers in the long run. The most consistent. And isn't that what's needed in the country?'

Sarcasm, cover for feeling, was gaining ground. She did not want to be disturbed to feeling. She wished no further involvement than the non-involvement of letting time pass. Anyway (in this mental projection of dialogue) Julia did not seem interested sufficiently to answer. Nevertheless her mother persisted in the same strain:

'The wayward Irish need a narrow consistency. Otherwise the growing young might find themselves imbalanced in a horrible jeopardy of experimental living and thinking. Iron strictures are the necessity of mad imaginations. That is a Church axiom. A people of tyranny and cowardice! And of them I am one. Therefore I can mock, criticise, condemn, propound, theorise, to my satisfaction. Not that it avails me or them in any way.'

But Julia had left.

A bell signifying the end of recreation sounded from the convent. Not always lady-like the sounds that issued from those teachers-in-the-making at the end of play.

'Raucous,' Sister Benignus thought, 'and something else. What? What else is it that they are? Animals? Yes. Dogs. Only human dogs. Snarling animals. Teachers in the making. They are putting away the balls, the camogie sticks, the racquets and croquet mallets, these last symbols of a refinement removed from animals. Personified in Mother Evangeline. Belonging to another generation, she is nonplussed by this rough-raw material. The day of the West Briton is definitely finished. She presides only because of the prestige of her seniority. Soon she will be replaced. The Dingle girls will not make croquet-players. Never. Maybe some of the aspiring socialites from other parts will?

'The wallop of a camogie stick; cows massing through a gap in the ditch. My children were like this. Walloping, crowding. Only I relinquished command. Trying for a gentler control in reaction against regimentation, I lost direction; bogged down. Swamped. I was beaten. Their fierce uncontrol triumphed. I have accepted failure. In the end they all went their own ways. I was needed no more. They were gone. Then Alec dead. Often I wished to be dead. Why he first? Was it fair? He left me without any final resolution between us. We never worked the thing out. I think the facade appeared whole. I think so. No one knew. Only the two of us knew the defeat, the problem unsolved. The unbridged islands. It *is* fair that he is dead. He is at least beyond the daily mortification of having a passionless wife, beyond the defeat of my unbelief, the waste of my uncharity. It is I who am, after all, dead. He is at rest. I have really been dead for a very long time. This that I walk about in is a cold clay case.'

She walked no further but sat in a wooden alcove, just aware of pelvic stiffness.

'Incipient arthritis,' her mind went on. There was no anxiety. 'Inherited tendency. It invades more rapidly when the wish to live is absent.'

The last prefects had left the field.

'Along the corridors I see them looking at me, these untried girls who have come here – Julia would triumph to hear it said – to have the clamps of dogma tightened about their already straitened thinking. So it was with me; long, long ago, at the very spring the stream was choked never to find a life-broad flow. Only last Sunday I heard Mother Evangeline giving them the weekly Adult Talk: "Always sit upright in the chair. Never, never lean back in a relaxed manner. A man, seeing you like that, will be bound to have evil thoughts." And each listening girl instinctively tightens muscles; braces herself afresh against the assault of man, the enemy. Of course later they will laugh – maybe. Silly old Mother Evangeline, they may say. Rubbish, they may think they think. But a poison, nevertheless, stays deep in the centre. It has already done its work to which no intellectualisation can be anti-dote. That poison was in fact lodged in them already before they came here and Mother Evangeline has added only a probably unnecessary booster to the earlier inoculation against innocent delight in the flesh.

'It is well that Alec is gone. Indeed I coldly killed him. Crime of frigidity. I see them looking at me, these gullible girls, wondering at my face. I have at last perfected the mask; its smiling ice is permanent. It pleases me to see the recoil in their faces.

'Soon the nuns' bell will ring. I will go to the mechanical prayer, kneel in my stall, the veil hiding my silence. Despising the cant. No word of it all makes me feel less cold. The routine, the order, the cleanliness of this place please me. Four pleasures: the Dingle girls talking Irish and these. But altogether I have five.

'There were other things I could have done. Turned to drink. The end is public, shameful. Everyone knows your sottish end. Privacy is a last necessity. Drugs? Worse than drink. More degrading, more confessedly selfish. And I never had money. Taken the offering lovers? And grown daily more dependent, more fearful because older. None of them would have borne with me as did Alec. I could have held no lover; I had nothing to give.

'I considered these things. I found no further hold in the outside world. In latter years my inclination had been more and more to retreat. I considered much. Once, they had wanted me here and I would not stay. Eager then, the insidious blights as yet unfelt, I went into the world to breed many years' puzzlements, confusion; and then knew myself barren. Then having lost any further urge to out-wardness, I remembered back to this retreat, a place to wait detachedly for the end I had not the courage to make immediate.

'I still possessed the things they once wanted from me here, brain, energy – which even if reduced could still be willed to efficient activity. The inner grave of no-belief was coldly secret, inaccessible to priest or mother superior. Confession? Profession of fervency? They did not bother me. I could now tell sinless lies, who had long striven to live to unattainable truth.

'It was not difficult to be accepted here. I was a prodigal returned. They were ready to forgive my humble heart and were unsuspicious of deceit. They were glad to refuge the erring widow whose family was fledged and provided for. Had she not also skills they could use, keeping in the convent useful money? They embraced my edifying vocation.

'I have felt relief in the changeless days. So then I practised the smile that very soon became a reflex to the rising bell. Now it serves me most usefully. When they speak to me and I am not disposed to conversation, I merely continue to smile and bow my head and pass along. Everyone respects my reserve. I am the widow who has known much sorrow. They forgive my eccentricity.

'Only when I play the organ – the fifth pleasure – a slow forgotten warmth sometimes stirs in me, and in the darkened chapel I know my smile is gone and I feel a wetness on my cheeks.'

YOU WOULDN'T THROW ME TO THE LIONS, WOULD YOU?

MAURA TREACY
Born in Co. Kilkenny, 1946, Maura Treacy won the Writers' Week in Listowel Competition in 1974. She has published one collection, *Sixpence in her Shoe*, and a novel.

The doctor hovered in the kitchen doorway, blinking in the fluorescent lighting that blinded him after the dim, economy bulbs of the bedroom, stairs and hall and he kept tapping his knee with his black bag, jutting out the knee to meet it each time as if he were about to genuflect. Otherwise he looked sleepy, amiable and forgetful.

'Well, that's that,' he said, with a tone of mournful finality but seeing Mary-Jo's puncturing glance he giggled and scratched his tousled head.

Abruptly she returned her attention to the five beakers of coffee she was making and he, recollecting that she might still be emotionally involved, cleared his throat and reached up to straighten his tie but there was no tie, only the rumpled collar of his red and green striped pyjamas over which he had dragged on his clothes.

She filled up two of the beakers and offered him one. Relieved, he came into the kitchen for it.

'Well,' she said dismally, 'did he urgently need your attention?'

He stroked and rubbed his wide nose with sterilised fingers and shook his head.

'Nothing a discreet and kind-hearted wife couldn't have tended to.' His voice became more analytical. 'You see 'em at it in the Westerns: just up with the skirt and tear a scelp off the petticoat and wrap it around the bullet wounds.' He sniffed aridly. 'Can I have a drop of milk in this? You'll ruin your nerves, girl, on black coffee.' He was fiddling with the air extractor over the cooker. 'I suppose that's why you never get a whiff of food around this place?'

'One of the reasons,' she said, hesitating over the half bottle of milk which was all she could find. She slammed the door of the vast fridge and two tins of sardines rattled obsequiously in the rack.

As they drank their coffee in silence, they looked around the modern, minutely equipped kitchen. They could hear on the floor above them the relentless footsteps of Marian and Julia, one on either side of Mel's bed.

'Will you remind me to tip off Marian not to pull the bedclothes too tight around him,' he said, betraying his line of thought too. 'Until we see what damage there is to his leg,' he added.

Mary-Jo nodded indifferently; she held the cup in both hands away from her mouth and her eyes were wide with joyless reflection.

'I could have sworn that was Mel I heard in the lounge,' Julia had said again. She went on shovelling dessert into her mouth with an expression of busy curiosity as if she still had hopes of finding something new and wonderful in the next mouthful. Nothing happened. The spoon rattled in the empty plate. 'Really, it's not worth the money,' she said, settling her arms on the table and shelving her rustling, tricel-covered bosom on them. She sealed her lips against a self-induced belch and uninhibitedly looked around at the people at the other tables.

Mary-Jo, eating her own dessert without expectation, lowered her calm eyes. Boredom ballooned in her mind, squeezing out every other passing sensation.

The waitress brought them tea and collected Julia's plate; she reached for Mary-Jo's but Julia shook her head and the impressionable girl left them.

'Eat it up, girl,' Julia said and reached across with her teaspoon and encouragingly did it for her. 'You won't get back your money because you're too finicky to eat what they give you,' she continued as if expounding a whole philosophy for life. 'Now drink your tea and we'll go look for Mel.'

'Julia, it's late. By the time we're home and unpacked . . .'

'They won't be waiting up for you at home, will they?'

'N-no,' she said, thinking of her tranquil father scurrying up to bed at the prospect of a midnight visit from Julia.

'Well then! And I'll drive, so come on!'

With their handbags on their arms they strolled down the broad silent corridor. They stopped to glance through the first glass door. Inside it was dark save for the blue flicker of a television set in front of which sat gentle, disappointed men who had expected to be doing something quite different by now. With them women in sleeveless dresses, pastel-coloured cardigans over their shoulders for the evening, and fragile shells of blue hair, women who thought in the weakness of relief that it was well to be so well.

'We won't find him there,' Julia said, moving on. 'What's that he used to say about letting it live our lives for us?'

Julia's careless attempts at quoting people always got under her skin. She paused to look again, to see how in ten or twenty years time she could hope to spend her holidays.

'Isn't it less likely that we'll find him here?' she asked as she followed Julia into the bar. She held the door as it glided and closed behind her. She was the first to see Mel and she knew even as she prayed how hopeless it was to pray that Julia would turn away now.

'Mel!' Julia was exclaiming as she loomed above his table in a dim corner.

'Zhulia?' He shook his light head to erase the image tossed up by his troubled imagination. As the illusion hardened into reality, a look of infinite sadness attenuated his features and he held up a gentle but unswervable hand. 'No! I'm not coming with you.'

'I'm not going home myself, yet,' Julia said happily and turned to wave Mary-Jo forward to the sport. 'Come on. Isn't this great!' But her eyes glinted, the first sliver of impatience with Mary-Jo's demurs showing through now that after a fortnight abroad when they had been dependent on each other for moral support, they were at last within reach of home and had met the first person they knew.

'And Merry-Jo came too,' Mel said with the dawning sad wisdom of Caesar when he saw who had put the knife in his back.

Julia bounced on the cushioned chair, thrilled that there was another kick left in her holiday, one the travel agent hadn't promised.

'Imagine meeting you here! What are you doing so far from home? Is Marian with you? And the kids, are they well?' She scattered questions over him as she opened her bag and rooted for her purse.

Meanwhile Mary-Jo sat down. 'Hello, Mel,' she said gently and then her eyes fixed on a point above and beyond Julia's money-counting fingers.

Julia left them and went to the bar.

'That stupid barman,' she said as she sat down again, washing heedlessly over the silence between them. 'Was Mary-Jo telling you about the great time we had in Spain?'

He raised his eyebrows, then nodded as recollection illuminated his hazy mind.

'Yeah, she was here writing it with her finger on the table. So that's where you're coming from. I had an idea I hadn't seen you around the place this while back.'

'Well, honestly,' Julia pouted, tucking in her shoulder as the barman placed their drinks on the table. 'We sent you a postcard; I don't know but that we sent you two and that's all the heed you put in it. We'll know better the next time. Now,' she hissed as the barman withdrew, 'back to what I was going to say. He nearly refused, didn't want to serve another drink for you; he said you'd had enough. I told him not to be an ass, you got drunk once when you were sixteen and you were a pioneer since and anyway the lemonade was for you.' But she took the empty glass out of his hand and sniffed. 'Mel! What came over you? Where's your pin?' She turned over the lapel of his coat. 'God,' she said and laughed but she was shocked. Mary-Jo looked on with a patient endurance that appalled herself.

'Little boys get tired of lemonade,' he said and his voice was sour and weary. He looked to Mary-Jo for insight and noted her glass of vodka. 'I see you have a working respect for anaesthesia, too. Do you remember the time you were here before?'

'Was I?'

'We were.'

'Did Marian change the carpet in the lounge yet?' Julia butted in briskly.

'What? Oh, you can pick it with her. I leave all that to Marian. I'm leaving all that to Marian,' he corrected himself introspectively.

Time passed unsatisfactorily. Julia's enthusiasm for Mel's company curdled as he became quieter and drunker. It seemed unlikely to Mary-Jo that Mel had ever acquired any taste for company for its own sake; years ago when he had been sober and self-contained, his preference for solitude had suggested some kind of philosophy that set him apart from everyone else she knew.

'We'll be back in a minute,' Julia warned him as she stood up, gripped her bag and jerked her head at Mary-Jo who tamely followed her from the room.

In the powder-room, Julia looked over her circumspect shoulder, then rounded on Mary-Jo.

'Well, what are you going to do about him?'

'Me? About Mel? What can anyone do?'

'That's what I'm asking you. After all, he's your responsibility.'

'Mine?'

'Well, more than mine, anyway. You're supposed to be his friend.'

'So are you.'

'It's not the same – you were nearly married to him, don't forget.'

'Don't let me, will you.'

'Well, anyway you can't let him get into a car and drive home – that journey and the state he's in! You'd have it on your conscience for the rest of your days. Imagine facing Marian if anything happened to him and to have to admit we met him here and saw how he was and did nothing about it. Wouldn't you rather confess to outright murder?'

Mary-Jo couldn't say, immediately.

'Well then, we had better book a room for him here.'

'No,' she discarded the advice she had extorted. 'He has to be at work tomorrow. He'd better sleep it off at home. Come on, girl, we'd better be going. I'll be with you in a minute.'

Julia led the march back to the bar, pausing first, tucking in her bottom and reaching back a prudent hand to make certain that nothing was being revealed that had better be concealed. Then she stuck her chubby, uncontradictable chin in the air and with a final flick to her creased skirt, advanced.

She resumed her seat, looking like the chairman of a returning jury.

The barman, polishing his counter, breathed soft relief as he watched Mel leave, walking with dignity for three steps, then slumping between the two mature ladies who bore him away with strength and desperation.

They held him in the open doorway while the cool autumn air revived him briefly and they withdrew slightly, thinking he could walk alone, but with the second step he stuck his toe in the grating and they were just in time to catch him. Julia, startled out of her disapproving silence, swore and in turn startled the sedate people in the foyer who were watching with discreet sympathy the brave way she bore her burden. Mary-Jo's apparent detachment invited no sympathy.

Julia swore a second time when, having unloaded Mel into the back seat of her own car, she slammed the door and instead of closing, it bumped softly and gently swung open again. She looked down for the obstacle and found Mel's leg slung out of the doorway.

'Lord, I nearly took the foot off him.' He groaned as she dragged up the stray but still attached foot and, more annoyed with him than ever, flung it into the car and closed the door on him.

Mary-Jo guided her through the city, warning her of traffic lights and one-way streets. After Inchicore she sat back and leaned her head against the window, the tangled irritation of her mind frozen at last with tiredness.

She must have dozed; Julia called her and rapped her knee as they drove across the Curragh. Her tired eyes were hurt by the unshielded lights of the oncoming cars.

'What's up?' she asked, resentfully rubbing her knee where Julia's cumbersome souvenir ring had stung her.

'Have a look back there and see if he's all right. He sounds as if he's strangling.'

Mary-Jo twisted around and knelt on her seat. Mel was cramped in one corner of the back, their parcels taking up the rest of the seat. His head was turned awkwardly, his chin stuck in his shoulder. His breathing was alarming. She gripped the lapels of his coat and tried to heave him up into a better position. The car bounced flippantly over a bump and he slid from her grasp.

'You'd better stop.'

Julia veered off the road and they jolted and rolled over the wide open grassy plain.

'Men,' she said as she jerked to a halt and Mary-Jo looked at Mel's drowned face and silently apologised for not having managed to steer him clear of Julia's ultimate derogation.

As Julia stepped out onto the grass, Mel opened his eyes. 'Where are we?' he asked.

'What's he saying now?' Julia asked irritably as if he had pestered her for years.

'He wants to know where we are.'

'Tell him we're crossing the Alps. With Hannibal.'

Mary-Jo handed out the parcels and Julia took them back to the boot.

'She says we're crossing the Alps.'

'Ah that's grand,' he said with sleepy contentment. 'So long as we're not going home.'

'Why? Don't you want to go home.'

'We went home once too often, yourself and myself.' He looked at her through half-deadened eyes, then his head drooped again. His hair fell across his forehead and after a moment she reached out and lifted it gently back into place, but it fell forward again immediately.

'What could we do when they came looking for us? I'd better get out and give Julia a hand.'

He looked up at her and she wasn't sure if he knew her.

'Julia? Is she with you? Jo? You wouldn't . . . throw me to the lions, would you?'

'Well, is he awake?' Julia called. 'Come here and open the door.'

Julia knelt on the edge of the seat and vigorously rearranged him. 'His hair and everything,' she complained as she dug her fingers into it and pushed it back off his face, subtly transforming his rakish appearance to one of youthful austerity.

Out on the road again, Mary-Jo huddled in her own corner. Now and again in the stream of light from passing cars she would watch Julia's squat form behind the wheel, her breath bated with efficient philanthropy as she rhythmically dimmed the lights for every oncoming car, her busy, stubby little fingers excitedly in touch with the switchboard of the entire world around her. The sight oppressed her.

In the back seat Mel snored mindlessly, as he was borne, unconscious and unresisting, back over the miles he had travelled that morning with such irreversible resolution.

ACKNOWLEDGEMENTS

For permission to reprint the stories specified we are indebted to:

John Banville: 'Nightwind' from *Long Lankin* (Secker & Warburg), copyright © John Banville 1970. Reprinted by permission of Sheil Land Associates.

Maeve Binchy: 'Shepherd's Bush' from *London Transports* (Century Hutchinson), copyright © Maeve Binchy 1978. Reprinted by permission of the author.

Clare Boylan: 'Technical Difficulties And The Plague' from *Concerning Virgins* (Hamish Hamilton and Penguin), copyright © Clare Boylan 1989. Reprinted by permission of Rogers, Coleridge & White Ltd.

Helen Lucy Burke: 'Trio', copyright © Helen Lucy Burke 1970. Reprinted by permission of the author.

Evelyn Conlon: 'As Good A Reason As Any' from *My Head Is Opening* (Attic Press), copyright © Evelyn Conlon 1987. Reprinted by permission of the author and Attic Press.

Shane Connaughton: 'Ojus' from *A Border Station* (Hamish Hamilton), copyright © Shane Connaughton 1989. Reprinted by permission of the author.

Emma Cooke: 'A Family Occasion' from *Female Forms* (Poolbeg Press), copyright © Emma Cooke 1974. Reprinted by permission of the author.

Ita Daly: 'The Lady With The Red Shoes' from *The Lady With The Red Shoes* (Poolbeg Press), copyright © Ita Daly 1975. Reprinted by permission of the author.

Anne Devlin: 'Five Notes After A Visit' from *The Way-Paver* (Faber and Faber), copyright © Anne Devlin 1986. Reprinted by permission of Sheil Land Associates.

Mary Dorcey: 'A Country Dance' from *A Noise From The Woodshed* (Onlywomen Press), copyright © Mary Dorcey 1989. Reprinted by permission of the author.

Anne Enright: 'Fatgirl Terrestrial' from *The Portable Virgin* (Secker & Warburg), copyright © Anne Enright 1991. Reprinted by permission of A. P. Watt Ltd.

Dermot Healy: 'A Family And A Future' from *Banished Misfortune* (Allison & Busby and Brandon), copyright © Dermot Healy 1982. Reprinted by permission of the author.

Desmond Hogan: 'The Last Time' from *The Diamonds At The Bottom Of*

The Sea (Hamish Hamilton), copyright © Desmond Hogan 1979. Reprinted by permission of the author and Rogers, Coleridge & White Ltd.

Peter Hollywood: 'The Dog' from *Jane Alley* (Pretani Press), copyright © Peter Hollywood 1987. Reprinted by permission of the author.

Neil Jordan: 'Mr Solomon Wept' from *Night In Tunisia* (Brandon Book Publishers), copyright © Neil Jordan 1982. Reprinted by permission of the author.

John B. Keane: 'The Change' from *Death Be Not Proud* (Mercier Press), copyright © John B. Keane 1976. Reprinted by permission of the author.

Sam Keery: 'The Studios' from *The Streets Of Laredo* (Jonathan Cape), copyright © Sam Keery 1986. Reprinted by permission of the author.

Maeve Kelly: 'The Sentimentalist' from *A Life Of Her Own* (Poolbeg Press), copyright © Maeve Kelly 1976. Reprinted by permission of the author.

Rita Kelly: 'Trousseau' from *The Whispering Arch* (Arlen House), copyright © Rita Kelly 1986. Reprinted by permission of the author.

Adrian Kenny: 'Bend Sinister' from *Arcady* (Co-Op Books), copyright © Adrian Kenny 1983. Reprinted by permission of the author.

Mary Leland: 'Windfalls', copyright © Mary Leland 1979. Reprinted by permission of the author.

Bernard MacLaverty: 'The Break' from *The Great Profundo* (Jonathan Cape), copyright © Bernard MacLaverty 1987. Reprinted by permission of the author and Jonathan Cape.

Seán MacMathúna: 'The Atheist' from *The Atheist* (Wolf-hound Press), copyright © Seán MacMathúna 1987. Reprinted by permission of the author and Wolfhound Press.

Aidan Mathews: 'In The Dark' from *Adventures In A Bathyscope* (Secker & Warburg), copyright © Aidan Mathews 1988. Reprinted by permission of the author.

John Morrow: 'Place: Belfast. Time: 1984. Scene: The Only Pub' from *Northern Myths* (Blackstaff Press), copyright © John Morrow 1979. Reprinted by permission of the author.

Éilis Ní Dhuibhne: 'Looking' from *Blood And Water* (Attic Press), copyright © Éilis Ní Dhuibhne 1988. Reprinted by permission of the author and Attic Press.

Gillman Noonan: 'Heat' from *Friends And Occasional Lovers* (Poolbeg Press), copyright © Gillman Noonan 1982. Reprinted by permission of the author and Poolbeg Press.

Kate Cruise O'Brien: 'Henry Died' from *A Gift Horse* (Poolbeg Press), copyright © Kate Cruise O'Brien 1978. Reprinted by permission of the author.

Mary O'Donnell: 'After The Match' from *Strong Pagans* (Poolbeg Press), copyright © Mary O'Donnell 1991. Reprinted by permission of the author.

Brian Power: 'Kyrie Boom-Boom-Boom' from *The Wild And Daring Sixties* (Tansy Books), copyright © Brian Power 1980. Reprinted by permission of the author.

Ronan Sheehan: 'Universitas' from *Boy With An Injured Eye* (Brandon Book Publishers), copyright © Ronan Sheehan 1983. Reprinted by permission of the author.

Eddie Stack: 'Time Passes' from *The West* (Bloomsbury), copyright © Eddie Stack 1990. Reprinted by permission of the author and Bloomsbury.

Eithne Strong: 'The Bride Of Christ' from *Patterns* (Poolbeg Press), copyright © Eithne Strong 1981. Reprinted by permission of the author.

Maura Treacy: 'You Wouldn't Throw Me To The Lions, Would You?' from *Sixpence In Her Shoe* (Poolbeg Press), copyright © Maura Treacy 1977. Reprinted by permission of the author.

Ed. DAVID MARCUS

IRISH SHORT STORIES

David Marcus presents thirty-two outstanding examples of
the Irish prowess at short story writing, capturing the
characteristic wit, scope and sheer entertainment provided by
authors who range from George Moore and James Joyce to
William Trevor and John McGahern.

'Shows a consistency of talent that seems almost unfairly
bestowed upon one rather small land'
Janice Elliott in the Sunday Telegraph

'A very rich and varied collection, a real feast of a book'
Robert Nye in The Guardian

'The Irish are great lads at the short story, and here's
another generously varied collection to prove it'
John Cronin in The Times Literary Supplement

'Excellent'
Gerry Colgan in the Irish Independent

'An excellent and definitive anthology'
Hibernia

'An impressive collection'
The Listener

'No one has done more than David Marcus to foster young
and unknown talent, especially in this particular form . . . So
the volume comes with the best possible credentials: and
lives up to them in every way . . . A very important
collection of magnificent work'
John Broderick in The Irish Times

sceptre

AIDAN MATHEWS

ADVENTURES IN A BATHYSCOPE

'This is indeed an exhilarating collection . . . One of the characteristics of the bathyscope is that it illuminates the hidden, and Mathew's powers of observation are masterly, his prose pellucid and revealing, his imagery exquisitely accurate. The stylistic range is impressive, moving easily from dark tragedy to metaphysical comedy'
The Times Literary Supplement

'Set variously in an Irish church, along a California freeway, in an English village, on a Greek isle and in Nagasaki on the morning of August 9, 1945, these rare and wondrous stories remind us of how the best Irish writing – like any art – is universal . . . A brilliant first collection of stories, nothing less'
The Irish Press

'A unique event in Irish fiction'
Neil Jordan

'A book to savour . . . its like doesn't appear too often'
The Sunday Press

'A conjuror with words, dealing us fourteen stories in which jokers, queens and tragic spades are shuffled in hypnotic succession'
The List

'Splendidly odd and oddly moving stories, the product of a unique talent . . . A very exciting debut'
John Banville

'These stunningly individual pieces breathe new life into the Irish short story . . . Excellent'
Image

LIAM O'FLAHERTY

THE SHORT STORIES OF LIAM O'FLAHERTY

O'Flaherty's reputation as one of Ireland's outstanding writers rests as much on his short stories as his novels. This selection of nearly sixty of his stories demonstrates to the full his genius. Lyrical, impassioned, combining hard realism and compassion, their economy of style and range of mood evoke Irish life in all its variety to perfection.

'Mr O'Flaherty goes deeply into the situation with a mind joyously full of intelligences and original sin'
Rebecca West in The Daily Telegraph

'I do not hesitate to compare his work with that of the most expert writers of the short story . . . Stephen Crane, Katherine Mansfield and H. G. Wells'
The Spectator

'O'Flaherty enters body and soul into the life of his subjects, transporting the reader . . . to the poetry of his own vision'
Sunday Press, Dublin

sceptre

CHRISTOPHER BURNS

ABOUT THE BODY

An inventive and unusual collection of fourteen short stories,
ranging in style from the traditional to the innovative and in
subject matter from the extraordinary to the apparently everyday – for Burns' acutely observed characters are rarely quite
what they seem.

'Nearly every story has some valedictory touch, some neat
shift in perspective that lifts it onto a higher level of
engagement . . . This is a peach of a collection'
D. J. Taylor in The Independent

'Carefully crafted, sinister little gems'
Judy Cooke in The Listener

'An uncommonly good first collection of short stories'
Robert Nye in The Guardian

'Very assured, inventive, hard-edged'
Anthony Thwaite in the London Review of Books

'A writer of formidable talent and imagination'
Digby Durrant in the London Magazine

sceptre